Shadow Coven

Shadow Coven

S. ISABELLE

Scholastic Press / New York

As a play on the *Macbeth* line "By the pricking of my thumbs, / Something wicked this way comes," the witches in this book perform magic by sacrificing blood by way of a thumb pinprick with a needle. This action is described numerous times throughout the novel, and characters cut themselves in other ways before performing spells.

In addition to depictions of self-harm, other content warnings include: blood, violence, gore, death of a parent, and body horror.

Library of Congress Cataloging-in-Publication Data
Names: Isabelle, S., author.
Title: Shadow coven / S. Isabelle.
Description: First edition. | New York : Scholastic Inc., 2023. | Series: The witchery ; book 2 | Audience: Ages 14 and up | Audience: Grades 10–12 | Summary: After defeating the wolves Jailah, Logan, Iris, and Thalia are ready to pursue their separate studies, but when witches start going missing, and Thalia is convinced her father is responsible, the coven is surrounded by magical and mundane threats and must work together to protect themselves and their magic.
Identifiers: LCCN 2022059707 (print) | LCCN 2022059708 (ebook) | ISBN 9781338758993 (hardcover) | ISBN 9781338759006 (ebook)
Subjects: LCSH: Witches—Juvenile fiction. | Magic—Juvenile fiction. | Friendship—Juvenile fiction. | Schools—Juvenile fiction. | Fantasy. | Adventure stories. | CYAC: Witches—Fiction. | Magic—Fiction. | Friendship—Fiction. | Schools—Fiction. | Fantasy. | BISAC: YOUNG ADULT FICTION / Fantasy / Wizards & Witches | YOUNG ADULT FICTION / Paranormal, Occult & Supernatural | LCGFT: Witch fiction. | Fantasy fiction.
Classification: LCC PZ7.1.K554 Sh 2023 (print) | LCC PZ7.1.K554 (ebook) | DDC 813.6 [Fic]—dc23/eng/20221220

10 9 8 7 6 5 4 3 2 1   23 24 25 26 27

Printed in Italy   183

First edition, September 2023

Book design by Stephanie Yang

For Mom.
And for the kids who spend all
of class time dreaming up stories.

We, the members of the Haelsford Witchery Council, do pledge to protect Haelsford and its people from wicked forces—magical or mundane, internal or external—and from all forms of harm that may come to pass. With the powers granted to us as elected members of this honorable society, we vow to shelter our town from the hexed Wolves that plague our Swamp.

We pledge to lead our young witches toward success and to offer judgment on misdeeds with fairness and respect. Covenhood is our lifeblood, our strength, our duty, our salvation.
—from the pledge of the Haelsford Witchery
Council, updated 2006

BEHOLD, CHILDREN OF MINE, WHO ARE BLESSED AND CURSED WITH THE POWER OF THE DEAD. YOUR PURPOSE IS A SINISTER ONE, BUT THIS BOOK IS YOUR LOYAL COMPANION. STUDY ITS TEXTS. GUARD ITS SECRETS. FEAST ON ITS OFFERINGS. FOR AS LONG AS DEATH EXISTS, NO NECROMANCER EVER WALKS ALONE.

MAY THE DARK KEEP YOU SAFE.
—from *Death's Compendium* as transcribed in
the *Necromantic Diaries of Anonymous*, year unknown

part one

reunion

1

iris

May

As the young deathwitch stepped onto the dark sand, she took in a comforting scent. Fresh citrus fruits. Salty air. Long-spilled blood.

Home.

Sun Harbor sat on a little island in the Florida Keys. The land was covered in headstones, unmanaged and neglected, wrapped in cobwebs and cracks. It was a village whose only inhabitants lived underground. A bleedbay once, thriving on making shows of its tortured witches and their mundane collaborators, the very ones whose bodies now fed the earth. The early morning sun seeped through the heavy clouds, revealing bare trees and yellowed grass. Stony House waited in the distance, a once-glorious manor burdened by years of neglect, its dark paint and gray stone covered in vines. Smaller cottages surrounded it, all touched with the same decay. Like Haelsford, Sun Harbor had its own hex, but unlike the Swamp, the dark magic here felt like a hug to Iris Keaton-Foster.

"Miss?"

Iris, enchanted by the literal ghost town, had forgotten the boatman behind her.

"Thank you," she said politely. "I'll see you in a few days."

While she took this trip yearly and should've long ago procured her own boat, or looked up a waterwitchery spell to make the lake solid enough to walk on, a sick little part of her relished the mundane's expression as he looked upon a land he couldn't truly see. He only saw a thick black fog and Iris's back as she disappeared into it.

With every step Iris took toward the three-story home, the setting around it transformed. The grass twitched and straightened, growing a deep and vibrant green from dried husks. The garden bloomed, bearing roses, daisies, violets, fresh tomatoes, and a mango tree, its branches heavy with fruit. Looking at the house was like twisting a holographic card; one moment, it was as corroded as the rest of the island, and with a blink, it was restored to its old glory.

At the wrought iron gates, something dragged against Iris's witchy senses. The house was already brimming with protection spells and death magic, but this sensation didn't feel familiar to the necromancer who had served as architect for much of them. Not malicious, just . . . new.

The gates opened with a sharp creak. Witchy or not, only a Keaton or a Foster would be granted access, so Iris was doubly qualified. She entered Stony House and called out, *"Honey, I'm Home!"*

The door shut behind her. Iris took a deep, bracing breath as her magic did what it always did here. It *shrank*. Her witchery receded, leaving her feeling empty and spent, as if someone had dimmed the lights of her soul.

4

Groggy, like waking up from a nap that was only meant to be a few minutes long but had stretched into hours. She was still a witch, and this price she paid wouldn't change that, but when she crossed the threshold into her family home, she was essentially mundane.

Iris pushed back the thick red drapes and opened up all the windows. The morning light revealed an untouched living room, foyer, and kitchen. It had a bohemian feel, from the colorful rugs and comfy blue sofa to the modernist paintings of naked Black bodies on the wall. The walls themselves were painted dark orange, except for the kitchen, which was drenched in baby's breath blue. Her parents' old things were neatly arranged. Mortimer's beloved record player rested atop a table alongside a stack of anatomy and biology textbooks bearing his in-line scrawls and sticky tabs. A case of his pristine surgical tools glimmered in the corner, but as impressive as they were, her father's collection was not the one that drew the eye.

An entire wall showed off Sage Foster's collection of necromantic texts. Before she died, she'd dedicated her life to recovering the books and artifacts that had been bought, stolen, and traded by mundanes. The sight always took Iris's breath away. She touched the spine of a grimoire that her mother had been working on translating from its original Mandarin. Her fingers came away with dust on them. Out of habit, her hand twitched toward her wand. *Clean It Up* would do the trick, but she couldn't use her witchery here. It was part of the bargain her mother made to keep Stony House standing—and safe.

An apparition of a woman flickered in the den, across the living room, and in the kitchen, all at once. Images of a man flashed in reflections, his skin dark, his coils thick and just barely gray. He smiled wide on the surface of a teapot, in the glass of a window, in the light bouncing off the mirror in the dining room. A gust of wind surrounded Iris, lifting her onto her feet and spinning her around. She giggled girlishly at the welcome.

Finally, Sage Foster settled at the top of the stairs. The woman was dressed in a deep purple cape with a large hood and long black gloves.

Iris swallowed thickly, blinking back fresh tears. "Hi, Mom."

Her mother grinned wide. *"If you knew how much I missed you, little death."*

Iris rubbed her eyes. "I missed you, too."

Her mother smiled, then shouted, *"Mortimer!"*

The antique tuner on the lovely oak sideboard burst to life, filling the house with the sound of static, and then the classics—Motown, jazz, old-school hip-hop—as if someone were flipping through stations. The voice, like an old-timey radio announcer, cut through the noise. It said, *"Ain't God good! My little heathen's home!"*

Iris felt a warm wind caress her cheek and flow through her fresh brown-and-blond braids. "Hey, Dad," she whispered, voice cracking. It felt so damn good to be somewhere where she was unequivocally loved for being herself and especially for being a deathwitch.

Across from her, Sage's apparition sat in the armchair with three quick violent flashes, as if she were being projected and the film kept getting stuck.

Dread bloomed in the pit of Iris's stomach. "Are you okay?"

"No—" Sage laughed and flickered, her words cut off. *"But you being here makes it better. It's been harder and harder to take form without you, and even now . . ."* She gestured vaguely with her gloved hands.

"Does it hurt?" An odd thing to ask an apparition, but Iris didn't know how else to ask if her mother's spirit was pained in some mortal way. Sage's presence was abnormal by default, a consequence of skilled necromancy fed by Sage's own death wish, Iris's young magic, and a fraying thread between life and death. The fragility of it all was suddenly impossible for Iris to ignore.

Sage shook her head. *"It's more like exhaustion."* She waved the words away. *"Now, get me up to date. Almost a senior, I'm so proud of you, Rissy!"*

From the radio, her father blared Kool & the Gang's "Celebration."

Sage rolled her eyes lightheartedly. *"How was your year?"*

Iris managed a nervous smile. She pulled a small book from her knapsack and placed it on the coffee table. *The Most Wicked Works of Olga Yara.*

Her mother's demeanor changed at the sight of it. Sage growled, inhuman and low. No one could mistake her for a mortal now, not with the inky-black aura spreading around her, or the way she slowly rose into the air, hovering above the seat. Iris felt her mother's emotions—anger, concern, confusion—pressing against her skin like steam. *"Tell me you did not cast from that book!"*

A bead of sweat dripped down her back. "I guess I should start from the beginning."

She told her mother of the last Haunting Season, how it began and how it ended. She spoke of her old friends Jailah and Thalia, and her new ones, Trent, Logan, and Beaumont, and the tethering that still perplexed her. And finally, she explained that against every rule of magic she knew, she'd resurrected the Wolf Boy and discovered the secrets of the Haunting Season. The Roddin Witch was Adelaide Strigwach, the architect of the curse, who had used Iris as a tool to bring back Theodore Bloom, the Wolf Boy.

7

When Iris was done, her mother's calm presence returned. She pulled back her hood. *"You've tethered a mundane boy."*

Iris wrinkled her brow. Of all she'd just said, that seemed like the wrong point to focus on. "Is that a thing? Tethering a mundane?"

A wisp of a man flashed in Iris's peripheral vision. The television turned on to static. *"Now just wait one damn minute. A boy? Did I hear that right?"*

"Mortimer."

The radio-announcer voice grew irritated. *"Well, if Rissy's got a boyfriend, I gotta shake his hand! Y'know, look that boy in the eye—"*

"And how in the hell do you plan on doing that?"

Groaning, Iris slunk down into the vintage couch. Spirit-parents could still be so embarrassing. "He's *not* my boyfriend," she muttered.

It's worse than that. He's my tether.

Before she could refute her father's teasing further, Sage's presence changed again. More than a flicker, it was as if Sage had been doused in a beam of red light, revealing a face writhing in pain.

Iris jumped to her feet. "Mom!"

From the stereo, a raspy voice growled her name. Iris turned, heart pounding. The dial spun back and forth, and her father's voice returned with laborious breaths, as if he'd been running, or *fighting*.

However useless, Iris pulled out her wand. "Dad? What was that?"

"Iris, what is it?"

Iris jolted to her mother. The apparition was back to, well, whatever *normal* was here. She examined her mother's face. "I just saw something. It was like you were screaming for help, or hurting somehow. And Dad's voice wasn't his own."

Sage stacked her shaking hands on her heart. She said nothing, but her gaze was angled to the now-quiet radio. Iris may not have been able to hear them, but she knew when her parents were talking in secrets the way that any child could. "Tell me what's going on!" Iris demanded, hating how petulant she sounded.

Sage wrung her hands. *"Every year it gets harder. You know that, baby girl. We were never meant to be kept for this long. Just until you found your way with your magic. Until you knew enough about necromancy to put us to rest yourself."*

Iris's heart dropped at her mother's tight voice. She didn't like where this was going.

"It's time we think about saying goodbye."

Not yet, Iris thought sadly.

Sage was the last deathwitch she knew. There was no necromancer on the Mesmortes staff. Her courses were essentially history and theory—learning about death magic, but never truly practicing, not the way her mom had once done and had taught her. Not the way the Roddin Witch had spoken of. A sticky anger bloomed in Iris's chest, but it wasn't enough to keep the sadness at bay. Even after the betrayal, the blood, the violence, Iris was left distraught at losing Roddin and the Emporium.

She had tried looking for necromancers like herself, who'd been contacted by Death, or saved from the afterlife the way that she was. Being a necromancer might've made her special in Haelsford, but deathwitches had existed since the beginning of time. She couldn't have been the only witch Death had spoken to or had spared.

The internet could be a perilous place to research witchery that wasn't the everyday things learned in a coven academy. First, there was the Witchery Web Safety Act, established after a rogue witch had posted his intentions to use magic to commit mass murder, a spell that not only promised death but also *worked*, unlike a lot of the dark magic drivel people posted for attention. Then there were the witch-obsessed hexeaters: mundanes who either pretended to be witchy or would pay good money to any witch who offered themselves up for dissection in misguided pursuits to become witches themselves.

Still, Iris had found a few interesting leads. There was a boy in Delhi who claimed he'd seen Death as well. Unlike Iris's vision of a great grim reaper, he'd seen a man dressed in red who spoke to him after he was almost crushed by a vendor cart a few summers ago. The boy's blog hadn't been updated since, and his contact form gave Iris an error message. But looking at his past posts, she could see that he was a true deathwitch. Between the silver pentagram on his wrist and the way he spoke of necromancy, his witchery didn't ring false.

Another necromancer, a ten-year-old in Jacmel who received her blessing early, vlogged of a man in dark glasses and a crooked top hat, who had taken her hand in her dreams and told her that she was bound for a higher purpose. The words turned Iris's spine into ice, and she knew for sure. Death approached necromancers around the world, appearing to them in different ways depending on their backgrounds or beliefs.

But this was a small comfort. With Adelaide either dead or disappeared and Sage passing on, who did Iris have to understand her death magic?

Her face warmed.

The closest living connection she had to her own necromancy was

Mathew Beaumont. A mundane. For once, she found herself wishing that he wasn't. She wished desperately that he was her true tether, the way Jailah and Vero once were. Two witches, their magic made to complement each other's.

Iris had . . . *other* wishes about Beaumont. Ones that she locked up tight, would never wear on her face, would rather die than admit.

"Iris?" her mother prodded gently. *"I don't want to frighten you, but my magic's running thin. You need to put us to rest before it's too late."*

"Too late?"

"A soul who overstays its welcome is a nasty sight. If you put us to rest now, we get to say goodbye together. You'll be eighteen in August. Still a child, yes, far from grown. But those are the terms. I don't want you to come back here and find us . . . gone. Or worse."

Sage's words were soft, but her expression was hard with urgency. Iris hadn't been in the Swamp with Trent when his mother appeared to him, but the way he spoke of the apparition worried her. Even if the Swamp's mind-altering hex was a part of it, the thought of her parents corrupting into horrors chilled Iris through.

A gentle breeze of her father's doing wrapped around her. Iris wanted to hold her parents, and to be held by them. "Before the end of summer. I'll put you both to rest."

⸱⸱•◆ ✪ ◆•⸱⸱

Three days passed with the sweet laziness of early summer. Thalia had given Iris a handful of seeds to plant in the clearing behind the house, which quickly blossomed into fruits and veggies, their colors witchy vibrant. She'd packed snacks and frozen hot dogs, and made the Simmons family lemonade

11

recipe that left her teeth sticky with sweetness. Iris spent the mornings curled up on the couch under the quilt, flicking through her mother's collection of grimoires. The house was freezing at night, unlike every other house in the state, and while Iris could have lugged wood into the fireplace, she relished the cold. Knowing that it was a result of the ghosts, her spells, and Sage's magic left Iris comforted by the chill.

On her last day in Sun Harbor, there was no goodbye hug. Only a stuttering of the radio as it cut off, a slight chill against her cheek and the feeling of holding back tears. It was the last time she'd be home like this. In August, she would finally put her parents to rest. After that, she'd come to Stony House and find it lifeless. She missed them already.

"You'll be able to Call us like you Call any soul, baby," said Sage gently.

A short necromantic Call here and there wasn't the same, but Iris nodded, if only to reassure her mother.

When Iris stepped outside, her witchery burst into her chest like a kerosene-soaked match. She inhaled, relishing it, even if she didn't feel quite whole yet.

This time, when she reached for her wand, the magic in her blood thrummed.

2

thalia

As a small child, Thalia Blackwood had spent the majority of the year counting down to the summer months. Summer break was a respite from schoolyard bullies who hated her for nothing other than her tawny brown skin and the magic that had rooted in her veins. But before that—before the blessing, the bloodshed, and her escape—Thalia spent the sweltering days firmly in her mother's orbit. The two tested new recipes for short-bread and lavender cakes because it was never too hot for Fiona Turner to quit baking. And when Pastor Abraham Turner came home after long days of preaching and pontificating, little Talullah would leap into her father's arms, neither caring that the front of her shirt was covered in flour and icing.

How adorable, Thalia thought sardonically. Her stomach turned with anger and disgust. She didn't recognize the little girl in those memories, and good riddance to her naivete.

Summer in Haelsford was a different beast. The air was as thick with humidity as it was with the chattering of overeager tourists, though the small witchtown attracted visitors year-round. Those who wanted to see the notorious hexed Swamp without the risk of being slaughtered by its hungry Wolves chose the summer months to do so, while others made a point to visit during the Haunting Season. Thalia wasn't sure who annoyed her more: those who wanted to brag about seeing the Swamp with little danger to themselves, or those who foolishly snapped videos of themselves dancing over the edge of the protection spells during autumn.

From the porch of her cabin, Thalia watched the Segway tour roll up to the edge of corrupted earth, rotting vegetation, and an atmosphere that was ripe for mind games. She knew it all too well. She'd been taken into the Swamp just months ago and had seen it up close and way too personal. Maybe *she* should've been the one guiding the nosy tourists. Shit, she could do a whole haunted Haelsford tour, and maybe even get Iris to rouse up some ghosts to make it something really special.

As Thalia genuinely wondered how much money she could make doing just that, she touched her index finger to the little green sprout in her thumb. After protecting Mesmortes with her greenwitchery, she'd earned this sprout. It was proof of her growing magic, her connection to the earth. Thalia touched it and remembered who she was. A greenwitch. A powerful one. One who'd survived the Swamp.

The one who might finally cleanse it.

Thalia turned back into the cabin. She'd learned that watching the Segway tours at this point often led to curious looks leveled at her, and she hated feeling like a fixture of the land rather than a living, breathing being. Maverick trotted in after her, his claws clicking against the hardwood floors.

She gave him a stern look from behind her wide-rimmed frames. *You ready to let me take care of those nails, or what?*

With a whine, her scruffy dog scurried into his bed.

Thalia glanced at her phone. It was new, bigger than her last phone, and she was still getting used to the way everything on her home screen was arranged. It was a splurge, but as it turned out, there were plenty of people in Haelsford and beyond who thought she and her friends deserved a reward for their actions on Hell Night, as Iris called it. The GoFundMe was in Logan's name at Thalia's request; the last thing Thalia needed was for her image to be plastered online. Besides, a girl who looked like Logan Wyatt was bound to inspire more clicks and donations. And when bloggers and journalists and fame-hungry YouTubers came around to dig up information for exposés, Jailah took care of them with that southern sweetness, tucking her threats into cute little quips.

The phone buzzed. Thalia had six unread messages in the group chat with her girls called *red coven*, but she clicked the notification above it.

The message was a picture of a Black boy smiling wide. Trent Hogarth was in London and had found an absurdly overgrown bush. His fingers were stretched out toward it, and the text read:

on my Greenwich shittttt

Thalia laughed. After an anxious moment where she tried to determine the perfect response, she settled for an eye-roll emoji, and allowed herself to ask **when do you get back again?**

She swallowed. Watching those dots bounce and pause and bounce again gave her heart palpitations.

15

End of summer. I want a welcome back party. gonna smoke you at beer pong.

Oh yeah, she replied as if she hadn't known. As if she wasn't mentally counting down the days.

This summer, she wanted to be normal, as she'd told Aunt Nonni on a tense phone call after the semester ended. She didn't want to be a witch with a bounty on her head, blood on her hands, a tangle of repressed Catholic guilt in her belly. She wanted an average teen summer, like in movies. She would do her RA job, go swimming, and chill with her friends. She wanted to be a girl who didn't worry about money. A girl with a little crush.

Thalia hadn't realized she was smiling until she saw the flash of her teeth in the dark screen of the phone. She almost didn't recognize herself. Her brown curls had gotten bigger, longer, messier. Her cheekbones seemed a little more defined, and her smile—well, it appeared more often these days. Her time in the Swamp had changed her—for better, for worse—and Trent was the only other person who knew what it was like to have that cursed land sink itself so thoroughly into their consciousness. Even now, Thalia could still feel the damp soil under her nails from when Adelaide Strigwach's Wolf had dragged her into the Swamp.

It was worse at night. Thalia had never been an easy sleeper—being wanted by a violent town of witch burners will do that to a girl—but she now relied on sleeping drafts to silence her mind. Her greenwitchery had always allowed her to feel the Swamp's hexed presence, but it felt different lately. Unsettling still; a low hum against her witchy senses, droning on in the back of her mind. But rather than a fearsome thing to avoid, the presence now felt more like a *beckoning*. With her guard down at night, that hum often grew into a buzz, but she could ignore it if she tried.

She couldn't ignore the sleepwalking.

It'd happened twice since the summer began. The first time was two days after the semester ended, and a normal day by all accounts. She'd taken a walk with Jailah after dinner, then the two went back to Jai's and video-called Logan, Trent, and Mathew, the latter two joining even though the European time difference was killer. Thalia could've just stayed in her dorm room, but she always preferred the little cabin in the woods that had been passed down to a Mesmortes greenwitch for generations.

That night, she laid her head down on the pillow in the creaky old bed.

Just before dawn, Thalia woke up near the Swamp. She'd jolted upward, the shock more potent than her terror. She used to look at the Swamp like it was something to fear, but now? After she'd already been dragged into its depths by Adelaide Strigwach, a creator of its curse? How could it scare her now?

Then again, Thalia had never experienced such dark witchery. She wasn't a sleepwalker before this. Her psyche had clearly been altered, whether she felt afraid of the Swamp or not. That was the rational explanation.

You're okay, she told herself on the way back. *Be gentle with yourself.*
You are safe.

At the cabin, she'd found Maverick sleeping soundly, completely oblivious to Thalia's absence. Her bed looked hardly ruffled, and her glasses were on, which meant that she'd woken up gently and gone out as if it were a normal morning stroll.

She was eager to call it a random occurrence until it happened again this week. This time, Thalia awoke *in* the Swamp, a few yards from the border. There was dirt under her nails like she'd crawled or tried to dig something up. Without the Wolves, the Swamp was mostly quiet, but she'd left quickly, not wanting to hear her name in menacing birdsong.

Thalia rubbed her wrists. She now slept with enchanted vines tied around them that connected to a larger fearmonger shrub. If she broke it during the night, thorns sprouted from the vines to wake her.

Thalia sat on the windowsill and took in the afternoon sky. Dark clouds gathered in the distance, as they did every summer day around this time. Against the backdrop of the threatening sky, the earth looked even more menacing. Her phone lit up once more, and the immediacy with which Thalia's excitement turned into dread left her breathless.

A text from Aunt Nonni at an unplanned time, on Thalia's real phone, not the dinky throwaway in a spell-locked box under her bead, was code-red shit. It was a crack in the perfect summer of easiness that she wished to have.

We need to talk.

Thalia's fingers hovered over the buttons for a moment. **Right now?**

Her aunt's response came too long after. Thalia's heartbeat was already racing.

**No, never mind. Enjoy your weekend. Call
me Monday. Love you.**

Thalia felt a flood of relief, though a small knife in the back of her mind needled her. Something was up, but her aunt was choosing to spare her the details. She tucked the phone away.

A normal summer. Already she felt that goal slipping out of her grasp, and perhaps it was foolish to think she could have achieved it. Thalia was not a normal girl. She'd murdered a boy in her hometown and spent the last four years running away from her past. And, truthfully, there was one thing she wanted more than a simple summer break.

Thalia was going to kill her father. To do that, she had to be a fiercer greenwitch than she'd ever been before.

She touched the sprout in her finger again. Thalia knew of powerful greenwitches who reached a higher plane with their gift of the earth. White-haired elders with sprouts growing all over their bodies like creatures of a forest. The witches of the Coven of Flowers were much older than her, had studied decades in their craft, and had unlocked a connection with nature so great that earth branded them hers.

Thalia didn't have decades of witchery, but she had her first sprout. It'd broken skin after she'd pulled up trees from the earth with nothing but her own blood and magic. It was clear that everyday witchery wasn't going to heighten her power. She needed to do something else, something big.

She would cleanse the Swamp, once and for all. And when Thalia went back to Annex, Abraham Turner would see what he'd fathered. A creature of the earth, ready for vengeance.

With a smile, Thalia lifted her brand-new cauldron onto her desk and got to work.

3

jailah

The Haelsford Witchery Council was the town's judge, jury, and hexbinder.

There were no cops in Haelsford, and the three numbers used to dial in emergencies were—fittingly—666. Everything was handled by the board of seven witches who comprised the Council and those who worked under them. Council appointments weren't lifelong, and residents voted every three years on re-electing members or selecting new ones. The mundane mayor, Louis Everett, wielded no real power, aside from bargaining on behalf of the mundanes, though the Witchery Council took care of its mundanes as it took care of its witches.

Unless, of course, a witch had done something unforgivable.

That called for a hexbinding, voted on by a majority of the Council, a punishment that could last as short as a few months or as long as *forever*. Lifelong hexbindings were banishments, and Jailah always wondered how the Council could dole out such a sentence. The thought of being without her witchery sent chills up and down her arms, though Haelsford in May was as *hot as Satan's asshole*, as her pop-pop would say.

Jailah joined the Junior Witchery Council for all the connections, perks, and letters of recommendation that it promised, and as High Witch Lucia's intern, she'd hoped to see the inner workings of Haelsford's most powerful witches.

Unfortunately, today's assignment was not as exciting.

Jailah sucked her teeth. *Boring-ass filing.*

She flicked her wand and put another piece of paper into the to-be-shredded pile. "Why ain't this all digital?" she asked under the sound of shuffling papers and the whirring copy machine.

"Could be worse," said Danny Chen, a rising sophomore and new addition to the JWC. He slammed the top of the scanner bed shut. "We could be fetching lattes."

"I'd take that over this," she muttered. At least that would've meant being outside, where people could see her outfit. Jai was dressed in a modest blue pantsuit and short heels. She'd gelled her curls back into a sensible puff. She wore small silver studs and just a slight wash of gold glitter on her eyelids. She looked too damn good to spend the whole day going through trivial citizen complaints in the Council Chambers' mail room, but like every branch of the Simmons family tree, she took the motto *Dress for Success* to heart.

The mail room of the Council building was home to as much of Haelsford's history as the town's public library. Between the rows and rows of filing shelves, tall windows, and wide wooden tables, Jai thought it looked a little like a library, too. She and five other JWC members were on filing duty today, assigned to move all items from 1975 and earlier into storage to make room for new items. It was tedious work, and everyone was too focused to socialize. The quiet unnerved Jailah, her unease compounded by a low hum of guilt. She kept expecting to look up and see Jenna Prim frowning over a stack of papers. She wanted nothing more than for the young witch to prod her with pointless questions while obnoxiously popping bubble gum or loudly video-calling her friends.

Jailah rolled her shoulders, as if grief and shame were feelings that could be so easily shaken off. As much as she knew that Jenna's death at the hands of Theodore Bloom was not her fault, her heart didn't quite believe it.

A stack of papers slammed onto Jailah's table, jolting her out of her thoughts. For efficiency, they'd enchanted the filing cabinets to automatically spit out the next stack of papers once the witch was done with their current workload. Jailah groaned. Two more hours of this, and she could go 'round Thalia's to chill. Haelsford felt so empty without the rest of their coven, and she couldn't wait for everyone to be back in town. Logan was with family at least, as were Trent and Mathew, but Iris . . . The deathwitch was more than capable of handling herself, but that didn't stop Jai from worrying relentlessly about her. She worried about all of them. Everything that happened with Adelaide Strigwach and Bloom left her tense and paranoid, more feelings she wished she could shake off.

Jai flipped through the next stack of documents. Most were minor events—witches whose green ivy bushes were growing into their neighbors' yards; a mundane who'd planted blackthorne alongside the hiking trail— *what a dick*—and the parents of a former Mesmortes student who complained that Haelsford was making their child sick. Something about the air quality or limited vegan options. Jai felt her eyes glazing over and took a long draw of her iced vanilla latte.

There were occasional bits of juicy gossip, at least. She didn't know that

Professor Ethan Whittley and Professor Elizabeth Circe were married, even though she'd had classes with both of them, or that in 1981, a witch had tried to concoct a spell for *Irresistible Attraction* and ended up infecting the entirety of the town with something akin to gout. Then there was the depressing stuff. Obituaries for those who were taken by the Wolves, who heard the Swamp's call and went past the seasonal protections. Though rare, there were awful crimes. Witches who murdered mundanes, mundanes who murdered witches, witches who murdered one another, and so on. With a heavy sigh, Jai arranged them by year.

As if listening to her thoughts, Haelsford's High Witch appeared in the doorway. Lucia Alvarez was a tall woman with light brown skin, a severe black bob, and charming smile. She was one of the younger witches on the Council but carried herself with the confidence and knowledge of an elderly witch. Lucia was a respected firewitch, and her past accomplishments were Jailah's current goals: excellent grades from Mesmortes, an impressive list of extracurriculars, a highly coveted internship with a Council, and then acceptance to a top coven university.

As the interns rose from their seats, Lucia lifted a hand. "Don't let me interrupt you."

She met Jailah's eye, and Jailah's heart leapt into her throat.

"Simmons, can I steal you for a moment?"

"Of course. You can have my whole afternoon! Not that I don't love the work! I'm so appreciative of the opportunity—" She scrambled out of her seat, wondering when the hell she got so anxious.

Mercifully, Lucia only smiled as she led her up the shiny oak steps to the second floor, where the Council had their personal offices. Jailah had only been in the High Witch's office a few times, and never for very long. Most of her time was spent in the mail room or out and about to sit in on meetings with community members. The room was decorated with throw pillows, flowers, and pictures of Lucia's husband and kids. Jailah took a seat in the stiff leather chair opposite the High Witch.

"Coffee?"

Jailah ran a hand over her slicked-back hair. "No, thank you."

Lucia's levitating coffeepot topped off the mug beside her keyboard. "I'll get right into it, then. The High Witch of the Americas is arriving next week."

A cold trickle of sweat inched down Jailah's spine. She'd known this was coming. There'd been rumors about the Highest Witch in the country, Evelyn Estrada, making a trip to Haelsford since the spring. Jailah had been mentally preparing herself for this moment but found herself floundering. Theodore Bloom was dead. Adelaide Strigwach was in the wind, if not dead. And the Wolves had retreated into the Swamp where they belonged. But there was so much more to the story, and the truth of how Haelsford was almost completely overrun with Wolves could never come out.

Jailah cradled her hand in her lap. The scar that wouldn't fade still circled her wrist. She'd given too much to Mesmortes and to Haelsford to let the Council bind her witchery.

"The Highest Witch? How exciting!" she said, even managing a sweet smile.

Lucia met this with an unamused scoff. "She'd like a few firsthand accounts of the incident last Haunting Season, and I gave her your name. You were there, and it would be good for her to get to know one of

Mesmortes's brightest witches. These connections are important if you'd ever like to see yourself in the continent's Council, I'm sure you're aware. I said you'd meet her for tea."

Tea with one of the most influential witches in the world? This was a huge deal. Jailah should've been honored, but she was only apprehensive. She had to get her story straight. Her coven, the boys, they all needed to be on the same page in case Highest Witch Evelyn grew curious.

Jailah grinned, widening her big brown eyes. "It would be my honor."

"Great!" Lucia drew her wand over the fancy leather-bound planner on her desk, then commanded it shut. Between the strained smile and the snappiness of her movements, Jailah felt like Lucia couldn't wait to be done with this conversation. "It's been a few weeks since your internship began, but I promise, you won't be sorting files all summer long, I've just had a lot on my plate between the hexeaters—"

"Hexeaters?" Jailah interrupted.

Lucia winced, then sighed. "We're seeing more mundane visitors than usual, and more witches have reported being . . . accosted by hexeaters offering who knows what in exchange for witchy blood." She waved the words away nonchalantly. "More importantly, I've been busy preparing for Evie's— *High Witch* Evelyn's—visit." She cleared her throat. "Once it's over, I promise to be a more present mentor."

Jailah grinned for real this time. "No need to apologize, I'm happy to help in any way I can."

"While we're here, do you have any questions for me? I've got ten minutes until my next meeting."

Under the mixture of excitement and apprehension in her belly, Jailah felt a twinge of guilt. She'd had another reason for wanting Lucia's ear, and it had nothing to do with herself or the future she wanted, but everything to do with a past she couldn't forget and a promise she intended to keep.

Unlike some of the older Council members, Lucia never cared for displays of deference, so Jailah straightened her back and looked directly into the High Witch's dark eyes. "I do have a question, actually, if you don't mind. It's about Veronica Dominguez."

Lucia raised a thin brow. "Oh? What about her?"

Jailah felt like she was already losing a battle that'd barely begun, but she continued, doling out the southern sweetness known to melt even the coldest hearts. "I respect the Council's decision regarding her hexbinding, but with two years already gone, I guess I wonder if her punishment could be—"

"I'm going to stop you right there, Simmons." Lucia folded her hands together in a way that made Jailah think of her mama when she was about to be chastised. "There are some members of the Council that are still . . . apprehensive of you."

Stunned, Jailah blinked. "Of me?"

"You were very close to Ms. Dominguez, and while you did the right thing in telling us of her intentions, well, let's just say that there are questions about whether a witch who was so close to a radical could serve well on a Council in the future. You're still so young, and you're so *bright*. Don't let your past mistakes jeopardize your future."

Jailah's grip on her knees tightened, her long pink acrylics digging into her skin through her pants. She wanted to ask who exactly on the Council doubted her, and why. Assuming they knew nothing about Jailah and her friends' role in the last Haunting Season, what was there to doubt her for? She'd been nothing but dutiful in her role in the JWC, as a student at Mesmortes, rising captain of their archery team, and as a damn teen. *Everyone loves Jailah.* That was the type of thing she heard all the time, whether genuinely or jealously, and it was always so easy to believe.

It was Jailah who stood before the hungry Wolves, making Mesmortes's last stand before Logan killed the Wolf Boy. It was Jailah, armed with a bow, arrow, and her expertly crafted knowledge of spells, who stood up to the most fearsome beasts on the planet. Did Lucia have any scars? Jailah did: one around her wrist where she nearly gave up her hand as a last resort.

And where were you and your fellow Council members that night? she wanted to scream. *Oh yeah! Sleeping soundly under a goddamn spell!*

Even with her internship, Jailah knew that a teen witch likely wouldn't be able to influence the Council's decision on a hexbinding. Still, she'd hoped to chip away, planting the seeds for leniency in Lucia's mind. It probably wouldn't have worked, but at least she could've said that she tried. For Vero, and for herself. How wrong she was.

Lucia sipped her coffee. "You were such good friends, and I know it's hard to think of someone you care for suffering, but you'd do well to let Veronica Dominguez go." She offered Jailah a placating smile, then whispered, as if they weren't already alone, "By the end of the summer, you'll see how much more there is to magic when you've got the right connections."

The guilt grew heavier, because the look in Lucia's eyes reminded Jailah of what she wanted for herself and for her future. Jailah could never forget Veronica entirely, but for a few seconds, nothing existed but the High Witch's secretive promise and the daydreams quickly filling up her mind.

Jailah wiped her slick palms on her pants and took a deep breath. She managed an embarrassed little laugh. "You're right, High Witch Lucia. Thank you for your time."

That evening in the mess hall, Jailah filled Thalia in over steaming plates of pasta. As she explained that they'd need to be ready for High Witch Evelyn's visit, Thalia considered everything with her usual skeptical brow.

Jailah pointed at Thalia's face. "Mmm, I don't like that look, girl."

"Why the hell did you bring up Veronica?"

Jailah groaned around a mouthful of ciabatta.

"You still feel like you owe her, don't you?"

"S'like I keep wondering what would've happened if I hadn't reported her—"

"Jai, you know what would've happened. If the spell worked, then all of us would've been without our witchery. And if it hadn't worked, then Vero would've *died*. Olga Yara's spells are—" Thalia cut herself off, no doubt remembering that Jailah and Iris had used one of Yara's spells to save her after Adelaide Strigwach pulled her into the Swamp. As if reading Jailah's mind, Thalia huffed. "Y'all used *Convergence* for good. Veronica wanted to use *The Culling* to wreck shit. Even if she did succeed, what would that have been for? Another Council would've come to Haelsford and set everything to rights, and Vero would've been fully banished."

It wasn't like Jailah hadn't thought all this through before. But seeing her in that abandoned industrial complex in the winter left her mulling it over and over again. "You right."

"I know about guilt," Thalia continued, pushing a few stray beans around her plate. "Have you even thought about what it would be like if she came back here?"

Oh, Jailah had. And she'd keep those thoughts to herself. "Like I said, *you right*. Forget Vero, I'm moving on."

Thalia rolled her eyes. It was obvious that she didn't believe her.

"No, real talk, I need to focus on my meeting with Highest Witch Evelyn—we *all* do. When the crew gets back, we need to make sure our stories are straight. Nothing 'bout that Haunting mess can come back to us, yeah?"

Thalia glanced at her thumb, then nodded.

Jailah rolled her shoulders. It was good to focus on a problem she could solve rather than one she couldn't. Be it the HWC, or the Highest Witch, or the whole damn Swamp, she'd put herself and her friends first. It was her coven above all.

4

trent

Trenton Hogarth was cold—not because living in Haelsford had significantly diminished his tolerance to the unseasonable London chill, but because he was standing in the room where his mother kept her knives.

The room had largely been left alone since she died. The walls were pristine, the knives fastened in a methodical arrangement. Short wooden pillars held jewelry in dainty glass cases, as if this were a showroom or a museum. Trent plucked a single opal ring from one of the displays and slid it onto his finger.

He'd expected some sort of otherworldly, paranormal acknowledgment, but Lourdes Hogarth didn't speak to him the way she used to. Their connection was severed.

Trent spent the years since his mother's passing under the watchful eye of her soul, her spirt, her . . . demon? Trent wasn't sure what to call it anymore. He used to feel like there was a guardian angel on his shoulder, but after what he'd seen in the Swamp, he wasn't so sure. She'd come to him as a specter from a nightmare. The image of her wrinkly gray skin and lidless eyes didn't scare him as much as it motivated him now, but those first days after Hell Night were difficult to get through. Thalia had eased his mind with some spell called *Dreamdaze,* and Mathew was always there to distract him. Trent had avoided the thought of her, but now? Now he was back in, headfirst.

"What did you do?" he whispered. "What was the bloodpact? And—"

He swallowed. He couldn't bear saying this next bit aloud.

Who did you promise me to?

"Trenton?" His father's voice traveled up the stairs. "You up there? You have a *guest.*"

Trent frowned. There was a lot of animosity in that last word, and sure enough, a black Jaguar was waiting just under the window. Eighteen-year-old Rixton Barnes leaned up against it in a tailored red suit, looking perfect with his short locs and flawless brown skin. Trent looked down at himself. He hadn't bothered changing out of the ripped-up hoodie from when he and his old crew went skating at the park earlier this afternoon.

"Trenton," his father repeated, closer this time. Trent turned and saw him there in the doorway, his father's dark brow furrowed in annoyance. "Didn't you hear me?"

"Sorry," Trent offered simply.

Damien Hogarth's eyes softened as he smoothed his tie. He was tall and gray-haired, broad-shouldered and stately. He looked around the room, then sighed as if it hurt to do so. "I keep meaning to take these down."

"Don't."

His father nodded absently. "Are you okay?"

"Yeah. I'm okay."

Damien angled his head at his son, like it was the first time he'd really

31

looked at Trent in the two weeks since he'd arrived in London. "It's that Barnes boy. Shall I invite him for supper, or send him on his way?"

Trent swallowed hard. Everyone who knew Trent knew that Rixton was his weakness. But suddenly, he just couldn't summon the desire to care. He looked down at his phone, at the picture of him and Thalia grinning with Maverick tucked between them, the dog taking a big lick at Trent's cheek. "Tell him I'm sick?"

Damien raised a brow.

Trent sighed. His father was all about being straight up with people. He found these little white lies to be cowardly; if Trent wanted nothing to do with Rixton, then he'd better go down there and tell him himself.

Trent was preparing to do just that, but Damien shook his head suddenly. "All right. I'll get rid of him." He looked around the room once more, then cleared his throat. "Be down for supper."

"You two again?" Troy asked the second Trent sat down at the table. "I promised the lad a proper smack in the face and haven't yet had the time to deliver."

Trent could do nothing but laugh. For once, Troy getting all into his Big Brother role wasn't entirely annoying. "Never. Rixton and I were incompatible. I had on first-love goggles, my vision was all fogged up. Besides, *someone* hated Rixton."

At the head of the table, Damien's eyes didn't leave his plate. He cut up his steak meticulously. "I did not hate Rixton."

Oh, and this was so like him. Revisionist history was his specialty. Trent chuckled humorlessly. "You kept saying he wasn't good enough for me."

"I didn't hate Rixton," Damien repeated.

"Sure."

"What I hated was the way he treated you."

Trent's eyes darted to Troy, wanting confirmation. Troy only shrugged.

"You couldn't see it, Trenton, but I could. He didn't deserve you; you're better than that. Pass the salt."

Troy and their father carried the conversation away from this, but Trent was uninterested in more talk about properties and stocks. He was stunned. His father had never said anything like this before, not when Rixton was spending entire summer days at the Hogarth house.

Trent and Mathew often complained about their parents to each other. They were dealing with legacies and expectations, and Trent was further tasked with continuing his father's success as a self-made Black man without the financial safety that ran through Mathew's entire family. Mathew went on and on about how his parents saw him and Rebecca as necessary things to carry on the name, obligations to fulfill, duties long assigned. But Damien . . . as much as he loathed his father's detachment, Trent never doubted that his father loved him. It seemed inherently wrong that a parent not love their child, but Trent wasn't sure that Mathew could say the same about his.

Trent turned to his father. "Dad. Do you know what a bloodpact is?"

Troy's gaze bounced between them.

Damien stopped cutting his steak but kept his eyes down. "No."

"Okay. Do you know what Mum was up to . . ." His voice trailed off. Damien lifted his eyes in warning, but Trent pressed on. "When she was in the Haelsfordian Coven Troupe, who did she hang out with? Who were her friends?"

"Enough."

33

"She did something, didn't she? She made a deal—"

His father's voice was rough and sharp, the equivalent of slamming his palm on the table without actually doing so. "I said *enough*."

Trent sat back in his chair. Troy looked away from both of them.

The rest of the meal was mostly quiet. Trent said nothing more about his mother, not out of anger or sadness but out of fatigue. He was exhausted with trying to pry information from his father.

Perhaps he was looking in the wrong place anyway. Lourdes Hogarth had moved from the States to London to be with Damien, but Haelsford was her true home. She wasn't born there, and only lived in the small witchtown to be a part of the troupe. If his father wasn't going to help him, then he needed to go back to the place where she'd left her mark.

Later that evening, Trent found his father in his study. Damien was listening to soft jazz as he worked on a sudoku set, a half-filled cup of tea at his side.

"I'm going to Haelsford tomorrow," Trent said stiffly.

Damien tightened the grip on his pen. "So soon?"

"I'll stay with the Beaumonts since the dorms are closed. And I'll make a trip back before the semester starts." His father said nothing, so Trent moved to close the door behind him. "Night."

"Wait."

Trent turned and found his father looking at him with heavy eyes.

"My boy. I love you. You know that, right?"

"I know."

"And sometimes . . . love means doing anything to keep the people close to you safe."

Trent had a million burning questions. *What are you so afraid of me finding out?* he wanted to ask. *What aren't you telling me?*

But the iciness of his father's posture returned, and Trent was certain that this conversation was over. So, he said, "I love you, too, Pop," and shut the door.

Hand still on the doorknob, Trent's fingertips suddenly flooded with heat. His mother's ring glimmered in the moonlight streaming in from the window, an opal gem cradled in a crest of gold. He rubbed his hand and flexed his fingers, but the prickly heat remained, like flames dancing underneath his skin.

5

mathew

June

Mathew Beaumont had only been in Haelsford for three days, and his anxiety was already reaching its peak. Uneasy stomach, twitchy heart, a constant sweat—or maybe that was from the relentless Florida heat.

Alone in his bedroom, he kept the windows open. The chatter of his neighbors' kids, the buzzing mosquitoes, and the whip of the wind kept him here in his bed, *safe*.

Stay grounded, Dr. Birch had told him. As if it were that easy to stop his mind from drifting toward that night at the Necromantic Emporium, or from remembering Iris's sweat-slick face as she held on to him, ignoring his pleas to save herself. The hexed flames that Adelaide Strigwach set inside her shop visited him every night, and every quiet moment he could muster was interrupted by the smell of burning wood. He thought of Jailah Simmons staring down at them in the rubble after the crooked shop had been burned to ash. *How are you both okay?* she'd asked, relieved and worried and awestruck all at once.

Mathew hadn't known the answer to her question then, and he still didn't know now. He shut his eyes hard, trying to focus on the dog barking somewhere in the neighborhood. It didn't help. All he wanted was to yell at it to shut up.

Frustrated, he forced himself upright and checked his phone. Trent was on his way over, thank god, and Mathew delighted at the pic of him at Heathrow. In the group text called *children of the (organic) corn*, Logan showed off a loaf of homemade bread—**tastes better than it looks, and I did it all wandless!! Ahh!**—to which he replied with a burst of confetti. Jailah sent a very excited voice note, and Thalia was her usual self—an LOL here, an emoji there.

And then there was Iris, nowhere to be found.

He had to scroll all the way up to the beginning of the message to see her only update since the summer started.

I'll be back on June 3. y'all won't hear
from me til then, but I promise I'll be okay.

According to Jai, Iris did what she'd always done—just up and left in the middle of the night. Unlike Hammersmitt, the Mesmortes dorms were open year-round for witches who'd been born into witch-averse families, and for anyone else who considered the coven academy to be their one and only home. Thalia checked with Iris's RA, and the deathwitch had filled out the required checkout form. Under *Reason for Leaving*, she'd written *parental visit*.

Mathew had one more day until her return. It made him anxious to think about the conversation they both knew was coming, the one she'd managed to avoid before he left on a family trip to Italy. Well, *family trip* was putting it nicely. He and his twin sister did three days with their mother in Venice, four with their father in Rome, and spent the entire time texting each other about how hard divorce sucked.

From down the hallway of the quiet mini-mansion, Mathew heard a stream of expletives delivered with a valley-girl edge.

He trudged out of his room and to the door that was decorated with a homemade flower arrangement. Rebecca's one weakness? Seasonal decorations. He knocked softly.

"Yeah?" she snapped.

He pushed the door and found Rebecca lying in bed, holding her Nintendo Switch above her face.

She glanced over at him, blue eyes dazed. "I'm about to beat your score in *Starlit Oblivion*, bitch."

"Have you slept?" Mathew asked, though the answer was obvious.

A warning tune chimed from her game and she cursed under her breath. "You're distracting me, leave!"

Mathew sighed, heart growing tender. Her room was messier than usual. Their mother had been calling Rebecca a walking hurricane since she was little, although the nickname had become less cutesy and more chastising as she grew older. He stepped over a pile of clothes, a spilled box of tampons, paperbacks, discarded school assignments, a tin of weed, then plopped onto the edge of her bed.

When he looked over at her now, the shining, platinum-colored mark at the base of her neck was apparent, even though the black turtleneck—one of ten that now comprised her entire wardrobe—should've obscured it. A death mark, Mathew knew. He was the one who had told his sister what she was now and what she could do on that stormy night when her witchery revealed itself. Their parents went hysteric as Rebecca's aura grew, that undeniably witchy heat pulsing around them.

A necromancer? Rebecca had asked, the word coming out with equal parts fear and exhilaration. *Like your . . . friend?*

And at the mention of Iris, Mathew's stomach had tangled up in a mixture of pleasure and pain.

"Trent's gonna stay with us this summer," Mathew said softly. "He'll be here tomorrow."

At that, Rebecca did smile, at least. "Good. I miss him."

"Me too." Mathew rubbed his hands. "We're throwing a party, just so you know."

Now, a frown. "Here?"

"Since Mom and Dad will be gone—hey, don't look at me like that, you used to throw parties all the time. And it's not even going to be a big thing. Just—"

"You and Trent and your witch friends?" There was something sharp in her voice. "No thanks."

"Maybe it would be good for you, Becky. You could learn about your magic."

"*Hello.* They'll cut me out of the will."

"They wouldn't really do that."

Rebecca lowered the game just enough for her angry eyes to be seen.

"*Or.* I'll split with you." He rubbed his hands again, his palms sweaty. "Have you thought about . . . everything . . . yet?"

Everything was the manila folder on Rebecca's bedside table, currently being used as a coaster for three lipstick-stained mugs and a cereal bowl. *Everything* was them choosing who they would live with until graduation.

"Whatever." Rebecca turned onto her side. Her dark hair fell away from her face, revealing deathly pale skin. Mathew's stomach turned.

"Becky, you're making yourself sick," he pressed on. "Your magic is just trapped up inside you—"

"Me? Have you looked at yourself? Any mention of the d-word and you start looking like your dog just died."

Mathew wiped his brow. For once the trigger causing his heartbeat to tick up had nothing to do with witches and hexes. It was the impending breaking of his family and, most importantly, the health of his sister that left him scrambling. Between the supernatural and the mundane parts of his life, he desperately needed everything to be okay.

"We don't have a dog," Mathew said finally. "Don't worry about me, you need to be taking care of your witchery—"

"Oh my *godddddddd*!" Rebecca whined, dragging that last syllable for as long as she could. "I'm fine. Stop worrying, you sound like Mom."

It was a lie, they both knew, because their mother wasn't concerned about Rebecca, or at least not for her well-being. She was concerned that Rebecca wouldn't be able to hide her witchiness forever. As for their father—he spent most of his time on the phone, scouring the web, riffling through books to find a *cure for witchery*. That was the reason for their latest blowup; Mathew had called him a fuckup as a father, and neither had spoken to the other since. This big house was quiet, haunting, and miserable, and all Mathew wanted was to have his friends and his sister here to make it better.

He hated seeing Rebecca like this, but he didn't know what to do when she refused to meet him halfway. "I've got therapy. You wanna come?"

Rebecca made a sound like a cat hacking up a hairball.

"Got it." Mathew shook his head and left.

PORT BARROW SUPPORT GROUP FOR

VICTIMS OF PARANORMAL PHENOMENA

As always, Mathew cringed at the little sign taped onto the door at the Port Barrow rec center. *Paranormal phenomena* wasn't so bad, but *victim*? It was true that he'd been left with nightmares and cold sweats, and was jumpier than ever, but. Well. He just didn't like the word. When Trent had texted him a picture of the flyer before he left for London, Mathew had simply replied, **I'm good**. He'd been getting help at the time from Dr. Birch, a therapist who his parents had brought him to. Mathew liked Dr. Birch well enough, but whenever he tried to explain the constant replaying of fire and death, of blood and Wolves—in vague enough terms that didn't give away the coven's secrets—she just wanted him to count backward, or to *breathe*. The grounding techniques were only so helpful when he could clearly recall the worry in Iris's perfect dark eyes. He took up boxing between moments spent on the fields with his beloved horse, Ruby. Punching things helped him forget everything, if only for an hour.

But when Mathew had flinched hard at the click of Trent's lighter, had

gone pale at the sight of the flame, Trent gave his shoulder a squeeze. *Mate.*
You need help.

So, Mathew ended up here, in group therapy, two towns over from
Haelsford. He took his usual seat—four down from the center of the
circle—and balanced the napkin of cookies from the refreshments table
on his knee. People liked to mingle before sessions started, but Mathew
always felt awkward and out of place.

Usually, there were only one or two other kids his age at these meetings,
and they kept to themselves as well. Mathew assumed group might've been
something their parents forced them into, judging from their inability to
put their phones away, but today, he noticed a freckly redheaded girl on the
other side of the semicircle. She looked up at him, and then quickly turned
back to her phone to cut the awkward moment short.

As always, they went around the room for introductions, first names only.

"I'm Chloe," said the new redhead. "Uh, first meeting."

Pamela, the group's leader, welcomed her with open arms. "We're happy
to have you, Chloe. What brings you here? Share as little or as much as
you'd like."

The girl flushed but nodded appreciatively. She glanced around the
room, her eyes landing on Mathew briefly. "I was . . . under the spell of a
witch. It made me forget who I was."

The group murmured empathetically. Lorelai, the group's eldest member, even gasped and prayed.

"That's all," Chloe whispered. She pulled her sweatshirt sleeves down
and shrugged.

"This seat taken?"

Mathew turned to the elderly man gesturing to the open seat next to him. He swallowed down a mouthful of cookie and said, "No, go ahead."

"First time, and I'm late." He presented his hand. "Name's Robbie."

"Mathew." He took the man's hand.

Heat seared in Mathew's palm. His vision flashed to a moment far from here. He saw Robbie on the floor, gasping for breath, the light winking out of his eyes. He flinched hard and jerked his hand out of the man's grasp.

Robbie eyed him worriedly. "You okay, son?"

Mathew resisted the urge to dig his nails into his palm. "Just zoned out for a second."

Intrusive thoughts, Dr. Birch had said, writing it out for him on a bright pink index card. *You'll see things that happened, and sometimes, your brain will simply make things up. Remember that these are only thoughts. They can't hurt you, no matter how violent or unsettling. They're just in your head.*

In the beginning, Mathew couldn't go a few minutes without picturing Adelaide Strigwach's face. Her *true* face, not the one she'd put on during her masquerade as the town's resident outcast, the Roddin Witch. His mind showed him alternate endings where he was stuck in the Chasm, scrambling in the sea of souls to get back to Earth. Now this. Picturing a stranger dying violently on the floor of the rec center.

Across the room, the new girl raised a brow, silently asking, *You okay?* He forced a smile, and she returned it before refocusing on Pamela.

Mathew clenched his fists, even though Dr. Birch tried to steer him away from using tension or pain to ground himself. But he needed to do something to keep himself here, and not in his nightly dreams of Iris wearing a dark hood around her skeleton-painted face, speaking of his true purpose.

43

6

logan

The Wyatt household was busy with gossip, food, and magic.

Logan, one of the youngest in the house, had been seated at the grand dining table while Margot, two years older, was relegated to the kiddie table a few feet away. Go sat grinding her teeth between their rambunctious cousins, and Logan chuckled at how things had changed.

Uncle Tobin, three cups deep, laughed with Logan's mother. He said, "I knew she had it in her."

Diane Wyatt placed an affectionate hand on Logan's shoulder. "Wyatt blood is always blessed." She smiled at Logan, though it faltered at the sight of the thin scar across Logan's eye. "All it took was a little time, but we all knew she'd ring true."

Logan smiled back.

Liars.

The evening was excruciating. Conversation came and went, but always turned back to Logan. *Show us that glow,* Aunt Tana said sardonically, wriggling her fingers. At first, sticking it to gossipy Tana and perpetually scoffing Uncle Mark was thrilling. Not only was her magic obedient, but being a proxy meant she didn't need a wand, hardly required incantations, and could complete a spell in an instant. Her mother enjoyed it as well, parading Logan around these parties with the smuggest *I told you so* face on earth. Logan delighted at showing off to her bratty army of cousins who had always looked down on her.

A year ago, she wouldn't have wanted anything more than to be welcomed as a true Wyatt, one who was, like all the others, powerfully witchy. But Logan hadn't forgotten how brutal those years before she received her blessing were. And then when her witchery *had* come to her—a whole three years late—it hardly mattered, as her magic was temperamental, explosive, and weak all at the same time. She didn't know what was worse: to be a mundane Wyatt, or to be a weak witch.

Now, with magic-rich blood and full control over her ability to proxy, those feelings of insecurity were replaced with something else. A wistfulness.

She looked out of the floor-to-ceiling windows behind her. Night was falling on Wicker, a tiny village on the outskirts of Toronto. *I miss Haelsford*, Logan thought, hardly believing it. She loved Margot and her nosy mother deeply, but she also missed the space that came with being away from her massive family. She missed her little coven of witches, especially now that their covenhood had been sealed in something bigger than shared jokes and sleepovers. She missed the way the air smelled like freshly cut grass and wildflowers, and the way it was always thick with dark magic.

Her smartwatch buzzed, and Logan knew before looking at the notification that it was a text from Margot. Her sister was texting furiously with one hand and shoveling mashed potatoes into her mouth with the other. Logan glanced down at her phone.

Do you need saving? Let's take a walk.

Or maybe I need saving

I'm pretty sure baby Melody needs a

diaper change and JE REFUSE.

After quietly excusing herself, Logan found herself out in the summer night tucked next to her sister.

"You've got thirty-six hours before you're back in Haelsford, so let me get my sister-time in." Margot ran her fingers through her hair, or what was left of it. The left side was shorn, and what she kept had been freshly cut so it reached her nose. Logan's hair, on the other hand, had gone over-grown like weeds. Her bangs were too long, her strands perpetually shaggy, and her ends could probably use a good chop. But she looked into the mirror every morning and decided that she liked looking a little unkempt, a bit feral, a look compounded by the scar a Wolf had left over her eye. The messier it got, the more she felt like herself. Also, she knew it annoyed her mother, and that was always a plus.

They came up to the empty park, and predictably, Go hopped onto the railing and proceeded to cross it as if she were a trapeze artist. "I'm gonna miss you, as always. Don't have too much fun without me."

"Never."

Go laughed. "You know, when I picked you up from the airport, I thought, is that really my little sister?"

46

Logan stopped walking. "What do you mean?"

Go hopped off the end of the railing and turned to her. "You were just—"

She shook her head. "You smiled. It was like you were *totally* happy."

Logan looked away, hiding a grin.

"I mean, like, after all the shit you told me about Haelsford and Mesmortes, I don't know what I expected. I keep meaning to ask you . . . what happened? What made you proxy?"

Heat crept up Logan's neck. She wasn't the best liar, and this was Go, who knew how to spot her lies better than anyone. "The Wolves, I guess. That night was *so* scary."

"Thank fuck you weren't hurt!" Margot shook her head, sharp locks swaying. "What a nightmare."

More than you know, Logan thought. She'd sworn a pact with Thalia, Iris, Jailah, Trent, and Mathew. No one could know what they'd done, not even a sister as close to Logan as Go was. It wasn't just the resurrection of Theodore Bloom that Logan desperately wanted to tell her about. She wanted to rest her head on her big sister's shoulder and cry over the first boy to break her heart. When she thought of Bloom now, she felt more anger than sadness—an improvement, in her eyes—but couldn't shake the needling feeling that he was still there. Under her skin. She'd passed a brown-haired boy in town and felt goose bumps up her arms. A neighbor's dog got too close? She thought of snarling teeth and bloodred eyes. Logan swallowed. The touch of Bloom's violent fingers around her throat was a difficult thing to forget.

But Logan kept her mouth shut. She imagined she'd confess to Margot someday, but it was still so fresh and, truthfully, Logan was a little scared of how the Red Three might react if they ever found out. Their commitment to secrecy wasn't a bloodpact, but it sure felt like life or death. It was Logan who had enabled Bloom to wreak havoc on Mesmortes. No one had spoken of her betrayal after she killed the Wolf Boy herself, but Logan was adamant on proving her loyalty.

Margot snapped her fingers suddenly. "Go ahead, do that thing you do."

Logan raised a brow.

"Being the Wyatts' only proxy means you're our own personal glow stick—don't make that face! Come on, flashlight!"

Logan groaned, even though she wasn't all that upset to have a reason to use her magic for her sister. "Fine."

She lifted her hands, aiming them at the pile of trash some passerby had left on a park bench. *"Azuamorraille!"* Logan shouted.

Even now, with the glow rising in her hands and the heat of her magic warming her blood, doubt crept in. Anxiety hummed in her belly. Shame warmed her cheeks, as it always had since she received her blessing.

But her witchery responded. Like a slow-rolling wave, Logan's witchery grew in her chest, pulsing, warming her skin. Her hands lit up, glowing as if the sun were alight under her skin.

Margot laughed. "There it is!"

Logan focused, threw her magic outward, and levitated the trash into the bin where it belonged.

Baby witch, she thought fondly, imagining the Red Three watching her now. *Look at her, getting all excited about doing a freshman-level spell.*

Margot threw her arms around Logan. "Not just cool, but environmentally conscious, too."

Logan sputtered a laugh.

Margot squeezed tighter. "I'm gonna miss you, Lo."

Logan's arrival in Haelsford was different this time. She knew her way around town and didn't have to keep looking at her phone for directions. She didn't feel like people were staring at her—though, okay, they probably never were in the first place—and when she passed other witches, she felt that irresistible pull of covenhood, even if it was entirely in her head.

Best of all, she had friends to look forward to seeing. Judging from the excitement in the group text, tonight's party at the Beaumonts' was going to be exactly what she needed before digging into what she was considering her first *real* semester at Mesmortes now that she could use her magic. Unlike every other person in town, witchy or mundane, Logan couldn't wait for school to start.

But first, a strawberry shake.

As she grabbed her order from the counter at Sugar, her thoughts were cut off by a whistle. High-pitched and nearly unbearable.

Out of her magic's own volition, her witchery bloomed, her body warming. Sweat beaded on the back of her neck. Logan's heart pounded in her ears as she snapped her head around to look for the source. Clearly, someone was playing a prank. The Haunting Season was over. The Wolves were hibernating. No one else at the busy ice cream shop seemed to have heard it. Was she having a panic attack? Maybe her blood sugar was low. She took a long draw from the shake—

Then there was a hungry and vicious growl, and Logan knew she wasn't just hearing things. The sound vibrated through her body and rattled her bones. Suddenly, everything was too loud, and she had to get away from the sound that contracted around her. She pushed through the chatty crowd of teenagers outside Sugar's entrance and nearly collided with a boy her age.

"Whoa!" he gasped, clutching her arms to steady her. "Are you okay?"

The dizziness subsided, but Logan's pulse thundered under her skin—a searing, foreboding feeling. She craned her head up and looked at the boy, and a thought in her head said to *run*.

But his hands were so tight around her arms.

She thought of Bloom. His smile, his eyes, his hold on her.

Heat flooded her fingertips. She exhaled. "What are you doing?"

The boy didn't seem to hear her. His eyes were wide at the sight of her glowing hands. She'd wished it was in fear, but the fire dancing in his eyes signaled dangerous delight.

"Logan?"

She saw Mathew Beaumont approaching over the boy's shoulder, wearing his Soma Café apron and cap. He smiled at her, then looked at the boy from the shake shop. His face furrowed in concern.

Before Logan could react, pain shot through her side. She jolted back, and the boy sprinted away.

Gasping, Logan scrambled to make sense of what just happened. Mathew was there then, a gentle hand on her shoulder. With the other, he whipped out his phone to take pictures of the fleeing boy.

"Who was that?" Logan asked, her side burning.

Mathew's voice was tense. "You're bleeding."

She looked down. A red stain seeped into the white fabric of her tee. She lifted it and saw the long but shallow cut that the boy had made. She hadn't even seen the blade. The pain wasn't totally unbearable, but her stomach turned at the sight of the wound.

From nausea and fear, a heady anger flashed wildly through her. Her witchery still pulsing, she snapped toward the direction of the boy and jerked up her glowing hands—

"Logan!" Mathew sputtered next to her. He teetered between stepping closer to her and stepping away. "Hey, he's gone!"

Logan didn't want Mathew's plea. She wanted to watch the boy writhe in pain, to hear him scream apologies and beg forgiveness. She was a real witch now. Her magic was not something a boy should test.

The warm feeling of blood dripping down her hips melted away the furious daze. The pain, numbed for a few cold seconds, returned with sharp throbs.

Logan looked up at Mathew, the sight of him grounding her. She looked down at her hands. The yellow glow dissipated slowly, leaving little pointed tips at the ends of her fingers.

Mathew looked her up and down, brow furrowed. "We need to report it to the Council—"

"No, just . . . take me to Thalia." Her hand clutching her side, Logan steadied herself. She felt foolish. All that time spent showing off for her family, and she hadn't practiced any practical spells, like ones for healing. "Did you get a good picture?"

Mathew shook his head. "Not of his face, but . . ."

He angled his phone to her and zoomed in on the picture. The pale skin of the back of the boy's neck was marked with black lines.

···•→ ✴ ←•···

"Hexeaters," Thalia spat, closing up the jar of green healing salve. "I forgot it's your first summer in Haelsford. There's more of them in the summertime. You'll see them traveling in weird little packs, trying to get the attention of every witch passing by. It's super annoying."

From Thalia's bed, Logan looked at the greenwitch's handiwork. There weren't any stitches, but a few thin silver lines shimmered on her skin where the wound had been.

"Usually they just talk some mess about buying your blood or offering to be your lackey. Others are straight-up violent," Jailah added, shaking her head. "High Witch Lucia says that they've been real aggressive lately."

"Right before it happened, I . . ." Logan's voice trailed off as she considered how likely it was that the howls were real, and not just in her head. She'd been so sure before.

Jai's brow twitched. "You what?"

Shame grew in Logan's cheeks. There were many reasons for Jailah to be suspicious of Logan. If Logan still felt guilt about it, then it made sense for them to have reservations, too.

"You looked confused," said Mathew, swirling his chipped mug of sweet tea. "I couldn't tell what was going on at first, I just felt like something was wrong. And then I saw his tats, so I knew he was trouble."

Logan nodded. "I *was* confused. I thought I'd heard a howl."

To her credit, Jailah didn't flinch.

"I think I was having a panic attack," Logan added quickly. "Maybe being back in Haelsford triggered it."

Mathew chuckled humorlessly. "Yeah, well, you're not alone." He looked down at his hands, then cleared his throat.

"We went through something no one else in this town has," Thalia said matter-of-factly, a blush just slightly visible on her cheeks. "No telling how our minds are gonna handle it."

"You should come with me to the Council, Logan," said Jailah. "That creep needs to be punished."

Logan waved her hands frantically. "No, let's just forget about it. Trust me, I'm okay."

Thalia sputtered, "You were just assaulted!"

"I'm fine!" Logan tried to smile. "I don't want to think about hexeaters or Wolves or whatever. We have a party to get ready for, and summer school is starting, I just want to relax and have a boring summer!"

Jailah threw her hands up. "Fine, but if you change your mind, let me know." She held out a hand to Logan, who took it gratefully. "And don't worry, this summer *is* going to be perfect."

Logan grinned back, for real this time. It was easy to believe Jailah, and she so wanted it to be true.

7

iris

Iris arrived last to Beaumont's, her legs still wobbly from the long drive to Haelsford. She showed up with three bags of hot chips, a liter of Sprite, and a bottle of whiskey from her parents' house—not like they could drink it anyway.

A light flickered in one of the second-story windows. Iris caught the edge of something, or *someone*, behind blue lace curtains. That was odd on its own, but the prickle of heat on her death mark was even more curious.

There was a joyous scream from inside the house, and Iris reflexively braced herself.

Jailah Simmons threw open the door. "There she is, *ay*!"

The pure glee on Jai's face warmed Iris's skin and brought a full smile to her lips. Jai flung herself into Iris's arms with little care for her snacks or her ability to breathe, but Iris was more than happy to catch her.

"Hi, Jai," Iris choked out. "Those are my lungs—"

There was no helping her, because here was Logan with a flash of blond hair, a red scar, and a new, dense feel of witchery against Iris's own. She hugged them both. "You're here! Finally!"

"Yep! And slowly losing oxygen!"

"Will you give her some space?" The voice of reason, bless her. Thalia Blackwood peeked at her over Logan's and Jai's heads to meet Iris's eye. "Hi, deathwitch. Answer your texts much?"

Iris laughed. "I did warn y'all."

Thalia joined the snuggle, and then there were four, the coven complete, holding one another like the world was ending when they'd only spent a few weeks apart.

Jai sighed, breaking the hug. "Yeah, but after what happened, maybe we shouldn't go 'round deserted islands without a hot spot, yeah?"

Iris grumbled in agreement. Jailah did have a point. She looked at Logan. "Look at you. Baby witch, all bursting with magic."

Logan straightened and mimed a runway walk down the Beaumonts' cobblestone driveway.

Jailah tutted. "Logan, right foot over left, stand up straight—ugh, *here*—" Jailah walked beside her, pulling out one of the pageant walks that surely netted her first place in some Miss Alabama contest. They took turns showing off, Thalia laced her fingers between Iris's, and it was so perfect that her heart squeezed.

Inside, there was the strangely alluring and slightly intoxicating sound of laughter. Boy laughter. Her Hammersmitts.

Grinning, Jailah cleared her throat in that exaggerated way that signaled trouble. "Come on. The boys'll be wonderin' where we went."

Iris played with the frayed strings of her denim skirt. "Can't we just stay here for a moment? Like, isn't this so nice?"

Thalia bit her lip against a laugh.

"Just the four of us! Like old times, us girls!"

Logan blew up at her bangs. "I literally just got here, so. My memory of *old times* is digging up an asshole from a grave."

Iris snapped her fingers at her. "Exactly!"

With a laugh, Logan turned on her heel. Thalia, pumping her brows upward, followed.

Jai looked at Iris deviously.

Iris held up a hand. "Whatever you wanna say, keep it."

"I'm just warning you. I'm a whole lesbian, and even I can see that Matty is looking *foine*—"

"Okay, going in now!"

Beaumont Manor was exactly what Iris expected from white people with too much money. Everything was very clean—sterile, rather—the art was boring, and the house felt suffocatingly unlived in. But as they followed the laughter into the den, which was littered with couch cushions and had beer pong set up on an expensive piano, Iris's shoulders relaxed.

For a moment, she just watched him. Mathew Beaumont stood behind Trent Hogarth, directing him on the video game he was playing—*You've gotta hold B, then aim, Trent*—and she savored what he was like when he didn't know she was looking. The way he rubbed the back of his neck and rocked on his heels. His eyes popped open when he laughed, and he played with his sleeves, all antsy.

Jailah cupped her hands around her mouth to announce Iris's arrival, but before she could get the words out, Beaumont stilled. And he turned. And he took her in, up and down and back again.

"We're back!" Jailah sang. "And we brought a deathwitch!"

It was Trent who rushed over to her, throwing himself over the back of the enormous sofa to get to her as quickly as possible. "Keaton-Fooooosterrrrr!"

Iris laughed. He hugged her, and she hugged him back, stunned by how much she missed his subtle cologne and easy smile. She'd been used to missing her girls for a bit every summer and knew how to stave off the loneliness and longing. But she hadn't quite realized she'd miss Trent like this, too.

Clearly, she wasn't alone. She felt Thalia's eyes, the quick glance.

Trent leaned back and looked at Iris, his fist cupping his chin. "Okay, *I see you*, new hair, same scowl, you look good, girl."

Flipping her blond-and-brown braids, Iris set her stuff on the counter. "And you. You look drunk."

"Well. I am drunk. *So*." With a lazy shrug, he pointed back to the den. "Come on, you got next on beer pong."

"One sec," said a voice from behind him. Beaumont's blue eyes glistened from beneath long, dark lashes. He was still the boy she knew and missed, Mathew, her tether, but a bit tanner, dark hair a little longer. Her eyes grazed over the small brown freckles on his cheek.

Trent scooted away with a giggle.

"Hi," said Mathew, more of a sigh than a word.

She couldn't look away from him. "Hi."

He snuck a peek behind himself. Thalia and Jailah were facing Logan and Trent at beer pong, and judging from Logan's little frown and Trent's words of encouragement, it'd been a close match.

"Can we talk?" Beaumont asked.

"We are talking."

He rolled his eyes and smiled. "Outside?"

Iris let him lead her to the large back patio. There was a pool, a flower garden, a shed bigger than a small house, and a little basketball court.

Iris blew out a breath. "That's a lot."

He sat on the top step. "Want a hit?"

Iris dropped beside him. Mathew had his fingers angled toward her, the joint held gently between his callused fingers. She was careful not to let her lips brush his fingers. The thought sent a chill down her arms, and she wasn't quite ready for it, though this—locking eyes as she drew a breath—seemed a strange intimacy of its own.

She lay back, the brick cool against her skin. He lay next to her, and the feeling of his arm brushing against hers brought warmth to her face. A few days ago, she was drowning in books, desperate to uncover something that could tell her what her connection to Death was, and what *purpose* could possibly mean. And now, she was lying down next to a boy, brain fuzzy, the two of them staring up at the night sky.

"I missed you," he whispered.

She looked at him and nearly gave in to her sudden desire to trace his jawbone with her fingertips. "Ditto."

He turned to her, eyes glassy. "Not like that." Iris felt his hand move. He found a frayed edge of her skirt and wrapped the loose thread around his finger. "I wanna hear you say it."

"I missed you, too, Mathew Beaumont," she whispered.

He turned his whole body to her, propping his head up on his elbow as if needing a better view. Dutifully, he brought the joint to her lips, keeping his eyes on hers as she drew.

She heard her name from somewhere in the distance, but she couldn't move. Didn't want to move. She was looking up at the stars, and into her tether's eyes, and they were one and the same.

"How was Italy?" she asked.

He shrugged. "Food was good."

"That's it?" She laughed. It felt loud in her ears, and that only made her laugh harder.

He inhaled sharply. "I like it when you giggle."

"Ugh, shut up."

She laughed again, and he laughed, and she felt it as if it were her own. When had he gotten so close? Their bodies were nearly pressed together, his head still propped up on his fist but angled toward her.

Meet any cute girls? she thought shamefully.

"None that I noticed," he answered.

"Oh." She bristled. "I didn't mean to say that aloud."

"But you were thinking it."

"I *think* I'm high."

Mathew chuckled, sweet and perfect. Iris wanted him to laugh again. She wanted to touch the mole on his neck, right below his Adam's apple.

There was something like a screech behind them—Iris lifted her head and saw Trent, his hand on the porch door. His eyes were wide and his smile contagious. "Ooop! Never mind me, just— Oh, what's that, Jai, you need help opening a jar?" He shut the door and sprinted.

"Ew," Iris mumbled. "Now he's gonna tell everyone."

"What's he gonna tell them?"

"That you and I . . ." Her voice trailed off.

Mathew's eyes flicked to her mouth. "That we're what?"

He kept curling that loose thread on her skirt. A million unspoken words passed between them, another thread going taut, a wheel in Iris's chest turning in time with his.

"You're my tether," Iris blurted out. "I already care about you too much, and I'm worried it'll get me—and you—into trouble."

"I like trouble." He retreated, lying next to her as they were before, staring at the stars.

"I almost died for you," she whispered, mostly to herself. "Is that not enough?"

"It is." He released the thread. "It is."

They stayed there like that until the fuzziness began to wear off, and maybe Mathew wanted that before he said, "Tell me what happened after the fire."

Iris swallowed. "We died."

Beaumont's voice lowered. "Then how are we here?"

"Death denied us."

At the Necromantic Emporium and House of Souls, Adelaide Strigwach was intent on severing the tether between Iris and Beaumont. If the rogue witch had her way, Beaumont would've been burned alive, but Iris argued for his life. She could still hear Death's deep, reverberating voice.

NOT. YET.

Mathew turned to her, eyes sharp. "What?"

The patio lights behind them went out. Without them spilling through the glass doors, the night was darker than before, not just in brightness but in *feeling*.

Iris jolted onto her feet, wand ready, heart pounding. She looked around but found nothing wrong. The rest of the group was laughing inside, completely oblivious to the change in energy.

She turned back, expecting Beaumont to be right behind her, but he was still sitting on the top porch step, cupped in a sliver of moonlight. His hands were clenched fists, but even with the distance between them, Iris saw the faint glow seeping through his fingers. He kept his head bowed as he unfurled his hands, revealing twin necromancer marks—glowing pentagrams—branded into his palms like stigmata.

Iris took a tentative half step forward toward him. "Mathew?"

He turned to her. Beaumont's eyes were no longer blue. Instead, they were all black, the irises and the whites.

Iris's muscles tensed. "Oh shit."

With a small smile, Beaumont—or Death, rather?—angled his head to get a better look at her. Mathew grew paler by the moment. The thin skin under his eyes grayed, his facial bones protruding sharp and skull-like. From his lips, the deep, dark voice of Death said, "YOU WOULD TREAT YOUR LORD DEATH WITH SUCH DERISION? YOU SHOULD BOW AT MY FEET."

She tightened her grip on her wand. "I've never bowed to anyone."

Death lifted Mathew's hand and touched his fingers to his lips. A cold bead of sweat slid down Iris's spine. That small movement felt so real and mundane, but heady with Death's presence.

"I have a request," said Death, now fully in Mathew's voice. "I am in need of Reapers."

Lord Death leaned in, offering a hand.

8

mathew

Mathew was flooded with his own stark fear, a sense of urgency, and Death's righteous determination. He was in two places at once, and yet so solidly in each.

In the ether of utter darkness, a world away. Sparks of blue light flashed as souls floated through its domain of peace and death. Lord Death, the Keeper of Souls, Protector of the dominion and the border between worlds, had one purpose since the universe came into existence.

The underworld was shrinking, as was its power. Death felt the boundary that divided the living and the dead weaken with every soul that clung to their earthly lives. And if the mortal world and the underworld ever met, both would be left in ruin . . .

And Mathew was here—home, with Iris's hand in his. Both parts of his consciousness relished the touch of her skin and the way her gaze was locked so unwaveringly on his. He wanted to stay just like this, *but there are such important things to be done.*

Mathew knew it, because Death knew it, and right now, they were one. This possession should have terrified him, but Death's presence against his own only felt like a tight hug, sharp cold against his skin.

Mathew's mouth was moving before he knew what he needed to say.

"I have chosen you, and I will teach you the way."

"Release him," Iris hissed, furious.

Mathew couldn't help but smile. "I am not harmed by this, deathwitch. As your Harbinger sleeps still, I come to you in the body of the deathling who comforts you most."

Iris's nostrils flared. "I—"

Death grew impatient. "HOLD YOUR TONGUE." Iris flinched from the commanding echo of Death's voice, and Mathew was forced to keep from reaching out to her. "I HAVE SUMMONED YOU, AND YOU WILL HEED MY CALL."

"To be one of your Reapers?" the deathwitch spat shakily. *Oh, she was a young one, and impulsive as they often were.* "What, you want me to run around, bringing you dead people's souls?"

"Not quite." With Iris now attentive, Mathew regained his voice. "When a soul is sent to me after its mortal existence has passed, I keep it forever in the land of the dead. It is *mine*. Souls converse with my children, and ancestors often speak to their mortal seed, but death is never undone, not truly." Mathew spoke as if these were words he'd said a thousand times before. "But sometimes, a witch might create an opening for a soul to take shape in this world."

"Take shape?" Iris questioned. She withdrew her hand, but only to take a better look at the new marks that had appeared in his.

"When a soul has not completely passed on and accepted its fate, it might cling to the magic of the witch that has Called it. Kept too long on earth, and it corrupts. It may become corporeal, feeding off the energy of witches

63

and mundanes. When a demon spawns and takes root in this world, not even I can banish it back to the otherworld."

"A soul can become a demon?" Her voice went low with fear. She was thinking of her parents, no doubt. Death walked alongside its necromancers like invisible shadows, and now Mathew could see what Death had. *A daughter of Death, like her mother before her, the blood of a legendary Harbinger running through.* "What happens after that?"

Mathew rubbed his palms together, relishing the heat of the pentagrams against Death's icy presence. "A demon left in the mortal realm frays the barrier between worlds. A demon no longer has mortal thought or understanding and wants only to feed on the life force of anyone in its path. It is a bloody sight, deathwitch."

Mathew said this because he'd seen millennia of such chaos. Demons that devoured scores of men, destruction held at bay only by the hands of Reapers. *She will make a worthy addition to my ranks.*

"Reapers, plural? How many more are there?" Curiosity danced in Iris's dark eyes, though fear remained present in her shaky voice. "And where are they?"

Mathew angled his head at her and smiled, the feeling tight on his face. "I have had Reapers since the earth birthed witchery. Necromancers, true deathwitches with my mark, are not common, but while you are not the one and only, you *are* one of few." He was Mathew, and he was Death, and when he leaned in, his pulse raced. "Show me your death mark," he whispered against her ear.

The deathwitch's eyes widened. "What are you—"

He stretched his hand toward her. She watched him carefully but didn't move away. Mathew palmed her thigh, just under the hem of her skirt, pressing the new death mark on his own hand against hers. Lips parted, she released a soft gasp of surprise, her gaze still boring into his. Icy magic billowed around them, but Iris remained still as he showed her the vision of a house that haunted his own thoughts.

Iris exhaled. Mathew felt like he could hear her pounding heartbeat alongside his own. She took a moment to gather her thoughts. "This house . . . There's a demon in it?"

"It has begun feeding on the surrounding earth, insects, animals. Soon, it will grow strong enough to seek mortal life force. You must destroy it before then."

"How?"

"I will arm you with death magic like you have never seen." He sent her another vision, of the three necromantic runes she would need to learn to conquer the demon house.

Iris swallowed hard. Watching her process everything was a wonder of its own. Mathew couldn't read her, even if the magnetic pull between them made him feel like they shared the same dark soul. Finally, she lifted her chin defiantly. "What do I get in return?"

He smiled at the gall of her.

She shrugged, holding firm. "I made no bargain for Mathew Beaumont's soul. You said this was an offer, not an order. So, Lord Death—" She spat this title sardonically. "What's in it for me?"

And isn't she a sharp one? Mathew fought the urge to slip his hand onto her neck and feel her pulse against his fingers. "A power you've never known. One that hasn't been seen in your mother, or in your mentor."

He watched Iris falter over the mentions of Sage Foster and Adelaide Strigwach. She recovered quickly, biting her scowl back with an unimpressed raised brow.

"Consider your parents' souls."

Iris said nothing, but Mathew knew that it was done. Her eyes grew wet, and her fists loosened.

"I see the depths of your heart, deathwitch. I bless all my Reapers with the highest necromantic power of any walking witch. This is no command. This is no payment. This is your purpose."

And then Mathew felt Death recede in a voice meant just for him.

As it is yours.

Iris cursed. She looked away from him, rubbing her top teeth over her bottom lip. An eternity passed before she flashed him a wry smile. "Do I get, like, a scythe or something?"

The cold pulled back. Mathew rolled his shoulders. Death's weighty grip loosened, but its last words came out fierce and deep. "UNTIL NEXT TIME, DEATHWITCH. MAY THE DARK KEEP YOU SAFE."

And to you, Runekeeper.

Though the heat of the air returned, Mathew remained cold. Hearing Death wish them both well—if *May the dark keep you safe* was indeed a well-wishing—was as discomfiting as it was intriguing. Death had not just claimed Iris, but Mathew, too. And Runekeeper? The knowledge that Death shared hadn't explained that phrase. His head spun with the possibilities.

"Mathew?" Iris asked softly.

He nodded. "Yeah?"

"Welcome back."

Mathew didn't react with the same wide-eyed fear and shock he'd felt when they went into the Chasm for the first time, all those months ago on Hallowe'en night. "I never left."

He looked at the scarred death marks in his palms. Unlike Iris's, they didn't glow, not without Death's presence. He thought back to his last session at group therapy. He'd shook that old man's hand and had seen—

No. That wasn't real. That was an intrusive thought.

Except now, looking at the pentagrams Death branded him with, he wasn't so sure.

"Dude. Death just used you to speak to me."

Mathew flexed his fingers, then relaxed them. "No. No. That was me."

Iris's brow twitched.

"Iris, I was here the whole time. I said those words. It's like I was Death, and Death was me." He flushed deeper, his eyes flicking to the hem of Iris's skirt.

For a moment, they both said nothing. The air between them was heavy and loaded, about to combust. Mathew could hardly think. He wanted to put his hand on her again to feel death magic flowing mutually through their skin.

He cleared his throat. "So. Demons?"

Iris released a disillusioned little laugh. "You tell me."

Behind them, the party grew loud with excitement. Trent was gloating about making a tough shot in beer pong, and Jailah was drunkenly shouting along to the music. No one seemed to notice how they'd been affected by Death's presence.

"That house you showed me?" Iris asked.

Mathew pulled out his phone, typing fervently. "898 Appleton Lane, Port Barrow. Oh, it's like forty-five minutes away."

He showed her the screen. There it was, a picture-perfect house in a picture-perfect neighborhood, along with a news article about a few grisly pet deaths.

"A spirit's causing issues," Iris said sharply. "I didn't even know something like that could happen."

Mathew sighed nervously. "You'll go?"

"I . . . I don't know if I have a choice." She looked at him, eyes deep with concern. "Are you okay?"

Mathew exhaled a laugh. "Honestly? Yeah, I am." Everything in the past few minutes should've sent him running in fear, but he felt oddly content and motivated. For all that his home life was spiraling, he had a true focus now. Family issues and marital squabbles were hardly worth a worry when the entire mortal world was at stake without the role of deathwitches and their tethers. He glanced at the blue curtains above them. *Your Harbinger sleeps still.* Mathew had work to do.

Iris remained frowning. "Y'know, that night at Roddin's, Death told me it had a purpose for me. I guess this is it, huh?"

Mathew nodded. "I know. Now I know." He looked at her with a tender sweetness and relished the shy way her eyelashes fluttered under his gaze. He grazed his knuckles over hers. "Iris, I remember everything."

9

thalia

A perfect summer.

The party had ended, but Thalia was still grinning. Wasn't this the loveliest thing in the world? Stumbling home, squeezed between her best friends, still buzzed from a mixture that tasted like heaven when sipped out of a Solo cup.

Jailah recounted an embarrassing story from her pageant days, something involving chest padding popping out of her dress and into the lap of a very serious judge.

"And *that*," she slurred, wagging her finger for emphasis, "is why you gotta stay ready! With double-sided tape!"

Thalia wanted to hold this moment close to her chest.

They made it to the cabin with a loud crash. Jai and Logan decided to race up the porch, and Iris jumped on Logan's back to slow her down.

"No fair!" screeched the baby witch, and the three fell into another fit of drunken giggles. Maverick looked on from the window with a grumpy *hmph*, like an exhausted nanny.

The little coven scrubbed their faces with Thalia's homemade face wash, changed into the matching pajama sets that Jailah had purchased—because of course she had—and climbed into bed. Thalia fell asleep tucked between Maverick and Logan, warm, held, cared for and content.

She woke up alone, gasping for air in the Swamp.

Thalia's sweat-soaked pajamas clung to every inch of her skin, and her nails were caked with soil. Had she been crawling? Or digging? Like last time, she had her glasses, which were splattered with dirt. Her feet were bare, and she cringed at the feel of muck under her soles.

"Not again," she wheezed, stumbling to her feet. Her whole body was sore from the hours spent sitting against a gnarled tree trunk. She placed a hand against the heartbeat thrumming rapidly under her chest.

The party, the drink. She hadn't even thought to connect her wrist to the enchanted vine. Had the others noticed? She looked around for a sign of them, but the Swamp was dark and quiet.

She balled up her fists at her sides. "What do you want?" she screamed.

There was no reply but the soft rustle of trees and the sounds of birds, their unnaturally high-pitched cries reverberating through her bones.

"I'm not afraid of you anymore! Leave me the fuck alone!"

The weight of the Swamp's hex settled onto her. She knew the deal—first, the suffocating humidity. Then the voices. There were no Wolves, but the Swamp was avoided year-round for good reason. Her witchy senses buzzed with a sickly premonition. She had to get back to the other side.

"Thalia?"

She jolted, only just biting back a scream.

A figure stepped out of the shadows. Trent, wearing the same blue jeans, black tee, and simple gold chain that she'd seen him in a few hours prior. "Sorry!" he said, throwing his hands up.

Thalia closed her eyes and took a deep breath. "What are you doing out here?"

Trent sighed a chuckle. "Was gonna ask you the same thing."

"I . . ." Her first inclination was to lie. She trusted Trent, but there were some habits that she'd never be able to shake.

Trent glanced briefly at Thalia's filthy bare feet and her mud-caked nails. "I couldn't sleep," he said quietly, eyes going dreamy. "I just wanted to take a walk, but then I thought about the last time I saw her."

His mother, Thalia knew. After all, she was the one who had eased his mind from the images of Lourdes Hogarth's zombified body that plagued him after Hell Night.

"You should know, my mum's protection spell, or spirit—" He hesitated, searching for the words. "She's not with me anymore. S'like our connection broke after whatever happened that night."

He kicked his heel against his opposite ankle, a movement Thalia recognized. Trent still wore the dagger his mother had used during her time as a knife-thrower with the Haelsfordian Coven Troupe.

"I'm sorry," Thalia replied. "Maybe Iris can help you get to the bottom of it? She still owes you a Call, right?"

"Shit, that feels like years ago, huh?"

Thalia sighed. "I've been sleepwalking."

"What? For how long?"

Thalia shook her head, trying—and failing—at playing off her own concern. "This is the third time."

Trent's eyes widened. He looked back at the Swamp. For a moment they just stood there together looking into the black, unending darkness. It was quiet again, and with the two of them here alone on magic land, there was a small part of her that hoped, well, if *Iris's* tether was a mundane boy . . .

But nothing quite so witchy and fated was happening here. That didn't make it any less intense.

"Should we . . . investigate?"

Thalia whipped her head around to look at Trent. And there was the fearless, mischievous expression that she hadn't realized she'd missed until now. His cheekbones were illuminated by the moonlight, dark skin all aglow. His presence was so easy to get lost in. Those round brown eyes, his perfect wide nose, the hint of trouble in the little smile he flashed her.

Still, worry sprang into her stomach. *Logan's hearing the Wolves. I'm sleepwalking. Trent's protection spell is gone.*

"T?" Trent whispered.

Thalia looked up at him with a watery smile. "It's supposed to be the perfect summer."

He reached for her hand, and her heart swelled. But his fingers settled on her sleeve, and he tugged on it. "It will be. I'll make it so."

The weight in her chest lightened. She cleared her throat and took a step forward. "Shall we?"

"Following you into the Swamp? Like old times."

They walked together, quickly falling into each other's rhythm. As they trekked deeper into the hexed land, the overt wrongness of the Swamp thickened around Thalia. Little voices whispered in her ear like devils on her shoulder, asking her how she could let Jenna die, how she could leave her mother, how lovely Trent's blood might feel in a spell.

"It's awful," Thalia exhaled with a strained, humorless laugh. "God, why are we doing this?"

Trent looked tired under the muted glow of the moon. "Exposure therapy, innit? In some ways, the Swamp still terrifies me. But I'm also like . . . I was here, once, and I walked out. Same as you. We did that."

Thalia fidgeted. The air was heavy on her shoulders.

Trent sat on a wide, mossy rock, scooting to give Thalia some room.

"Exposure therapy," Thalia scoffed. "I think normal people would put on, like, whale sounds, or something."

Trent laughed, and the sound eased Thalia's heartbeat like slipping into a favorite sweater, warm and comfortable. That was how he made her feel. And considering how few people she could say she really cared for, it was a wonder that she'd managed to find another, that he'd managed to become one.

"Guess we're not normal people." Trent's voice went soft as he said, "I was over at the Beaumonts', and they started talking all about college and next steps, and now I can't turn my mind off thinking about it. I used to be able to picture exactly what was going to happen next in my life, and now I just don't know. Not since I met you." He exhaled. "You witches."

She wanted to comfort him, to offer some perfect advice, but everything she thought of rang false to who she was. "I've never really known what the hell I'd do in the future. I mean, a greenwitchery track at a coven university makes sense, but, like, I can't focus on anything that far ahead when . . . you know. Daddy issues."

Trent laughed once more. Thalia was becoming addicted to the sound of it and the feel of being the one who made it happen.

"It sucks, huh?" Trent said finally.

"Yeah."

And that was all she needed. *It sucks.* Like they were talking about a disappointing cookie or a movie.

"You feel anything?" he asked softly.

Aside from the sudden uptick in her heartbeat? "Nope. Do you?"

But Trent was distracted. He was looking at her neck, just under her ear. "Is this one new?"

Thalia ran her fingers over the skin there, and her heart leapt into her throat. "Oh my god."

A small clover had broken skin, like the sprout on her finger.

Trent was smiling, too, even though Thalia figured he probably didn't know what this meant. "I'm going full greenwitch," she said excitedly—it was all she could do to stay seated instead of jumping to her feet. "And I'm gonna cleanse it."

Was that why she kept showing up here in her sleep? She wondered if the Swamp knew her intentions and was trying to scare her, or if it was her own subconscious leading her here.

She pushed up her too-big glasses. "I'm making a spell. It's mostly high-level cleansing incantations, nothing that would make a dent on their own, but together . . . Anyway, at first I thought a really strong greenwitch would need to do it, but then I was thinking, if the big magic I did in the spring heightened my greenwitchery, then it's gonna be more big magic that gets me full greenwitch, you know?"

Thalia quieted, suddenly out of breath. She never rambled like this, but it was Trent's widening eyes and raised brows and sudden smiles that encouraged her along the way. Even now, he looked at her like she was made of the same starlight streaming down on them.

Thalia flushed under his gaze. "Probably a long shot—"

"Nah, fuck that. I *know* you can do it. Shit, after what happened in the spring, I'll believe whatever the hell you lot say."

Thalia thought, *I could stay here forever.* But the voices were growing loud, slipping doubts and threats into her mind. For all Trent was attempting to ignore them, she could see that they were bearing down on him, too.

"Thanks. Um . . ." She rose to her feet. "We should get going."

Trent gazed up at her. "Can I be there? When you destroy the Swamp?"

Thalia lifted a brow. In spite of herself, she said, "Yes."

"Cool." He jumped to his feet and rubbed his hands. "It's a date."

She followed him, grateful to the dark for hiding her satisfied smile.

They walked quickly, craving the feel of clean air and the peace of their own thoughts. But as they went on, Thalia's witchy senses heated up under her skin.

Trent looked at her, his own brow furrowed, and that confirmed it for her.

Something's wrong.

They quickened their pace. When Thalia finally felt the satisfying release of the Swamp's pull, the relief was short-lived.

She turned and looked back at the mouth of the Swamp. A healthy forsythia shrub grew ten, maybe twenty steps from the border where the hex began. Or, it *should* have. Thalia approached the bush, her nails digging into her palm. She pushed away the thick leaves to inspect the roots, and she was showered with its loose, dying petals. And *there*. The mossy, red-green rot of the Swamp dotted the plant's roots, having snaked up its limbs. She smelled the slight scent of sickly sweet decay. Thalia swallowed a curse.

Trent stood next to her, shoulder to shoulder. "What's up?"

Thalia touched the sprout on her thumb. "The Swamp is expanding."

She felt the cut of air from Trent whipping her head to look at her.

Thalia gestured to the shrub. "The border between Haelsford and the Swamp is supposed to be, like, half a mile behind this bush."

"Okay. Where does it stop now?"

"*On* the bush. The rot's in its roots."

Trent said nothing, but Thalia heard him swallow. The defiance they were trying to exude in the face of the Swamp dissolved. Thalia hardened her heart, if only to keep her fear from drowning her.

"We should go. Night, Trent."

"Wait, the Swamp—"

Thalia walked forward, ignoring Trent's raised hand. "It's late. If someone sees us out here with everything going on, it'll look sus." She glanced at him over her shoulder.

"Oh. Okay. Night, then."

Thalia ran her teeth over her lip. *Logan's hearing the Wolves. I'm sleepwalking. Trent's protection spell is gone.*

And the Swamp is growing.

10

jailah

Jailah woke up in Thalia's cabin with Logan's hand in her face, a scruffy dog curled up against her neck, and Iris staring at her from the edge of the bed.

Jai screeched. "Why are you watching me sleep?"

"I wasn't watching you," the deathwitch scoffed. "I was sitting here waiting for the rest of y'all to finally get up, and you moved, so I looked over at you, and you woke up!"

Jailah extricated herself from Maverick, who was sleeping between her and Thalia. "Okay, I think we overdid it last night."

"*You* overdid it," Iris corrected. "I tapped out around midnight."

Jai rubbed her eyes. Her head was spinning. "Was that before or after I tried to convince everyone to go streaking through Hammersmitt?"

"After," Logan whispered at the same time Thalia sleepily said, "Before, I think."

Iris nudged Thalia's leg. "Okay, everyone's up. Let's go, I'm starving."

"Wait!" Jailah rolled out of bed to Logan's protests and then stood in front of everyone. She was thrilled to see them all wearing the matching silk pajamas she'd bought for them. She vaguely remembered ditching the boys and walking over to Thalia's, arm in arm. It had been a perfect night. Happy and tipsy and surrounded by her very best friends, she'd thought, *I won't let anyone try to take this from me again.*

"Ooh!" Jailah exclaimed. "We look like a girl group!"

Thalia smiled, but Jailah saw that it didn't quite reach her eyes. And what were those yellow bits in her hair? They all looked rough, but Thalia looked particularly exhausted.

The greenwitch fidgeted under Jai's gaze. "What?"

"You look like you got somethin' to say."

"*You* look like you need to puke," Iris added.

Thalia rummaged through her shelves of plants, jars, and half-filled tins of salves that bore her fingerprints. She presented a tiny vial. "Here. Hangover cure."

Jailah sipped the muddy red liquid. It tasted like strawberries and flame. She relished the ease of the pain in her head, the clarity in her eyes. She planted her hands on her hips. "Actually, I been thinkin'—" She paused, pacing, waving her hands around a little. "We need to talk, to let it all out. I'm talkin' secrets, feelings, fears, worries!"

Logan said, "Wait, is this an intervention?"

"It's not an intervention," interjected Iris. "It's clearly . . . therapy?"

Jailah waved their words away. "We almost died a few months ago, like *damn*. None of that woulda ever happened if we'd just been talkin' to one another." Jailah rubbed her right wrist. "Iris, you didn't tell us that Mathew was your tether."

"Unfortunately," Iris quipped.

"And then there was Logan, hooking up with the Wolf Boy in her dreams."

Logan made a small choking sound, her scar wrinkling as she cringed. "Well, don't put it like that!"

"And Thalia—"

"Yeah," Thalia offered coolly. "We know."

Jailah looked around at them with an invitational shrug. "So, maybe we need to just put all our secrets out here and make sure some shit like *that* doesn't happen again. The next time one of us is in trouble, the others should know exactly what to do." She stared at them, her little coven. "Who's first?"

They looked at one another.

Logan lifted her head, blue eyes shimmering. "I don't have any secrets anymore. You guys know everything. Now I'm just a boring old normal witch." She looked at her fingers and smiled to herself as if *boring old normal witch* was the best thing that anyone could ever be called. "I'm just here to do my remedial classes and eventually graduate, hopefully without getting held back along the way."

"You said you thought you heard Wolves when you got here," Thalia said pointedly.

Logan's voice wavered a little. "I mean, I feel like that's like . . . a normal trauma response? I googled it, I don't know."

Thalia laughed sadly. "Okay, so we *do* need therapy."

"What about you, T?" Jailah looked her up and down. "You sleep okay?"

With an annoyed sigh, Thalia rose from the bed. "Don't freak out."

Jailah frowned. "You know, you say that, and it just stresses me the hell out."

"I've been sleepwalking. It happened last night, but no one noticed."

Jailah resisted the urge to gasp. Thalia told them of how she woke up in the Swamp with no memory of leaving her bed. That was horrifying enough, and it took all of Jailah's self-control not to throw her arms around Thalia, but that wasn't the worst of it.

"The Swamp is *growing*?" Iris spat, face furrowed in disbelief.

"I'm assuming that's not a thing that's supposed to happen?" Logan added quietly.

"You're sure?" Jailah asked, even though she knew Thalia wouldn't be mistaken about something this serious.

"I'm positive. I planted some bushes even farther into Haelsford land. If the rot touches it, I'll know."

"Think the Council's noticed?" asked Iris.

"I ain't heard a thing 'bout it," Jailah replied, her thoughts turning anxiously. She looked at the others, and it was obvious that no one wanted to be the one to say it, so she did. "Y'all think this has to do with us?"

Thalia bit her lip. "The century-old hex changing for the first time right after Hell Night? It can't be a coincidence."

"It had to be Roddin," Iris offered, her tone icy. "Adelaide, whatever. She lied about being hexbound, she lied about *everything*. She's a whole Strigwach Sister! We don't know what magic she was capable of."

Jailah couldn't find fault in Iris's reasoning, but Thalia looked skeptical.

"Whatever's going on, we need to make sure it can't come back to us, right?" Logan asked.

Jailah nodded. *Exactly.*

"Roddin's an easy culprit. She's already on the Council's shit list, *and* she's missing, if not dead," Iris said.

"Okay, I'll keep my ear out with the Council," said Jailah. "If anything comes up 'bout the Swamp, I'll let y'all know. T, maybe you should sleep in your dorm from now on?"

"Mav likes the space here," she whispered, annoyed.

"Then we'll all stay here. One of us will stay up and keep watch—"

Thalia crossed her arms. "I don't need babysitters. I think it's better if I keep an eye on things here."

Jailah looked at Thalia with wonder, her heart squeezing. Sleepwalking aside, Thalia seemed lighter lately. Still nothing like Jailah's consistently sunny disposition, but Thalia smiled more, laughed more, and just seemed . . . happier. Surely, the secret of the accidental murder she'd committed had always been much too much for one person to bear.

In fact, Thalia looked pretty damn pleased with herself when she walked to her untidy desk covered in dirt, plants, and seeds, and pulled a messy, battered notebook from the drawer. Sunlight glinted beautifully off her silky green pajamas. She hugged the book to her chest. "In other news, I've been working on a way to cleanse the Swamp."

She said this with all the weight of announcing she was going for a walk.

At the sight of Jai's impressed grin, Logan's abject confusion, and Iris's skeptical brow, Thalia added, "I'm working on my own spell."

That got Iris's attention. "You're doing spellcraft?"

For the average witch, any spell they could possibly need in everyday life was something they could look up—in a book, online, in an app on their phone. Spellcraft was a required course for seniors at coven academies, where young witches could learn how to tie intention, blood, and magic into a spell of their own making. It was harder than reformation, where a witch could change a necessary incantation from their language or another's into something easier to remember and incant.

"It's not entirely original," Thalia continued. She splayed out the pages, loose sheets dropping to the floor, sticky notes jutting out of the margins, a chaotic smudge of ink and graphite before them. "I've been researching cleansing spells, but specifically for sickness rather than dirt or mess or whatever. Magic meant to purify. And then I got some hexbreakers—well, some of them are made for breaking bloodline curses, which is probably the closest thing we could call the Swamp, right? Anyway, I figure if I find the right mix of purification, healing, and hexbreaking, maybe I can make a spell that fixes it. Forever."

She looked up, and the three of them must've been looking at her in awe—Jailah certainly was—because Thalia flushed slightly.

Logan's eyes were wide as she ran her fingers lightly over Thalia's work. "Holy— This is—"

"So fucking dope!" interjected Iris. She lifted the book, examined the pull-out pages of plant diagrams and *witchy maths*, as Trent would've surely put it.

"I'm just . . ." Jailah sniffled, her heart soaring. "So proud of you."

"Oh god!" Thalia grabbed her book but was unable to hide the excitement in her voice. "I don't even know if it works yet. I mean, it probably won't. Hundreds, maybe thousands of people have tried to break the hex."

Still, it was impossible to not have confidence in her, with the prideful way she looked down at her notes. "And how many could say they went face-to-face with Adelaide Strigwach, got pulled into the Swamp, survived, and saved the day?" Iris replied. "Only you, T."

Logan played with a few strands of golden hair. "Did we? Save the day, I mean? Is the Haunting Season really over?"

Thalia considered this. It was an unspoken question that had hovered between them for some time. "Theodore Bloom is dead, as Mathilde Strigwach had advised."

Jailah nodded. "But he wasn't taken by the Wolves since Logan went all vengeful witch on his ass."

Logan offered a strained, unamused smile.

Thalia said, "If we assume that the Swamp and the Wolves are connected, then the Swamp still being here means that the Wolves are, too."

"Only, they answer to no one," Logan muttered. "And that's better than them answering to Adelaide or Bloom, right?"

"I guess we'll see." Jailah didn't like it. The end of the last Haunting Season had increased her discomfort in being caught off guard. Waiting until the fall to know if the Wolves had been at all affected by their actions was a frightening thing.

Iris cracked her knuckles. "Okay, my turn."

"Can't wait to hear this!" Thalia teased.

Jailah flopped down onto the bed, clutching her heart. She added a chill to her voice, serious and cool. "Ooh, I'm Iris Keaton-Foster, Death itself, and I'm madly in love with a boy, and it sucks, 'cause feelings!"

Thalia threw her head back with laughter. Logan was a little nicer, using a pillow to stifle her guffaws.

Iris's dark eyes took them in before she offered a slow, insidious grin. "Death came to me at the party last night."

Jailah exhaled roughly. "Whew, of course it did."

"It spoke to me through Beaumont and asked me to be a Reaper."

Thalia nearly choked on her breath. "Oh, is that all?"

Jailah turned onto her stomach. "Where the hell was I when this happened? Wait—was this before or after I got up on the island?"

"And what's a Reaper?" Logan interjected.

Iris bared her teeth in a little grimace. "Something that involves banishing demonic souls to the underworld."

Logan's eyes popped open. "Uh, how do you sound so calm?"

Iris shrugged. "After what we just went through, does anything *really* freak you out anymore?"

Jailah supposed she could understand that. She looked at her girls and felt reassured to have a coven who knew exactly what one another had been through. This was something a friendship bracelet—as much as she loved them—couldn't touch. They were connected in ways that couldn't be severed. If they were bound by the Haunting Season, Bloom's resurrection, and a dark night where they all nearly died, then they had to keep one another close. And yet, she had an odd prickle in her stomach that things could change . . . that things were still being hidden.

Jailah pulled herself onto her feet. "Highest Witch Evelyn Estrada is coming to Haelsford next week. High Witch Lucia wants me to have tea with her."

The tension in the cabin stiffened. Jailah remembered the other parts of her conversation with Lucia and held back her anger.

"There's no reason to think she knows anything about anything, but just in case, we need to make sure everyone's got their stories straight," she continued. "Just 'cause she's talking to me doesn't mean she won't wanna talk to y'all."

The others wore various shades of worry, but Thalia looked like she might barf. Though Thalia already knew about Evelyn's impending arrival, that was before she'd discovered the Swamp's shifting borders. Jailah figured Thalia was running through worst-case scenarios the same way she was.

"Thalia. You got any sevdys? I think we should take a little bit every day."

Thalia refocused. "I can make some. It won't be as potent as what you'd get from an apothecary, but I guess we shouldn't be seen buying it either."

"This is a lot," Iris said sharply. "I'll take the sevdys, and I'm not saying we shouldn't be careful, but, Jai, you're the Council's favorite Junior Witch. You really think Evelyn's gonna roll up with truth serum to interrogate you?"

Favorite Junior Witch. A few weeks ago, Jailah would've thought the same, but Lucia had made it clear that if Jailah wanted to succeed in the JWC and beyond, then she couldn't be associated with any forbidden magic, whether through Vero or not.

"No, Jai's right," Logan said before Jailah could reply. "She knows Lucia and the HWC, but we don't really know Evelyn, and *she* doesn't know Jai. I'll do whatever it takes to keep our secrets." A glimmer of yellow light bloomed from Logan's hands. She played with it, threading her witchery around her fingers. "And if it comes down to it, it was *me.* I was the one who enabled Bloom, so I should take the fall."

Iris sucked her teeth loudly. "Look, that's noble and all, but *I'm* the necromancer, no one's going to believe you."

Anger and sadness welled up in Logan's eyes. "I'm the legacy witch, I've got the powerful family, and even if I didn't? You all already know that trouble for you would look different than trouble for me, and it's not like I don't deserve it!" She leveled her gaze on Jailah, so steady now that it was like she'd snapped into a different person in a matter of seconds. Her witchery pulsed with her growing resolve. "I went to the MidWinter Celebration with Bloom, we got drinks at Soma, we were out all over town! There'll be witnesses of the proxy witch and the strange boy from nowhere. Isn't it obvious?"

Of course it was obvious. Jailah had already thought all this through, a worst-worst-case scenario: giving Logan up to protect herself, Iris, and Thalia. Their memories of Logan betraying the coven and attacking Iris in this very cabin was proof enough, not to mention the evidence of Bloom at her side that Logan just mentioned. *An accidental resurrection. Strigwach's manipulation of Iris. It was Logan who didn't want to report it all*, Jailah would say. *Logan loved him, and she hated Mesmortes, so she helped Theodore Bloom and his Wolves breach town.* A believable story precisely because it wasn't far from the truth.

And here was Logan, putting the whole plan out there. Even if Jailah held no resentment toward Logan after she killed Bloom herself, there was a part of her that thought, *You owe us.*

Thalia opened her mouth, then closed it. Iris's impressed smirk chilled Jai's blood.

"You used *Sanguirremorr* on Bloom," Jailah said for all of them. "That spell is goddamn vicious, and you had to mean it. That's not nothing."

"*Please,*" Logan scoffed impatiently.

"What?"

"I know you trust me, and you forgive me, and I appreciate that and all—" Logan pushed back her bangs, her golden strands falling over her scar. "But you don't have to baby me. If you think they're coming for us, you *need* to pin it on me. Or I'll do it myself." She cleared her throat, effectively ending the conversation. "So. Breakfast?"

"Thank you!" Iris said dramatically.

Thalia nodded. "Scheming makes me hungry."

Nerves still shaky, Jailah sputtered a laugh. "Wait, we need a pic of this first!"

Ignoring the groans, Jailah set her phone on the desk and set the timer.

"We should jump!" Iris suggested, taking Jailah's hand.

When the phone beeped, Jai was the only one to jump, of course. As the others broke into laughter, she held her phone like it was a precious thing. They looked so cute and happy, even if Jailah was definitely doing way too much. It was perfect, the four of them.

She was going to keep them all this way, whatever was coming for them next.

11

logan

After the weekend, the remains of Logan's stab wound had mostly vanished. She still felt a twinge in her side if she stretched too far, but Thalia's healing salve left her skin untouched.

Gingerly, she pulled on her Mesmortes summer uniform, packed her knapsack, and took a good look in the mirror. Aside from the longer locks and the hairline scar across her eye, she looked the same as she had on her very first day of school. *Poor baby witch*, she thought, amused. *You had no idea what was coming.*

"This is no big."

She gave herself a small smile in the mirror, then paused. There was a smudgy red stain on her teeth. She ran her tongue over it and tasted a metallic tang. Likely bit her cheek during dinner, she figured, or during sleep. She made a mental note to look up spells for bruxism after class.

Logan looked over her schedule. There were two empty slots that had to be filled in before the first week ended. She could wait on choosing these electives, but seeing the blank spaces turned her stomach. In the past, she'd been so obsessed over her own lack of magic, over the Wolf

Boy and the Haunting Season, and now that those worries were mostly settled, what would she do next? Thalia was a greenwitch; medicine was a natural path. Jailah had goals to serve on a Witchery Council, and Logan envisioned her moving to a great big city or even running for High Witch of the Americas someday. Iris's future was more difficult to envision, but perhaps there was a life to be had as a deathwitch that Logan didn't know about—Calling deceased loved ones, giving mourners closure, running a funeral home?

School hadn't been a focus at all in the last year, and Logan had managed less-than-stellar grades. Now she had to prove that she was a capable witch. To the professors, to her friends, to herself.

If she could survive Theodore Bloom and Adelaide Strigwach, she could totally survive summer school.

Logan gathered her stuff and set off. Though the halls were emptier than they usually were, Mesmortes dorms were open year-round, and a few witches stumbled out of their rooms for breakfast, or were busy packing beach supplies for a trip to the lake an hour away. In the past, Logan couldn't do something as simple as walk to class without the crushing weight of her own insecurity. Today, she strode through the main building like she really, truly belonged here.

Logan decided to cut through Odd Hall, an enchanted hallway in the middle of the arts building that spat you out *Wherever You Needed to Be*, as the spell went. It was how Rowe Adler, a rising junior who had been there when the Wolves breached campus, was said to wake up three minutes before homeroom and be the first to arrive. Logan had always ignored the shortcut; she'd convinced herself that the enchantment would've had disastrous circumstances with all her weird witchiness, but today, she entered the candlelit hallway lined with photos of notable Mesmortes alumni.

The air was cool. She stood before the wooden doors at the end of the hall, her heart pounding. She called forward her witchery, and lifted her glowing hands.

"Take Me to Where I Need to Be."

That small, fleeting moment before the magic obeyed always made Logan nervous. A bead of sweat dripped down her back, and she winced for the worst. Then she heard a sound like shifting stones and felt a slight vibration under her polished loafers.

She grinned. A simple spell, yes, and the enchantment in place was already doing the heavy lifting, but *still*. Logan's pride swelled . . . until she opened the door.

Odd Hall didn't take her to the herbalism labs.

Instead, she found herself staring at the Swamp in the distance. The hallway had spat her out at the eastern exit outside Mesmortes.

Logan couldn't move. Her throat tightened, her blood chilled, and the sweat from her palm left the doorknob slick. The howl she'd heard a few days ago could be chalked up as a phantom sound, something her subconscious had conjured up in response to returning to Haelsford. But this? Was it a fluke, a mistake? Those options didn't seem satisfying, considering what Logan knew.

The Swamp is growing.

Logan had a bad feeling, but she didn't have time to dwell. Heart pounding—partly because Professor Fournier was notorious for issuing tardies—she ran back through the hall and took the usual route to the herbalism labs, texting the girls on the way. **Weird thing just happened, talk after class.**

"Must be an interesting meme if it's got you late for the first day," Professor Fournier mused sweetly as Logan stepped into the second row, the elder witch not looking up from the bubbling cauldron on her desk.

Logan quickly stashed her phone. "Sorry, Professor Fournier. Won't happen again."

With a flick of her fingers, Logan levitated her notebook, pen, and sticky notes out of her bag. According to the notes on the whiteboard, today's class was about healing bases, simple concoctions that could be used as the groundwork for an infinite number of drafts and salves. The cauldron of bubbling blue goo on Fournier's desk smelled like mint and lilacs.

As her pen independently took notes, Logan looked around the classroom. It was a small group, mostly comprising younger baby witches who wanted to start school early, likely due to overbearing parents. Logan recognized two witches she'd seen around and were probably here for poor grades, like she was. If there were any who had gotten their blessing late as she had, Logan didn't know.

"Pair up! You have ten minutes to make one hundred grams of healing base. You'll be testing them on yourselves, so be careful!"

Logan glanced at the boy nearest to her, a shaggy brunette whose wand was decorated with the symbols of a sports team Logan didn't recognize.

He threw up a peace sign. "'Sup?"

His name was Bobby Wiles, and he spent more time peppering her with questions like this was a first date than working. Logan finally got him to shut up by letting him use the mortar and pestle to grind up the herbs.

Everything worked as expected, but the excitement never came. Just this morning, she'd squealed with delight at successfully using Morgan Ramirez's enchantment for waking up to the smell of French toast and the sounds of pretty birds. She was going to enjoy the hell out of her witchery until she was dead, but seeing the Swamp knocked all the enthusiasm out of her. Being back in a classroom to learn basic magic was a little underwhelming, considering the dark magic she'd seen in months past.

Logan turned to the sound of laughter and found the rest of the group huddled around Evan Hofferson. They were watching something on his phone, and whatever it was, it freaked out the other witches as much as it enthralled them. Logan joined them, peering over Rosie Nelson's fro to get a look. "What's going on?"

Rosie spoke over her shoulder. "Some mundane got attacked by a dog."

The video was posted to Bitchcraft, Haelsford's annoying anonymous gossip app. It showed a boy in a bed at the local hospital, his arms all bandaged up.

"I know it was a familiar," the boy spat. "That was not a normal effing dog!"

Logan's blood turned to ice. She'd seen him before.

"Hexeater," Logan whispered.

Evan snickered. "Yeah. What a freak!"

"I'm team dog," Rosie said with a lazy chuckle. "Been waiting for them hexeaters to get what's coming to 'em."

Professor Fournier cleared her throat loudly, and everyone jumped.

"Hofferson. Put it away," she warned. "You've got five minutes to finish up your work."

"Professor!" One of the younger girls raised her hand. "How do we protect ourselves from hexeaters?"

Amid a few whispers, Fournier offered an amused smile. "A question for Professor Circe, yes? This is herbalism, not protections."

"I heard that hexeaters have been walking around in groups, trying to corner witches," Evan said.

Worse than that, Logan thought anxiously.

"Leah Dover's dad got tricked by one," said another young witch. "He thought he was meeting someone to buy an old spellbook, but a hexeater met him and tried to cut off his hair!"

The volume grew as the witches traded increasingly exaggerated stories about hexeater attacks in town. Logan used the chaos to slip out her phone and pull up Bitchcraft. The video had originally been posted to Insta, and Logan went to the heaxeater's page.

His name was Blake, and he attended Devereaux in the next town over, where most of Haelsford's mundane kids went. Logan didn't dare click on his stories, but the newest post on his page was the same video filmed from the hospital bed.

Though Logan hadn't quite shaken her memories of Theodore Bloom, she suddenly felt his *presence*, as palpable as if he were really sitting next to her. His voice slipped into her thoughts.

What have you done, my little wolfgirl?

Logan shook off the thought. She linked the Bitchcraft post into the group chat. **Have you guys heard about this?**

Jailah replied as she always did—immediately. **Ok but like he deserved it tho, right? I can tell he's an asshole just by looking at him.**

Normally, Logan would've laughed—hell, she managed to get a curse out of Jailah Simmons. But she only chewed on her lip, her fingers hovering over the screen. Jailah had made them all promise that there wouldn't be any secrets in their little coven, but she wasn't even sure if there *was* a secret here.

That was the kid who attacked me, she typed back quickly.

That there was no instantaneous response left Logan's nerves buzzing. She knew that they were thinking what she was.

It was Thalia who typed it out. **A wolf? There's no way . . .**

"Wyatt!"

Logan jumped at the sound of Professor Fournier's voice. The professor stood before her with her hands on her hips, her pen and clipboard hovering next to her. "Where's your head today? I thought you of all people would want to take this seriously."

Logan's cheeks grew hot. "I'm sorry—"

"Hand it over."

Logan dropped her phone into Fournier's open palm. At least the professor looked pleased with the potion bubbling away on the hot plate. She glanced at Bobby, who flashed her a self-satisfied smirk before turning back to Logan. "Good work, you two. Careful not to overstir, however; looks like there's been one or two turns too many."

"Yes, Professor."

Her pen made a note on her board. "I have high expectations for you this summer, but you need to take this class seriously. Proxy or not, the basics are vital to making a strong witch, understood?"

Logan nodded.

The professor moved on. Bobby pumped a fist to his chest. "Nice!"

Logan ignored him to look out the window. She held her trembling hands together and thought of the Wolf she'd come face-to-face with at the end of the last Haunting Season. It had given her a scar, and she'd left it blinded.

That was not a normal effing dog, Bloom's voice teased. *And you have never been a normal witch.*

12

trent

Unlike his mother, Trent didn't have an entire wall-sprawling collection of knives. He had *one* knife, however, and balanced it on his taped knuckles in the corner of the Hammersmitt School fitness center.

This knife held magic. He'd known it for years; his mother had died and left him this, a last protection against a threat he still didn't understand. When he thought of Lourdes Hogarth, he wanted to picture her smiling, singing, chasing bluebirds in the garden. Not driving her car off a cliff, or . . . monstrous.

The Swamp had reunited Trent and his mother. She'd appeared to him in a broken body, a haunted specter, and told him that his soul had been promised to another. Call it a gut feeling or sheer fucking foolishness, but Trent didn't believe that it was just the Swamp's mind games. It was real, and Trent couldn't change what she had done, but he would find out what she'd left in her wake.

Even this blade had been touched by magic in new ways. Trent watched it grow to the size of a sword before cutting through a hexed Wolf, at the command of Jailah's spell. He'd pulled it from the mess of black blood afterward, marveling at how the glittering handle fit in his hand. Jai had offered to change it back, and he'd accepted, but part of him wanted to hold that magical weight once more.

He meant to spend the day scouring for clues about his mother's life here, but Mathew insisted they fit a workout in. Matty had never been one of those gym bros, aside from the necessary training needed to keep up with the equestrian team, but lately, he was verging on obsessed.

"One more go," Mathew said impatiently from the ring, his chest heaving.

"You got a death wish?" Trent replied with a playful smirk. "Bruv, you're not gonna beat me."

Boxing was perhaps the only interest Trent and his father shared, although Trent didn't like it as much as he tolerated it. He hadn't done lessons since the summer prior, but even his casual sessions were worth a lot when going up against Matty's clumsy, untrained skills.

Mathew jumped out of the ring and wrapped an arm around the punching bag. "Fine, spot me, then?"

Truthfully, Trent would rather be sitting with a book and a cup of tea, but he put away the knife and trudged over to the bag.

Unrefined, sure. But Trent couldn't say that Mathew's movements lacked power. Trent watched the heat flicker in his determined eyes. "What you training for? 'Bout to finally do us all a favor and knock out Petey Haelsford?"

"I won't be the weak link." Mathew jabbed the bag. "Next time, I'll be ready."

Trent dropped his hands from the bag. "Ready for what?"

Heaving, Mathew let his fists fall at his sides. "I died, you know."

Trent pursed his lips.

"Iris didn't want to talk about it before she left, but I know it." His voice caught in his throat. "You all did something that night. Me? I died."

Trent blinked. Then he *guffawed*. He couldn't help it. They'd all narrowly survived Hell Night with their lives, and Mathew was concerned about *this*? Being seen as weak? It was such a privileged little worry that Trent keeled over.

"Dude," Mathew muttered softly. "Really?"

Trent shook his head. "What the hell are you thinking? You gonna punch a Wolf in the mouth?" He could barely get through it without laughing. "Come on, man."

At this, Mathew peeled off his gloves and threw them in his bag. "Thanks, noted, will not fight a Wolf."

Trent stood in front of him, cutting him off. "Mate, you know how much I care about you. I'm so fucking happy that you're doing your therapy thing, you're getting help—" He waved his arms. "Shit, we *all* should be. But I don't want you running face-first into trouble because you think you need to prove yourself."

Mathew nodded, but Trent knew him too well to be fooled. Whatever was bugging Mathew, it was dug too deep for Trent to excise it just now.

Mathew's eyes found the knife on the corner table. "You feel it yet?"

The change of subject took the air out of Trent's lungs. He needed to be eased into talking about his mother these days. "Not yet."

As they walked toward Town Square with the sun beating down on

98

them, Mathew asked Trent if he wanted to hop into the pool. Maybe pull Rebecca from her bed and drop her into the deep end.

Laughing, Trent rubbed his thumb over his bottom lip. "Nah. I got shit to do. I'm going to the library."

----◈ ⊛ ◈----

Talk to me, Mum.

Trent twisted the opal ring around his finger, needing to do something with his hands.

Protection spells could be as simple as putting up a barrier to keep something menacing out, like what the witches did every autumn out on the border of the Swamp. Protection spells could also be placed on people, whether witchy or mundane, at the behest of a witch. This seemed to require some type of connection between the caster and the protected, and simple spells were severed if the witch died. So whatever Lourdes had done was *not* a simple spell, but he'd already figured that much.

Trent changed gears. He pushed away the piles of literature on protection spells and slid forward what he had on the Haelsfordian Coven Troupe, a traveling circus composed of witches who used their magic to put on shows. There was plenty about the troupe in the HPL's holdings; actually, there was possibly *too much* about the troupe, which presented its own problem. And yet, Trent had a hard time finding anything about his mother aside from her name being listed as an "alumna" of the group, and a single blurry picture of her eye peeking out of the corner of an old photo. The man in the picture wore a ring that matched the one on Trent's pinkie finger. Smooth, shiny black opal crested in solid gold. Trent's mum never spoke much about her time in the troupe, the same way she'd rarely even used magic around their family, but he knew she'd spent years with the troupe before she met Trent's father and moved with him to London. And he knew she worked with knives.

Trent strolled up to the service desk. "Hi, Mrs. Lopez."

"Trenton." The frizzy-haired librarian pushed up her glasses. "That book you're looking for isn't in yet."

Trent furrowed his brow, trying to remember.

Mrs. Lopez sighed. *"Perilous Protection Spells,* third edition? They're mailing it over from a library in Houston, so may be a few days."

"Got it, thanks—actually, I wanted to know what else you had on the Haelsfordian Coven Troupe."

She looked over at his workspace, which was so covered in stacks of books and newspaper clippings that the legs creaked.

"I'm looking for my mum, she was a knife-thrower." Saying those words made him a little proud, but also a little sad.

At this, Mrs. Lopez looked up, brown eyes popping open a little. "Oh! That's pretty cool." She said *pretty cool* like she thought it was what a teen would say, but it didn't quite fit naturally in her mouth. "Unfortunately, there's not much you can do *but* look. The Coven Troupe requested that materials not be digitized, so we keep our research and artifacts here, in special collections." She shrugged. "We do have a few films, however."

Trent perked up. "Oh yeah?"

"You'll have to use the VCR." She pointed casually to the dusty machine in the workroom and laughed. "You're probably too young to know what that is, aren't you?" She waved him into the workroom, which was cluttered with empty library carts and unsorted donations. It smelled like old paper and ink, which Trent liked.

Mrs. Lopez opened up a door to a small closet, just big enough to fit three, maybe four people. Shelves lined the wall, heavy with jet-black tapes.

Trent smiled. "Oi, this is just fucking fantastic."

Mrs. Lopez raised a brow.

"Apologies, I'm just excited! All I need is the footage from 1997 to 2000."

"Well . . . good luck!"

It was then that Trent realized the tapes were all unmarked, unorganized, and essentially looked identical.

The librarian opened her hands awkwardly. "I know, I know. We've just never sorted through them all."

Trent rubbed his hands together. "Do you guys give out service hours?"

He spent the next three hours plugging tapes into the VCR, noting the dates, punching the details into the label maker, and assembling the tapes in order. It would've gone faster if he wasn't scanning each tape for his mother, fast-forwarding and hoping for a flash of zigzagged curls or the dimply smile she gave to him. Most of the tapes were from before Lourdes's time with the troupe, but even then, he kept hoping to see a young woman who looked like him in the crowd, marveling at the witchery on display before her.

Trent gave a bleary-eyed look to the neat rows of labeled tapes to his right and the remaining boxes of unsorted tapes on his left. His fingers felt a little sore from all the unpacking and labeling. The room now smelled more like pizza than old books—Mrs. Lopez had dropped off a slice for Trent's lunch—and he cracked open the window for a little air.

On what must've been the hundredth tape that Trent pushed into the old VCR, he found her. The shot made him jump so hard, he nearly knocked over his half-filled orange soda.

The footage lifted the hairs on Trent's arms. It showed the fun and mischief behind the scenes before a show. The acrobats dabbed powder on their faces and stuck their tongues out at the camera, a trombonist showed off his impressive skills, and Trent's mother flitted off camera, feigning shyness before giving the lens a big kiss. The troupe was a family, clear from the way they all looked at one another.

Trent hardly blinked. He didn't want to miss anything. And when the scenes changed from the backstage camaraderie to the start of the show, he gasped.

Trent couldn't keep the wild grin off his face. *Look at her.* His mother, draped in a glittering black dress, her hair done in elegant bantu knots. She wielded no less than six long knives in her hands and wore a devious smile, something he'd seen on his own face from time to time.

The footage was marked with the year 1998, which meant she was, what, twenty-five? A spark in her eyes, Lourdes began throwing the knives in the air, higher than Trent had ever seen any performer go.

Lourdes closed her eyes. The blades lit aflame.

With a silky tone, the announcer hyped up the crowd. "Lourdes DeVry, the firewitch!"

She spun around the length of the massive stage, throwing and catching, the firelight dancing against her jeweled dress. It was mesmerizing, and Trent's soul burst with pride.

My mother was a goddess.

"With Odeah and Quincey, the magical DeVry Siblings!"

Trent's heart flipped, his face furrowing in confusion.

At first, he thought, *Maybe this was part of the act.* Three witches fashioned as siblings who performed as a trio. But as Odeah and Quincey joined his mother, the resemblance was too strong to ignore.

Trent had an aunt and an uncle. He'd never met them. He never knew they'd existed.

Did they know about him?

Mesmerized, Trent watched the three witches circle one another in their glittering outfits, the crowd swelling with similar anticipation. Odeah and Quincey broke off, the two standing on opposing sides of a target painted onto a backdrop. They locked arms, then stretched away from each other so that the target was centered between them.

Fire danced on the blades, the smoke coiling into shapes of animals, delighting the children in the crowd. With a smile and a wink, Lourdes sent the first blade hurtling toward her siblings. It hit the target in a burst of colorful flames: orange and red, pink and purple.

Odeah and Quincey took a step toward each other, the space of the target growing narrower. Lourdes hit it again, and this time, the flames burst into tiny firebirds, eliciting gasps of wonder from the crowd, and from Trent.

With every go, Lourdes's siblings thinned the gap for the target between them. She hit every target and laughed as the crowd roared in approval. For the final throw, where the distance between her siblings was but three inches, Lourdes pulled out a small, gilded knife that had been strapped to her leg. The very one Trent now carried with him. It hit the target with a perfect *thwip*.

Trent fast-forwarded through the alligator charmer's bit until the footage was backstage again. Dressed in a modest T-shirt and jeans, Lourdes swiped a cotton pad over her makeup. Her sister was beside her, pulling off a fake eyelash and making eyes at one of the acrobat ladies.

Lourdes squealed suddenly and threw her hands around a dark-skinned, well-dressed man.

Trent clutched his chest.

Damien Hogarth had a toddler in one hand and lifted his mother up with his free arm, spinning her around. Baby Troy giggled gleefully between them. They looked picture-perfect. Quincey playfully wrapped his arms around them with a teasing kissy-face.

The video shifted to a few younger members of the troupe balancing stacks of glasses on their heads, and when it returned to Trent's family, Lourdes was different.

Her face dropped, just for a second, before she regained her smile and the tape ended.

What had she seen? There was something, or someone, off camera. Trent replayed the video over and over and over, looking for someone in the shadows whose presence had affected his mother so. The look of fear on his mother's face couldn't be denied.

"Trent?"

He turned. Mrs. Lopez gave him a small smile. "Did you find what you were looking for?"

"Yeah, thanks." He nodded and felt a few tears slide down his face. He hadn't realized he was crying; no wonder Mrs. Lopez was looking at him like she wanted to give him a hug.

She looked at the shelves of organized tapes. "Thank you for your help. We close in fifteen, but feel free to finish up."

He nodded again. "A few minutes, and I'll be out of your hair."

Trent watched the tape one more time, but this time, he savored the memories of a family he'd never met, and had never known.

Adrenaline cut through his sadness. Odeah and Quincey DeVry. Trent had his next leads.

13

mathew

Mathew Beaumont began his day with a ride on his beloved horse, Ruby; a shouting match between his parents that resulted in a glass vase thrown at his feet; and, according to Trent, *pining*.

It was a lazy afternoon, as all afternoons were in Beaumont Manor. In the wide-open living room surrounded by Serious Art, untouched bookcases, and fresh flowers, Rebecca, Trent, and Mathew were like spots of oil atop a glass of water. Trent bounced a basketball with one hand and held up a book with the other. He'd gotten close to knocking over a crystalline jar of untouched candy but managed to catch it. He made circles around the room, an excited energy pulsating about him.

Mathew picked a piece of glass out of his sock. It was bad enough when the Beaumonts argued over their divorce settlements, but somehow it was worse when they agreed. Ainsley and Frances were adamant that Rebecca needed to remain in hiding until the issue of her *affliction* could be solved. Some quack of a doctor was supposed to visit next week, and there was even a conversation about blackthorne supplements, which was where Mathew lost his shit. He'd happily take a thousand more hurled vases in defense of his sister, his twin, a baby witch. *The Harbinger.*

Rebecca sat sprawled across the old settee, twirling a black lock of hair around her finger as she flipped through a thick magazine. Her dark turtleneck was pulled all the way up to her chin, though no one in the room was unaware that she was a witch. Not like the turtleneck was hiding anything. A witch's aura was palpable, and Becky was like a radiator in the winter. She'd called dibs on the stereo system, and nineties pop bumped through the floorboards. Mathew didn't know when Death would call her, and though he was diving into the world of necromancy headfirst, he wished Rebecca could remain in this blissful ignorance.

He picked up a drawing pad and retreated to the wide windows overlooking an acre of perfect grass. Back before he'd discovered his love of horses, his parents had thrown money at dozens of potential hobbies, desperate to make one stick. Art landed in a close second, though he rarely indulged these days. Even now, he didn't know what he was doing, or why the itch in his palm led him to pulling a pencil from his largely untouched art supplies.

Hammersmitt was in the distance, and farther back, the spires of Mesmortes poked out, refusing to be ignored. He flexed his hands. He watched the pentagram scars in his palms wrinkle and smooth. They fascinated him like he was holding two precious gems.

"Where are you, Matty boy?" Trent crossed him up—even though Mathew was standing still—and mimed shooting a three.

Mathew shrugged. "Thinking about my new battle scars."

Trent cocked his head at him, wearing unease on his face. "So freaky."

"I thought you'd think they were cool."

"That was before . . ." Trent shifted his weight from foot to foot. "Before everything."

Everything. One easy word to encapsulate the immense shit show that was the end of the last Haunting Season. Mathew reached out to touch Trent's shoulder, then stopped himself. Trent was too busy pretending to throw the ball at Rebecca to notice how quickly Mathew jerked his hand back. He dug his nails into his palms, but the images came anyway: the flames, the Wolves, and the new one—the vision of the old man from therapy crumpling to the floor.

He turned back to his blank page and began to doodle the grass, the sky, the schools in the distance. Anything to distract himself. His knee bounced to Rebecca's music, his hand flying across the page.

Suddenly, he couldn't stop. His hands moved of their own volition. He flipped the page and drew a house he'd seen only once before, tendrils seeping from its walls and into the sky. He sketched a hundred pentagrams, scores of circles and triangles, into something resembling a Venn diagram. Death's presence slipped in, guiding his hand as much as his thoughts.

"The runes," he muttered in a voice that wasn't entirely his own. "Purging, confining, exterminating."

Trent looked up from his book. "Huh?"

Mathew's work wasn't done. Barely thinking, hardly breathing, he put aside the illustrations and began scribbling out the laws of Death that would guide his Reaper to the work that needed to be done. Neat text filled up pages and pages, and when he was done, his wrist and arm were sore.

Finally, his fingers relaxed. He looked up from the daze and saw Rebecca and Trent standing behind his shoulders in the window's reflection. They shared a tense look.

"Yeah, so this is, like . . . supremely satanic," said Trent, flipping the pages back toward the diagrams.

Rebecca leaned in closer. "Mathew. What the f—"

Her voice cut off. She clamped down on her neck, a sudden sweat breaking all over her forehead. A cold wind rolled through the room, the lush curtains billowing.

Mathew turned to Rebecca, and she gasped.

"Matty!" Trent choked out. "Your eyes!"

Ignoring Trent, Mathew opened his hand toward Rebecca, the pentagram pulsing in his palm. "YOU CANNOT HIDE FROM ME, HARBINGER. WHEN I CALL UPON YOU, YOU WILL ANSWER."

Rebecca swallowed hard. She had the front of her turtleneck balled up in her fingers, as if her skin burned where it'd touched.

"YOUR DEATH MARK." He moved closer, but Rebecca scrambled back.

No matter.

Death lifted Mathew's hand, the pentagram in his palm burning with new life.

White light streamed from Rebecca's neck through the spaces between her fingers. The glowing tendrils met Mathew's hand, smoky wisps dancing in the space between them. Rebecca gritted her teeth, her eyes determined and angry, as if she could fight off the power of her own necromancy. Mathew hated himself for being unable to stop this, but the part of him he shared with Death knew that it was necessary.

A new heat burst beside him suddenly, strange flames licking at his side. He snapped his head to the source of the sensation, but it was only Trent. "Matty! Stop!"

Mathew stared at him. This unholy heat—it disrupted the Death connection and hurled him back into the Emporium.

With a pained gasp, Rebecca dropped to her knees. At the same time, Death released his grip on Mathew, the heat of Trent's presence broke, and the world slammed back into place.

Immediately, Mathew jolted for his sister. "Shit. Are you okay?"

Rebecca exhaled a slow breath before peering up at him. To his relief, she looked more alive than she had in months. Healthy color flushed her cheeks, and her eyes brightened with a witchy glow. And her *witchery*. Magic pooled out from her into a warm aura that pulsed with her every breath.

"I'm gonna *punch you in the face*!" she screeched.

Mathew held back his smile. "It feels really good to hear you say that."

"Shit, man." Trent stared at the two of them. "Death just takes over your body like that?"

Mathew nodded. "That's the second time it's happened."

"Harbinger," Rebecca spat. "The hell does that mean?"

He waited until she pulled herself onto her feet before going back to the pages he'd worked on. He understood why Trent and Rebecca had been concerned. The drawings, doodles, and pages and pages of text looked to be the work of a man possessed. He skimmed the instructions that Death had him transcribe and found a section on its *Unholy Trinity.*

REAPER. HARBINGER. RUNEKEEPER.

He read the commands for the Runekeeper, his heart racing with every word. *They, who serve the Reaper, whose blood is given willingly in the quest to protect the mortal realm from Death's enemies . . .*

Mathew swallowed hard. A horrible realization clicked into place. "Rebecca, listen to me. You need to take care of yourself. Don't let them give you blackthorne. No more holding back your power. You need a wand, you need a needle—"

"What are you talking about?" She dropped the armor, and her voice shook with fear. "You're scaring me."

"Please. Just." He held her arms, grateful for the thick fabric of her turtleneck against his death marks. "When Lord Death calls you, you won't have a choice but to answer. You need to be ready." She stammered for a response, but he held up a hand. "I need to talk to Iris."

Trent gaped at him. "Wait, wanna tell us what's going on?"

Mathew scrambled for his phone and his keys, the unbound book of Death tight in his grip. "I'll be back ASAP. Just. Wait here. Don't worry. Everything's good."

From the look on their faces, his words did anything but reassure them.

Ignoring both of them, Mathew sent a frantic text and hurried out of the house. With all he'd read about the roles they had to play and the personal cost he'd have to pay, Mathew should've been terrified. The fact that he wasn't should've been alarming in its own right. But as he sprinted away from the rows of houses and made his way into the center of the witchtown, he felt a weight ease off his shoulders.

Death had blessed him and cursed him in one inky-black scrawl. And finally, Mathew knew his life's true purpose.

14

iris

Under a dark sky and heavy clouds, Iris made her way to the Green. Unlike Thalia or any of the other witches practicing plant magic and healing magic, Iris didn't ever have much cause to enter that sacred magical garden, but she felt comforted by its existence. After all, she and her friends had been the ones to barter for it before the last Haunting Season. A drop of rain hit her shoulder, and she put up a *Sealing* spell around herself right before the sky opened up.

Hot, humid, rainy. The weather was miserable, but Iris preferred the town when it was quiet like this, with all the tourists taking shelter rather than running all over the Hill. She thought of Logan, attacked by a hexeater. They were getting better at hiding their motives. A few days ago, a girl had asked Iris for directions to the town apothecary. Iris, in a good mood, led the way. She was headed for Soma anyway and would pass the apothecary en route. The girl seemed normal enough, until she caught the flash of Iris's death mark peeking out from the hem of her shorts.

The girl's face grew *hungry*. The red-and-black tattoos that usually signified a hexeater were nowhere to be seen on her.

"Deathwitch!" she'd screeched, falling to her knees in reverence. "Please, I just need a bit of your blood, I'll give you anything, anything you want!"

"Ew, fuck off!" Iris spat in response, but the girl clutched at her Forces like a child. At the threatening sight of Iris's wand, she only became more fervent. Thankfully, Suzette, the elder witch who owned a garden shop, heard the commotion and threw a spell between them, one that physically separated the hexeater from Iris.

Her stomach twisted at the memory. If it were up to her, hexeaters wouldn't be allowed to step foot in the town, but according to Jailah, they spent a lot of money in Haelsford, and those tourism dollars couldn't be ignored. Iris didn't think the safety of witches should've been given up for money, but it looked like she was going to have to deal with the next one who tested her herself.

As the rain pattered against her invisible bubble of magic, Iris quickened her step through the quiet Hammersmitt campus. It wasn't open for their students the way Mesmortes's campus was, and she was happy for it. No boys puffing up their chests, no curious eyes watching from the windows. Aside from Mathew and Trent, she had no love for Hammersmitt boys.

Mathew was waiting for her in a flat patch of grass surrounded by bushes bursting with purple and yellow flowers. He was clearly unprepared for the rain. His clothes were nearly soaked through, water dripping from his dark hair and onto his face.

"You're here," he said, exhaling in relief.

"Of course I am." She expanded the *Sealing* bubble around him.

"Thanks." He shook his hair like a golden retriever, and Iris's heart warmed at the sight.

He sat back on a large rock, and that was when Iris noticed the palm-sized stones laid at his feet. Before she could ask, he said, "All right, so . . . something weird happened today." He riffled in his knapsack. Iris heard the shuffling of paper.

"Weird for a mundane and witch, or weird for *us*? 'Cause like, a lotta weird things been happening."

Mathew chuckled. "Lord Death took over my body and made me write you a guidebook—how do we classify that?"

Iris's breath caught in her throat.

The aforementioned book was a loose stack of drawing paper covered in strange diagrams that Iris didn't recognize.

"You did this today?"

"Yeah, just an hour ago—" He gasped, the words dying in his throat.

Iris's chest tightened. "Beaumont?"

"I'm fine." He sighed as his eyes darkened to that glossy jet black. Through him, Death said, "I REQUIRE YOUR BLOOD ON THE BOOK, DEATHWITCH."

Gritting her teeth, Iris pricked her thumb and sprinkled a few beads of blood on the pages. With a sharp cut of cold air, the stack of pages in Mathew's hands transformed before her eyes. From nothing, a dark green binding of thick leather grew around the sheets. She stared, speechless, as an invisible tool etched three entwined pentagrams into the center of the cover. Where the pages were tan, they were now gilded as if dipped in golden lacquer, the text in dark red ink rather than graphite. It was a thin book, but when Mathew dropped it into Iris's curious hands, the weight of it nearly toppled her.

"*Death's Compendium*," Mathew whispered, his voice returning to him. "This book is yours, and yours alone."

Iris exhaled slowly. "Cool, cool, cool."

She held the book tightly. Her body buzzed. While this entire thing was *batshit*, the curious part of her magic-hungry mind spun in anticipation. She was being taken under the wing of Death itself, and though she said she was doing this to become powerful enough to preserve her parents' souls, there was no version of herself who would've ever denied the call to her purpose.

How long have I been destined for this? Iris wondered dreamily.

She looked up at Mathew's deathly dark eyes. "Not that *I* want to be randomly possessed, but why aren't you—why isn't Death—just putting the things I need into *my* brain."

Mathew tutted his tongue, almost amused. He reached out. Iris didn't know whether to lean in or flinch, so she just stood there as Mathew—*and Death? Or Death?*—rested his knuckles on her cheek. "Imbuing a Reaper's soul with Death is a dangerous proposition. Your frail, mortal body would not withstand the necromantic power. Imagine dousing yourself in gasoline and walking into flame."

"Uh. I'm good." Iris swallowed, heart racing.

As Death released its hold on her tether and blue replaced the black, Iris felt an odd tug in the pit of her stomach. Mathew drew his hand away slowly, knuckles trailing on her cheekbone. Was that Death's action, or the mortal boy he used as a vessel? Either way, her stomach flipped, and Iris was unable to stop herself from imagining those rough, slender fingers elsewhere.

Shit.

"Okay, so too much death magic is bad," Iris sputtered quickly. She leaned back on her heels to put some distance between them.

Mathew did his own awkward side step. He shoved his hands into his pockets before sitting on the rock. He gestured to the book, a wordless command.

Iris sat beside him and balanced the book in her lap. She wanted to go slow and take in every word, but she felt like a child with an assortment of candy before her—she didn't know where to start, what to linger on. She forced her hands still and started at the beginning.

Tears sprang into her eyes within moments. There were pictures from the beginning of time, faces blinking back at her from under dark hoods, death marks glowing silver.

"Oh my god . . ." Iris said breathlessly, excitement rising in her chest. She leaned into Mathew, comforted by his presence. "These are the other Reapers!"

He smiled sweetly at her, taking on her delight as his own.

Most of the photos were monochrome in what Iris assumed signified a Reaper's death. Though she knew her mother was never called for it, she still checked the pages of necromancers with last names beginning in *F*. She did not see Sage Foster's face, or any Foster at all. But there was a dapper man a few pages later who gave Iris pause because his face was so much like hers. Dark skin, wide nose, high cheekbones. Unfriendly eyes.

DAVEED KEATON.

HARBINGER TO IVAN HALLOWAY.

HARLEM, NEW YORK. PERISHED NOVEMBER 1931.

Iris released a delirious laugh. "Looks like it's in my blood." She rubbed her eyes with the heel of her palm before flipping through and finding Ivan Halloway's picture. Another Black man, lighter-skinned, with round spectacles and wide grin. He died a few years after Iris's relative, but his title was Reaper, like hers. "What's a Harbinger? And a Runekeeper?" She continued flipping through, past the roster of necromancers and toward the end of the book. Her knuckles landed on a section titled "Lord Death's Runes."

Mathew's smile tightened. "There are hundreds of necromantic runes, but three essential ones to take care of a corporeal demon."

And there they were, centered on the first page. "A rune for confining, a rune for exterminating." She ran her fingers over the illustrated glyph: several interlocking pyramids for confining; a whirlpool of circles descending in size for purging; and a simple skull drawn in thin, quick strokes for exterminating.

Runecrafting, as Mesmortes put it, was a tool for lengthening the effects of magic without doing physical maintenance on a spell. Iris herself had runes drawn on enchanted parchment in her room that kept spirits at bay while she slept, as ghosts needing rest never seemed to care about *her* own rest. "Okay, so I need to make these before going to Port Barrow—"

Her eyes snapped to the three stones on the ground. Now she saw that their smooth surfaces were carved with the rune marks.

Mathew winked. "Too late."

Confused, Iris sputtered for the words. "You're not a witch, though."

"No," he said proudly. "But I am your Runekeeper."

The energy in the stones chilled Iris's witchiness, the same way

Mathew's presence did when Lord Death was near. She shook her head. "Hold on, is this another rule? *I* can't make the runes because . . . why? Also, if you're my Runekeeper, then who is my Harbinger?"

Mathew looked away. "I don't know."

"You're lying," she replied instantly. At some point, she'd learned him well enough to know how to spot his lies.

Mathew nodded sheepishly. "Yes, but I have a good reason for it. I promise. You'll have to trust me for now."

Iris didn't know what to do but nod back.

"As for the runes . . ." Mathew quieted in a way that twisted Iris's stomach.

The instructions on creating these runes looked simple enough at first, but as she continued reading, her heart dropped.

"This is why," he said too calmly, looking down at the damning words with her. "Creating a necromantic rune involves imbuing it with life force, not blood."

Iris's heart pounded in her ears. She looked at him for a long moment, her words in her throat. "Beaumont. What. *What?*"

She glared at him, waiting for him to explain himself, but to her horror, his voice was steadfast and sure. "Three runes? Can't knock that much off my life. Maybe a few days, a few months?" He rubbed the back of his neck casually. "I figure we see how you do in Port Barrow, and then you can tell me if you need any others—"

"Oh my god, do you hear yourself?" Iris jumped up to stand before him, holding her fists at her sides to keep herself from shaking some sense into him. "You never, ever should've made these if that was the cost!"

His gaze was as stubborn as his voice. "I don't regret it."

"You should!" Iris spat desperately.

"Iris. I've had my life planned out for me since before I was even born, okay?"

She closed her eyes. "*Don't.* Do not give me this whiny, rich, white boy bullshit—"

"But this is bigger than getting into an Ivy, or getting a good job, or, fuck, whatever!" He ran his hands through his hair with infuriating nonchalance. "Maybe this is *my* purpose: helping you keep the border between the mortal world and the underworld intact."

Purpose. The word now left Iris itchy with discomfort. "Chipping away at your life force to help me put down some demons? You're not a necromancer, why do you even care?"

He stood to meet her, the height difference forcing Iris to look up at him. "I know that you want the power Death has promised you—to keep your parents' souls tethered to earth. Besides, you argued for my *life.* You saved me. Let me repay you."

"No," she whispered. "I never would've asked you to do this. You shouldn't have done this."

He gave her a smug smirk. He dipped his head toward her, and Iris's stomach leapt into her chest just before he tilted his head to her ear. "And you should've left me to burn."

The words unraveled her, pulling her from the Green and back into the Necromantic Emporium on the night Adelaide Strigwach tried to kill them both. Before the fire, Adelaide had offered to spare Iris.

You have your weaknesses, but you are young. I can rip them out.

Iris pulled herself back to face him once more, and his knowing look pierced her straight through. *I see you*, he seemed to say, and for all Iris wanted to bury her feelings for him, it would be a lie to say he was wrong.

"You don't owe me anything," she managed. "Death made the decision itself, it saw what you were to me and my necromancy."

"Yeah, well, like I said before. *Too late.*"

With one hand, he held both of hers, palms upward. He flinched suddenly at the touch of her skin.

"What was that?" she asked.

Mathew only shook his head, a tight smile on his lips. One hand still cradling hers, he dropped the stones atop her palms.

Power cut through her body with an icy vibration. Like jumping into a frozen pond, she trembled while her witchery usually only warmed. She'd never felt magic like this before, and now that she had, she wondered what else she would discover that her education was keeping from her.

Iris was torn between her fear of Mathew's actions and her dark delight at this new necromancy. As if he could sense her conflicting feelings, he stroked her fingers in reassurance.

"Never again," Iris whispered. "I'm serious. No more runes."

His fingers moved up from her hand to her arm, the heat of them more palpable than the scorching air around them. "No more sacrifices."

15

logan

Logan had done plenty of foolish, risky, and potentially life-threatening things in her life. There was coming to Haelsford, for one, a town way out of her comfort zone and surrounded by a hexed Wolfpack. Then fostering her connection to Theodore Bloom in secret, and, of course, falling for him. But *this*—walking into the Swamp with a backpack full of Maverick's dog treats—was on a whole other level.

"Here, Wolfy, Wolfy," Bloom teased, his presence like a touch of silk against her ear.

Logan ignored him. She had one hand opened outward, and her glowing witchery—the gift of a proxy—lit up the tunnel of rock before her. The complete quiet of the Cavern was a thunderous distraction in its own right, and Logan was focusing hard for any movement that might signal that she wasn't alone.

The Cavern smelled like moss and the faintest hint of a wildfire. Logan dripped with sweat and had been since she'd made the trek away from Mesmortes and up the surrounding hills. Navigating the Cavern was deceptively difficult, and her calves were beginning to burn.

Bloom's otherworldly footsteps made no sound beside her. When Logan glanced at him, something she was trying very hard to refrain from doing, she thought he looked like a kid. His fists were in his pockets, his shoulders raised in a little shrug. Was it her imagination's doing, the vulnerability of his appearance? He now seemed a separate entity from her thoughts; if it were up to her, he wouldn't be here at all. Whatever this was, she needed to sever it, and quickly.

And if her gut feeling was right, this wasn't the only connection she needed to sever.

"I've never been this far in," Logan whispered. "Not since that night."

Bloom touched his fingers to his temple, as if feeling a headache. "I can still smell the smoke."

Logan turned to him. "How did you do it? How did you call the Wolves?"

The sly, crooked grin that grew on Bloom's lips made Logan regret asking. How was it that she could still feel wanting when he looked at her like this? Logan never thought of herself as someone who truly hated people, but she knew she hated him. And yet, *and yet*.

"Well, I don't know." Another shrug, another coy look. "But I trust you'll figure it out, Wolf Girl."

Yeah, she hated him.

With a scoff, Logan picked up the pace, or as much as she could without tripping over the uneven, rocky ground. She was going lower, she knew it from the way her ears were starting to pop. As the path ahead of her grew narrower, Logan remembered Hallowe'en night. She'd thought the Red Three were testing her tolerance for tight spaces, when they were really

trying to dissect her fears. She laughed a little at the thought. *Baby witch,
you really had no idea.*

Logan stopped. The entrance to the tunnel that connected Haelsford to the
Swamp was quiet, dark, and musty. She swallowed and sat in a little nook of
rock before it and pulled out the dog treats—to Bloom's intense amusement.

"What else would I bring, a bit of human flesh?" she muttered.

"If you think the Wolves are heeding your thoughts, then why not just
call them here?"

"I've tried," she muttered. She'd done nothing but think of them in the
week since that hexeater Blake was attacked. Never once did a Wolf come at
her internal call, whether intentional or not. She looked down at her glowing hands, at the unzipped sandwich bag of dog treats at her feet.

What the hell am I doing here?

It was getting late, she was tired, and her stomach twitched with hunger. She should've packed snacks for herself. Logan looked into the tunnel
and wasn't sure what she wanted to see looking back at her. She flung a
handful of treats into the dark mouth of rock, leaned her head back, and
closed her eyes. Twenty minutes. After that, she would leave and have a
normal night. Dinner with the girls, a movie, and bed.

When Logan jolted awake, she nearly screamed. She didn't remember
falling asleep, and the unending darkness mixed with the smell of blood
disoriented her.

Wait. Blood?

Logan jumped up and threw out the light from her hands. She was
alone. Bloom was gone and the Cavern was silent. She frantically felt along
her body for a sign of a wound, but she was untouched—

She looked down, bile rising in her throat. Two dead birds rested at her feet. They'd been placed there carefully, wings overlapping, hearts cut out messily but with intention. She didn't bother looking around; Logan had never seen birds in the Cavern, and it was clear that this was no accident.

It was an offering.

She needed no further proof. She sent a text to the group chat: **In the cavern. If you don't hear from me in 20 mins, something's wrong. Love you guys.**

The text was met with a red exclamation point signaling an error in sending. *Duh*, she chided herself. She was surrounded by stone a few feet underground. Whatever happened next, there would be no rescue mission.

Logan opened the SpellCheck app, grateful that her past self had been dutiful enough to download its contents for offline use. She searched for something like a bungee cord, a tether to pull her back. The spell she found was close enough.

She pricked her finger and lifted her hands. *"An Anchor to Steady Me."*

Her witchery warmed; that was always a good sign, but Logan felt a strange resistance against her magic. It wasn't like it was before Hell Night, back when her power felt uncontrollable and chaotic. No, this was as if her witchery was being held back even as she pushed it forward.

Teeth clenched, Logan reached deep into the inner well of magic that ran through her veins and pushed with all her might. Finally, a beaming, purple rope of witchery shot out from her hand and buried itself in the opposite wall of stone. Though the spell was denoted as suitable for beginners, Logan was exhausted.

With heavy breaths and glowing witchery, Logan stepped into the dark tunnel.

Her heart raced with every step, a mixture of fear and anticipation. These tunnels hadn't been used in a century, aside from Bloom's use of them for the Wolves. Sweat trickled down Logan's neck as she gingerly stepped over the rocky terrain and jutting stone. Was there enough air down here? A wave of nausea twisted in her belly and chest, and she had to blink hard to refocus her blurred vision. Though she walked slowly, she nearly tripped over her own two feet. With help from the *Anchor*, Logan caught herself but had to take a moment to regroup with her hands on her knees.

Please don't vomit.

Logan looked around and realized three things at once. First, the *Anchoring* spell had dimmed. What was brilliant shining purple just a few moments before was now a dull mauve. Second, and more concerning, the proxy glow of her hands *flickered*. Sure, she'd only awakened this part of her magic a few months ago, but she'd never seen it flicker so violently. And third, there were little black vines embedded in the Cavern's walls, and Logan felt silly for not immediately realizing what was happening.

"It's—" she choked out. "Blackthorne."

Being surrounded by the one plant on this earth made to disempower a witch should've convinced her to turn back, but she only swallowed her nausea and steadied herself. She had to push through. She needed to know what was waiting for her at the end of the tunnel.

Every step forward sent her proxy magic flickering. She was plunged into near darkness every few seconds, but as she dragged herself forward, she saw a strange light up ahead.

The blackthorne in the Cavern walls grew into thick, dark vines and large petals, the air pulsing with its suppressive energy. Both Logan's magic and her mundane energy dwindled, and by the time she reached the break in the rock that opened up into a massive stone chasm, she thought she was hallucinating.

In the middle of the circular room of stone was an enormous, glowing bulb. Its heavy vines and tendrils snaked through the ground and were embedded in the walls. Pain shot through Logan's limbs. The scar across her eye throbbed with heat, and the proxy glow of her hands dimmed entirely. She heard a distant cry, a scream. Not her name, but something that the last bit of her consciousness responded to. With all the strength she had left, Logan thumbed the button on her camera and passed out.

·····✦ ⊗ ✦·····

Heat pressed down on Logan, an invisible blanket growing tighter.

She gasped, worry and witchery pulsing in her heart. She was on the ground. In the Cavern? No, the Cavern was made of cold rock. As she fidgeted, her knees and fingertips sank slightly into the sludge beneath her. As her surroundings settled into focus, Logan thought of Thalia, who'd found herself waking up in the Swamp in the middle of the night.

But as she turned toward the steady sounds of animalistic breathing, Logan knew she hadn't been sleepwalking.

There, half-shrouded by thin branches and dead leaves, a red Wolf waited.

Logan had taken the Wolf's sight, but she felt that it could sense her like she sensed it. The Wolf was much bigger than she remembered, though still not as large as the Wolves that ran rampant on Hell Night.

Gingerly, Logan rose to her feet. She presented her hand the same way she had in front of the Cavern after she'd killed Bloom. Did it remember? This Wolf had felt her anger for that hexeating boy and went after him. This Wolf heard her rumbling belly and left food at her feet. Still, her hand shook. Those teeth were awfully sharp.

"Careful," said a familiar, unwanted voice. To Logan's annoyance, Bloom's specter was still with her. He sat perched on a boulder and watched with smug curiosity. But the Wolf only nuzzled her palm. To say that the Wolf was just an oversized dog was foolish—the thing was bigger than a mastiff and between its crooked teeth, mangled face, and the way it stalked rather than walked was not something of a pet. But when it sniffed her hand, Logan nearly forgot that it had tried to kill her at Theodore Bloom's command.

She didn't know what to say. So, she whispered, "Hi."

The Swamp began to move and shift. Branches swayed, bushes rustled, and all around her, bright red eyes danced in the dark. Logan pulled her hand away. One Wolf was terrifying; a pack was a death wish. They breathed and huffed around her, each keeping their distance as the smaller one circled Logan protectively.

The biggest of the pack stepped forward.

Bloom snickered. "You really let yourself be lured here—"

"Shut up," Logan snapped. She didn't look around for Bloom, not wanting to take her eyes off the pack's leader. But his words hit her, as much as she hated it. All she had was her magic—which was still so new—and an intuitive feeling that now seemed more foolish than hopeful.

The leader didn't howl, but it growled deep and loud as it approached. Logan was awestruck and frozen in fear as the Wolf circled her. When the others stepped away, leaving Logan with the leader of the pack, she understood.

The Wolf jerked back, then lunged.

Logan was ready. She brought her glowing hands together in an arc. "*A Shield!*"

The Wolf lurched away, avoiding her and the glimmering barrier of gold light that she'd put up. It set itself back into a defensive stance and circled her once more. Logan could've wrapped the shield all around herself and run, but there was that *really* foolish gut feeling once more.

The Wolf bolted for her again, mouth wide.

"*Insanora!*" she shouted, an un-reformed spell from her greenwitchery texts. The earth opened just enough to trip up the Wolf's back left paw, but it didn't hold. Its teeth caught Logan hard by the wrist.

The pain was unimaginable, but a thunderous, feral energy ruptured through her and drowned out the agony. Logan tasted copper in her mouth, and the world went red.

Instinctively, Logan drew her head back and bit down hard on the Wolf's ear.

The Wolf howled loudly, but Logan didn't relent. A moment passed, then another. Logan and the Wolf glared at each other, neither wanting to give up. Logan aimed her free, glowing hand in its face. Finally, the Wolf released her, suddenly cowed in the face of her magic. Logan held her hand there until the Wolf slowly lowered itself to the ground.

The adrenaline slipped, and Logan collapsed next to the beast. She stopped her bleeding with a quick healing spell, but she'd need to get to Thalia soon.

Theodore Bloom looked down on her sweetly. "Look at the witch you've become." His presence grew unstable. He slipped in and out of the moonlight. "You're welcome."

Logan couldn't find the energy to fight her own mind back.

"Thank me. I brought out your witchery, didn't I? And I—" He went in and out of view, arms open toward the pack of Wolves watching her. "I gave you *this*."

"Maybe," Logan whispered as his image flickered away. She choked out a vicious laugh. "Or, maybe, I *took* it from you."

Finally, she had silence. Well, almost. The Wolves stepped toward her, leaves and twigs crunching under their enormous paws. And though their leader was curled next to her, hiding its wounds, it looked at her with murder in its red eyes. Actually, that may have just been its resting expression.

Shaking, Logan pulled herself to her feet. Her little Wolf stepped forward, head lowered slightly.

"No more . . . hurting people, okay?" Logan whispered, almost laughing at how ridiculous this was. She petted him gently. "I think I'll call you Shadow."

The Wolf circled her slowly, his body close to her legs, claiming her the way she claimed him.

16

thalia

Thalia jerked awake with a gasp, her wand readied. To her shock—and relief—she was in her bed, and the enchanted vine around her wrist was unbroken. *Finally*, a night of uninterrupted, peaceful sleep, the first since she'd discovered that the Swamp's hex was stretching outward. This had become so foreign to her that she woke up expecting the worst.

Thalia undid the vine around her wrist. For all her relief, she was curious about why last night was different. As cathartic as it was to yell at the Swamp to leave her alone, she wasn't convinced that her efforts made any difference.

She checked her phone. It was ten; she needed to get to the cafeteria quickly if she didn't want to miss Waffle Wednesday. Her stomach twisted in agreement, but the unread text in her messages left it twisting out of fear, not hunger.

We need to check in.

The number was unsaved, but Thalia knew who it was. She deleted the text immediately, then reached under her bed and pulled out a small wooden box. Though its lock looked simple enough, only Thalia could open it. She pricked her thumb. *"Darkest Secrets."*

The case snapped open, revealing old letters from her mother and her aunt, neat wads of emergency cash, her backup wand, and an ancient cell phone. She dialed a number she still knew by heart.

Fiona Turner answered on the second ring. "This is Fiona, owner of Salty Sweet Bakeshop."

The sounds of the aforementioned bakery filled up the background: the ping of the cash register, the sound of children, staff calling up customers. Thalia's heart ached. She could almost smell fresh vanilla cupcakes and buttercream frosting. "I'd like to order thirteen cupcakes."

"Of course. By when?"

"The next new moon."

"Absolutely. We have vanilla, chocolate—" Her mother paused. Thalia heard a door closing in the background before Fiona said, "Hi, hi, I just needed to make sure that you were safe."

Thalia hardened her voice. "Finish the code."

"Okay, okay." Fiona chuckled. "Vanilla, chocolate, and coconut almond. There."

Technically, Thalia was supposed to end with *extra frosting, please*, but she could tell that her mother wasn't in the mood, and maybe didn't have the time. "Yeah, I'm fine. Everything's okay here." Well, as okay as things could be, considering. "Why, what's going on?"

"I'm sorry, lovey, I know we shouldn't talk without planning a call first, but with those witches still missing, I guess I thought maybe—"

Thalia's pulse jumped. "Wait, *wait*. What do you mean missing witches?"

Aside from Fiona's small intake of breath, the line was silent.

Thalia scurried to her desk and opened up her laptop. "Mom? What missing witches?"

"I thought your aunt told you, baby."

Thalia thought back to the very beginning of summer, when Aunt Nonni had mentioned needing to talk before dropping it. "She didn't."

Thalia typed *missing witches* into the search bar. That yielded an absurd number of results, so she added *Annex, Arizona* to the end of it.

That got her close enough.

To the south of Annex was a larger town called Fey's Landing. Not a bleedbay like Annex, but it wasn't a witchtown the way Haelsford was. There were several witchy families according to the demographics data, and . . . three young witches had gone missing since the spring. Thalia skimmed the headlines quickly—the first two had vanished at the same time, and the third shortly after. All young, about Thalia's age. New, inexperienced witches. After the third disappeared, witches in Fey's Landing placed tracker hexes on their kids, and the disappearances stopped.

Then, just two weeks ago, a city to the east of Annex reported two missing witches, seventeen and nineteen years old.

"What the hell?" Thalia whispered. Maverick whined worriedly.

"I can't talk long," her mother said quickly. "I just needed to hear your voice."

"Wait, you think he's . . ." Thalia swallowed the words down, too nervous to say them. Her father hated witches, that was true. But he wanted Thalia to pay, specifically. Not only had she been tainted, but she'd gotten away. How he would've loved to burn her, to prove to his congregation that he was so holy, he'd even put his own daughter to death. *I tried to love her,* she imagined him saying, fake tears glistening in his gray eyes. *But she left me with no choice.*

Thalia had no proof that her father was involved, but it was easy to spin a tale of a man scorned and the revenge he took out on other young witches since he couldn't find her.

If this is his doing, then it's his sin, not yours.

Thalia desperately wanted that sharp, rational thought to take. She wanted to close the laptop and forget that her monster of a father existed. And yet, her heart stuttered with guilt. This wasn't on her, but god, it felt like it.

"What have you heard?" Thalia demanded, her voice going shrill. "Are there leads?"

Fiona sighed. "I'm beginning to think that Nonni was right in deciding not to tell you. You're just a child, and we don't have any proof."

A little late to claim my innocence, Thalia mused.

Fiona's voice lowered into a murmur. "I don't want to worry you. But . . . if this *is* the work of your father and his followers, there needs to be a reason for it."

"Anger." Thalia clenched the hand at her side. "Revenge. Hell, *fun*?"

"Nonni thought . . . maybe it's practice."

A chill trickled down Thalia's back. "He doesn't know where I am."

Her mother confirmed what Thalia was thinking. "But he'll never give up."

And he wants to be ready.

"Listen to me." The fatigue in Fiona's voice twisted the knife in Thalia's belly. "I will *never* let anything happen to you. That's why I'm here at his side. The second I think he's coming for you, you'll know. Nonni's in your corner, and the Coven of Flowers will protect you if you need to run. Once you graduate, baby, we're gone."

"I know," Thalia whispered. Shamefully, she often forgot that she wasn't alone, and that her mother was sacrificing her own happiness, her own freedom, to keep track of her husband's movements. Aunt Nonni, Abraham's own sister, was the one who'd bought Thalia her first wand and reassured her in secret calls after her witchery manifested. And the greenwitch sanctuary run by the Coven of Flowers of the Southeast had housed them both during the long drive to Haelsford. She had people fighting for her safety.

Those missing witches . . . who do they have?

Fiona pulled the phone away from her face to answer a question, then returned. "I love you. Let's talk soon."

"I love you, too."

The line clicked. Thalia set her box of secrets to rights and slipped it back under her bed. Her mind was itching to comb through the articles about the disappearances for signs of her father's doing. But first, waffles. She threw on a light tee and sweats, and hooked Maverick onto his leash.

Thalia stopped on the porch's top step, the immediate wrongness of the air hitting her witchy senses like insects crawling all over her body. Maverick growled at her side, his tail inert. Thalia didn't remember drawing her wand, yet here it was, steady in her right hand.

But she didn't need it, not to fight off an intruder anyway. There was no one dangerous around. Thalia recognized this sensation, and it was worse than any violence that Abraham Turner could bring to her doorstep.

It was the heady, oily, decayed touch of the Swamp.

Horrified, Thalia looked at the grass surrounding her cabin.

The rot resembled a plant's roots and tendrils, the too-bright green moss snaking through the otherwise healthy grass.

Without really thinking, she ran back into the cabin and began assembling the ingredients on her desk. She knew her spell wasn't anywhere near good enough to cleanse the Swamp of its hex yet, but maybe it could slow the rot in her front yard enough to buy her some time. Wishful thinking, but considering the dreadful scenarios currently running through her head, she was okay with a bit of silly optimism. She grabbed her notebook and took three deep breaths before stepping outside.

Back in the buzzing heat, Thalia knelt to a patch of affected earth. She looked down at her notes though she knew the incantation by heart. It grounded her, seeing her scribbles, the margins filled with the mentor texts she'd pulled from. Aurora Xie, called the mother of modern green-witchery, was all over the page. Thalia had researched her strongest cleansing spell, translated it into English, and began reforming it into something of her own making. A legendary witch named Esther Bassey provided the healing spell, and Thalia added the toughest hexbreaker she could find to complete the trifecta. She'd connected the spells for three separate purposes—cleansing, curing sickness, and hexfighting—into one mighty spell.

She named it *Cut Out the Rot.*

Thalia pricked her thumb and felt the warmth of the witchery in her chest well up with the intention of magic. She spoke the incantation in a careful whisper and waited. Her heartbeat thrummed in her ears.

Before her, the tendrils of dead grass moved. Thalia held her breath, and *there.* The rotting earth shifted, and a lovely, vibrant green twisted up the tendrils from their roots, inching slowly toward the tips of grass.

Thalia's heart swelled with excitement. The spell was working. "Oh shit, *oh shit—*"

Then the earth pulsed beneath her knees like a faint heartbeat in the ground.

The rot *swelled* around her blood. The movement was so much like . . . consumption. And under Thalia's flesh, she felt several sharp pokes. She looked on in shock as scores of little sprouts broke skin. They blossomed in the space between her knuckles, in the dip of her collarbones, and along the soft underside of her elbow. These new sprouts weren't the same vibrant, witchy green as the one on her thumb. They were slightly taller, and dotted with the glistening rot of the Swamp. At first, Thalia thought they were fluttering in the wind, but the air around her was still. The sprouts moved, each one angling down toward her skin.

She'd thought the border between Haelsford and the Swamp was shifting, but now she knew the truth. If the Council saw this, she'd be questioned, and everything would unravel. Not just her involvement in waking the Wolf

Boy and everything leading to Hell Night, but her old life, her true name, the murder she'd committed—

Her blood thrummed to a manic beat. She'd have to run, *again*, because she'd fostered a connection with the Swamp in the spring, and it wasn't just expanding. It was reaching out for *her*.

And the sprouts in her flesh reached back.

17

jailah

At the sight of Iris and Logan waiting for her on the steps of the Council building, Jai planted her fists on her hips. She usually met the girls for dinner after interning, and after a day of preparing for Highest Witch Evelyn's impending arrival, all she wanted was to sit and stuff her face. "What now?"

"Thalia wants us," Logan said quickly. "I grabbed Iris, now I'm grabbing you."

"Sounds important," Iris added.

Jailah shrugged even as worry grew in the pit of her stomach. "A'ight, let's go, then."

They met Thalia at her dorm room in Bramblewynn House, and that only deepened Jai's worry. The room was messy as always. Vines bursting with flowers obscured the back wall, and her desk was covered in last semester's notebooks and spellbooks. Maverick rested comfortably in the canopy of vines that was Thalia's bed, thus avoiding the maze of mason jars on the ground and his greenwitch's frenzied pacing. She didn't seem to notice that they'd arrived until Iris sighed dramatically. "What's this, an extra-credit project?"

Logan shook her head firmly. "That's the Swamp."

So, she'd noticed what Jailah had. Within the jars of soil, there were little flecks of electric-green mold. Only one of the jars looked to be filled with regular, unhexed soil.

Jailah waved a hand to get Thalia's attention, to calm her. "T, are you okay?"

"Look at this," Thalia whispered shakily. She drew her sacrificial needle, pricked her finger, and let the blood settle atop the dirt in the jars.

The Swamp dirt curdled and twisted around the bright red beads of blood as if it were alive and hungry and Thalia's blood was a delicious offering. Even though Jailah only thought it as a simple observation, one look at Thalia revealed how close she was to the truth.

"The Swamp is moving toward me! It wants me, it's reacting to me!" She pulled back her sleeves to reveal several dark green clovers protruding from her brown skin. Once revealed, they all *shifted*, bending toward the jars in unison.

Iris's eyes danced between Thalia's sprouts and the jars of Swamp-dirt. She muttered, "Well, fuck."

"Yeah!" Thalia screeched, throwing up her hands in disbelief. "Fuck!"

Jailah couldn't think of anything comforting to say. She bit her lip, a twin movement to Logan's own uncertain fidgeting.

Jailah rubbed her forehead. "We have two days until the Highest Witch arrives. I wanted us all to get together to get our stories straight, but now I'm thinkin' we're in more trouble than I realized. If the Council finds out that the Swamp is actin' up and Thalia might be the reason why, hell, she'll probably forget all about me."

Thalia pushed up her glasses, her eyes suddenly focused and fierce. "I'm leaving. I'm going to Annex."

Jailah chuckled, but the sound grew high-pitched as she realized that Thalia was *not* joking.

As the others protested, Thalia lifted and lowered her hands to get them to calm down. "There's something going on with the witches in nearby towns, like they're going missing, and my dad might have something to do with it. Considering... whatever is going on here, it's the perfect time for me to settle this."

"So, you're going straight *to him*?" Iris shrieked. She went to Thalia and gripped her arms. "No! No! Absolutely not!"

Thalia smiled, genuinely pleased. "It's really cute when you freak out like this."

Iris pursed her red lips into a tight line. "I won't let you. You're gonna have to duel me, bitch."

"Sounds fun." With a sad laugh, Thalia shrugged off Iris's grasp. She glanced at Jai. "Think I can take her?"

Jailah was too stunned, too furious to play along. "Don't go, T."

"Guys, I've made up my mind. If Abraham's hurting innocent witches because of me, or using them to practice killing me, then I need to stop him because no one else will. And with the Highest Witch coming, you can't tell me the timing isn't perfect."

Jai planted her shaky hands on her hips. "If the Swamp's reacting to you, what happens when you get back? Have you thought of that?"

Thalia blew a curl out of her face. "I'd thought that cleansing the Swamp would make me stronger, strong enough to take on my dad and his followers.

Maybe the reverse is true. Next time you see me, I might have gone full greenwitch."

"Just dye your hair white if you want it that bad," Iris muttered.

Thalia rolled her eyes. "At least the Highest Witch won't be snooping around by the time I get back, so."

"You shouldn't . . ." Logan's voice trailed off, her pale brows furrowed in horror. "Wait, I'm coming with you!"

"We all are," Jailah added suddenly, forgetting everything on her plate. "I can quit my internship—"

Iris was already pacing, typing on her phone, looking up tickets to Arizona.

Thalia threw her arms around them. "Love y'all, but I'm going alone. Jailah, I know you know you can't skip the meeting with Evelyn Estrada. Iris, you're literally helping Death preserve the barrier between worlds, dude. Logan, you've got summer classes, and even if you didn't . . . Annex isn't a safe place for witches, not even white ones like you."

"But you're going?" Logan choked.

"I have to."

Silence fell over them. Jailah felt like she could hear everyone's hearts pounding. The self-preserving side of her was impressed with Thalia's decision, particularly in light of the Highest Witch's visit. It was always the two of them who were ready to make the tough decisions, even if it meant putting themselves at risk. But the fiercely protective side of her scrambled for a way to make Thalia stay.

"You're sure?" Jailah forced herself to say.

"Sure enough that I already bought my tickets."

"We need to get you to a shadewitch."

Thalia chuckled. "Jai, I already got Rowe Adler's brother coming over tomorrow. I've got this." She looked down at her arms. "Just hope he can take care of these."

"On the subject of horrifying discoveries," Logan said quickly. She tapped her phone, then turned it around to show them all a picture of a terrifying plant, black and green, slick tar seeping from its pores.

Silently, Jailah brought her hand to her mouth in shock.

Iris leaned in, brow furrowing. "That's . . . a lot of blackthorne."

"Where was this?" Thalia sputtered, the color draining from her face.

Logan swallowed. "I went into the Cavern last night."

Jesus.

She told them about her little experiment and the offering left at her feet. A Wolf, servient to Logan? The pack, *bowing* to her? Was this the result of her killing the Wolf Boy herself? It was difficult for Jailah to picture the beasts as docile, but then she remembered the strangeness at the end of the last Haunting Season. After battling them nearly on her own, they'd retreated, and Logan stood there as they ambled back toward the Swamp.

"I passed out. I didn't get to the Swamp on my own, I was dragged there," Logan finished.

"Been there," Thalia whispered darkly. She walked over to the opposite wall and pulled off the large map of Haelsford that they'd all been given at Mesmortes orientation. Pushing vials and stray leaves to make room on her messy desk, she splayed the map across the wood. "How far did you walk into the Cavern?"

Logan grimaced. "Maybe ten minutes? I didn't start feeling the blackthorne until I reached the tunnel, so it was pretty far in. Wait!" She clicked through her phone for an app that tracked steps. "Looks like I took six hundred steps south, and then I passed out—I started east after that."

"Okay, so when you snapped that picture, you would've been . . ."

Jailah's stomach twisted. Thalia's fingers traced the route that Logan had taken and landed on the castle marked with a wolf's head.

Silently, each witch dropped their head to look at the floor beneath them.

"Here?" Iris said, dismayed.

"Under the school," Logan whispered. She looked up at Jailah, as if asking for an explanation.

But Jai was just as shocked as the rest of them. "I've never heard anything about a damn blackthorne plant growing under the school. I—" She searched for something to make this make sense but came up empty. "Adelaide, ya think?"

Iris nodded, but it was more a movement of habit than agreement. She didn't seem convinced, and so neither was Jailah.

Thalia shook her head, curls bouncing. When she spoke, Jailah heard a new fear in her voice. "Logan, pull up that picture again." Logan obeyed, and Thalia narrowed her eyes at the sight of the toxic plant. "That plant isn't new. A blackthorne bulb this big has been around for decades and decades, and maybe before Mesmortes was even built." She pursed her lips into a pale, thin line. "I'm not an expert on blackthorne, but there's no way this was planted anytime recently."

"How does blackthorne work, exactly?" Logan asked. "That was the first time I'd been around a whole plant like this, aside from the night we resurrected Bloom."

"Blackthorne is a man-made plant, deriving from belladonna, monkshood,

144

and a few dozen other poisonous flowers that harm us but can be defended against." Thalia whipped her wand outward and levitated a massive plant compendium before them. A four-page foldout was dedicated to blackthorne in its many forms. It said a bulb, like the one Logan saw, was blackthorne at its purest. Its tendrils could be cut and rooted into the more commonly seen vines, which were easier to tend to. The vine-tar could be distilled into serums and used as poison, and boys at Hammersmitt were given jars of the stuff for emergencies, a policy that made Jailah angry and sick.

"When we say 'blackthorne,' we're usually talkin' 'bout this stuff"— Jailah pointed to the illustration of a glass jar filled with inky black liquid—"'cause that's what anyone can buy at any old store. But real, pure blackthorne grows in a bulb . . . like the one under us."

Logan looked disgusted. "Who's the mundane that created blackthorne?"

"Not a mundane." Thalia grimaced. "No, only a greenwitch could have crossbred the plants into something as strong as this. Some historians think it was at the command and patronage of some mundane ruler, others think greenwitches were locked into a lab and forced to create it. But most think that making a witch-repellant was simply a greenwitch's own desire."

Iris tutted her tongue. "Just 'cause someone's witchy doesn't mean they're for all covenhood. A witch can be just as shitty to another witch as any mundane can."

Thalia nodded. "Blackthorne can't kill a witch on its own, but there's no real antidote against its effects, so putting up a *Shielding* spell is the best option outside of avoiding it altogether."

Jailah's thoughts drifted to the person who would've reacted to this discovery with smug acceptance, a confirmation of something already known. She pictured Veronica grinning wickedly, pressing her lips against Jailah's ear to whisper a million theories.

"Theoretically," Logan started, "could this bulb have been grown elsewhere, then planted under the school?"

Thalia shrugged. "I don't know exactly what Roddin and Bloom were capable of." She pushed up her glasses. "But, purely guessing? I'd say this is a holdover from the days of old Haelsford."

"A Hunting Season special," said Jailah glumly. Long before Haelsford had become a witchtown, it was one that hunted down magical folks for sport. That was how they got here. It all began with the tyranny of mundanes.

"Why hasn't the Council done something about this? Could they really not know about it?" Iris asked.

Logan considered this. "Dunno how anyone could know about it unless they walked through the tunnels themselves. It's not like we can feel it up here, right? We live here, and we're not affected by it."

"True," Jailah offered, her thoughts spinning. "That far down, guess it's harmless to us."

But even as Jailah said it, her uneasiness only grew.

"I'll have to leave the mysterious blackthorne to you guys." Abruptly, Thalia yanked out a few of her curls straight from the root. "A perfect piece of corporeal witchery can last a few months before needing to be reinforced, but Stevie Adler only graduated a few years ago, so I've got a week or two before it wears off. I'll try to contact you guys if I can, but let's just call July thirteenth my homecoming. If I'm not back before then . . ." She held out the brown strands to Jailah. "Come rescue me."

18

trent

Odeah DeVry left no trace that Trent could find, but it wasn't difficult to locate her brother, Quincey. In fact, Trent was a little annoyed with himself for thinking of all the magical ways to find his uncle before the more obvious one; he'd considered asking Jailah for a powerful spell that made use of his bloodline, or convincing Iris to Call his mother for real this time so that he could demand to know his uncle's whereabouts. It was Logan who suggested the easiest option.

Did you google him?

Trent's uncle kept his first name but changed his last. Professor Quincey Connors—Dr. Connors—was a professor at Ilterra College, a private coven university a few hours away in North Florida. Trent could call his office or send an email, but he decided that he needed to stand in front of his uncle, look him in the eye, and understand the connection between them. So much of the information he needed had been kept from him by his parents, and he wasn't going to let an unanswered call or ignored email leave him floundering. And if Quincey wanted to keep things hidden, too, then Trent certainly didn't want to give him a heads-up.

"What time are you leaving?" Thalia asked over a steaming plate of French toast piled so high, it nearly reached her chin.

"Right after this," Trent replied.

She chewed silently. Though they were seated at the same outdoor table as the other four, for a moment, it felt like they were alone. Maybe Trent was thinking too hard about it, but he'd noticed how she'd slowed her pace to the table so that Logan would sit first and she could be at the end across from him. Maybe because he'd watched them all enter and was ready to push Mathew forward if he needed to do the same.

Her knee slid against his. Accident or intentional, his heart leapt all the same. "I hope you get your answers," she said. "Partly because I'm dying to know what your mother did—I mean, it's none of my business, but."

He smiled. "You'll be the first to know."

Mathew glanced at the two of them and gave Trent a small nudge. Trent responded with one of his own, and then the two began an elbow-off that grew increasingly violent.

"Guys!" Logan's glass of orange juice nearly tipped over from the motion.

From the other end of the table, Jailah pointed her fork menacingly at Trent. "You'll be back by tomorrow night, yeah?"

"Should be—"

"Assuming you aren't kidnapped by your evil uncle," Iris added, then cringed. "Sorry, I've been a little pessimistic lately."

"Lately?" Thalia, Logan, and Jailah said at the same time.

Iris flashed a middle finger.

"What's tomorrow?" said Mathew.

"So." Thalia's light brown skin grew slightly red. "I'm . . . going home for a little bit."

It took all of Trent's strength to remain calm. Next to him, Mathew speechlessly looked to the other witches for some sort of explanation.

"It's a long story," Thalia said coolly. "Before you ask, no, you can't come with, yes, I'll be disguised, and no"—she lowered her voice—"he's not going to hurt me."

"You're not going alone, are you?" Trent asked quickly, ignoring that first bit.

"Absolutely not," Mathew added sternly.

Thalia crossed her arms. "I can take care of myself."

"Don't bother," Jailah said, waving that fork again. "She ain't changing her mind. We're sending her off with a little get-together tomorrow night."

Trent thought that made it sound like she was going on a long vacation and not to the town that wanted her dead, but he held his tongue. Under the table, he bumped her knee with his own.

She looked up at him, and he forgot the plea he was going to make. Her steady gray eyes were so full of determination and hate for her father that Trent's breath caught in his throat. He felt her power. She'd escaped that town once. She'd survived the Swamp. She'd protected Mesmortes with magic like he'd never seen. He couldn't *not* be worried, but with one look, she reminded him of who the fuck she was, and he felt a wash of pride.

A calendar reminder popped up on Trent's phone. He had to be at the bus station in an hour. Mathew had offered to drive him, but Trent declined. Though he loved Mathew like a brother, he wanted to do this alone. "You're leaving day after tomorrow?"

She nodded.

"Okay. I'll be back. Don't leave without letting me say goodbye."

Her eyes softened. His stomach flipped.

Ilterra College seemed to sing to Trent.

Though just a few hours north of Haelsford, the air felt so different. Trent's nerves eased once he stepped out of the car, though the rideshare driver eyed him and the school suspiciously. The campus was small, a circle of gray stone buildings capped with orange roofs. The building's windows were perfect rectangles without decorative molding or stone statues. Minimalist, modern, and crap.

The driver took off, leaving Trent to do nothing but go forward.

So much of the campus was outdoors, and as Trent tried to find the main building, he was distracted by the central lawn. It was summer, so campus wasn't busy, but there were a fair number of students having picnics and study sessions, getting that sunshine in before the rain clouds in the distance worked their way over.

On the opposite side of the lawn, Trent saw a group of students and parents trekking up the path, led by a young woman in a bright yellow dress. She spoke with an animated flair and stopped every few moments to point out something or spout what Trent figured were fun facts. He grinned. Considering how little he was able to find about Ilterra online, orientation was exactly what he needed.

There were about twenty in the group, and none seemed to notice Trent slipping in. He looked the part anyway—nearly eighteen, wearing a backpack, a curious attention to the orientation leader's every word. Her name was Winnie and the name tag on her dress was decorated with cutesy plant stickers. A greenwitch, then? When she looked over at him, Trent tensed, ready to explain that he wasn't a witch, but that he was here on behalf of his sister, who wasn't feeling well. But Winnie only smiled and continued her talk. If the others in the group noticed that he didn't have that distinct witchy aura, no one said a word.

They entered the President's Building, the one that held Ilterra's assembly halls and larger classrooms. Trent could hardly pay attention to Winnie's well-practiced speech; he was mesmerized by the summer courses in session, the way the classrooms were bursting with light and magic. In one, a woman hovered in the air while two witches reattached her leg with nothing but their wands and a glittering substance resembling a spiderweb. In another, a firewitch and a waterwitch sparred, the rest of the class sitting in a circle around them taking notes. He saw a professor who had no arms manipulate his magic without a wand, similar to Logan's proxy skills. It had been a long time since Trent felt that stab of jealousy in missing out on magic, but here it was again.

"Hi, got any questions?"

Trent didn't see when Winnie had sidled up next to him, but now he realized the group had largely dissipated while he was still hovering, taking everything in.

Trent smiled. "Not really, but Ilterra seems dope."

Winnie grinned back. "I was between Ilterra and Michigan Coven

University, but I like the weather here better. Plus, we've got one of the most extensive greenwitchery curriculums in the country, so it was kind of a no-brainer."

He mentally logged that for later. Maybe Thalia might want to know more. "Is there a directory of professors I could look at?"

Winnie nodded and led him down to a large study space. A group of students passionately debated the use of a rose-infused poultice over aloe for severe burns, their books and wands scattered across a large table. The walls were lined with shelves full of plaques and trophies, framed newspaper clippings, and portraits of distinguished staff.

Winnie eyed the plastic panel of brochures and pamphlets before plucking one from its holder. "Here's a list of all the professors, their studies, and their office hours. Good on you for taking the initiative to look into this stuff early. Most high schoolers I meet only want to know which dorm has the most parties."

"Well, now I feel boring." With a laugh, he snapped the pamphlet against his palm. "Is it cool if I chill here for a bit?"

"Oh yeah, but don't forget dinner, we'll be meeting back over at the dining hall. Shout if you need anything in the meantime."

"Will do, thanks, Winnie."

She left, and Trent plopped his bag onto an empty armchair. The study group was now arguing about nettle seeds, and Trent forced himself to refocus his curiosity to the packet in his hand. He wasn't here to play at being a witchy student, he was here to find the person who knew his mother.

He flipped through the alphabetical directory. Dr. Quincey Connors was an award-winning researcher in the field of *thermalwitchery* and *earthbound runes*, whatever those were, and had been serving at the school for nearly two decades. Trent's blood pounded in his ears. Two whole decades. His mother had never mentioned Quincey. His uncle never sought him out, though he was just a few hours away. Anger flickered in his chest. Trent left the room with such haste, he nearly tripped over his own feet.

Quincey worked on the third floor of the Eastern Building. At the end of the quiet hall, Trent found the office door half-open. A bald man was dipped over his desk, his glasses slipping down his nose. He had tweezers in hand as he examined what looked like a tangle of twigs. He blew on the bundle of wood. A bit of smoke rose from it, and he jotted down a few notes.

"You just gonna stand there?" the man said, never lifting his head.

Trent jumped, heart pounding. Suddenly, this felt too real, and he wondered if he'd made a mistake coming here. But there was no turning back now, was there? He was only a few footsteps away from the truth.

Still jotting down notes with one hand, Quincey used the other to wave Trent in. "If you're here to ask about extra credit, please note that your syllabus states that none will be provided."

"I'm not in your class."

With a sigh, the professor looked up. His reaction took the air out of Trent's lungs. Quincey stared at him slack-jawed, eyes wide, disbelief dancing in his pupils. Then he tensed his jaw and furrowed his brow. After a few breaths and a hard swallow, he said, "Well. *Damn.*"

That . . . was not the reaction Trent was expecting.

His uncle slipped off his glasses and rubbed his eyes. A small smile grew on his lips, and Trent's nervous anxiety eased. That smile was like one of his mother's: warm and welcoming. "You look just like her," said Quincey.

Trent found himself smiling back. "I'm Trent."

"Yeah, I know." Quincey laughed. His voice was deep and rich, he had a slight southern drawl, and his gaze was full of wonder. "I know my sister's own kid."

Do you? Trent wanted to say. *'Cause you never even tried to know me.*

Quincey adjusted his glasses and gave Trent another long, hard look. He seemed to be searching for something, or analyzing Trent's presence to make sense of it. He gestured to the seat across from him. "How'd you find me?"

"Google." Finally, Trent's feet unstuck, and he took the chair. Quincey looked like he had a few other questions, but Trent cut him off. "What's with the name? You're Quincey DeVry, not—"

"No, I, yeah." He fumbled with his pen and chuckled. "I changed my name after I left the troupe."

Trent's heartbeat raised a tick. "Why?" He knew there were only a few reasons that people changed names and left towns, and they all seemed to be decisions shaped by trouble, if not violence. "I watched some old tape from your time in the troupe with my mum. I saw something, I mean, I think I did. Something that freaked her out on one of the tapes—did that have something to do with it?" The softness in Quincey's face faltered, but Trent couldn't push back his excitement. He'd been waiting so long for answers, and now he was finally going to get them. "I'm here to know what my mother did. What was in the bloodpact?"

At this, his uncle's face went pallid.

"Oh, and I still have her dagger." Trent pulled out the gilded knife and flipped it into the air. He flashed a smile at his uncle. "Although it's not like it used to be. Not since—well, it's a long story, but my mother came to me, truly, the ghost of her. I mean it was scary as shit—"

"Trenton—"

"But I know she's been keeping me safe from some force, or some witch—right, you know all this already." He rubbed his sweaty palms on his knees. "I just want to know why, or who, or what the hell this is all about. Tell me everything."

Quincey leaned back in his chair. "And here I was, hoping *you* might be able to tell *me*."

Trent's heart plummeted. "What do you mean?"

"The bloodpact. Silverhand. The hexbinding?"

As Quincey spoke each word, the hopeful expectation in his expression faded into worry as Trent grew more visibly confused.

"Silverhand? What's that? And who was hexbound?"

Quincey rubbed his temples before pressing his hands together as if in prayer. He went silent and still for a few moments, and though adrenaline coursed in Trent's blood, he forced himself to be patient as his uncle thought something through.

Finally, Quincey looked up at him. "You said the Haelsford library? You live there?"

"Just during the school year, yeah."

Now Quincey's voice wavered. "And you go to . . . which school?"

This seemed unimportant, but Quincey looked as if this question were one of life and death. "Uh. The Hammersmitt School for Exceptional Young Men. The only other school in town is for witches."

And that, evident in Quincey's slow nod, seemed to confirm something. "I'm happy I got to see you, kid. But you shouldn't have come here. Stop asking around, stop snooping through old tapes. It's better that way."

Trent's grip on his knees grew tense, his fingernails pressing into his jeans. "I'm not leaving until you tell me what I want to know."

Quincey remained silent.

"Fine, I'll ask my aunt Odeah." Trent crossed his arms petulantly. "Where is she?"

"In the wind." At Trent's worry, he waved a hand. "Last I heard, she was backpacking through Peru. Nothing to do with any of this. Odie's just restless. She pops in every few months—hell, like you just did—then takes off."

This only frustrated Trent. He should've known this about Aunt Odeah already. He pictured her, an older version of the woman he'd seen on the tapes, stopping by Haelsford with souvenirs and stories about her adventures. Instead, he'd been severed from this part of his family because of whatever secret was being kept from him. It wasn't fair. Trent didn't know when he got to his feet, didn't feel himself raising his hands, but he slammed his fists hard against the desk. "I'm done with the bullshit. If it's my life that's been bargained, I deserve to know!"

Quincey tightened his jaw. "I feel you, kid, and you're right. But you don't come to my office and talk to me like that."

Truly, Trent hated talking to an older family member like this, but he was over it. "Man, whatever."

Uncle Quincey wore the same look as he had earlier, as if piecing together the puzzle before him, with Trent being the puzzle in question. "Did you know that mundanes can't walk through the doors of Ilterra College? Not unless accompanied by a witch, that is."

An anxious prickle crawled up Trent's spine.

"I thought she would've told you." To his credit, Quincey looked genuinely saddened. "I'm sorry, Trenton."

A slice of heat cut through Trent's chest. "Sorry for what?"

"That I have to be the one to tell you, because you should've known all this time. You should've known since you were thirteen. And this—" Uncle Quincey waved a hand lazily over Trent's presence. "This is the last protection your mother gave you. A hexbinding, the strongest I've ever seen."

Trent's voice wavered so strongly that he barely recognized the sound of it. "I'm not. I've never been—"

"You can *see* Ilterra. Mundanes can't, son. If they stumble upon the address, all they see is an abandoned amusement park."

Trent stilled. He remembered the driver's odd expression before he drove off. *You're wrong,* he wanted to say, but the words caught in his throat.

"I'll bet Silverhand isn't looking for Lou's fourthborn child," Quincey continued, voice sharp as a blade. "She's looking for her firstborn witch."

In all Trent's abject confusion, his jumble of thoughts settled. That word again. *Silverhand.*

"I can't help you, even if I wanted to. The only people who know what your mother did are your mother and . . ." Quincey lowered his voice. "Silverhand's what Odeah and I used to call her."

"You don't know her name?" Trent asked quietly.

"I reckon I did, once. You ever see memorywork done on a witch?"

Trent almost laughed. Witnessing memorywork was perhaps the first time he'd been really terrified of magic. "Yeah."

Uncle Quincey managed a small nod. "Whoever Silverhand is or was, she's mostly gone to me now. All I remember is that she wasn't in the troupe, and I don't even know if she was Haelsfordian. And she wore these wild rings." He held up his hands and wiggled his fingers. "Silver snakes curled around her fingers. But that's all I got after she, presumably, wiped herself from my mind. Well, I always thought it was Silverhand, but now looking at you, maybe it was Lou who did it."

Trent felt a chill down his spine. He eased back into the chair. "Mum told me that I was promised to a witch and that she would do everything to keep that witch from collecting. Do you know why she would make a deal like that?"

Quincey fumbled with his hands, and Trent was already preparing to be lied to. But when his uncle looked up at him, all he saw was sadness in his eyes. "Lou-Lou had big dreams for all of us. And she'd wanted to live comfortably. Glamorously, you see? We teased her when she started going 'round with Damien, used to joke that he was the only one on earth with pockets deep enough for her tastes." He laughed, but it sounded more resentful than amused. "Or maybe there was something else that she wanted. Believe me, if I knew . . ." He leaned in, his voice racked with anger. "You think I wouldn't have already put Silverhand down if I could? You think I *wanted* to let my sister suffer under that bloodpact? That I would let Silverhand come for you? *Tuh.* You and your brothers were everything to her, and believe it or not, that makes you everything to me. You don't know shit, kid. You don't know what I've been through trying to break the memory spell, and Imma need you to understand that you're not the only one left in the dark. You lost your mama, but I lost my sister, too."

Trent's breaths came out in frustrated huffs. It was hard to pull back his anger, but the shame did it for him. "Sorry," he whispered.

Quincey leaned back. "If I know Lou, and I do, I'd tell you that her protections go far beyond that blade. The fact that you haven't been sought by your mother's debtor isn't a mistake. But if you keep digging, you might undo everything she did to protect you."

The disappointment was like a wave, pulling Trent under. "So, what, I'm supposed to just go through life knowing that my mom cheated a witch out of a bloodpact that offered up my soul? I'm supposed to *hope* that her protections are strong enough to keep Silverhand away?"

"Yes. *You are.*"

Trent released a disgusted scoff.

"We're talking about your safety. Look, I know going to that mundane school probably ain't much fun, but keeping your hexbinding intact is the safest thing you can do."

Trent could only sit there, stunned. He hadn't known what to expect from this conversation, but the news that he was witchy and hexbound was never in the realm of possibility. After all he'd been through, hearing that he needed to *let things go* was still unsatisfying, even if the reasons had changed. Grief struck him, a piercing blow right through his heart. He had so much love for his mother and never considered that her secrets from him were a form of love, too. He felt guilt and frustration. Was it better to search for Silverhand to know what he might be up against? Or was digging up the past an act of betrayal to the pains his mother went through to protect him?

Uncle Quincey went to the mini fridge in the corner of his office and pulled out a small water bottle. He placed it on the desk in front of Trent. "I just dropped a lot on you, and you were probably hoping this conversation would be different. I can't change the past, but I'd like to know you better, if that's all right with you." He shrugged. "If you're not in a rush to get back home, I can give you a tour, take you to dinner, share some happier memories about your mama. Maybe next time Odie's back, we can come down to see you?"

The hopefulness in his uncle's eyes was like a life raft in the heavy waves of Trent's grief.

"I know I'm basically a stranger. I haven't been able to really be your uncle in the way I should've, so you don't have to say yes—"

"No, that'd be—" Trent cleared his throat. He'd promised Thalia he'd be back before she left, but he would have to make it up to her in another way. "Yeah. I'd like that."

Quincey clapped a hand on his shoulder. "Good. Let's not let time take away more from us than it already has."

19

mathew

The next night, Jailah pushed them all into a booth at the pizzeria-slash-arcade that had seen better days. It was busy enough that their voices didn't carry, but clearly, the townspeople and tourists had better places to be than the teen spot that was in desperate need of a renovation. And Mathew supposed that was why she'd chosen it.

Iris slid in next to him, her arm brushing against his. She wore a simple white halter top and was barefaced aside from the dark purple color on her full lips. Her braids were pulled into a high ponytail, her shoulders bare before him. His face warmed at the sight of her. His stomach twisted with a desire so piercing, it felt closer to an animalistic hunger. And here she was, exposing her neck.

She was angled away from him to speak with Logan on her left, but she turned her head to look at Mathew over her shoulder. Their eyes met. Whatever Iris saw in his gaze left her with a raised brow, and her eyes flicked briefly to his mouth.

Though they were tethers before, being her Runekeeper felt different. They'd spent the last few days meeting up in the blissful, lovely solitude of the Green. Per her plea—that was more like a threat—he hadn't attempted any other runes. Instead, he watched her pour magic into the carved stones and practice the three spells she would need when Death deployed her to the house in Port Barrow. He was happy to support her, and even happier to be the one she turned to with a satisfied grin after successfully using the runes for the first time. She'd looked at the triangle of glowing witchery extending from the stones and squeezed his arm in delight, leaving him dizzy with happiness.

He inched closer to her, their thighs now pressed together in the ripped plastic booth. Mercifully, she didn't move away.

"I thought this would make us all feel better, but I'm actually just worried sick," Jailah exclaimed, lifting a pepperoni to her lips. She pouted at Thalia.

"I'll be back before you know it," Thalia replied softly. She was in a sour mood, understandably, but it felt gloomier here without Trent to poke her with bad jokes and that disarming grin of his.

"Remember when our only focus was saving the town from Wolves?" Logan added with a little laugh, though her mouth seemed to stutter around the word *Wolves*. She reached for her soda and took a big gulp.

"I don't like us splitting up," Jailah said. "Y'all, it's like the number one rule in scary movies, or Scooby-Doo. You should've gone with Trent, Matty!"

"Hm?" Mathew muttered absently. Iris had dropped her hand to the side of her knee next to his, the backs of her fingers resting against his thigh. "I asked him!" he added defensively.

Jailah returned to Thalia. "And someone should be going with you!"

"The fewer witches in Annex, the better. Now hurry up and eat so I can embarrass you in air hockey."

Three pizzas and a jug of lemonade later, the group dispersed from the table. After Mathew had been thoroughly walloped at Ping-Pong by Jailah and her wicked serve, he found himself being waved at by a girl as he exited the bathroom.

"Mathew!" she said, and it was her voice that placed her. Chloe, the redhead from therapy. "Hey. You weren't at the last meeting." Before Mathew could answer, her eyes went wide. "Oh my gosh, are we not supposed to talk outside of sessions?"

Mathew gave her a friendly smile. "It's okay, I don't mind."

"Oh!" She sighed with exaggerated relief.

Thankfully, that gave him an out in discussing the meeting he'd missed because Death had him carving sigils into rocks. "Good to see you," he said, inching his way back toward the arcade. "I'll catch you at the next one."

"I also wanted to say that I'm sorry about Robbie. Did you know him well?"

Mathew froze. There, in the bottom of Mathew's chest, he felt a pang of nausea. "Robbie Kidd?"

Chloe blinked. Her freckly, pale skin reddened. "You didn't hear? He had a heart attack last week. I'm so sorry, I thought you knew."

The blood drained from his face. "I'm sorry to hear it." He cleared his throat. "I'll, uh, see you later."

The smile returned, and she touched his hand to stop him. "Wait."

Chloe said something about a party, but while Mathew watched her lips move and heard her speak, the words barely registered. He looked at her and saw something else, something awful, and for a moment thought he was simply going to faint.

He flinched hard away from her touch. Mathew looked down at her, and he surely looked pained because her eyes widened and her voice tensed with concern. "Hey, sorry, are you okay?"

Mathew's stomach turned. "I have to go." When he left her this time, he kept his fists in his pockets. He wondered what she thought of him. A boy who got nervous and sweaty at her touch, who couldn't string together a sentence in her presence. She was quite pretty, and maybe she was used to it.

But the stir in his chest was borne of dread and fear, not sweet butterflies.

A month ago, he had touched Robbie Kidd's hand and had what he'd thought was an intrusive thought of the man clutching his chest and collapsing.

And when Chloe grazed his hand, not only had Mathew seen her soon-coming death, but a vision of her dying at the gleeful command of his deathwitch tether.

He felt Iris before he turned the corner and saw her at the pinball machine. The tether in his chest tugged in delight at her presence as his chest seized in fear. Silently, she moved aside for him. He took the first player knob, and she took second. They played without saying anything, each one flipping the paddle dutifully until the little silver ball finally dropped through the middle.

"New high score," Mathew whispered shakily.

"Meh. We could do better." Iris laughed. She looked him up and down. "You okay?"

At some point during the game, they'd gotten closer, arms nearly touching. Mathew pulled away from her. "What? Yeah."

"You're lying." She cocked her head at him. "You're my tether, you can't lie to me."

Mathew looked at her for a breathless moment. A few months ago, after the fire at the Emporium, he could hardly get Iris to say more than two words to him. Now she was throwing around the word *tether* like it wasn't supposed to give him heart palpitations.

She smiled coolly. "Tell me a secret, Beaumont."

He thought of a warm summer day in the Haelsford Cemetery. He'd asked her the same, and she'd said, *I will not kiss your scars.*

He looked over at the rest of the group. Jailah and Logan were playing foosball while Thalia was at the edge of the table, typing away on her phone in intense conversation. Mathew still couldn't wrap his mind around what Thalia was thinking, going into the mouth of a lion as she was.

Mathew tugged his sleeves down. As careful as he'd been to keep his death marks out of sight, he remembered now that Chloe and Robbie weren't the only people whose skin had met his fingertips recently. During his first meeting with Iris in the Green, he'd held her hands under the runes he'd made for her. The vision had been too quick and too shadowy for Mathew to make sense of it, though the sudden change made him flinch anyway. Perhaps his power didn't work on Death's children. Or perhaps the feel of Iris's skin was too distracting for him to focus.

Iris lifted a brow. "Mathew? You look like you're about to fall over."

"It's . . . this shit with my parents," he muttered quickly.

Iris dropped her crossed arms. "The divorce?"

"Yeah, uh. It's getting uglier every day, even though my dad's not in the house anymore. And each of them wants us to live with them, but not because they actually want us, they just want to *win*. Every meeting with their lawyers ends in a screaming match, and they keep trying to get us to turn on the other." He scrubbed the back of his head with his knuckles. "My dad promised me a new car if I told the court my mom was mentally unwell, and my mother told me I wasn't her real son if I didn't choose her."

"Holy shit." Iris's mouth twitched. "Why didn't you tell me?"

Because I didn't realize it would feel this good, he thought.

Mathew let himself sink into her dark, attentive eyes for a few moments before chuckling. "I'd rather talk about saving the world from demons, to be honest."

Iris sighed a laugh, her full lips curving into a perfect smile, before melting back into worry. "You can tell me about this sorta stuff, too, yeah? I might be a deathwitch, but I'm not *totally* heartless. Just a *teensy* bit. Okay?"

He nodded, face hot under her gaze. "Okay."

At first, Mathew wasn't sure why he'd even decided keep the truth of his death marks from her, but now he knew. Things between them were *perfect*. Iris had admitted to fearing her closeness to him, her care for him, as if that was something to fear. And here she was now, laughing in his presence, calling him her tether, seeing through his discomfort and smiling in return. It was what he wanted. Though he wasn't magic like she was, being her Runekeeper made him feel like they were on more similar footing, or at least that he could be more useful to her and, in turn, the coven. Mathew had meant it when he'd said he wasn't going to stand by and be the weak one.

He could fix this. He couldn't save Robbie Kidd, or mend his parents' marriage, or make them love their witchy daughter, but he could find a way to change this vision's course. Between Death's call, the demons, and the corrupting souls of her beloved parents, Iris had enough to focus on without his strange visions.

But a sliver of doubt needled him like a prick of the thumb.

If his vision was correct, then she was going to kill a girl. And though Mathew had seen Iris at her angriest in the face of Adelaide Strigwach, though he knew all about her death magic, though he once overheard her say she'd kill anyone who hurt her friends, he knew all that intensity was just who she was. That was how she spoke, like death was nothing. But the vision showed her following through, and he thought . . . *maybe I don't know her at all.*

Thalia had killed once, but Mathew thought that accident was justified. She hadn't been cruel; she hadn't savored it. Hell, even Mathew himself had floated the idea of getting rid of Theodore Bloom before they'd known who he really was. He ran with this coven now, and knew what witchery could be. But why Chloe? What could she have done to deserve death like that? The Iris in his vision looked happy, and the image of her sadistic grin left him reeling.

For the first time since they'd met at the Box Chant on Hallowe'en night, Mathew truly feared the girl he loved.

20

thalia

July

It'd been so long since Thalia last prayed, she barely remembered how to do it.

With her mother's old rosary in tightly folded hands that were more like fists, she said, "I know it's been a while, but I'm asking nicely. Watch over me."

Maverick nuzzled her ankle impatiently. Gently, Thalia eased him off. Her familiar wasn't used to this behavior from Thalia either.

"Least you could do," she continued through gritted teeth. "Considering how you *abandoned* me before. So, yeah. Thanks."

She skipped the sign of the cross, tucked the rosary into her bag, then double-checked everything. Her cash, her altered ID, her wand in an invisible compartment. She packed lightly—nothing she really liked or treasured was going to cross Annex city limits, and that included her beloved Maverick. He'd been an anxious mess since she came back to the cabin with a new face and the news that he wouldn't be joining her.

While Thalia's magic was superficially dampened to mundane senses, her face was changed, and her sprouts were concealed, she felt that bringing her familiar was pushing it.

She checked her phone. Trent had texted her an apology in the middle of the night for not making it back in time, and Thalia still couldn't come up with a response that fit what she wanted to say. So, she left it unanswered, and hoped she could say it to his face when she got back.

Thalia slung on her backpack. She nearly jumped at the sight of herself in the dusty desk mirror. Her skin tone and scrawny shape were the same as they had always been, but she borrowed things from her friends; Stevie said having references made things easier, and he was still a novice shadewitch. From Jailah, she took perfect full lips that were lovely in a scowl, but much lovelier in a smile. From Iris, cheekbones deep enough to cut glass, and from Logan, Thalia took blue eyes and blond hair. Stevie had done a fantastic job, but he warned her that the work would fade little by little each day without maintenance, and that she needed to be back in a week's time before it depreciated enough to cause issues. That was fine with her. Thalia didn't want to be in Annex for longer than she had to anyway. He'd also told her that emoting too hard might cause the disguise to slip for a second, like a loosely fitting mask would. So, no getting worked up while returning to the source of so much trauma. *Easy.*

Maverick looked up at her with wide, dark eyes. She felt his pleading in her chest, and his whine was a gut punch. They had never spent more than a school day apart since they'd found each other. Tears welled in her eyes. "Watch over the gang for me?"

He dropped his head and licked her ankle.

"I love you, too." She hooked on his leash, then took him into her arms. "Iris is waiting."

Thalia opened the door and was met with a blast of unnatural, heady warmth. It wasn't just the rot on the grass anymore. The *feel* of the Swamp was terribly strong now, the border nearly finished devouring her cabin.

Safe on the Hill, Thalia let Mav down. Iris was waiting for them in a set of silky purple pajamas and a matching head scarf. She yawned. "Why did you have to choose the *earliest* damn train?"

"To annoy you, specifically. Also, cheaper tickets."

"See how she treats me?" Iris asked Maverick with a grimace. She pulled Thalia into a hug, then tilted her head to her ear. "Know what happens if you die there?" Iris whispered threateningly. "First, I'm sending an army of zombies to kill everyone in town."

"Not something you can actually do, but okay."

"*Then* I'm gonna raise your ass up from the dead and force you to help me cheat in physics."

Thalia grinned amid the pain. "We both know there are necromantic wards in the classrooms for that reason, Iris."

They both laughed for a few moments, the sounds growing thick with tears.

"I mean it." Iris pulled away to hold Thalia at arm's length. "Don't let them hurt you, T."

"I'll see you in a week." Thalia blinked out a few tears. She'd done all her goodbyes last night, but it seemed as though Iris held her emotions in for this moment. "Love you," she added, at the same moment that Iris said the same.

It was a ten-minute walk to the bus stop in town. The journey was a simple one. The local bus would take her to the train station half an hour away. There, she'd take the Charioteer Express, a high-speed train that ran cross-country on enchanted wheels and tracks. Thalia had always wanted to ride on this great witchy invention, though she felt like it should've been called the Hexpress, but anyway. She would arrive in Phoenix in just under three hours before taking a mundanely slow bus to Annex.

Thalia's anxiety dulled once she was settled on the bus, then heightened after she arrived at the train station. Her mind was similarly split; one moment she was buzzing with energy, the latent rage in her heart melting into anticipation. The next, she was terrified and kept picturing herself walking into a trap set by her father. But never once did she consider turning back. How this ended was still to be seen, but Thalia was going to Annex no matter what.

Thalia boarded the Charioteer with three minutes to spare. She had hoped for an empty table, but there were two others playing cards at the one she was assigned to, and Thalia nearly burst into tears at the sight of them.

Trent Hogarth caught her eye over Logan's blond head. He smiled.

Thalia threw her bag into the overhead compartment. "You guys! *Get off!*" She was going for angry intimidation, but her tears left her choking out the words.

Logan looked at Trent with uncertainty. His smile never faltered. He said, "You should sit down. Train's about to leave."

Unable to speak, Thalia simply jabbed a finger toward the train doors.

Logan found her voice. "We've made up our minds." She looked up at

Thalia with the strangest thing. Admiration. "After everything, you deserve to be looked after for once. I know I'm still learning things. I know you're so much stronger than I am and that you don't need my help. But I'm not letting you do this alone. If any of those mundanes wanna get to you, they're gonna have to go through me."

"Damn it!" Trent sucked his teeth. "I was gonna say that."

Thalia sputtered a teary laugh before regaining her composure. "Logan, Annex is the last place for a witch to be."

Oddly enough, Logan only shrugged while Trent fidgeted uncomfortably. He averted his eyes and absently twisted the opal ring around his finger.

"You still haven't noticed," Logan said. "I asked Stevie to work on me, too."

Thalia paused. In all her emotion, she hadn't realized that Logan's magic was dampened. She could still sense it slightly, but there were so many witches on the train that she didn't notice, and surely no mundane would either.

With the shake of her head, Thalia sat next to her. "What about your classes?"

"Oh—" She grimaced playfully. "I had my sister imitate my mom. As of right now, I'm on the way to Ontario for my great-grandmother Eunice's funeral."

Thalia could do nothing but drop her head into her hands. The train lurched forward, there was no going back.

When she looked up, Logan and Trent had resumed their game. Having the two of them here wasn't part of the plan. One new face in Annex was cause for neighborly nosiness on its own, and there were three of them, two being hidden witches. Thalia would have to adjust her expectations of how this would end. Trent and Logan might have been here to protect her, but Thalia felt like the feeling was mutual.

"I do have one question," Trent asked. "Shouldn't this train be called the Hexpress?"

Tears sprang back into Thalia's eyes, though this time from laughter. She was hurtling toward the most dangerous place in the world. She was delirious with joy. Thalia felt angry, vengeful, terrified, and uncertain all at once. And her heart was so full.

part two

retribution

21

jailah

When Jailah was young, her parents took her traveling every summer to run the pageant circuit.

Jailah begged to continue year-round, but pageants weren't something they'd pull her out of school for. Neither Etta nor Charlie Simmons pushed her to aspire to become Miss Alabama, or America, or Universe, or whatever. But when little Jai had walked into her auntie Tish's dress shop and seen the older girls in their lace and heels and big, big hair, she wanted that, too. It was probably for the best that Jailah was only in it for the fun, unlike some of the girls she'd run into at shows. She might've gotten *really* competitive. Even at seven years old, Jailah had a hard time losing.

Thankfully for everyone, she rarely did.

Jailah remembered one particularly hot summer in Memphis. Auntie Tish had doused her in setting spray, which annoyed her, because she was trying to watch her favorite cartoon on the hotel room's flat-screen. *Hol' still, baby*, Tish pleaded, and Jailah obeyed, though not for her auntie. Her father had flipped the channel to the news in an effort to bore Jailah, but she was only more mesmerized. There was a witch on-screen, and she was beautiful, and she was capital-W Wanted.

Covered in glitter, rhinestones, and mesh, Jailah watched with wide eyes as the report spoke of how a witch got her sweet, sweet revenge on a mundane man who had wronged her, who had wronged a whole lot of women. Little Jai didn't quite understand exactly what he'd done before her father flipped the channel, but she knew he deserved it. The witch on the screen had been smug and unrepentant.

And Jailah wondered why witches obeyed anyone but themselves. Why was there a mundane president separate from the World Witchery Council and the High Witches of each region? What mundane effort could stop a legion of like-minded witches?

These were questions that Jailah largely abandoned once her own magic manifested and she enrolled in Mesmortes. Her parents had high expectations for the first Simmons witch, which was fine, because she did, too. Her priorities evolved. Good grades, but a better social life. A diverse slate of extracurricular activities. Invitations to rub elbows with senior witches who would offer up recommendation letters and referrals that were more like golden tickets. She worked hard so that when graduation came, she'd be set. Her parents were respected in their fields and had money to keep them all comfortable, privileges that Jailah never took for granted. But in the world of witchery, she was going to have to pave her own way.

To think that the Council had doubts about *her* when there was a small mountain of witch-repellant hidden under their feet.

In their summer uniforms of skirts and shorts, sleeveless white shirts and black vests, Jailah was melting right along with the other young witches of the JWC. They were arranged in two neat lines on either side of the tall steps leading up to the Council building. The elder witches of the Haelsford Witchery Council stood in a semicircle on the middle of the first landing. Between their dark robes and the overcast sky, this was one depressing-ass welcoming committee.

Five large white SUVs rumbled in the distance. The *Haelsfordian*'s reporting team was here, along with news crews from Tallahassee, Miami, and Orlando. Jailah remembered that this visit wasn't just a big deal for her, but for the whole town. She straightened her back, adjusted her top hat, and prepared to smile.

The moment the line of cars stopped, there was a flurry of coordinated movement. Witches dressed in odd suits that looked like a cross between armor and athleisure jumped out of the first and last cars. It was the Highest Witch's security detail, surely. Jailah rarely stood before witchery that felt as commanding as this. The magic flowing from their auras fell around Jailah thickly, though not uncomfortably.

They opened the doors to the middle cars, and it was obvious that Evelyn brought along a small army of assistants as well. They looked around expectantly, but seemed a little disappointed by what they saw.

Finally, the last remaining door was opened by a grizzly man whose wand resembled a two-pronged fork. The High Witch of the Americas looked younger in person. Where her security team resembled a crew of assassins, she was awfully . . . colorful. She wore a shiny, lime-green jacket over a simple lime-green dress, and her headband bore a pattern of neon daisies. Were those Louboutins on her feet? The fit was flashy, well fitting, and probably worth more than Mesmortes's entire faculty salary. It looked like it belonged in a photo shoot and not on the gloomy steps of the Council building.

"Reminds me of someone," Danny Chen muttered behind Jai.

"Please," she scoffed. *Maybe if she was wearing pink, though.*

In the pictures Jailah had seen of Evelyn, her long brown hair was always styled in neat waves, but today, she wore a bob so severe that the playful glee-fulness in her expression felt off.

"What a sweet welcome!" she crooned on her way forward, arms open like she meant to hug everyone, including the building.

Jailah couldn't hear Lucia's response over the sound of the reporters and the cameras, but she felt the tension. When Lucia presented a hand, Evelyn pulled her into a tight hug and rocked her side to side. When Evelyn finally released her, Lucia looked like the energy had been sucked from her.

Lucia cleared her throat. "Highest Witch Evelyn, on behalf of the entire Witchery Council, I hope you'll make yourself at home during your time here."

"I think the real question is whether I'll have time to," Evelyn teased. "You've given me a healthy itinerary."

Lucia pursed her lips. Jailah had sensed some irritation in the way Lucia spoke of Evelyn a few weeks ago, but her sour expression now told Jailah all she needed to know.

With a sweet grin, Evelyn clapped her hands together. "Now, which one of you is Jailah Simmons? I'm ready for tea!"

Jailah's well-practiced smile faltered as the others young witches stepped aside for the Highest Witch. Jailah glanced at Lucia, who looked on with annoyance. The next thing she knew, Evelyn was wrapping her up in a vanilla-scented hug, and the Council was ushering them both toward the Chamber doors.

····•⦾ ⦿ •⦿····

High Witch Evelyn kept her wand to the left of her teacup. With just the two of them at the Council's wide table, the room felt so much bigger than usual.

Jailah didn't like tea, unless it was chamomile with honey or her grammy's sweet tea, but she sucked it up. She turned the bitter black tea over in her mouth, trying to discern any added potion while thinking of a way to buy time.

No, she was ready. She'd practiced her story and could answer any questions about the last Haunting Season, even if the meeting was supposed to take place tomorrow, and not moments after Evelyn arrived. She'd been taking sevdys every day. She just had to calm down, focus, and smile.

"I hope you had a pleasant trip," Jailah said sweetly, adding a little wobble to her voice. While High Witch Lucia might not have liked reverence, Jai could tell that Evelyn wanted that attention.

Predictably, Evelyn pouted at Jailah like she was just the *cutest thing.* "I did, thank you so much for asking. I hope it's okay that we're doing this now. Honestly, I think you'd probably like to be hanging out with your friends, so thank you for taking the time, baby witch."

Baby witch? Sure, compared to her. Jailah had to remind herself that being underestimated was a good thing here.

"I don't mind at all!" Jailah spun the teacup in its saucer. "We have a tour to do, I actually put together a whole thing—"

"Oh, don't you worry about that." She peeled off her jacket and slid it over the seatback. "Formalities get so boring when they're all you do. I don't want the little tour, I want you to tell me about what Haelsford is *really* like."

Here we go.

Evelyn eyed Jailah like she was the prize hog at the Bama state fair. Her fluttery, musical tone matched her admiring gaze. "I've heard so much about you. Lucia talks about you as if you're her own child. It's nice to have an elder witch as a mentor, I'm sure."

Jailah smiled back, though she wondered if she was being fed compliments for a reason.

Relax, Thalia would have said. *You're being paranoid.*

"It is," Jailah replied, "and I actually mentor a lot of the younger witches, too. In Archery Club and here on the Junior Witchery Council."

"That's so lovely. It seems like you're well known around school and the community. Haelsford's *such* a small town." Evelyn smoothed her hands over the table in awe. "I haven't been in a town this small since . . . well, ever, I think. You'd think a place as unique as Haelsford would merit a check-in every so often, but your Council is a well-oiled machine. That's why the reports about the events in the spring were alarming, to say the least. And all the hexeaters!" Evelyn hissed. "A nasty little group of them trailed us here. One of my guards had to put up a spell to make them all think my car was going in the opposite direction."

Jailah nodded. "I've heard that they're more . . . enthusiastic this year."

"Oh." Evelyn chuckled. "You *are* good at that, no wonder Lucia's chosen you as her pet."

Jailah felt a muscle in her eye twitch. "Good at what?"

"Good at making things sound less awful than they are. I think we both know that hexeaters aren't *enthusiastic.* They're annoying pests who shouldn't be allowed to step into a witchtown like this."

Jailah took a long sip of tea. Already this conversation had veered from the path she'd envisioned, but something about Evelyn's tone and her attitude signaled to Jailah that she wasn't the only one with an ulterior motive, though Evelyn's felt more like a game.

"Sorry, I'm rambling." The elder witch ran her thumb over the lip of the porcelain teacup, her fingertip coming away red. "All right, tell me. How did you find yourself fighting off a pack of Wolves? I've read the notes, and according to a young witch named Lilly Han, you saved the day."

Jailah didn't have to muster up any fake emotion. The chill that entered her voice was real. "It all happened so fast. I was gettin' ready to hit the MidWinter Celebration, and all of a sudden, there were Wolves on the Hill, and then they were up against our door. Most everyone was already at MidWinter, and some were found in the hollow rooms after everything was said and done. But I wasn't alone. My friends and I gathered some witches on the roof and . . . it was a group effort."

"Was it?" Evelyn angled her head slightly. "Perhaps, but you were the captain of the ship. Humility is nice and all, but your bravery can't be understated."

She pulled a tissue from her purse and handed it to Jailah.

Jailah looked at it for a moment, confused. She was so focused on getting every word out in the way she'd practiced that she hadn't noticed how full her eyes were. It was like she was back on the staircase, scrambling over displaced granite to get out of their way, wondering if she was going to live or die. The scar that would never fade still circled her wrist, and though it was currently covered up with foundation, Jailah dropped it into her lap. "Thank you, Highest Witch Evelyn. I appreciate your kindness."

"Hm." Evelyn took a long, hard look at Jailah. "You know, you can stop now."

Jailah blinked away a few errant tears. She considered a hundred different responses in only a few seconds, but none seemed appropriate for the sudden shift in Evelyn's energy. "I'm sorry?" she sputtered.

"I know you just met me, but I know an act when I see one." Her gaze softened. "God, I was just like you when I was your age."

Pulse like a jackhammer, Jailah toyed with the elegant bracelet on her unscarred wrist. If this was a game, and now she was sure it was, then she needed to decide whether to play it safe, or to knock the board off the table.

Jailah dropped the overly sweet tone. "You aren't here because of the Roddin Witch, are you?"

Evelyn paused to rap her fingers against the table. "I do have to make a report. You'll learn when you're older that there are plenty of nasty, violent witches in the world, but it's not every day that a heretic witch compels an entire Witchery Council and tries to murder everyone, and punishment must be dealt there. You wouldn't believe how many potential High Witches want to use this . . . occurrence as a blemish on my record."

Jailah was stunned and hardly able to comprehend what she was hearing. The High Witch's investigation was purely for pretense, a way for Evelyn to save face.

"But there's another reason that I wanted to speak with you, and it's not about the Haunting Season."

Jailah waited, not wanting to seem too eager.

Evelyn smiled. "Lucia is an old friend of mine. We went to Butler Coven University together in Philadelphia. Did she ever tell you that?" At Jailah's headshake, she shrugged. "I'm not surprised. It's hard to be an ambitious witch when your friends don't have the same goals."

Unease slipped into Jailah's belly. With one look from High Witch Evelyn's piercing eyes, Jailah felt like her soul was being held out in front of her for the world to see.

"You decided to attend a school in a town under a hex. You risked your life for it, even though you could've run. And I think I know why. Witches like us are different. We crave safety and happiness for our loved ones and for all witchkind. Now, I'm not an extremist like Roddin was. I don't think that only certain witches deserve magic, but do you ever feel like witchery is wasted on those who don't *love* magic like we do?"

Jailah found herself speaking before she had a chance to mull over a response. "It's like . . . what's the point of being blessed with magic if you're not going to try and be the most powerful witch you can be?"

"Magnificent." Evelyn's brown eyes twinkled. She settled back into her chair. "Jailah, have you seen anything in Haelsford, aside from the Wolves, of course, that concerns you? Because if there is, perhaps we can fix it together. And after that . . . maybe you'll mentor under me after you graduate."

Evelyn's words were like a lullaby to induce Jailah's most ambitious daydreams. The Junior Witchery Council and an internship under Lucia was nothing compared to what Evelyn was offering post-graduation. An appointment with the High Witch of the Americas was even bigger than what Jailah had dreamed for herself.

But she had to consider the consequences. There was something tense and antagonistic between the two elder witches, and Jailah knew that how she answered here might unravel all the work she'd done to impress the HWC. On top of that, she felt a bit of disappointment that the most powerful and influential witch in the Americas made this trip to check a few boxes and, what, dig up dirt about an old rival?

Then again, wasn't it Lucia herself who said the HWC had doubts about her? The memory stoked a fresh flame of frustration. Jailah considered her options. She would be graduating in a year and would likely never return to this cursed witchtown. More importantly, she and her friends had done some banish-worthy things in the last Season. There was the matter of Thalia's past as well. Jailah was sitting here with the Highest Witch's eye, her ear, her favor. Perhaps this was the key to ensuring not only her future, but safety for those she loved.

Jailah lifted her head. "There is something, yes."

Evelyn's lip twitched. She was pleased.

"I tried to go through the tunnels once," Jailah continued, wringing her hands as if ashamed. "It was foolish, I know, but I thought I could do something to stop the Haunting Season. But, um ... well, I didn't get very far on account of the—"

"Oh heavens," Evelyn interjected. Her expression was one of pride. "You incredible girl. You found the blackthorne."

Jailah's stomach flipped. "Y-you know?"

Evelyn rose from her seat. She pulled a card from her purse and placed it in front of Jailah. "It's going to be a joy to teach you, Jailah. I know my colleagues will be impressed that I snagged a baby witch who discovered her school's blackthorne bulb. It's very rare! You should be proud."

Jailah was confused and growing increasingly angry. She rose as well, not liking the feeling of the High Witch looking down on her. "Forgive me, but I have to ask that you explain."

The elder witch's voice was maddeningly even. "You are a smart witch. Think about what the world would look like if witches had access to every bit of power that they were born with."

Jailah could only stare. It was a wonder that her mouth was closed in all her shock.

"Chaos, of course." Evelyn placed her wand in a lush, velvet-lined case. "Us witches, we still make up so little of the world's population, and, well, you live *here*, you know what mundanes can do if they get worked up enough. Fear and power are such incredible motivators. There was an agreement, back before either of us was born. It was decided that coven academies needed to be regulated. It was a way to keep us all safe, happy—"

Subdued, Jailah wanted to say.

"But when you've made connections with people like *me*, you'll learn ways to really unlock your potential. I see you, Jailah. You are destined for greatness."

Jailah wondered if High Witch Lucia knew about the blackthorne, and then realized...*duh*. She's in on it. They're all in on it. Keeping young witches supressed while rising up through the ranks to become powerful witches.

Evelyn tapped the business card on the table.

An invitation was being extended to her. Jailah was on a path to power, and if she played her cards right, she, too, could be given the keys to this kingdom.

For the first time, Jailah didn't want it.

So much of what Evelyn said was true. Jailah loved magic and had always felt like being a witch was the most incredible thing a person could be. And yes, Jailah was self-motivated, and even selfish when it came to her own magic. She'd betrayed her tether to save herself, an act that could never be undone. But in one vital point, Evelyn was wrong. Jailah cared so much about magic that she believed that every student of Mesmortes deserved unencumbered access to their true power. She wanted Thalia to ascend in greenwitchery, and she felt that with proper instruction, Iris could rival Adelaide Strigwach in necromancy one day. Watching Logan master her proxy magic was something Jailah genuinely looked forward to. And for all the baby witches like Morgan Ramirez, Lilly Han, and Danny Chen, she wanted their witchery to thrive. Jailah wanted to be the best, but this didn't feel like winning.

If Evelyn looked at Jailah and was reminded of her younger self, then Jailah looked up at Evelyn and saw a witch she never wanted to become.

"That would be amazing," Jailah said with breathless excitement, like the perfect witch she was.

After a blur of conversation-ending pleasantries, Jailah ambled back to the Hill. Her plans for the day, as dictated by her meticulously organized bullet journal, were buying school supplies with Iris and Mathew, video-chatting her parents, and looking through the class syllabi that were dropping onto the Mesmortes student portal at exactly midnight. She'd wanted to keep herself busy to stave off stress over Thalia, Logan, and Trent. But the errands seemed trivial after what she'd just learned.

She knew the right thing would be to run and tell Iris. They could complain together, then determine what to do, if there was anything *to* do against a school that lied to them from the start. This was not a place to become a powerful witch. This was a place to have their magic dampened and their witchery controlled. Jailah had always known that the Mesmortes curriculum wasn't meant to create the type of powerful witch that frightened mundanes, or other witches at that. Iris and Thalia had known, too—they'd learned so much about their Pulls from sources outside of the coven academy.

But this? Blackthorne under the school? Was it in their water, their food? Jailah's head spun with anger and shame.

She was supposed to meet Iris, but Jailah didn't want to speak to anyone aside from one specific person right now. The only one who ever tried to tell her the truth.

She pulled out her phone and sent a message with the picture that Logan had snapped.

For an excruciating moment, she wondered if Vero had blocked her number. But the responding text came within a few minutes.

LOL. I fucking told you so.

22

trent

In a filthy stall of a seedy bus station bathroom, Trent pricked his thumb.

It wasn't the first time he'd done it. As a kid, he'd once unlocked the case of his mother's sanctified needles, the ones she'd kept hidden and rarely used. Lourdes Hogarth had treated her witchery like a personal trait or a quirk, not something that had imbued her blood with literal magic. It never made sense to him when he was younger, but knowing what he knew now, Trent was starting to understand why.

Nothing magical happened. He was left with a sore, bloody thumb instead of a hot burst of witchery in his chest. For a moment, he doubted what his uncle had told him. But as he recalled Uncle Quincey's serious face and tense words, he felt an irresistible twitch of nervous excitement.

Her firstborn witch.

Trent's witchery seemed to be the key to the bloodpact and a "beacon" to Silverhand, whoever that was. There was skilled, powerful magic at play here. *I'm a witch*, he thought, releasing a disillusioned chuckle. What was a witch without their magic? How cruel was this, to be given the one thing he'd ever wished for, only to be told, *Don't touch.*

Trent washed his hands, pressed a paper towel to his thumb until the bleeding stopped, then returned to the lobby where Logan and Thalia were waiting. The small bus station was surprisingly busy. Like Haelsford, Annex attracted its own tourists every summer. Families on their way up to see the Grand Canyon, thrill seekers looking to lure rattlesnakes for their social media accounts, and Bible-thumpers. Annex was one of three surviving bleedbays in the country, and there was a certain audience that liked the idea of being in a place where witches could be hurt without recourse. He shivered at the thought.

"Ready?" Thalia asked.

It was weird to hear the higher-pitched voice, but it was her face that was going to take some getting used to. He wanted her mess of wild curls, her shy smile, her big gray eyes. This version of her was too smooth and perfect. "Yeah. Are you?"

"As I'll ever be," she whispered. She looked to Logan. "You get the reservations?"

Logan turned her screen for them. "Two rooms at Annex's finest motel. Looks like they offer cornhole every evening at six, so exciting!" She smiled stiffly.

"Can't miss that," Trent agreed.

Thalia adjusted her backpack, then paused. Trent followed her gaze.

The bus station announcement board was covered in missing-persons posters. While Thalia's eyes didn't linger, Trent took in their names, their faces. Five different witches, all gone missing in the span of a few months. A stark reminder that witches weren't all-powerful and that a mundane with hate in their heart could be just as dangerous.

"Let's go," Thalia said quickly.

They skipped the rideshare line and started on the mile-long trek into town. The heat was blistering and the air shimmered, but Trent understood that the fewer people they came into contact with, the better.

"Let's go over everything one last time," Thalia said, her index fingers pointed up like a schoolteacher's. "My name is—"

"Annie Swift," Logan said quickly. "You're a runaway from Texas, where your witchy boyfriend tried to kill you."

"Except *we* don't know that 'cause we've never met her," Trent added, brow raised.

"Oh!" Logan facepalmed. "Right."

"Well, I'm glad you studied." Thalia smiled. Though Trent thought it was so odd to see such a familiar smile on a stranger's face, it comforted him.

"I need a name, too," Trent exclaimed. He racked his brain. "Should I hide my accent? I should hide my accent, though it's close enough to *y'all's* these days anyway."

Logan grimaced. "Trent, your American accent sounds like you've got a mouth full of food."

"Fine, I'll be Canadian. Me and Logan, a couple of Canucks, eh?"

Logan groaned, and Thalia laughed so hard, Trent felt like he was floating. They quieted as a couple of hikers passed, then Thalia said, "You don't need to have a disguise, no one here knows you."

He shrugged exaggeratedly. "Well, damn, can I get a fake name, at least?"

"Fine, think of one. Logan, you'll be my eyes and ears in town while I'm with my mom. Get to know people. See what you can uncover about the missing witches." Thalia glanced at her, squinting from the sun. "Time to put that white privilege to good use."

Logan pulled up her hair into a bun. The ends were damp with sweat, her bangs sticking to her forehead. "What do we do if we're in trouble? What's the signal?"

"I'm gonna put us all under a tracker hex. If it's an emergency, use your magic to activate it. Trent, you'll have to hang tight, but your blood will lead me to you..." Her voice trailed off as they reached Annex city limits. "That's new."

Up ahead, there was a sign that said WELCOME TO ANNEX, ARIZONA. HOME OF THE THIRD-DEADLIEST RATTLESNAKE! Below it, the entrance into town was surrounded by what looked like a canopy of thorny branches growing from two enormous trees. The path was completely out of place on the dusty desert road.

"Blackthorne vines?" Logan asked.

Thalia nodded. "There must be a well underground to keep it alive."

Trent's stomach flipped. Was he daydreaming, or did he feel a slight tingle against his skin? They were all sweating, but the beads rolled off Trent's dark forehead quickly. "How are we—how are you gonna get through it? Maybe there's another way."

"Our witchery can't be detected by any mundane trap," said Thalia, her voice hard. "The blackthorne's an issue, but we'll just have to force ourselves through. Besides, this is a lot less than what you just dealt with, Logan." She pulled a dark glass vial out of her backpack. "There's no true antidote to blackthorne, but this will help numb the pain." She took a small draw, then passed it to Logan.

Trent trudged along after them. He hadn't told anyone about his uncle's claim, at Quincey's stern request. Blackthorne had never bothered him before, so it shouldn't now . . . right? Still, he held his breath as he approached the poisonous canopy.

"How the hell is this legal?" Logan whispered.

Because it's America, Trent thought, biting his tongue. He glanced over at Thalia with a look of frustration and understanding. Neither felt compelled to explain to Logan how Annex may have been anti-witch, but there were still places where Thalia and Trent wouldn't have been welcome for being Black, regardless of their magical capabilities or lack thereof. And though Trent's hidden magic was locked up, he still felt apprehensive about this small Arizona town.

"Ready?" Logan asked.

Thalia nodded, already wincing.

Trent watched as they started on the trail, each witch pushing forward with a clenched jaw and tight fists. It was nothing like Iris's reaction to blackthorne during what Trent would call his most embarrassing moment in the spring, but looking at them closely, it was clear that they were in pain.

"Just a little bit farther," Trent said, trying to sound supportive.

"Ugh, such a mundane thing to say," Logan quipped. She attempted a smile, but it didn't quite land.

With heavy breaths, the three reached the end of the blackthorne canopy. And there was Annex. A small, dusty town that circled a man-made lake. It looked like something out of an old storybook. Brick buildings, cozy shops, and statues of what Trent presumed were old white men with white-washed histories.

The church loomed in the distance. Great spires and stained glass towered over the town, its medieval design clashing with the strobe lighting set up at either side of the wide iron doors. There was an enormous digital billboard advertising church services, accompanied with a clip of a middle-aged man with cold gray eyes.

Trent knew immediately. He knew before the sharp intake of Thalia's breath. Those eyes were hers.

"Also new," she muttered quietly. Her expression hardened, but her body shrank. Watching this change angered Trent, and he made a quick promise to Thalia and to himself: He wasn't going to let that man touch a single hair on her fucking head.

"We made it," Logan said, a similar hardness in her voice.

By force of habit, Trent knocked his heel against his ankle, tapping the knife strapped there.

23

iris

Holding *Death's Compendium* felt like holding history in her hands.

When Iris wasn't practicing using the runes with Mathew here in the Green, or trying to soothe Jailah's anxieties, or worrying over Thalia, Logan, and Trent herself, she thumbed through the book like it was a precious piece of art. A few days she'd had it and found herself discovering new segments of the book, relishing the scribbled margin notes, those little insights into the necromancers she was connected with but didn't know. The part that interested her most was the list of runes and their uses, but considering how these necromantic runes were made, she kept herself from indulging. She wouldn't ask anything more of Mathew.

A peek won't hurt, she thought, flipping through the gilded pages. There was a rune for stasis, whose carvings consisted of ten thin lines in neat little rows. Such a simple diagram, but according to the accompanying text, could effectively pause a beating heart, thus sending the afflicted to Death's realm for an unclear amount of time. Alternatively, it could also be used to briefly give a dead body life. And the cost?

Iris shivered. "Three years," she whispered shakily.

Just as she went to flip the page, she found a note in the bottom left corner. Vital trick to skeletal puppeteering! There were plenty of shorthand marks and jotted footnotes, but this one . . . well, the words glistened as if the ink had not yet dried.

Beside the note, she scribbled a small question for herself to come back to.

skeletal puppeteering?

Iris watched the ink dry on her own scribble and gasped. Another note appeared under hers in the same thin strokes as the first's.

New here, baby witch?

A mixture of excitement and fear sizzled over Iris's nerves. She wanted to slam the book shut and run away from it. No, she wanted to lean in and commit every word to memory.

Another note appeared then. Different handwriting, hot-pink ink, all caps.

DON'T SCARE THEM! Then, in the same handwriting and pink ink: I'M DARCY. WHO ARE YOU?

Iris paused. She didn't know what this was, or if it was safe to write back, but the name Darcy was immediately familiar. She flipped to the front of the book, scanning the list of Death's roster.

There they were. Darcy Lohman, a Reaper from Australia.

But Darcy Lohman was dead.

Back on the page with the live notes, Iris found herself in the middle of a squabble.

YOU SCARED HER, RILEY! Darcy had written.

Then she needs to stick to the front of the book, the first annotator—Riley, apparently—replied.

Iris quickly scribbled back. I'm Iris Keaton-Foster.

KEATON?

Yes, she answered quickly. **That Keaton.**

There was a small pause before the next note came. New handwriting. A new spirit. **I've been waiting for this. My own blood.**

The book nearly slipped out of Iris's hands. This must've been Daveed Keaton, her great-uncle.

You have my name and my face. What you waiting for?

Iris bristled. Calling him should've been her first response to seeing his portrait, but perhaps Bloom's resurrection had left her more messed up than she'd realized. Now it seemed obvious.

But she was without her supplies, and Mathew was on his way. **Can't, busy.**

Too busy to Call your own damn kin?

Iris groaned. She could *hear* her father's annoyed tone in these words. **What's skeletal puppeteering?**

You got a dedicated Runekeeper? Lotta Reapers don't have that.

That was one thing she could say that without a doubt, Mathew Beaumont was. Her stomach twisted. **I do.**

Good.

Below that last word, a small image was sketched onto the page. It was a crude, quick rendering of skeletons bursting from the ground. Above them, a pair of hands held what looked like the strings of an old-school puppet connected to the skeletons' bodies.

Behind her, Mathew said, "I know the Green is like a big witchy space, perfect for what we need to do, but, Iris. The *heat*."

Iris slammed the book shut.

Mathew's pale skin was wet with sweat, but his eyes were still his own, and narrowed in annoyance. He smelled faintly of shampoo and sunscreen, a scent that had become familiar and comforting to her. He was the most casually dressed that Iris had ever seen him: a loose, sleeveless tee that showed off his well-toned arms, athletic shorts that ended just above his knees, and sneakers. Next to Iris in her oversized top and bike shorts, they looked like a pair about to go for a hike, not practice destroying a demon.

Mathew said, "Please tell me that you have a spell for dumping a bucket of ice water on me."

Iris snickered. Lifting her wand, she pushed out a *Sealing* bubble, then looked up a cooling spell in her app. When the invisible barrier pulsed with chilly air, his face visibly relaxed. "Thanks. Ready?"

Iris nodded. She opened up the pouch of stones slung around her shoulder, but her gaze was immediately pulled back to him.

Light flickered in his palms.

"Mathew?"

He suddenly slammed his hands down into the earth with a strength that Iris couldn't understand. When Mathew lifted his head up to look at her, she found his black eyes glistening. There was a deep hole in the ground between them. Iris's chest tightened.

"A TEST, LITTLE REAPER!" Death shouted, wearing Mathew's crooked grin. "BANISH IT, SHOW ME YOUR STRENGTH."

Adrenaline flooded Iris's body. "Wait—"

The ground lurched, and a horrible sensation seeped into the air.

The demon ascended from the earth in a red cloud, a jolting mass of death energy. Its aura scratched roughly against Iris's. It had no eyes, no face, no physical body that she could see. The cloud constricted suddenly, and the air went taut like the demon's energy was a slingshot being pulled back. Iris heard a high-pitched squeal.

Before Iris could duck, the demon sent a sharp gust of wind toward her, so strong that she barely managed to throw up a *Shield* before she was sent sliding backward in the damp grass, her sneakers unable to keep purchase. Her knees hit the ground hard.

Iris scrambled to her feet and braced herself. Out of pure anger, she sent two tiny fireballs from her wand toward the demon, but they only dissipated once coming into contact with the red cloud.

The next gust was like little needles against her skin. Hell, little needles dipped in *lava*. She gritted her teeth but managed to keep her footing this time.

"The runes!" Mathew yelled, fully himself. He circled her and the scene, watching her work intently.

"Got it!"

Iris dodged another gust, then scrambled to place the runes around the demon as it regrouped. One knee on the ground, she knelt before the first one. *Confining.*

Quickly, Iris pricked her thumb over the stone. It vibrated immediately, and Iris couldn't help but puff out her chest when the demon screeched. The red smoke melted away, revealing a little catlike creature dripping in green ooze. Though *catlike* was generous. It was more like a child's interpretation of an imaginary clash between a cat and a zombie. Iris pushed back the threatening spike of fear. This was just a test. Whatever was waiting for her in Port Barrow was bound to be much worse.

"Good!" Mathew shouted, snapping her out of it. "Next!"

Purging.

Before she could make her way to the next rune, the creature spat out a slick green mass. It sizzled in the air, hot and acidic, and burned through Iris's *Shield*. She was forced to throw herself onto the ground.

Fucking hate cats.

She lunged for the second rune, the stone marked with several circles. It responded to her blood with a pleasantly chilly pop, the burst of air cool against her skin. A line of vibrating light jolted out of the stone and pierced the demon. It thrashed against the magic to no avail, now trapped in the air helplessly.

Iris glanced at Mathew and found him staring back with a look that melted her nerves away and replaced them with dangerous desire. *Girl, focus!* She forced herself to break this heady gaze and stand before the final rune.

Exterminating.

The last rune activated with a burst of magic that expanded around the demon like netting. It was gloriously frosty, and Iris relished the feel of it as much as the display of her own power. She thought of the names in the compendium. An entire legion of strong deathwitches who had ascended everyday magic and became more than necromancers. The feeling cut through her with satisfying electricity.

With steadily quieting wails, the demon succumbed to the runes. It burst with a loud *pop!* The remnants of its aura sizzled in the air. The runes stilled. Iris's breaths calmed. In the end, it was her and Mathew standing before a patch of scorched grass in the middle of a triangle of stones.

"I'm ready," she said, returning her gaze to Mathew's. "I'm so ready."

His voice was tight in his throat. "I wish you didn't have to do this alone."

But Iris smiled confidently. "I'm walking with Death. I've never been less alone."

His eyes flashed black. He was Death, and he was Mathew, and she was powerless against the *need* tightening in the pit of her stomach. And how could she not give in, staring at a boy who saw her call the Chasm at a party and immediately decided he would do anything for her.

She kissed him hard, a wild pull of an embrace. He caught her easily with his mouth, with his hands, pulling her so close to his body that Iris let out a small whimper at the impact. He tasted sweet, the faint lingering of summer fruits as he slid his tongue against hers. He held her with infuriating restraint, the loose fabric of her shirt balled up in his fists. But Iris couldn't stop running her hands through his hair and over his bare arms, relishing the feel of his scorching skin. She knew nothing but the feel of his body and the sound of her name catching in his throat with every breath.

24

thalia

If Haelsford summers were a sauna, then Annex summers were...hell. Literal hell.

Thalia cringed at the dry, hot air hitting her skin. Sweat was already pooling in places she didn't even know sweat could pool, and sure, the anxiety thrumming in her belly and all over her skin probably wasn't helping.

Welcome home, Tallulah. Four years away from Annex left her more unimpressed than fearful. She was a much different person now. She'd been tending to her witchery, not suppressing it. She knew spells that could alter minds, could hurt people, could drag this town down to its knees with a few carefully spoken syllables. Thalia had survived the Swamp and the Wolves, had pulled up trees from the earth with her blood. What could a mundane do to hurt her now?

With Logan and Trent settled into the motel, Thalia made her way into town. The gravity of her decision to come back bore down on her with every step. Her wand was tucked away in her backpack, disguised as a tampon. She had a burner phone for her friends back home, and Maverick was in their care. She missed Haelsford. She missed her *face*. But she also really missed her mom, and whatever happened here in the next few days, at least she had that to look forward to.

All roads led to the massive gray-brick cathedral on the southern edge of town. Where everything else had a dated feel, this was a Church of the Future. The top steps were bordered by two massive screens promoting upcoming services, random lines of scripture, and her father.

Gray eyes, gray hair, a perfectly tailored gray suit. It was like he was a celebrity. The screen displayed him giving some sermon, cut to him holding a baby, then showed him waving at a crowd. Though soundless, Thalia could hear his gravelly voice as he whipped up the congregation.

The last time Thalia was here, the church hadn't been tiny, but it was nothing like the massive structure staring at her. This looked more like a small arena than a place of worship. Her father used to stand in front of his congregation in simple clothing, not fancy suits. In fact, his ability to seem like the approachable everyman was part of what had drawn people to him. Now he looked like he wanted to sell Thalia a fancy car out of her price range.

Or like he wanted to kill her. Coming from her father, any look could be a murderous one.

Thalia turned away from the church. She was in a hurry to get out of view of her father's gaze and into her mother's.

Salty Sweet didn't have indoor seating. It was a tiny shop, just enough to hold the staff, the small kitchen, and her mother's growing collection of potted dandelions. Customers lined up at the service window to order freshly made peach pastries, chocolate-filled croissants, and fluffy doughnuts that were like biting into clouds. Thalia felt a little pang of jealousy at the girl working the counter. Those easy smiles, the apron bearing her mother's face.

That should've been her. Happy and safe, with a little job that was more legitimate than selling fake weed to the teens in her town. At least her mother had taken her suggestion to add lattes and macchiatos to the menu, judging from the chalkboard in front of the counter.

At the touch of an older woman's hand on her shoulder, the girl at the counter turned, then stepped aside for Fiona.

Thalia's heart swelled.

Her mother was radiant. Fiona's dark brown skin glowed in the sunlight, and her wide, heavy fro was a crown atop her head, even under the hairnet. She wore precious jewels around her neck and a small collection of rings on her fingers. Fiona looked up. She recognized Thalia, even though she shouldn't have.

It was hard enough to not run into her mother's arms, and now she had to act like she didn't know her at all. They'd practiced this, albeit over a spell, but neither Thalia nor her mother was prepared for the flood of emotions now.

Fiona swallowed. "How can I help you?"

"I was actually wondering if *you* might want some help." Thalia lifted Jailah's southern lilt onto her tongue—an impression, not a spell—and ducked her eyes. Her words had come too fast, and she took a breath to slow down. "I'm new here and looking for work. I can bake or work the counter. I can mop up or wash dishes. Whatever you need."

Her mother smiled. "Funny enough, I was just thinking of maybe getting another pair of hands around here. What's your name, sweetie?"

Thalia smiled back, a sheepish thing that required no acting at all. "My name is Annie Swift."

Her mother flipped up the counter as the other girl took the next orders. Thalia felt the girl's curious eyes on her. She was vaguely familiar; maybe an old classmate or member of the church choir. The girl offered a smile, and Thalia returned it.

Fiona led Thalia to her back office. It was cramped, more like a big closet with a window, but her mother had made it look cozy enough. The stacks of papers on the desk amused Thalia. It looked just like the mess in her cabin.

Fiona closed the door, then wrapped her arms around her daughter.

At first, Thalia didn't know how to respond. To hug her mother back was the obvious response, but this show of such affection sucked the air out of her lungs. It had been so long, and Thalia realized now that nothing compared to her mother's embrace. Was she weeping? Her cheeks were wet, and she buried her face in Fiona's shoulder.

"Tallulah," her mother whispered, as if her name were a small thing to cherish.

Thalia didn't know how long they stayed like that, hugging to make up for lost time. But when Fiona finally held Thalia at arm's length and looked her over, Thalia's eyes were dry and her smile was wide.

Fiona smoothed her palms on her apron. "Annie, was it?"

"Yes, ma'am." She would've killed to have her mother speak her true name again, but she was glad that Fiona was taking this seriously, at least.

"Where are you from?"

"Texas, ma'am."

"You like to bake?"

"No." Thalia smiled. "But I'm stubborn and determined, and that makes me a fine worker to have."

Thalia doubted anyone was eavesdropping or that their voices would carry into the shop, but she wouldn't take any chances. That hug and that *Tallulah*, that was all she could accept. From this moment on, she was Annie Swift, a sweet mundane girl in need of a job and a new home. This mask wasn't coming off until she was far away from Annex.

Fiona matched Thalia's smile with one of her own. "You can start tomorrow."

Thalia took in the room, the generic decor of signs saying random words like *peace* and *grace*, and landed on the photo of Fiona and Abraham at her desk.

"Your husband?" Thalia asked innocently.

"Yes," said her mother.

Thalia licked her lips. Looking at the picture, no one would ever think that the Turners had a daughter, too. "And where is he now?"

Fiona's smile didn't waver, though her brow lifted a tick. "Pastor Abraham works long hours with the congregation. He has a mass in about forty-five minutes actually."

Thalia didn't respond. Her mother giving her this piece of information— was that a direction to avoid the church? Or to go to it?

It was clear from Fiona's shaking of her head that she'd meant the former. But Thalia was already thinking otherwise. And maybe Fiona saw that, mask and all, because she quickly said, "I can show you around the town—"

"That's quite all right," Thalia retorted, sounding more like herself than she had in the past hour. "I think I can find my way. And I wouldn't want to put you out."

Fiona pressed her lips into a tight line. If Thalia hadn't effectively spent the last years of her life on her own, maybe Fiona could've forbidden her from going anywhere. But they both knew that Thalia would do as she pleased. It wasn't that she didn't love Fiona or didn't respect her, because she did, but their relationship didn't work on normal mother-daughter terms.

"Have you already found a place to stay?" Fiona asked softly.

"No."

"Then you're more than welcome to stay with my husband and me. We have the space."

This was another rehearsed moment for the sake of potential eavesdroppers, but Thalia still began to sweat at the thought of returning to her old home. She'd deal with the awkwardness later; first, she had to go spy on her father.

On the outside the church was daunting enough, but the inside?

The inside was a nightmare.

The sheer size of the stage was staggering. There were multicolored lights to illuminate the small choir on the stage, and a spotlight for the speaker's pulpit. And a DJ? She had hardly made sense of any of this when her father walked out from a cloud of smoke to raucous applause. They were indoors, but Thalia half expected fireworks to start shooting out from the rafters.

At the very least, all the commotion and the number of pews made it easy for her to hide in the back. Mask or not, Thalia was sure that her current expression of disbelief and disgust would stand out.

Seeing him was one thing, but hearing his voice was another. His smooth, deep tone poured out of the invisible speakers that were placed too close to

Thalia. His voice seemed to encircle her, trapping her, and her body went stiff at the sound.

He opened his arms to his followers. "My beloved brothers and sisters."

They answered in kind hellos and sweet little murmurs. Thalia tried to fix a smile, but it wouldn't take. Her attempt to reach that part of her that once fit in here left her grasping for something that didn't exist. Even before her witchery manifested, had she ever felt like one of them? Thalia had no beef with religion; what she didn't like were the actions of wide-smiling hypocrites who spoke in scripture in one breath and violence in another.

Thalia watched her father move around the stage. The sight of him, even from this distance, left her breathless with unease. But she was going to be under his roof once more, and she had to get used to this. He was older, he was taller, his blood was hers. And still, she would win. She had no choice.

Organs blared and the crowd jumped up, moved by the spirit in his words. Through the pews, papers were being passed around with the collection bucket, and when they finally reached Thalia, she resisted the urge to pocket some of the money out of spite.

It was the flyer that stilled her. Thalia expected a listing of dates and times for mass, mentions of Annex gatherings and social events. She didn't expect to see her own face staring back at her. Her true face. Tallulah Turner.

A small square was dedicated to her father's biography, and there was a nice bolded section about his great loss. His daughter, succumbing to the devil's witchery. The words were vague enough, but everyone in Annex knew that Thalia had killed Oliver Warner and nearly killed his sisters with a levitation spell gone wrong.

The flyer got worse. There was a QR code paired with it. Thalia scanned it, and it took her to the church's website.

Pastor Abraham has been tested and stays to speak the Lord's message!

Keep Annex witch-free and under the eyes of our Lord!

Donate today!

Thalia crumpled the flyer. She waited until everyone was on their feet in raucous song before fleeing the church, her father, and her own young face. All this time, he wasn't just hunting her. He was making money off her. Using what she had done and his self-professed pain to appeal to his followers. He hadn't built this church.

She'd built it for him.

25

logan

Within hours of arriving in Annex, Logan learned that the people here had nothing to do but gossip, pray, and whine.

After checking in to the motel, she spent the day patronizing the local establishments, including the drugstore, the bookshop, and an antiques dealer specializing in terrifying porcelain baby dolls. She learned way too much about people she didn't even know; of not-so-secret affairs, dog owners not picking up after their pets, the woman who distastefully brought a peach cobbler to a funeral—which honestly seemed fine to Logan—and of the de facto leader of the town's pride and joy. Its church.

"Oh, you *have* to attend a service," said the woman at the counter of Annex's diner. It was getting late, and this was the only place that wasn't about to close. The woman packed up Logan's pastries. "You know, I think hearing Pastor Abraham speak really is the closest thing we all have to God."

"Wow!" Logan managed. "Sounds . . . divine!"

"Mhm!" She counted Logan's change. "And you know, he's been through so much. I still think he should've married a good girl from town. A more appropriate wife. Maybe that's why his daughter—" She shook her head. "Here's your change, hun."

"His daughter—"

She could barely finish her question when the woman, predictably, put her unwelcome hand on Logan's and said, "Oh, it was an awful thing. That woman birthed a devilish girl." She lowered her voice. "A witch."

Logan's smile tightened. "How sad."

"More than sad!" A man in head-to-toe camo spun around on his barstool. He was a good ten years older than Logan. He took a long draw from his coffee mug before continuing. "That girl murdered an innocent boy in cold blood! Then she smeared that blood all over her face and went around cursing the town!"

Logan, who had come from Haelsford, definitely considered this town cursed.

He rubbed his shaggy beard. "The poor Warner triplets. I know they never got over it. Hard to heal when your brother's murderer got away with it."

"For now," the cashier said slyly. She looked a little too pleased to be speaking of a murderous witch and an awful tragedy. "Pastor Abraham and the Holy Healers are gonna bring that monster to justice, I'm telling you. And when it happens, I want a front-row seat."

The man at the bar raised his mug. "You and me both, honey."

Logan grabbed the bag of pastries, intending to leave. But she thought of Thalia and her plans for Logan here. To *infiltrate*. Logan had no desire to stand around with these hateful, ugly people, but if she had to bear it to get information, then she owed it to the greenwitch. White, young, seemingly mundane; the only other person in their coven who could've done this was Mathew, and Thalia didn't have him. She had Logan, and Logan would do whatever it took to keep Thalia safe.

"Holy Healers?" Logan asked, forcing her voice sweet and her expression awed. "Witch-hunters?"

"Protectors!" said the man. Logan stepped aside to let the next customer order and settled closer to him. "We're the ones that put up that witch-repellant. We've been trying to get everyone who comes to town to have to drink a concoction of the stuff, but the county put a stop to that. All Annex got is ourselves."

"Totally."

"I'm Bennett, by the way." He looked her up and down. "What're you in town for?"

Logan was prepared, but she didn't expect to be asked so abruptly. "Just passing through. Driving up to visit some family."

He groaned an affirmation, a rough syllable that sounded wordlessly lewd. "Need some company while you're in town? Annex is full of people who'd lay down their lives for a neighbor, but a sweet girl like you shouldn't have to wander a strange place on her own."

Sweet girl.

Those words hit Logan with a fleeting cut against her confidence. Her subconscious tried to drag her back to Theodore Bloom, but Logan was able to hold it off.

But this man Bennett *did* bother her. Logan looked into his eyes, and a strange thing happened. A chill passed over her, and she felt the odd desire to open her mouth, flash her teeth, and bite down hard on the man's neck.

The daydream was as palpable as something that had actually happened, a too-solid memory. The long, sharp teeth she'd pictured weren't hers, but the bloodlust felt oddly natural.

The moment passed quickly but left Logan's skin covered in goose bumps.

"Oh no, got my friends waiting for me." She was finding it harder and harder to keep the innocent grin. "But I know some girls who've been hurt by witches. When's the next meeting?"

Bennett let his eyes skate over Logan. "Tomorrow night, but Pastor Abraham doesn't let females in. That said, if you need someone to rough a couple witches up, I got a few friends."

There, again, that flash of witchy, feral anger. This time, Logan had to grip the bag tighter to keep her focus grounded.

"I gotta get going," she managed through the sudden rise of bloodlust.

"Maybe I'll see you around."

She nodded.

You'd better hope not.

Back at the motel, she found Trent lying on his bed, twirling a dagger, deep in thought. The room was nothing special, with overly bright curtains, a very busy sunflower wallpaper, and two creaky twin beds with thin mattresses.

"I bought croissants," Logan said softly. "Have you heard from Thalia?"

Relief passed over Trent's face at the sight of her. "No, but it's only been a few hours. I'm sure she's fine. Get any intel?"

Logan laughed easily. "I'm an okay spy, I think."

"Oh yeah?"

"There's a group called Holy Healers, and I guess T's dad is a big part of it. Sounds like it's dedicated to keeping Annex witch-averse. Didn't find out a ton else, except that everyone hates her."

Trent nodded, his expression like the too-calm ease of a man about to punch something.

"They only accept men, but—"

"Probably not a great place for me?"

"Yeah. I'm gonna go anyway, just to poke around." Logan pulled a pastry from the bag and offered one to Trent. "Weird that Haelsford is the least messed-up town we've been in lately."

Logan felt a tug in her chest. It was Thalia, their joint tracker hexes. It was the signal that she was okay. Logan called forward her witchery, the magic finding the spell between them. She wasn't totally sure how this worked, but thought in affirmation, and hoped that was enough for Thalia to understand that they, too, were safe.

Logan's proxy magic glowed in her hands as it always did when she did magic, but this time, the strange feeling of warmth became a hot poker in her hands. She looked up at Trent, whose hands emitted little wisps of smoke.

"Logan—" Her name came out in a harsh whisper that was so unlike him. "You need to step away from me."

Confused, Logan backed up. "Why? What's happening?"

"Well, you're a proxy, and I think you're doing something to my witchery."

Her eyes widened. "To your *what*?"

He sat there with his wondrous eyes on his hands. It was hard for Logan to not feel a little like she was seeing herself in him. The smoke died. He clenched his fists.

With her magic now drawn in, Logan sat beside him. "Is this about your mom? I never asked you how things went with your uncle."

"Guess I forgot to mention that my cool witchy uncle told me that I'm also a witch." He chuckled. "Shit just gets stranger every day."

Logan wasn't sure whether to be excited, nervous, or pitying. Trent's own expression seemed to oscillate between the three. "I can't feel your witchery, though."

"Yeah. One of my mom's many secret and super-powerful protections." He turned his hands over and looked at them as if it were his first time seeing them. "If I fully embrace my witchery, not only would it put us at risk here, but it might call the witch who owns my soul." He turned to her. "No one can know, especially not Thalia. She needs friends here, and if she finds out, she'll send me back."

"I know you're worried about her, I am, too, but, Trent, are you okay?"

Trent smiled. He looked like himself again. "I think so."

"If it makes you feel better, I think having a terrifying, potentially life-threatening witchy secret makes you a shoo-in for our coven." Logan offered him a warm smile. "Your secret's safe with me, baby witch."

26

jailah

Meet me at our old spot.

Verity River was the closest thing Haelsford had to a beach this far inland. There was grass, moss, and rocks rather than sand, and the cliffs made for a treacherous jumping spot, though that didn't stop rowdy kids from taking the leaps. The waters attracted more kayaks than swimmers, and the surrounding forest was full with campers this time of year.

Coming here was Veronica's decision, and though Jailah had doubts that she'd show up, she made the drive anyway, if only to get away from Haelsford for a bit. Highest Witch Evelyn had a full slate of events around town. A tour of Mesmortes, a meeting with the mundane mayor, and a photo op in front of the Swamp. At least the hexed land hadn't expanded any farther since Thalia left.

At the other end of the pebble-filled parking lot, an old sedan pulled into a spot, its body vibrating with reggaeton. Vero cut the engine, and the car stuttered still.

Jailah braced herself. *It was easier when there was distance*, she thought, catching the green streaks in jet-black braids.

Across a sea of cars, they locked eyes. Unlike Jailah, Vero wasn't one to hesitate. Swinging her keys and her hips, she strode up to Jailah.

"You're staring," Vero said curtly. "You miss me?"

Jailah rolled her eyes. "Definitely didn't miss that attitude."

But she did miss a time when they were both just baby witches.

Jailah had brimmed with childish excitement when she first stepped onto the Hill. Her wand had been newly shaved and plucked of splinters, her grimoires and herbal guides were already marked up, and the strange new power she owned begged to be used.

An anarchist bullet of a witch fit nowhere in her plans, but Jai couldn't help being fascinated by Veronica Dominguez. She'd watched Vero mutter her spells and create something somehow brighter than hers. Jailah had labored over her brews, while Vero just threw this and that into a cauldron and let everything writhe into something perfect and potent. Vero was the type to ace an exam the morning after a raucous night at the Box Chant while Jai relied on sleepless nights with color-coded flash cards.

As their competitive natures gave way to curiosity, they grew closer. Veronica began to show Jailah the way of real magic, the wild thing they were born with and didn't need instruction for.

Here's the thing about coven academies, Jai-jai, she'd said. *They give you rules and guidelines—don't do this, never do that. They don't even give you the chance to see for yourself, to figure out the limits of your power. They don't teach you that witches can do most anything they put their minds to . . . so long as you're willing to make a little sacrifice.*

They made forbidden elixirs off campus, where the charms couldn't sense them. They cast banned spells and researched illicit incantations. They only ever poked and teased, but there was something satisfying in knowing the things the school didn't want them to know.

Jailah couldn't resist their secret studies, or Veronica. Vero knew how to draw out her power when their classroom lessons only ever limited it. The tether that tightened between them made her more fearless in her magic, and in her desire.

Vero sniffled. "C'mon. I got other shit to do today."

Their spot was a cliffside patch of grass beneath a large tree. It had the perfect view of the cliff-divers and an ample amount of shade. Vero dropped down to the ground, dangling her legs over the edge.

Reluctantly, Jailah lowered herself next to her, trying not to think of the bugs. She could cast a *Repellant* spell to be safe, but she felt like doing magic in front of a hexbound witch was probably rude.

"I haven't been here in years," Jailah started. She avoided Vero's gaze, focusing on the cliffs instead. "Felt wrong to come here without you."

Vero smirked. "Whew, things must be really bad if you're doing all this sweet reminiscing." She leaned back onto her elbows. "Go on, butter me up for what you want."

"I'm not—" Jailah huffed. "I didn't ask to see you because I need something from you."

"Right, you're here because you're scared of what you found."

Jailah licked her teeth. "I'm here because you were right, and I wanted to tell you that to your face. That's all."

"Aw, que cute." She took in Jailah's outfit from the kitten heels to the pink cardigan. "God, you haven't changed one damn bit."

Jai flicked her gaze to the massive holes in the knees of Vero's jeans. "You're one to talk. That looks like the same thing you were wearin' when we became official."

"You remember that?" Vero asked, eyes on the water.

"Of course I remember," Jai whispered. "'Cept your shirt was blue."

Vero's lip quirked.

"See, I remember hatin' you for it because I was wearing green, and we were clashing, you know, and I'd wanted our officially together pic to be a li'l more coordinated."

Veronica threw her head back and laughed.

Jailah shrugged, a little smile threatening to break her cool facade.

"We were silly," Vero muttered, throwing a loose rock into the ocean. "But we were tethers."

Jailah closed her eyes. This seemed to be a liminal space for them. The cliff, where they had their first kiss while the other kids on the field trip were busy setting up campsites and putting up tents. Where Vero had entranced her, the two of them tripping over themselves to be the one to ask for official girlfriend status, because everything was a competition between them, even this. Where they had tethered, their magic coiling around each other's like puzzle pieces snapping into place.

And for what? A tummy full of butterflies and nights holding hands, a short-lived scream of a relationship. And maybe closure was what Jailah needed, too, if she could still feel the shadows of those butterflies. Two years pushing down feelings, and Vero was already working through them with ease.

Jailah sighed. "What was the point of it all, Vero?"

Veronica didn't respond at first. Her eyes were trained on the water and the slick bodies launching themselves into the blue-green crush. "All I ever wanted was the best for us," she whispered. "For you, for me. For us *all*. For witchkind." She looked at Jailah with eyes that had been soft but grew sharper with each passing second.

Jailah shook her head, exasperated. "Oh please, don't act like you weren't doing that spell for yourself. *The Culling* would've given you power that neither of us can even imagine. You keep acting like you're this big, misunderstood hero who's gonna save us all, but you're not."

With a humorless chuckle, Veronica nodded. "Right. Well, *I* regret nothing. Can you say the same?"

Jailah hesitated. "I regret not being able to convince you before I went to the Council. I should've called your mom, I should've—"

Another strained laugh. "Jailah, no one was going to stop me."

Jailah lifted her chin. "True, you are so damn stubborn. Then, fine. Never mind. I did what I had to do."

Silence fell over them, as heavy and thick as the approaching storm clouds.

"I don't regret *us* either, Jai. I mean, I want to, but." Vero shrugged. "I'd be lying."

Jailah turned to her. Everything was a force of habit. The way their bodies angled toward each other. Jailah's haphazard glance at Vero's mouth—

A high-pitched wail split the moment, followed by desperate shouts and anxious footfalls.

They turned together and saw a tween girl flagging them down. "Help! Please help!"

Neither hesitated. Jailah ran toward the screams, Vero keeping pace behind her.

A trail of blood glistened on the highest cliff's edge. Down at the drop, a boy was scrambling wildly in the river's fast currents, hardly able to keep himself upright. He was cradling another boy with blood-soaked hair.

The rest of the group tittered nervously, hands in hair, phones pressed to cheeks. One of them was explaining to Vero about how the first boy had tried to jump into the waters but slipped and hit his head. The second one went in after him and got caught in the currents.

Wordlessly, Jailah ran to the edge and pricked her thumb with her wand's retractable needle. A simple levitation or beckoning spell would work, but between her distance and the rushing waters, aiming her wand and gaining purchase on the boys was more difficult than she'd anticipated.

"He's bleeding," Vero said after they slipped from Jailah's magic once more.

"I know!" Jailah flung out *Come to Me*, and the spell only crashed into the waters. The boys went under again.

Vero dipped her fingers into the blood and flicked her eyes up at Jai. "Calm the waters. I'll get 'em."

"What?" Confusion and frustration flooded Jailah's senses. Vero and her smugness had a way of making Jailah angry with just a few words.

But Vero was serious. "Jai! The water!"

Cursing, Jailah focused her witchery on the roaring river now whipping the boys toward a dangerous cluster of rocks. *"Be Still!"*

Vero bent over her clasped hands. She whispered frantically in Spanish, and while Jailah didn't understand her words, she *felt it*.

Vero and Jailah might not have been tethers anymore, but their magic connected as if it'd never been broken. And though the spell tired Jailah—it would've required less strain if she were a waterwitch—the feel of Vero's witchery growing around her gave her a burst of power.

Impossible.

Vero's eyes flew open. She threw a hand outward, her finger still wet with the boy's blood.

Below them, the water roared. Jailah watched incredulously as a massive wave grew from the still waters and lifted the boys out of the water. In one swift movement, it dropped them onto the shore below.

The rest of the group scrambled to get to the boys. A girl fell to her knees before Veronica. "Oh my god! Thank you, thank you!"

If things were different, Jailah would've laughed at Vero's uncomfortable disgust, but she was too stunned to feel anything but bewilderment.

When the last girl ran off to join the others, Jailah managed four whispered words. "What did you do?"

She wanted to say more, but the look on Vero's face intrigued her. Vero looked utterly serious without that mischievous twinkle in her eye or a smug smirk. "I broke the hex."

Jailah's heart stuttered. "That's impossible. You would've had to *kill* the binder to do that, and your binder was the entire Council! So, how?"

Vero crushed a wayward piece of grass under her sneaker. "I can't tell you that."

"The Council—"

"The Council doesn't know, obviously!" Vero chuckled. "They didn't feel my magic the last two times they checked in on me, so."

"Impossible," Jailah repeated. She didn't know what else *to* say. She stood there speechless as Vero took a long, hard look at her.

"I forgot how upset you could get when you're confused."

Jailah didn't have the energy to clap back. An unwanted feeling settled over her; not fear, not desire. It was *worry*. "What kind of magic have you gotten into to break an unbreakable hex?"

Annoyance flickered in Vero's eyes. "You are still so damn patronizing." She cocked her head at Jailah. "I'm not going to tell you a thing, because I don't trust you. Go tell the Council. I'll take them all. And you know, you're right, Jai, with what you said before. I am no hero." She dipped her lips toward Jailah's ear, the same way Jailah had hoped she would. "But you know what? I'm still a better witch than you'll ever be."

Jailah now found herself confused, furious, and—regrettably—into it.

After a long moment, Jailah said, "I get it. You hate me. You'll never forgive me, and god knows I don't deserve your trust. But I called you anyway because you're the only witch I know who wouldn't be surprised that the Witchery Council is purposely controlling our magic. Highest Witch Evelyn knows. And only witches with an in to the elite get to really tap into their power."

She shook her head in disbelief at her own words. Vero's hand moved to the crescent moon gem hanging from her neck.

"You don't gotta pack up and follow me, you don't even have to reply. I mean, look at you. Clearly, you don't need me. I just had to talk to someone that understands." Jailah lifted her hands in finality. "That's all. Thanks for comin', though, I mean that."

She walked past Vero and in the direction of the parking lot. The divers

225

were piling into their cars, and one of them waved at Jailah in thanks. She clicked absently on her phone and acted like she hadn't seen it.

Footsteps crunched behind her. "Jai. What are you gonna do about it?"

Jailah scoffed. "Burn it down, obviously."

"Oh *shit*." Vero ran in front of Jailah and blocked her path. "Really? And how are you gonna get close enough to that thing to do that?"

Jailah lost focus for a second. Under the sun, Vero's gem sparked suddenly with light.

"And if you do burn it down, what happens after that when the Council gets ya, huh?" Amusement danced in Vero's eyes. "You tryna get bound like me? Nah, don't tell anyone else, and don't try to destroy it."

"I can't do nothing!" Jailah spat desperately.

"I didn't say we were going to do nothing."

Jailah stilled her shaking hands. "We?"

"Yeah, whatever." She stepped back from Jailah and ran her crescent moon gem over her lips. "I'm not going back to Haelsford, so meet me here Friday. I got something to show you."

27

mathew

In about nine hours, Iris was going to battle a demon in a haunted house, and here was Mathew at some party catching a contact high.

He didn't want to be here. He wanted to be back in the Green, relishing the taste of Iris's mouth as she murmured his name. It was impossible to concentrate on anything but the memory of it. It was real, it was real. He'd had the swollen lips to show for it. If it were up to him, he would've walked her back to Beaumont Manor, or let her lead him to her dorm room in Topthorne House, to the bed he'd laid in once before and desperately wanted to again. But Iris had said that she needed to clear her head and get a good night's sleep. Mercifully, he saw no regret in her eyes. And before they parted ways at the doors to Mesmortes, she'd lifted his palm and pressed her mouth against his pentagram scar. The memory of her lips on his hand tingled inside the fist he held at his sides. The resulting vision was slightly clearer than the last time he'd touched her skin, though Mathew only saw a flash of a hooded Iris in a blanket of shadows.

There was one thing that Mathew needed to understand and fix. So, he came here to a party with people he barely knew. He kept one hand tight at his side, and the other around a mug that said WORLD'S WORST DAD.

If it were up to him, Trent would be here to buffer. Watching Trent charm strangers was always fascinating to Mathew, who had to build himself up before social interactions with people he didn't know. On the plus side, there was alcohol. But Mathew needed to keep sober enough to see the vision one last time.

When Chloe, the girl who now sat next to him in therapy every session, had invited him here, Mathew's first thought was that he could hardly stand to look at her without seeing her death. Part of him wondered if it would be best for him to stay away; he was the only mutual connection between her and Iris, and if he just stopped attending the meetings, or at least stopped speaking to Chloe, then maybe the two would never meet. Could the vision change? Was he forcing Chloe and Iris to a bloody ending, or steering them away from it? The only way to know for sure would be to touch her again and see if there was something in the vision that he'd missed. This whole thing was terrible, but somehow easier to deal with than the shit going on at home.

He made his way around the party, which was spilling out onto the front yard, kids tripping over one another to refill from the keg that was set up on the porch. A few kids his age, maybe a little older, looked him up and down when he asked for Chloe. He hadn't been at a party like this in so long, where people looked at him and didn't immediately know him.

A few minutes later, he was sitting on the couch, muscles all relaxed and mind buzzing, but not with the usual fire-fueled ruminations.

"You made it!"

Mathew's mellow reverie was broken by an excited squeal. Chloe was happy to see him, and her smile made him smile, a knee-jerk reaction. "Hi, Chloe."

Her green eyes widened. They were lined with thin black eyeliner that gave her a vulpine look. Her freckles danced on her pale skin. Her hair was different—bright red, half-up, half-down—and Mathew might not have recognized her if he hadn't heard her first. Her therapy attire was usually a hoodie and mom jeans. Here, she was all done up, even though this party was more of a chill stoner attraction, judging from the smell. She tugged on her crop top a little. "I almost thought you weren't going to make it."

She looked at him expectantly, and his thoughts went muddy. He cleared his throat. "Well, I'm here."

One moment, she was in front of him, and the next, she was sitting beside him. She was close, her body warm.

"How do you know all these people?" he asked.

"School, mostly. But you know how it goes, throw a party, and people tell people, and ta-da!" She opened her arms out to the tipped-over potted ficus.

Mathew smiled. She turned away in a little moment of shyness, cheeks going pink.

"So funny how we ran into each other at that arcade. I didn't realize you were from Haelsford."

She said the town's name like it was unfamiliar, a word she'd only ever read but had never said aloud.

Mathew put down his drink. He needed to focus.

"This party must be so boring if you're usually hanging out with witches."

At this, Mathew tensed. "It's hard to not know a few witches, living in that town."

She nodded. "I know we're not supposed to talk about what supernatural phenomenon happened to us—" She paused, seeming to have the same annoyance with that phrase that Mathew did. "But it's hard not to wonder, right? Especially knowing that there's someone who might feel what I'm going through, you know?"

Her voice was low and tender. She grew antsier now, her fingers drumming on her knees. Mathew wondered if this was what he looked like at times. All uptight, knees jerking, on the verge of tears.

He couldn't touch her skin—not yet—but he leaned in closer and said, "Sometimes, it's all I can think about."

In the circle on the living room floor, a girl flicked a lighter on and off, on and off.

Chloe looked up at him, nodding. "Same."

As much as Mathew was tempted to tell her more, he clamped down on his alcohol-heightened emotions. He had a whole coven of witches to protect and keep secrets for.

Thankfully, Chloe wiped her eyes and blew out a laugh. "Sorry! We're supposed to be having fun!"

With that, she lifted her head to him.

She was still close, and this movement brought them closer. She was tearstained and willing, her lips slightly apart, his hand just an inch from her knee.

Mathew rose from his seat. "Sorry, I need to make a call," he sputtered quickly. "My sister. She's not feeling great. I promised her I'd check in before she went to bed."

"Becky? Oh no!"

"Yeah, be right back."

Chloe said something about how sweet that was, but Mathew couldn't hear over the blood pounding in his ears. He found a small coat closet across from the bathroom and slipped inside and pulled out his phone.

At the click of the call going through, Mathew whispered, "Iris?"

"Beaumont?"

Her voice was slow and thick with sleep. He leaned against the wall and savored it. "I'm sorry."

He heard her move, sheets rustling around her. "For what?"

"Calling you this late."

"It's only like ten, but okay."

"But you're sleeping." He shook his head, trying to clear his thoughts. There was something off about Chloe and their conversation, but he couldn't work out what it was. "I'm at a party. It sucks. I'm a little drunk, by the way."

"Okay—"

"And I know you said I can't come with you tomorrow, but maybe I should."

"Demons feed on life force. *You* were the one that told me that. You made the runes, I'd rather you keep your energy, like, inside you, yeah?"

Mathew chuckled.

"But *thank you*."

His chest squeezed. "Hey."

"Hey?"

"There's a thing coming up. The annual Hammersmitt Equestrian Banquet. Will you come with me?"

"I—" Her words caught, and that hint of surprise in her voice gave Mathew the sort of chill that he didn't want to go away. "What are you asking me right now?"

"This is me asking you to be my date."

"For your horsey prom?"

"Exactly."

His face was hot. Waiting for her response was excruciating. Why was this so hard when they'd already made out after banishing a demon?

Iris said, "There is nothing I'd like to do less than be surrounded by horse snobs and eating their unseasoned foods. Like, little slugs on pieces of lettuce or whatever."

And now Mathew smiled. "I don't want to make you uncomfortable. We go, we dance once, and we leave. No mingling, no tiny appetizers."

"Hm." She was amused now, her voice teasing. "One dance? You want me to get all dressed up for that?"

"We don't have to go home afterward. After that . . . I'll take you wherever you want to go. Away from all of that. Just us."

Suddenly, he wished he'd waited to ask her in person so he could drink in her dark eyes as she examined him.

But it was worth it to listen to her slow, little— "Okay."

"Okay?"

"Yes, Mathew."

When had his palms gotten so sweaty? He gripped the phone to keep it from slipping out of his hand. "Cool," he answered in breathless disbelief. "Cool."

"Is that all?"

No, no, of course not. There were a million other things he wanted to tell her. "Yes."

"Night."

"Wait."

"Yeah?"

"I think we should kiss again. Soon. Really, really soon."

"Good night, Mathew!" She gifted him a little chuckle before hanging up.

Mathew took two deep breaths to steady himself before going back to the party. But there were hushed voices on the other side of the door, and out of habit or instinct or pure nosiness, Mathew stilled to listen.

". . . Chlo's working on it," said the first voice.

Mathew squinted, wanting a better look through the slats of the closet door. The voice belonged to someone who looked only a year or two older than Mathew but had him beat in size and height.

"It's taking longer than it should," said the other voice. It was the girl with the lighter.

"Mara—"

"Like? Really? This is the closest we've been, Blake, and she's fumbling." She clicked the lighter. The flame illuminated the gold bands in her twists and her brown skin. "I'm just sayin', *we* can step in."

"We voted on Chloe's plan. You were there." Blake crossed his arms. "And we still have two weeks."

Mathew wanted to leave, but a feeling in his gut told him they wouldn't be too happy to see him coming out of the coat closet mere inches from their conversation.

The girl, Mara, nodded. Her voice went lower, and Mathew couldn't make out her words. Something about the moon? Maybe a sign? By all means, he shouldn't have cared, but he found himself interested. If it concerned Chloe, then maybe it concerned Iris. That was reason enough.

The conversation ended when the boy threw up his hands. "Fine. I'll talk to her. You stay out of this, Mara."

Mara sucked her teeth. "Aye-aye, Captain." She turned on her heels, the boy following. Mathew waited a minute before slipping out of the closet and into the hallway.

He felt her hand first. The gentle way she snaked her fingers up his back. "Mathew, there you are."

Mathew turned to Chloe.

"Your sister okay?"

"Yes."

"Cool."

Gently, Mathew brushed his fingers against her knuckles.

A vision obscured his gaze.

Iris moving her fingers with the grace of a conductor.

The flash of a bony hand.

The snap of Chloe's neck on a dark night.

28

iris

Port Barrow looked like Haelsford's preppy twin, and for that, it made Iris sick.

Even in the dark of early morning, she saw houses lined with perfect gardens and well-maintained paint jobs, each a clone of the one before it, every single one screaming picket fence and 2.5 children. The stores were picturesque, not a single sign advertising potions or tools for witchery. Iris was ready to do what she needed to and then head the hell back to Haelsford.

But. There was something interesting about Appleton Lane. Iris was rightfully terrified about what was in store for her, but a tinge of excitement bubbled in her chest. The house she'd come for pulsed with a sinister energy. Iris sensed it before it came into view. She couldn't see anything physically wrong with it, but she could smell it.

No, that wasn't the right way to describe it. She felt acid at the back of her throat, but it was more like an inherent feeling of the death energy, something that existed in a higher plane than mortal senses. When she stepped out of her car, she waited before approaching. She wanted to see if faces appeared in the nearby windows, or if any lights flicked on in the houses down the street. Was everyone just sound asleep while a house corrupted with death magic shared their idyllic little haven? Iris couldn't imagine falling asleep with such heady magic clawing at her witchy senses, but mundanes really had no idea about the things that existed within the arcane.

Iris tightened the bag around her waist. She felt a little ridiculous hauling around these incredibly important necromantic runes in one of Logan's Sailor Moon fanny packs, but it really was the most efficient option. And cute, so there.

Mere feet from the front door, Iris found that the house did stink. Like decay, like blood, like overripe fruit. She turned away, took in a deep breath of fresh air, and covered her nose before she used *Knock-Knock* and stepped inside.

She was met with the sound of buzzing. Above her, a cluster of fat, blood-thick mosquitoes hovered over a dark, greasy stain in the wall. Iris's stomach turned. She moved quickly, taking in the state of her dilapidated surroundings. The windows were cracked, the wallpaper ripped, and the little furniture in the sparse living room was tattered. Her every step pushed down on the loose, bending floorboards. Something creaked. At first, Iris thought it was her own footfalls, but she froze solid at the sight of the body at the kitchen table.

The man had been dead for a while. Iris understood the loneliness that might've kept a man's death from being reported, but the stench was unbearable. How had the neighbors not noticed?

Another creak. The slow opening of a door on rusty hinges. A call, a beckoning from the second floor.

But Iris remained where she was. She felt inexplicably pulled to the body. He was an old man and, judging from the mush in the discarded bowl before him, had been eating breakfast when death took him. Iris stood over him, examining the pale, papery skin.

Now, looking at it, she thought it was odd that he hadn't decayed further. Death had told her about this house weeks ago, so he had to have been dead for a while. The awful smell and the slowly decaying body didn't match up.

Death also told her that Reapers were meant to collect souls who had escaped death and were in danger of becoming malignant, corporeal demons.

A blast of searing heat grew all around her. Iris drew her wand, though she wasn't sure what she was supposed to be aiming at. She was so intent on finding the source of the malice around her, she almost didn't notice that the body was now sitting upright.

Iris lurched out of the way, and the body barreled to the ground, its rotting black fingers breaking against the floor. The crunch turned her stomach, and the stench was unbearable, but the sour, sharp energy coming from the upper floor was worse. Wand at the ready, Iris ran upstairs.

Every door was closed, but Iris sensed the aura weeping from the main bedroom. The door creaked open, then closed with a slam, as if there was an open window somewhere playing with the air pressure. Under the sound of her own tense breaths and pounding heartbeat, Iris heard a laugh or a cry, she wasn't totally sure.

Iris dropped to a knee and opened her bag of stones. She wanted to be ready with the runes, but she didn't get that far.

Her ears filled with the sound of screaming wind. The energy took hold of her. It lifted her off her feet, sucked her into the room, and thrashed her hard against the wall. Iris's world spun, and when her vision cleared, she found herself staring at something from a nightmare.

The demon manifested in a broken, rotting cross between a person and some sort of multi-limbed monster. Its head was covered in red eyes, and its body pulsed black blood.

Iris screamed.

She felt it again, an arm, or a rope, wrapping around her waist and taking hold of her.

But the demon flickered, its corporeal body disappearing, reappearing, in and out like a stuttering lightbulb. Iris was released. She hit the ground, and though her body screamed at her in pain, she was relieved. Whatever this thing was, it couldn't stay solid for long.

But how long?

Iris had considered asking Jai to come with and was sincerely regretting her decision not to. She thought she could do this alone and thought that Jailah, as a witch who wasn't a necromancer, didn't have a place here. And now she was in over her head.

Beaumont.

A mundane, but different. The boy was probably sleeping off a hangover, and yet Iris reached for the tether within. She put out a call for him in a way she never had before: desperate, and urgent, an SOS in this connection they shared. Port Barrow was an hour's drive from Haelsford, but if he woke up Jailah, and if Jailah blessed him with one of her speed spells, maybe, maybe they'd reach her before this demon took her to hell with it.

Lotta ifs and maybes, she thought helplessly.

If Mathew had sensed her desperate call, she didn't know, because the demon appeared once more.

It took shape with a blistering roar that made Iris's ear pop. The monster lunged for her on spindly spiderlike legs, but she got out of the way in time. It crashed through the opposite wall instead. The demon flickered hard, and Iris took the moment to run out of the room and down the stairs to put some distance between them.

Crashing down through the ceiling and to the first floor, the demon did something Iris couldn't explain.

The heat constricted her once more, but instead of being lifted, Iris felt herself getting . . . tired. Worse, it felt like the spell she'd done to keep Stony House alive—like she was being relieved of her magic. A siphoning of it.

Oh, absolutely the fuck not.

With a feral roar of her own, Iris sent a *Cutting* spell into the air. The demon screeched in pain, the magic severing its hold on her. She didn't wait to watch it flicker and disappear before pulling out the runes.

Hastily, Iris began arranging them. The triangle was nearly set when she felt two distinctly different sensations: the demon recovering with a sicklier energy than before, and the soft wheel of a turning in her chest.

Mathew! she called internally, unable to get the scream out of her throat as the malignant energy raced toward her in shock waves. The demon was latching on again, even as her tether's ever closer proximity imbued her with a new sort of energy.

Iris gritted her teeth, *Cut* once more, and called for a *Shield*. The air

239

around her glistened red, a barrier of her witchery. Like an angry child, the demon seemed displeased with its inability to keep its hold on her. It rebounded, broke her magical barrier, and lifted her up once more. Iris threw a cushioning spell behind her, just in time.

Regaining her footing, Iris scrambled to reset the stones and, narrowly missing a whack from a spider leg, she pulled out her sanctified needle and stabbed her thumb.

The stones vibrated on their spots. Magic grew, hummed, and twisted all around Iris.

The demon opened its mouth and laughed, revealing rows of green-slick teeth. It flailed, breaking the triangle once more. Iris was forced to duck and weave out of its way. Her heart fell into her stomach. She had to fight off the demon, rearrange the runes, and keep the demon in the middle of it long enough to banish it. *Awesome.*

She wanted to run. Thought maybe she could come back when she figured out a way to do this, but electricity exploded in her chest. It felt like something that should've stopped her heart, but instead, it forced her to stand taller. Her witchery was dancing in her veins, small pops of adrenaline racing though her body.

The tether inside her pulsed once more. Iris screamed, "Beaumont, the runes!"

But when she whipped her head to the front door, it was not Mathew standing there, heightening her power.

It was his twin.

Rebecca Beaumont was dazed, like she'd just woken up and found herself here. She was pale, covered in sweat, and the death mark at the base of her neck shone violently beneath her cool black turtleneck. Iris could hardly believe her eyes, or the force of witchery radiating in her chest.

With a lifted brow and determined eyes, Rebecca met her gaze and said, "You called?"

Iris had a million questions, but there was no time. "Look out!"

Rebecca lurched out of the way just enough so that the demon's leg missed her head. Eyes narrowed, Rebecca clapped her hands together and held them there for a moment, like she was praying. She pulled them apart, revealing two shimmering death marks on her palms. When Iris felt a blistering heat in her own fists, she knew before she saw them that they matched.

The demon sputtered around them, slamming into the walls and skittering on the ceiling. It seemed angry that there were two witches now, and that the power between them was growing. In her peripheral vision, Iris saw something happen to the flies hovering near that dark sludge in the corner. The black cloud grew darker, and then a clump of lifeless bodies hit the ground.

Rebecca jolted to her feet, eyes alert once more. "Tell me what to do!"

Now, hearing Rebecca this close, Iris didn't know how she could've mistaken her presence for Mathew's. They had utterly different energies. Mathew was a pull in her chest, a winding rope, a catch on a line. But Rebecca was a flash of lightning that burned up the rope and replaced it with unbreakable steel links. It was new, but somehow familiar, like Iris had always known her, like she always would.

The tether between them twisted, demanding her attention. But when Iris opened her mouth to tell Rebecca about the runes, the other girl simply nodded and said, "Got it. You'll lure the demon, I'll set the stones. And then you'll vanquish it."

Iris didn't have time to dwell on her confusion, or her new and absolute love of the word *vanquish*. "Easy enough," she spat.

"Wanna switch?"

"I want to go home and watch bad reality TV is what I want, Becky!"

The Beaumont girl ran to collect the scattered runes, yelling over her shoulder, "It's Bex!"

A clump of flies dropped to the ground, and the demon's presence was a fierce white light against Iris's witchery. Iris understood then. It couldn't siphon from her or Bex, so it went for the next best thing, the only other living creatures in its vicinity.

Iris felt an odd sense of calm. The witchery between her and her tether was growing mightily. Iris drew her breath. *"Stay Back!"*

The demon flew backward into the kitchen. Bex set the runes wider, muttering curse words to herself as she did it. She set them so that the triangle encapsulated the whole living room, and when she looked up at Iris, Iris knew what to do. She opened up her witchery. She let herself be a beacon to the demon, calling it with the irresistible promise of energy to siphon. As if she were weak, when that was the last thing she felt right now.

She tightened the hair tie around her braids and readied herself. *Come and get me.*

The demon roared back to her. Iris had to trap it here in the triangle, and that wasn't exactly easy, but it helped to have just one focus. When the demon connected to her, she let it. She let it have a little taste of her magic.

Its maw curved into a vicious smile, and Iris dropped to her knees, desperately trying to hold on to her consciousness even as she cut her hand once more.

And as the demon grew drunk on her energy, strong off her magic, and lifted her up to devour her whole, Iris felt Bex's warning well before her tether screamed, "Iris, now!"

Iris obeyed. Finally, she *Cut* from the demon and flung herself out of the triangle. When the aggravated demon tried to follow, a line of electric-blue light snapped at it from one of the runes.

The demon released a bloodcurdling scream as the energy it had consumed was purged from its being. It tried to break free, but the light held on to it like a shackle, keeping it in place. Iris glanced at Bex, who watched in childlike awe. The baby witch looked down at her blood-slick hands and then back to the work she had done.

The rune for extermination manifested in black threads. They slithered toward the demon and wrapped around its misshapen body. The demon's desperate cries shuddered to one high-pitched wail. With a flash of light that forced Iris to shield her eyes, it exploded into a cloud of lovely stardust.

The house was quiet. Without the thick, decaying magic, Iris gulped down clean breaths.

Bex looked to her, speechless.

Exhausted, Iris dropped against the floor. "It's *you. You're* my true tether. How the hell did you get here?"

Rebecca ran her tongue over her teeth before speaking. "I drove."

Iris rolled her eyes.

Bex shrugged. "I was going to sleep, but couldn't. Every time I closed my eyes, I saw a strange little house—this house—and . . . you. And then I started to feel shitty. Like, dizzy, but my magic—" She stumbled over the word like it was a swear and she was a child and had been told that it wasn't a word for her. "I couldn't ignore the feeling in my chest. Everything was telling me to go, and it was like my feet were moving on their own. I didn't even really know where to until I saw Matty waiting for me by the car. God. It was so freaky."

The front door creaked open. It was Mathew. It was Death.

"PERFECT," it said, glowing palms sprawled out before them as if they were about to be pulled into a group hug. "TOGETHER AT LAST. A TRINITY FORMED. MY LOVELY LITTLE DEATHLINGS."

"Never gonna get used to this," Bex muttered. She frowned suddenly, her fingers drifting back to the pentagram on her neck. Her eyes flicked to her brother, and Iris felt as though she was watching a silent conversation between them.

Sure enough, Bex straightened and said, "Yeah, got it."

Iris glanced between them. "Got what?"

Death addressed Iris. "I LEAVE YOU NOW, REAPER. YOUR HARBINGER WILL LEAD YOU HEREAFTER."

For a witch who'd just discovered her otherworldly ties to Death, Bex looked a lot like she'd just been assigned a massive stack of homework. "What is it about Florida that breeds so many demons?" She crossed her arms petulantly. "We got a shitload of work to do."

Before Iris could ask what Death had showed her, Mathew's hands curled into fists, then he opened them to reveal two glassy stones resembling red obsidian. *Runes?* Each had one mark etched in gold, glittering lines: a scythe.

"A PARTING GIFT. MY BLESSING TO PRESERVE TWO SOULS."

29

thalia

Thalia decided to spend the night in her room at the motel. She didn't have a lot of time to uncover the truth of the missing witches, but she needed to work herself up to being in her father's company. Seeing him at church was difficult enough, even with the sea of pews separating them. She needed to keep it together. She hadn't even come face-to-face with Abraham yet and was already falling apart.

At noon, she made the trek through town toward her parents' house. Annex still put on a farmer's market on Fridays, and she spotted Trent and Logan doing their best to blend in as tourists. According to Logan, a group of men calling themselves Holy Healers would meet tonight, and she planned to do some snooping. Thalia didn't like the idea but had to trust that Logan could handle herself.

As she expected, the door to her parents' house was unlocked. It smelled divine—like coconut, sugar, cleaning products. Thalia tried to avoid looking at her mother's silly porcelain figurines, the ones she used to play with like toys. The dining room table had been replaced, a tapestry hung where the old grandfather clock used to be, and the lines on the wall outside Thalia's room that kept track of her height had been painted over.

"Mrs. Turner!" she called out.

Her mother responded from the kitchen. When Thalia poked her head in, Fiona shook her head to say *he's not home*.

At the end of the hall, the door to Abraham's office was closed. Thalia walked over and threw it open. *No time to waste.*

Immediately, she pulled open the desk drawers and began rifling through his things. There were stacks of papers tracking donations, endless correspondence from pastors around the country, and her father's prized collection of copper bird statuettes. Feeling petty, she plucked a tiny blue finch and slipped it into her pocket.

Thalia opened up the filing cabinets, pulled out each folder, and flipped through them. She had to remind herself to slow down and keep everything looking untouched, but her anger with him only fueled her impatience.

As she opened the last drawer, something caught her eye. A small leather-bound notebook under a stack of receipts. Weird place for a notebook, and even weirder were the rectangular pieces of paper sticking out from its lined pages. Newspaper clippings, but from online articles rather than print editions. Thalia expected to see the faces of the missing witches from nearby towns, like trophies he was keeping. The reality was worse than her assumption.

Each clipping was from the *Haelsfordian*. Reports on the Haunting Seasons, articles about the Wolves.

He knows. Thalia used to curse her own paranoia, but here was the truth before her. *He knows.*

"Annie?"

At the sound of her mother's voice, Thalia jumped. Before she could respond, she heard heavy footfalls coming her way.

She knew that rhythm . . . that gait.

Quickly, Thalia shoved the book in its place and stood, right as Abraham Turner entered his office.

He furrowed his brow at her. "Hello there."

Hatred lanced through her.

"I'm so sorry. Oh heavens!" Thalia ducked her head. "Mrs. Turner asked me to fetch her order book, and I got lost, I thought this was her office." She glanced up, glanced back down. "I'm so sorry, Pastor Abraham, I see my error now."

Every word was like cutting her tongue on a knife. Apologizing to him, deferring to him. The anger welled up in her like the first flickers of a soon-burning wildfire.

But then, Abraham grinned. That was *worse*. "You must be Annie," he said. "Apologies for not introducing myself sooner. Late night, early morning, and my wife likes me to stay out of the bakery. *Her domain*, she calls it."

He offered his hand.

Forcing back bile, she took it.

He gave her face a hard look that sent shivers down Thalia's spine. Did he see her? Did he know his own kin despite the animosity between them and the mask she wore? Thalia was ready to reach for the witchery within to defend herself, but Abraham released her and said, "Thank you for your help. The missus has needed another employee for a while now. Glad you came along." He leaned in conspiratorially. "She's very picky."

Thalia forced a smile. "I'd say she's doing me the favor! I've been meaning to put down roots here for a while."

His brow twitched. "Have you, now?" He looked her up and down. "You're so young to be on your own."

"I'm coming from a difficult, um, situation. Long story short, I've been looking for a place where I'd be accepted, and when I saw your church online, I hoped Annex might be the right place." She swallowed hard, fiddled with her fingers. "My ex-boyfriend is a witch."

Her father nodded sagely. "Ah. I see."

"Anyway." Thalia wiped a few hard-earned tears from her eyes and chuckled. "I'm sorry to bore you with this stuff, Pastor Abraham. Just wanted to say my thanks."

"Oh nonsense. I try my best to know my flock." Another grin. He really had that thing down, didn't he? If Thalia didn't know him, she might believe him. "I trust that my wife has already invited you to stay with us, if you need a place till you get back on your feet. At the very least, dinner tonight, yes?"

Her stomach lurched. This was the plan, but she still felt so unprepared. Thalia was a teenager, not a sleuth, not a spy. Could she really make him trust her enough to reveal what he was up to?

Despite everything, she was his daughter, once. He'd loved her, once. Maybe she could make him do it again. And just when Abraham thought he'd found the perfect, God-fearing replacement for his lost daughter, she would put him in the fucking ground.

Thalia smiled up at him. It felt good and convincing. "That would be lovely. I'm honored, Pastor Abraham. Thank you for inviting me to your table."

Abraham Turner was just so *nice*.

Look at him, doting on his wife with passing glances and stolen kisses. He filled his guest's plate first, then his wife's, before settling down with his own. To the strange, pious girl sitting on his left-hand side, he offered a prayer of protection and love, a wish for her to be swaddled by God's care. An offering of thanks for her presence here now at his table, as if this was all his design.

When he offered his hand for grace, she wanted to jab her fork through it.

She swallowed down her nausea and took a small bite of her mother's curry-spiced meat loaf. It was delicious, naturally, but the combination of dangerous nostalgia and adrenaline made a perilous combination. Thalia managed a grin. "It's lovely, Mrs. Turner."

Fiona looked satisfied.

Thalia kept Annie's precocious little smile on her face, even as her father peppered her with questions. *Where's your family? Any plans to go to school? Oh yes, that troubled boyfriend, how unfortunate; where is he now? Well, lucky for you that you met my wife, huh?*

Thalia couldn't deny that there was something addictive about this one-sided game where she tricked him over and over again.

Thalia beamed at them. "You two are such a lovely couple. Do you have any children?"

It was good that her father's eyes were on her, for Fiona's mask fell completely, and she struggled to wrangle her shock and fear into quiet acceptance.

Abraham waited a beat.

Go on, she thought. *How are you gonna explain me?*

Her father dabbed his mouth with his napkin. "Yes, actually."

"Abe," Fiona whispered.

He patted her hand. If Thalia didn't know any better, she might think that was regret in his eyes. Or actual tears.

"I failed her," he said.

Thalia resisted the urge to scoff. "How, Pastor Abraham?"

Regretful eyes again. It was harder when they were aimed at her. His cheeks flushed, and his voice had a mournful lilt to it. "I should've . . . well, I should've taken care of her. I was weak."

Thalia swallowed. What was this? A trick?

But then he said, "I didn't put her down when I had the chance."

And there it was. Thalia's blood turned to ice. Her heart hammered in her chest so forcefully, she wondered if anger could make a person black out.

Her mother was quick to take the plates and ask for Annie's help in the kitchen, but Thalia ignored her. "Put her down? What do you mean by that?"

Abraham's eyes were still wet. Thalia had the strange urge to dig her nails into them. "She was an abomination."

"Abraham, please."

"She'll hear it from me, or from someone out there, my love." He gave Fiona a small, rueful smile before leaning back in his chair. "Somehow, my wife and I gave life to a warrior in Satan's plan."

Blood pounded in Thalia's ears. "A witch."

"Yes. The moment her arcane power showed itself, well, I should have—"

"Enough!"

For a moment, Thalia thought it was she who had screamed. But it was her mother. Fiona had thrown the dishes to the ground, but her cry was worse than the sound of shattering ceramics. Thalia couldn't tell if the grief was for the life she'd lost with her daughter, or a desperate plea to stop the conversation before Thalia acted on her impulses.

Purely for her mother, Thalia held back what she really wanted to say to her father. "I'm so sorry, Pastor Abraham."

Abraham's eyes were distant. "If I had only done my duty, the murder never would've happened."

He was right, in a way. If he had done his duty to Thalia as a father who loved his child unconditionally, maybe they'd all be living a different life, and Oliver Warner would still be alive.

Thalia unclenched her fists, her shoulders, her spirit. She willed herself to be light and rose from her seat. Standing behind him, she placed a hand on her father's shoulder.

"It's not your fault," she said. It was easier without seeing his face. "Your daughter. She made her choice. What could you have done in the face of pure evil?"

Relief flooded her mother's eyes. For that, it was worth it. Fiona wiped her palms on her skirt, then lowered her head as if in prayer.

When Abraham turned to Thalia, she thought, *I did too much. Laid it on too thick.*

But the fear was fleeting. Her father patted her knuckles just as he'd done to his wife moments before. "Thank you, Annie."

She was happy to follow her mother into the kitchen after that. They worked in a silence that was almost electric with the secret shared between them. If they were a normal family, maybe that secret would've been Thalia breaking a curfew, or getting into a fender bender. What they had instead was *this*, and Thalia was thankful for it all the same.

Abraham stayed at the table nursing a glass of red wine. Thalia gave him no attention until there was a knock at the door and he got up to answer it.

Under the sound of running water, Thalia only made out that the voice was young, female, and whatever this visitor said, it'd made her father laugh.

She found her mother's gaze and raised a brow. Fiona glanced toward the dining room, but looked just as confused as Thalia was. And when Abraham finally came in with this visitor in tow, Fiona's reaction was warning enough.

Thalia didn't recognize the girl at first glance, and that made the eventual understanding all the more terrifying.

Raina. The third point to the Warner triplets' sadistic triangle, along with her sister, Michelle, and her dead brother, Oliver.

Raina, who knew how to cut baby witch Thalia with both words and glares, who always looked a moment away from trying her luck with a blade, too.

There was nowhere for Thalia to run. Disguise or not, this was a surprise she hadn't prepared for, and it tipped the hand of this situation.

"You must be Annie!" Raina didn't offer a hand, but she held out a basket of home-baked treats wrapped in pink cellophane and nestled in a checked cloth. "I made this for you!"

The dead weight in the pit of Thalia's stomach wouldn't budge. Stiffly, she took the treats and smiled. "Thank you," she mustered. "Have we met?"

"Oh no, not yet, but Pastor Abraham told me there was a new girl my age in town, and I wanted to invite you to Bible study."

Now Thalia noticed the little flyer in Raina's hands.

She slipped a lock of dark hair behind her ear, just like she used to before levying a cruel insult at Thalia. Only this time, she paired it with a welcoming smile. "We meet Saturday evening, so you're just in time for our next one!"

Thalia couldn't think of anything she'd rather do less, but she couldn't exactly say no, could she? In fact, Abraham was looking upon this moment with such tender joy, he was probably already planning a way to turn Annie Swift into one of his loyal followers. The less suspicion on her, the better. The more he trusted her, the better.

So, Thalia took the flyer and thanked the girl who'd almost died by her hand. "I would be honored."

30

jailah

In the Mesmortes cafeteria, Iris and Jai found that their usual table felt too big without Logan and Thalia. The empty seats only reminded them that the others weren't just away for the week but were staying in the least safe place for witches like them.

"Wanna do a booth?" Jai asked.

They slid into a small two-seater. The table was a little rickety, so Iris slipped a stack of napkins under it, to Jai's amusement.

"What?" The deathwitch laughed. "Sometimes the mundane way is the easier way." She rifled in her Mesmortes-branded knapsack and pulled out a pink flyer. "You see this? Someone's handing them out in Topthorne House."

It was a petition to not only ban hexeaters from Haelsford, but also to give witches free rein to use their magic in any defense necessary. "Damn."

Iris took a big gulp of iced coffee. "Banning's never gonna happen. How do you tell a regular-degular mundane from a hexeater if they don't have the tattoos? I mean, all the ones I've come across made it very clear that they wanted my blood or to make me their queen or whatever, but wouldn't they just . . . stop doing that to gain access to town?"

"True. I used to think they were real goofy, but mostly harmless, until that boy went for Logan. Wish one of them would roll up on me like that."

"Just a look at him, and he would've skipped town and changed his name." Iris grinned. "Weird that the Council hasn't said anything about it."

Jailah pushed her home fries around her plate. "They don't really care about us like that."

Iris paused, mid-bite. "Huh?"

She lowered her voice and got Iris up to speed about her meeting with Highest Witch Evelyn. Though confusion flickered in Iris's eyes, her voice was even. "You told her about the blackthorne?"

Jailah frowned. "*That's* what you're concerned about?"

"I guess I just think we should keep everything within the coven."

With a petulant huff, Jailah leaned back into the booth.

Iris lifted a reassuring hand. "Not saying you were wrong, but the more we tell them, the easier it might be to let something slip, right?"

Let something slip? Jailah's grip on her fork tightened in response to this undeserved display of doubt. "But it was cool when I was using my position with the JWC to find out if they knew about Bloom, yeah? Or to hear anything about the Swamp growing."

Iris soured. "Whoa, okay, fair—"

"You really think I'd say something that got us into trouble?"

"No!" Iris shook her head in bewilderment. "That's not what I said at all. I trust you with my whole damn life, Jailah. I want us all to be safe from potential hexbinding just like you do. *Damn*. What's your problem today?"

256

"Forget it, forget this whole conversation."

"No, I don't want to." Iris began furiously opening sugar packets and dumping them into her coffee. "So, there's blackthorne under the school, and everyone knows about it but the students. What about faculty?"

Jailah shrugged. "Doubt it. It seems like only Council members and higher are in on it. Iris, if you had felt the magic from Evelyn and her guards . . . Never felt anything like it before. Shit ain't fair."

"Never has been," Iris replied. "You've heard me complain a million times about the deathwitch track here basically being nonexistent. I guess none of us have ever been shown the way to our full potential."

"And those of us without Pulls would never even look into ways to make our witchery stronger outside of school," said Jailah.

Iris turned an ice cube over in her mouth. "What are you gonna do?"

The words gave Jailah pause. Perhaps it meant nothing at all, and was just how it came out, but she immediately thought of how Vero had said *we*. "Nothing. Wouldn't want to get into trouble and let something slip."

Iris's face dropped. "Sis. Seriously?"

Laughing, Jailah rose and planted a big kiss on Iris's head. "I gotta go. You doin' another one of those haunted houses today?"

Glumly, Iris nodded.

"Don't get hurt."

"Where are you running to?"

"The mall, then my nails, then my brows. Wanna come?"

"Mmm, I'll pass. Might accidentally seduce a demon by getting all done up."

Jai laughed. "A'ight, see you later."

Jailah walked away with a familiar thrill. Lying about meeting Veronica . . . it was like she was fourteen again.

At Verity River, Veronica was waiting for Jailah by a dip in the cliff that almost resembled a shallow cave. Dressed in black Nikes, a thin beanie, a basketball jersey, and jean shorts, she was the opposite of Jailah in her pricey leggings and matching top.

Veronica was holding a small burlap sack in one hand and waved her forward impatiently with the other. "You're late!" she shouted over the waves.

"Yeah, 'cause *you're* always late." Jailah climbed down into the dip, shoes slipping against the wet rock. "What's in the bag?"

She held up a hand. "First things first. You look me in my eye and tell me that this isn't a trick."

Jailah held her gaze. "This isn't a trick."

"You're not working for the Council? Spying on me and shit?"

"*No.* I told you why I texted you, and I'm here because I want to be. That's the truth."

Vero looked Jailah up and down. "I don't have alítheia, so you're gonna have to swear on it." She pulled out a small switchblade and pressed the tip into her thumb. "When you came by in the winter, you were so desperate that you offered me a bloodpact. How desperate are you now?"

With her sanctified needle, Jailah pricked her own thumb and presented her hand. Vero took it, and Jailah was sure she wasn't making up the way the jewel Vero wore around her neck shimmered.

"Go 'head," Vero whispered.

A hundred internal voices shouted at her to stop, but Jailah ignored them all. *"A Contract Sealed in Blood."*

Purple vapor grew around their linked hands. Blood dripped between their palms and onto the ground.

Jailah continued. "I haven't spoken about this meeting or Veronica Dominguez's magic to anyone. Neither the Haelsford Witchery Council nor the Highest Witch of the Americas nor any other witch is behind this. I'm acting of my own free will. Should I betray Veronica hereafter, she in entitled to—"

Suddenly, Veronica yanked her hand away. The vapor dissipated, and the magic between them dimmed as the bloodpact broke before it could be completed.

"Well, damn, okay." Vero gave an impressed nod. "I believe you."

Half-dazed with relief, Jailah wiped her hand on her leggings. Had she really just attempted to bind herself to Vero?

Vero was unfazed. She dropped to the ground and sat cross-legged atop the damp rock. From her sack, she pulled out three pieces of jewelry that, like her necklace, shone strangely.

Jailah sat across from her, the anticipation building between them.

"When I was a kid I used to love watching my cousins do magic whenever we went to my aunt Simone's place in New Orleans," Vero started, rubbing the crescent moon gem in her palms. "Their magic always looked so fun, so *free*. My mama used to argue with her about putting my cousins in a coven academy, but Tante Simone refused. They were witchy but went to a mundane school. And you know what, Jai? They never needed no wands, no spells. Just a little blood, a lot of intention, and a connection to their witchy ancestors."

Jailah, in spite of herself, leaned forward. She was riveted by this new knowledge of who Veronica was, not to mention the way Vero's lips moved when she spoke.

"So, I get to Haelsford, and I'm like *cool*, finally, it's my turn. I'm excited by my wand, my books—I was never a great student, but this was different. Like, this was *magic*. Then one summer, I went back to my aunt's place with my cute little wand, and my cute little books, and I couldn't do *any* of the magic they could. Their witchery was like—" She paused, searching for the words. "Jai, their auras were like thunderstorms, and mine was like a little drizzle. My mama said that it was better to learn at an academy, because a home-trained witch could get in over their head. A witch had to know how to control the magic in them so the magic didn't run wild. But, like—"

"It's bullshit," Jailah agreed.

Vero nodded slowly. "We get assigned these spellbooks and learn all these incantations made by some witches we've never met, but why do we learn *those* particular spells? Yeah, I can reform some old witch's spell into one of my own, but what are we not learning? Every time I traveled home during breaks, it was like my witchery was taking deep breaths, and I was tired just trying to keep up. But then I'd get back here, and I was strong again. It was cozy and familiar, because I was used to it."

That was one heavy *it*. "You used to say that Mesmortes was sucking the magic out of its witches," said Jailah.

Vero chuckled, teetering on embarrassment. "Yeah, okay. I wasn't exactly right."

"But you weren't wrong; there's blackthorne growing underneath the school. They're dampening our power, why, to keep us weak?"

"We can have a little power, as a treat. But not *too* much. No, no. Imagine what witches could do to the world if we let our magic loose."

And that chilled Jailah to her core because it was exactly what Evelyn had said. "So how are you accessing your witchery if you're bound?"

Vero tapped her necklace and smirked. "A hexbinding doesn't take away a witch's magic, it just roots it deep inside and locks it up tight. But the magic is still there in my blood, and the blood of all the witches in my family that came before me. My tante Yaya gave me this necklace. This one—" She pointed at a gem resembling the sun, decorated with tiny gold crystals. "This one's from Tío Rafael on my dad's side. You know I never got along with my pops like that, but the witches in his fam are chill. We're all blood, we're connected. They give me a little bit of their magic, and I'm able to wield it."

Jailah heard herself laugh in amazement. Obviously, Vero was telling the truth, Jailah had seen her use magic with her own eyes, but everything she said conflicted with what she'd been taught.

Vero wore a satisfied smirk, but her eyes looked a little sad. "I could do more if I wasn't bound, but just being able to do what I can with my ancestral magic is nice. And, uh . . . I'm building up my tolerance," she added simply. "Not with the sludge, but with the actual stuff."

Jailah's eyes popped open. "You've been *consuming* blackthorne?"

"Uh-huh. Once my binding's done, I don't want anyone, mundane, witchy, whoever, to be able to control me."

Jailah stared at her. "I don't feel any different when I go back home. I've never heard anyone say that they left Haelsford and felt their witchery was stronger. Shouldn't being away from the blackthorne do that?"

But as she spoke the words, she thought of a file she'd read in the Council mail room about a witch whose parents claimed Haelsford was making her sick.

"Yeah, I can't explain that. My guess is it's like a dependency thing. You're exposed to so little of it that you can't register its effects on your magic."

Jailah grimaced. "I don't have any witchy ancestors that I know of, on either side. My folks always said I was the first."

"Doubt that. People like you and me lose our ancestral histories all the time. Unless you got a family tree, how you gonna know for sure that you're the first?"

Jailah couldn't argue with that. Still, she hadn't been passed down any enchanted gems to tap into the magic of her bloodline. "I still think we should tell people."

"Not this again." Vero rolled her eyes.

"We could get the *Haelsfordian* to do a piece, I think Suze from the plant shop is still on their board. But wait, if this is happening everywhere, at every coven academy, then maybe we need to go viral. Let's get some pictures of the plant—"

"Girl, I already went through this, and you know how that ended."

"A'ight, you don't need to be shady—"

"I'm not!"

"Vero, you used to talk about Mesmortes like you wanted to take a bulldozer to it. I should've believed you, or I should've tried to."

Vero's gaze went soft. "Well, now it's my turn to tell you to chill. Even without bloodline magic, there are still things you can do to resist. For one, stop using your wand. The quicker you learn how to pull your magic

262

without it, the better. And I can give you fresh blackthorne so you can start forcing your magic to resist it."

Jailah's stomach twisted uneasily. But she nodded. After all this, she trusted Vero.

Vero reached in and brushed a stray curl away from Jailah's eyes. "We can't take on the whole coven academy system, but we *can* rebel, even if it's just for us."

31

logan

Annex's Holy Healers met after mass on Friday evenings. Logan attended the service and found that every seat was full. *Fascinating*, she thought, watching Abraham Turner command the audience's attention. Logan's family practiced religion in the most casual ways. Most of her family attended holiday masses and celebrated Christmas, but the older she got, the less she'd been forced to go. She imagined that her mother considered herself a believer of God, but even prim and proper Diane Wyatt would've been annoyed by the theatrics here.

Logan hadn't originally planned to attend any of the service, but she thought it might be good to be spotted here before she followed Bennett and the others to the meeting. Now that she was here, it was hard to look away. Though, of course, the way scripture was being manipulated here was far more dangerous than the strobe lights and sound effects implied.

She spotted Bennett during the communion line, whispering to one of his friends before taking the eucharist. And when mass finally ended, Logan slipped out of her pew and into the crowd behind them. The two men joined up with three others, and Logan watched them descend a stairwell into the basement. She looked over her shoulder, and once the footsteps quieted and she was sure no one was paying her any attention, she went after them.

The stairs led to a dim hallway with a large room on the other end, one with shiny laminate floors and fluorescent lights. Judging from the seasonal decorations poking out of the stuffed supply closest, this was where they held their parties and gatherings. This would've been a great time to put some sort of eavesdropping spell to use, but Logan had to settle for a more mundane option. She stood just outside the open doors and listened.

Logan heard the men setting up tables and folding chairs. Chip bags crinkled as snacks were poured into bowls. Cans popped open, drinks fizzing under the sound of laughter.

A pair of quick footsteps sounded on the stairs behind her. Cursing, Logan scrambled into the supply closet, elbowing a frighteningly jolly Santa Claus statue out of the way.

Through the slim opening of the door, Logan saw Thalia's father dust off his sleeves and straighten his tie before entering the room. She didn't have to strain to hear the cheers that sounded at his arrival.

"Now, now, settle down, boys!" The pastor laughed. Though Logan couldn't quite see him, she imagined a puffed-out chest and an air of importance. "Oh no, none for me tonight, Ryan, thank you. Last time I drank with y'all, I nearly passed out up in the pews."

Logan frowned as the laughter grew.

"Anyway, anyway, forgive me for not staying tonight. We got company at home. Wes, don't forget to lock up, yeah?"

After a few parting remarks, Pastor Abraham returned to the hall and climbed the stairs.

From the meeting room, Logan heard the unmistakable tune of *Mario Kart*'s theme.

Logan's stomach plummeted, and she extricated herself from the closet carefully, not wanting to send everything crashing behind her. Though Logan was sure the men in that room hated witches, the Holy Healers were nothing but a cover for what . . . bro time? She'd been terrified about what she might see or hear tonight, but she hadn't expected to be left disappointed. They were fast approaching day four in Annex and she'd made no progress in helping Thalia find any evidence against Abraham.

She stuck around for another few minutes to be sure that this wasn't a more nefarious gathering, but after the third chant of *chug it, chug it!* she was confident that there was nothing here of importance.

There was an exit on the opposite side of the hallway, the red sign illuminated in the dark. If anyone was still upstairs, whether Pastor Abraham or otherwise, she'd have to explain herself. So she waited for another outburst of drunken cries, then raced across the hallway to the door.

On the other side, a man was seated atop a low wall with a cigarette hanging from his lips.

Shit. Shit!

Bennett grinned wide at the sight of her. He smelled like a seedy bar— cheap beer and ashtrays. "Sweet girl!"

Logan looked around. They were at the bottom of a brick stairway that led up to the street. The small alleyway was surrounded by shops with apartments stacked atop them.

Quickly, she put on a smile. "Oh! Hey! I remember you." She took a half step toward the stairs.

He scratched his head. "What are you doing around so late?"

Logan sighed a laugh. "I . . . got lost. This church is massive!" She hooked a thumb over her shoulder, then twisted to look back at it, using the motion to take a few steps away from him. Her voice was shaky, but she hoped he didn't notice. "Gave myself a little tour after mass and got turned around. Thought I was going to the bathroom but landed in the basement."

Bennett chuckled. "Gotta use the buddy system next time. Pair up with someone who knows his way around." He hopped off the ledge and stood before her. He was just a bit taller than she was, but broad-shouldered. He wore a high school football jersey under his camo vest, though Logan thought he must've been a decade out of school.

"Right," she said finally. The attempted perkiness landed flat. "Thanks. Good night."

She'd hoped she was overthinking the situation, but Bennett blocked her way. "Let me walk you back."

"No, I—" She wanted to sound tough, but her voice cracked and her face went hot. "I'm not interested."

This amused him. "We don't want you to get lost again, huh?"

Logan exhaled hard. "I can find my way."

Desperate, she pushed past him.

Though he was behind her, though she could not see Bennett, she *felt* him reach to grab her arm. As a witch, Logan possessed some inherent instincts and connections to other witches. Her gut feelings were sharper, and she could sense how strong another witch was through their aura.

This new feeling was nothing like that. Her body moved of its own accord, and when she spun and caught Bennett's wrist in her hand, it was like his body opened up to her. She felt his heartbeat stutter in complete shock at her countermove.

That makes two of us, Logan thought, stunned along with him. She tasted and smelled copper like her mouth was full of blood.

Her magic pooled around her fingers into clawlike points that dug into his skin. All the while, Logan wrestled back the sudden and heady desire to *bite* him.

What the hell is wrong with me?

Bennett's face screwed up in horror at the sight of her proxy glow.

Time slowed around Logan. She was here in Annex, and she was trawling through the Swamp with her pack. Her senses were aflame. She felt everything a hundred times over.

Before Bennett could yell for help, she assessed their surroundings. The streets were empty, but she saw a flash of movement behind a second-floor apartment above a café. The lights clicked on.

Logan had no choice. Before the shades were pulled open, she lifted her hands, pushed out an invisibility orb, and *Shunned* the noise.

"WITCH!" Bennett screamed, face screwed up in hate.

Now free from her touch, he lunged for her. Another burst of instinct and bloodlust rippled through her, and Logan kicked him hard in the stomach.

He fell forward and hit the ground. The sound jolted Logan. "Fuck! Are you okay? Wait, no, no, I don't care if you're okay . . ." Wincing, she peered down at him. "But you are okay, right?"

He groaned in agony.

Gasping, Logan bent over and grabbed her knees. Her mind scrambled for an idea. What now? Invisible to the eye and *Shunned* silent, she was safe at the moment, but she couldn't just leave Bennett here.

What do I do? What do I do? What would the Red Three do?

"Bitch," Bennett cursed, laboring to get to his feet. "I'm gonna make . . . make you pay . . ."

Logan lifted her head at him. Even in her fear, anger wicked off her in thick waves.

"Just so you know," she hissed, "the last two boys that put their hands on me didn't like what came next. Try it again, and you're gonna wake up tomorrow morning in the body of a black cat. Got it?"

His confidence melted away. Logan was grateful that men like him hated witches with such ignorance that they'd never thought to look into the limits of their power. He looked around desperately, and Logan thought for a moment that she really was going to have to find some . . . body swap spell, but he ultimately slumped in deference.

"Smart choice." She clenched and unclenched her fists. This was a dangerous idea, but she was here now. It was too late to turn back. The window above them was dark, at least. Might as well make the most of this.

Logan took a deep, steadying breath. "Tell me everything you know about Abraham Turner."

When she got back to the motel, Thalia screeched at the sight of her. "Oh my god! Where were you?"

Trent pulled her in, closing the door behind her. "Oi, you look like you just ran to Haelsford and back."

At this, Thalia stopped to really look at her. She was still clearly furious, but attempted to soften her voice. "You're supposed to signal me at nine. I had to make an excuse to leave the house and come here! We were just about to go look for you."

"I'm sorry, complete shit show—" Logan dropped herself onto the bed. "I don't think your dad has anything to do with the missing witches, T."

Thalia turned her head like she hadn't heard. "How do you know that?"

"It's a really long story—like I said, shit show—but I got everything out of one of his little underlings, this dude named Bennett."

Thalia's expression turned bleak. "Bennett Parsons?"

"I guess so."

"You know this dude?" Trent asked.

She grimaced in response. "He'd just started teaching at the high school my last year here. Had a reputation among freshman girls."

Logan's stomach twisted. "If you wanna see him now, he's taking a very deep nap behind the church. I think he drank too much."

Slowly, Thalia raised a brow. Logan had her to thank for the sleeping spell she'd used; it was one Thalia put on Theodore Bloom. Her hope was that when Bennett woke up, he'd think it was all a vivid nightmare. If not, Logan would be the second witch in their coven with a price on her head.

"There are no Holy Healers. They're just a bunch of sorry dudes hanging out under the guise of worship and witch hunting. It's a damn joke."

Trent's gaze shifted between them. "What's the point?"

"To make everyone think they're useful? To make the town feel safe?"

She turned to Thalia. "No one else saw me use my magic, I made sure of it. But now that I've used it, my dampening's not going to last much longer, and, Thalia . . . if you want to settle things with your dad for what he did to you, go ahead. But I had Bennett scared shitless under the threat of feline transformation, and I don't think he was lying."

Thalia chewed her bottom lip. "Parsons is a nobody. My father has real friends who would help him with his work."

Logan tried a different approach. "You said he does mass three times a week, then charity work and social events on other days. When would he have the time to go round up witches?"

Thalia scoffed, disgusted. "Yeah, he's such a saint! Why are you defending him?"

Logan jerked back at the accusation. "I'm not! T, I just gave myself up as a witch so that I could dig into his plans. I'm on your side. But you said yourself that even your mom wasn't sure if it was him."

Logan looked to Trent for help and saw that he was already deep in thought, scrambling for the right thing to say.

Thalia never gave him the chance. "Maybe you should go home, Logan."

As much as she wanted to protest, Logan kept silent for a few moments. She knew that Thalia was just upset that a few days here had yielded nothing, and Logan's questioning of Bennett Parsons only proved that Abraham's hands were clean of *this* particular crime.

Logan shook her head. "I'm not leaving unless you're coming with me."

Thalia's eyes narrowed. "What good's a baby witch who just started using her magic to me?"

It stung, striking Logan right where Thalia wanted. But Logan held firm, throwing her hands out in an exaggerated shrug. "I guess we'll just have to wait and see."

Cursing, Thalia jabbed a finger in her face. "You're not *me*. You can't wipe a man's memory without a ton of practice that we both know you don't have."

"All right, easy, Thalia," Trent warned.

Thalia snapped at him. "Stay out of this!"

Logan flinched against the flicker of witchery that Thalia exuded. Gray flashed in the blue eyes she'd been wearing for the past few days. "T, you need to calm down before your disguise breaks!"

Thalia ignored her. It was like Logan was talking to a completely different person. Thalia was always so calm, so reserved. She calculated before planning, she considered her words carefully. Logan didn't recognize her friend here, and it had nothing to do with the face she was wearing.

"What you did tonight put all of us at risk," Thalia spat. "Not only did you use your magic, but you *left Parsons alive.*"

Fear curdled in the pit of Logan's stomach. "What?"

"Go back and take care of him, or leave town before he wakes up and starts telling everyone to hunt you down."

"Thalia." The name trembled in Trent's mouth.

"I know you can," Thalia continued, voice dripping with animosity. "You killed Bloom."

"That was different," Logan whispered. "And we were in the Cavern. You want me to kill Parsons, then what? Leave a dead body in the alleyway outside the church?"

It was Thalia's turn to offer that exaggerated, sardonic shrug. "I guess you're just gonna have to go back to Haelsford and do your little lessons. You're in way over your head." Then she stomped out of the room and slammed the door behind her.

Trent and Logan didn't move. They shared a stunned silence that seemed to stretch for hours. When Trent finally sat next to her, his hands were trembling along with hers. "She's having a hard time seeing things clearly," he said gently. "Can't blame her."

"No, we can't," she agreed. "I'm not angry, I'm just . . . sad for her."

"We'll try again tomorrow."

Logan looked up at him. His love for Thalia was so clear in his eyes, and Logan had to trust that she'd be okay with only him by her side. "No, I think she's right. I should go."

Trent shook his head. "Come on, Logan."

She offered him a teary smile. "I'm okay, I'm not running home to sob about it. I mean, I might cry a little, but I'm just a crier in general. If I'd gotten some info about Abraham, it would've been worth it, but I didn't, and now Parsons's a loose end." Under Trent's sad expression, his silence confirmed that he understood. Logan cleared her throat and wiped her face. "I'm going to give you something, just in case."

Logan went over to her knapsack. There was a hidden pocket stitched into the lining. She called forward a small bit of witchery, and the enchanted stitches fell apart. From it, she pulled out a porcelain box, now covered in yellow gems that pulsed with suppressive energy.

Trent groaned at the sight of it. "Aw, *god*. That again?"

"Just in case! I'm a baby witch, after all. And so are you." She ran her fingers over the casing. "My sister helped me with this sanctifum. It's stronger, and—"

"I *cannot* use my magic, Logan—I don't even know how."

She placed the amplyfyr on the weathered dresser.

"We're in Annex. You might have to learn, not just for Thalia, but for yourself." She hugged him hard even as he was still processing everything. "Unlearned or not, bound or not, you're still a witch. Your blood is magic."

32

iris

Iris rapped her fingers against the steering wheel gleefully. "You know, I think we're getting the hang of this."

From the passenger side, half-covered in what Iris could only describe as *monster goop*, Bex Beaumont stared her down with the clear intent of murder.

The demon in St. Stephen Church in Rockburn, Florida, was smaller than the one they'd put down just a few days ago in Port Barrow. Though Bex had told Iris that it wasn't urgent, and that it had a few months before going fully corporeal, Iris wanted to see what a half-born demon looked like.

It was gross. A slimy, sluglike creature that moved through the church walls, only appearing after midnight. Bex, Iris's Harbinger, never spoke in Death's voice like Mathew had, but she was tasked with serving as Iris's source of knowledge for nearby places of concern. According to Bex, the demon was the result of a botched summoning performed by a novice witch with no necromantic Pull. Iris had a few words for this young witch but talked herself out of finding them.

Exterminating the demon was easy but messy. It perished in an explosion of glowing gel. Iris had brought up a *Shield* in time, but Bex had lunged to save the diamond earring that had fallen from her ear. Thankfully, the goop was harmless.

"Gonna let me clean that up yet?" Iris teased. "You're lucky I let you in my car like that."

Bex was stubborn. She was adamant in performing the cleaning spell, even though her brand-new, rose-gold-and-chrome wand still looked awkward in her hand. "I can do it," she spat.

"Suit yourself."

Iris refocused on the dark road. It was well past two a.m. Neither had wanted to stay in Rockburn, though the thankful clergy there offered up a hot meal and beds. Iris hadn't expected *applause* when it was done. She was so shocked to see the little crowd of residents and nuns that she had put up her wand, ready to defend herself against the mob. Instead, the nun offered a thankful hand. Sage and Mortimer had taught her proper manners, but Iris could only stand there in silent confusion in the face of such gratitude.

Bex whispered a cleaning incantation. The end of her wand fizzled.

One hand on the wheel, Iris used the other to press her thumb onto the sacrificial needle standing inert in the center cup holder. Eyes on the road, she swung her wand. *"Clean It Up!"*

The spell settled over Bex, melting away the goop and the slightly sour smell that came with it.

Bex scoffed. "Hey! I almost had it!"

"Girl."

"I just helped you destroy an evil blob of gel, I think I can do a simple spell!"

The slightly upturned tone of Bex's voice tickled Iris. She sounded so bratty, and Iris enjoyed putting her in her place. "You've really taken to being a deathwitch and all, but that's 'cause Death chose you." From her peripheral vision, she felt the heat of Bex's glare. "All that back there and at Port Barrow? You didn't have to learn it, Death gave it to you. *I* can do spells that have nothing to do with necromancy."

Bex didn't argue. She was helpful; Iris could admit that. Having Bex to heighten Iris's power, set the runes, and watch her back made everything more efficient. But Iris used both protective and offensive magic during these rituals, and Bex was useless in that regard.

"That's why we came here tonight," Iris confessed. "I thought a little demon would put up less of a fight, and I was right. Until you get your shit together, we can't face anything like the Port Barrow demon again. I don't want to get hurt, and I assume you don't either?"

Bex crossed her arms. Iris took the silence as acceptance.

She turned into the final stretch of road before Haelsford. "You should ask if you're too late to join summer session. You've missed a month, but it might help. Mesmortes has a fast track for late-bloomed witches, but it's still gonna be at least two years until you graduate if you can test out of the mundane courses—"

"I'm not going to Mesmortes."

Iris glanced at her. This partnership, if Iris could even call it that, was still new enough that Iris hadn't considered what she would do if her tether-slash-Harbinger moved out of Haelsford to attend a coven academy elsewhere. "Where'd you choose? Is it in Florida?"

"I'm staying at Devereaux." Bex reached to change the radio station.

Iris slapped her hand away. "The mundane school?"

"Yup."

"Are you getting a witchery tutor?" *I know your ass can afford it.*

"I didn't know that was a thing." Bex turned away to look out her window. "It's not really any of your business, but I'm just gonna teach myself."

"Uh." Iris faltered. "If you had a witchy family and support, that'd be fine—"

Bex laughed sardonically at that.

"But you can't do it on your own. And *I'm* not babysitting you."

"Never asked you to."

Iris needed to get this girl home before she bit Bex's head off. The cool nonchalance made Iris want to scream. "It is my business actually, because you're not going to be strong enough to handle a bigger demon if something happens to me during one of these rituals, and I'm not gonna be your little shield if shit goes down at our next one."

Bex shrugged. "Then I quit."

Now Iris laughed. "No, you don't. You love it too much."

Bex shifted uncomfortably in her seat. She was silent, but Iris knew she'd aimed true. The tether between them sizzled and tugged.

"You wear that smug look like you don't care about anything but yourself, but you jumped in at Port Barrow without even thinking about it. You didn't even know me, and I still barely know you. But I saw you. You *loved* watching that demon get blasted to bits. Two seconds ago, you yelled at me for doing a spell before you could, and now you're gonna quit? Come *on*.

"I can't tell you what to do, but at least be honest. It's because you're scared of your parents. You can't enroll in Mesmortes because they won't let you." Iris squeezed the steering wheel. "I don't know what that feels like, but I know it's not fair."

She pulled into the side street that held Beaumont Manor. Immediately, Mathew flung open the front door and walked toward them. He wore a dark blue pajama set that looked straight out of some bougie catalog, and had left the top buttons undone.

Iris lowered her window. "Really. Boobs out?"

He winked. "You love it." He glanced at his sister. "How'd it go?"

Before Bex opened the door, she gave Iris a hard look. Was it a thanks? The tether bloomed with satisfying energy. "Later," she muttered.

Mathew watched her walk away. "So. Good?"

"She's just in a funk. A lot's happened in the past week."

"Yeah." Mathew pressed his hand against his chest. "I don't feel it anymore. You said that it's really Bex that shares the tether with you, but I guess I didn't expect to lose mine."

Iris drank in the disappointment in his eyes. She liked him when he was undone like this. It made her feel less afraid of how easily he made her feel vulnerable, too. "We don't have to be tethers to be . . ."

He dipped his forehead to hers.

"To be two people that just happen to know each other and occasionally frequent the same space."

Mathew grinned, face crinkling in delight.

She tilted her mouth up to his.

"Goddamn it!" Up ahead, Bex screeched. Iris refused to turn away from Mathew, but she heard the violent jangling of a doorknob. "Matty! You locked the door behind you—OH MY GOD, ARE YOU MAKING OUT RIGHT NOW?"

"I wish," Mathew said, sighing quietly. "So, tonight? I was thinking... maybe we just do something chill instead of the banquet. That okay with you?"

Iris perked up. "*Hell* yes. But, like, if you want to go, then we can."

His lips softened into a sweet smile. "Let's skip it. Not really in the mood to socialize either—"

"MATHEW AINSLEY BEAUMONT, FOR FUCK'S SAKE!"

Iris's eyes widened. "Ainsley!"

Gaze still focused on Iris, he called out, "Spare's under the mat!" Then he popped a kiss onto her forehead. "I'll see you tonight."

Back at Topthorne House, Iris took a long shower, slipped into a pair of light sweats, and flopped onto her bed. Her body was exhausted, but her mind was running. She thought of Thalia, Trent, and Logan. Logan had sent a simple text that they were okay, but Iris still wanted them back home. She wondered what Bex was going to do and made a mental note to look into the compendium later. Could she still be a Reaper without her Harbinger? Or was Death going to strip her of the title?

Doesn't matter. I got what I need.

The glossy red runes were tucked away in Iris's bottom drawer. Two stones for two souls. Iris could keep her parents' spirits intact at Stony

280

House. She could spend time with them after graduation. Perhaps she would even bring her coven along, the boys, too, and have a real home away from Haelsford. And under the experienced eye of her mother and the care of her father, Iris would explore necromancy in ways Mesmortes never let her dream of.

33

jailah

After years with her wand, Jailah shouldn't have expected that her magic would be easy to wield without it. But she still suffered crushing disappointment when she couldn't call it forward. She felt foolish, sitting on the beanbag chair in her dorm room, her hand extended toward a stack of junk mail to levitate. The space between her fingers hurt with how hard she was flexing them.

"You really ain't gotta do alla that," Veronica teased, her face beaming on Jailah's phone screen.

"I'm used to holding a wand. Thought it'd signal to my body that I wanna do a spell."

"Well, don't strain nothing."

Jailah wiped sweat from her brow. "This is silly," she muttered. "I'm not a proxy, and I don't have an ancestral connection to boost my witchery."

"You've been at this for like a day, Jai. You *just* found out that there are other paths to magic. I know you're *you*, but shit ain't easy."

Jailah rubbed the scar around her wrist. "Yeah, but I'm still pissed."

Vero chuckled. "Not gonna lie, it's funny as hell to watch you struggle."

"Glad you're having fun." Jailah took a long drink from her water bottle. She didn't have a textbook to draw from, or a mentor to help. She had a feisty ex-girlfriend to heckle her, and perseverance that waned with every failed attempt. And the High Witches had everything. Magic unfettered, knowledge kept away from the general witch population. It was so easy for Jailah to picture herself at Evelyn's side in her office at the World Witchery headquarters. Her gut twisted. Was she so weak that a few days of failure had her scrambling for her old goals, though she knew the injustice at its core?

"Hey," said Vero. "Stop moping. And you've got that Council event soon, and I know how long you take to get ready."

"I'm not going. Ain't got the energy in me to fake smile and schmooze."

"They're gonna notice that you skipped it. Might get suspicious. You haven't told me, but I know *something* went down that you're hiding."

Jailah tensed. While she and Vero had found something like peace, she wasn't going to reveal any of her coven's secrets. "Evelyn isn't here to dig into anything for real. She just wanted to do her little speeches and rub it in Lucia's face." She cracked her knuckles. "Do you wanna get dinner later?"

She asked without thinking, like they hadn't just spent a few years apart. It slipped out as naturally as it would have if she'd asked her girls, and now she felt a flutter of embarrassment.

Vero clicked her tongue. An eternity seemed to pass before she shrugged. "You treatin'?"

Jailah rolled her eyes. "Fine."

"Lobster it is—" There was a knock on her end, and Vero turned away from the phone. "My mom's back, I gotta go. Jailah, go to the Council lunch. It's better that they think you're in with them for now, yeah?"

Jailah glanced at the yellow sundress hanging on her closet door. She had zero desire to see Evelyn, Lucia, and the rest, but Vero had a point.

The luncheon was set up on the massive back lawn behind the Council building. High-profile mundanes rubbed elbows with Council witches, and Evelyn was surrounded by a circle of Mesmortes staff and elder witches who ran shops in town. Her haughty laugh carried over the sophisticated sounds of Haelsford's community orchestra.

She spotted a couple of JWC members lingering by the refreshments. She felt the impulse to tell them that they needed to mingle with the higher witches and make connections instead of sticking to one another but couldn't muster up the energy.

She felt eyes on her. From a group of chattering adults, High Witch Lucia Alvarez met her eye. Jailah plastered on a smile and hoped that would be it, but Lucia excused herself from the conversation.

"There you are," she said, with a hand on Jai's arm to angle her away from the party. "I was beginning to wonder if you weren't going to make it."

"I'm sorry, High Witch. Just got a little sidetracked."

"Happens to the best of us. Well, I've been meaning to talk to you." She took a few steps forward, putting some more distance between them and the gathering. "I hear you made an interesting discovery this summer."

Jailah blinked. "Ma'am?"

Lucia smiled slightly. "Every few years, some curious witch discovers their coven academy's inhibitor. I should've known it would be you. Honestly, I guessed Blackwood—greenwitches often have the advantage—or last year's standout, Anika Johnson. I was wrong. Kudos, we're all quite impressed."

Jailah couldn't believe what she was hearing. "What?" she choked out.

"I know it must have been a shock." To her credit, Lucia did look remorseful where Evelyn was flippant. "Rooting inhibitors under coven academies was a decision made long ago."

"I don't care," Jailah sputtered, and she didn't care that she was getting emotional in front of a senior witch either. "How many witches could've been saved if they'd had their full power in the face of the Wolves? Maybe the Swamp could have been destroyed by now!"

"A few Councils in witchtowns across the country have actually uprooted theirs, but Haelsford's different. The inhibitor—"

"Blackthorne," Jailah interrupted. "Call it what it is."

Lucia lifted her chin. She glanced around before continuing. "Blackthorne doesn't only dampen a witch's power. In its natural form, it can also impede a hex or a spell. You understand? The blackthorne is also keeping the Swamp from devouring the whole town."

Speechless, Jailah thought of Thalia. She'd said that the greenwitchery she'd done in the Swamp forged a connection between them, but Thalia had no idea that the Swamp had *always* been alive, pushing at the border that the blackthorne reinforced. She just happened to give it a bit of new life.

"Simmons, even you don't know how truly dangerous magic can be in the wrong hands, or even in well-meaning but *inexperienced* hands. Keeping magic in check helps us stay safe from the treachery of our own kind. But Mesmortes's inhibitor also stops Haelsford from succumbing to the

Strigwach Sisters' hex." Lucia exhaled sharply. "And I wish I'd had the chance to explain all this before you fell in with Véronica Dominguez."

Jailah's blood curdled.

"I was a young witch once, too. I know how exciting it can be when you first gain your magic." High Witch Lucia squeezed Jailah's arm patronizingly. "I see that you still feel some loyalty to her, or some guilt, and I'm sorry that I can't consider your request to revisit her hexbinding."

Jailah resisted the urge to pull her arm away. Lucia seemed genuine. There was no joy here, no *wink-wink* conspiratorial coyness that Evelyn favored. Lucia really believed that Vero was a danger to Jailah and a blight on witchery as if the elder witches weren't actively impairing the younger ones themselves, and that was just as unforgivable.

Jailah looked Lucia in the eye. "Veronica didn't deserve what y'all did to her. Yes, Yara's spell was an awful thing, but seven years hexbound is too severe for a young witch."

Lucia's lips pursed into a grim line. "For your sake, I won't tell anyone that you said that."

"Tell whoever you want."

Lucia held up a hand. "We're done here. I think you should go home, Jailah."

Jai was already walking away from the conversation before Lucia got the last word out. She raced back home, needing to be alone, wanting to *scream*.

Inside her room, she pulled out her largest cauldron and dropped in a couple of twigs for kindling. With her wand, she added a spark.

Next year's spellbooks sat in a neat clean stack atop her desk. She took the first and began ripping out the pages with both hands, relishing how cleanly the paper separated from the binding. One by one, she pulled the books apart and gleefully watched them burn, occasionally using a purifying spell to suck away the smoke. She felt drunk off the smell of charred paper and burning ink.

Not yet satiated, she dug around in her desk drawers. Her eye caught a pristine grimoire with red sprayed pages. Hungrily, she licked her lips.

"Reveal Yourself."

The book twitched into the air. It landed as a small, tattered book. Bound in oily leather and full of crinkled, stained pages, it had doomed Vero once, and saved Thalia another time. Iris had it for a while, then handed it over to Jailah, who they both agreed had less of a chance of ever being searched for witchy contraband.

The Most Wicked Works of Olga Yara.

Jailah had desperately flipped through the book for a spell while the Wolves were waiting at the front doors. She'd found *Black Arrows* and was prepared to use it. How was it that she found a perfect spell so . . . conveniently? It hadn't occurred to her to be suspicious at the time, but now she wondered if Yara had embedded even more dark magic in the book than she knew about.

Jailah held the book in tight, trembling hands. "I need something to free my friend."

The book twitched once more, pages flipping violently. The page it stopped on offered a crude spell to rid the body of mortal pains. Jai was fairly certain that just meant death. Technically correct, but utterly wrong.

She closed the book.

This is dangerous.

She opened it again, its heady power dancing and diffusing against her fingers.

I need to be specific.

"I need a spell to break a hexbinding. A strong one. An unbreakable one. A spell to give my friend back her power."

And there, right in the middle of the book, where the seams were thick and black, where the thread perfectly parted the decayed pages, was a scrawled spell.

TRINITY SPELL III

EXCAVATION. FOR SEVERING BONDS.

34

thalia

Thalia spent the morning hating herself. Guilt like this couldn't be shaken off, as much as she tried. When she woke up and trudged back to the motel, Logan was already gone.

"She's taking the evening train home, but left early just in case," Trent explained. There was no judgment in his eyes, but Thalia's face grew hot with shame regardless.

"Sorry," Thalia whispered. She touched her thumb, momentarily forgetting that the sprout there had been pushed down into her skin by Stevie Adler's shadewitchery. "I wasn't very nice to you either."

"We're your friends. We know what you've been up against." He ran his hand over his face. Looked like Thalia wasn't the only one who had trouble sleeping. "I know I haven't been much help since we got here."

"Don't say that," Thalia interjected. "Ignore everything I said last night, this place just makes me lose my shit."

Gently, Trent approached her, like she was a wild animal that might snap back, and Thalia felt another punch of annoyance at herself. He said, "Maybe we should go home."

She dropped her head into her palm. It was hard to look at him when he had so much concern in his eyes. "Yeah," she whispered. "Maybe."

Trent looked like he had something else to say but kept it to himself.

Awkwardly, Thalia retreated toward the door. "If you want to go back now, you should. I've got another day left with this face, and I just need to be sure that I'm not missing anything with my dad. I'll head back tomorrow morning."

"I'm going back with you, T." And he was adamant about it, leaving no doubt in his deep brown eyes. "Have you heard anything about that dude from last night?"

Thalia shook her head. "Best-case scenario, his friends dropped him into his bed to sleep it off. Here's hoping he really doesn't wake up until tonight."

"What are you gonna do today? Need me for anything?"

"I've got one last lead I need to poke at. Stay here. I'll shout if I need you."

Trent nodded. "Be safe out there, T."

---•> ✦ <•---

Raina Warner and her cohort of prim and proper girls were more exhausting than Thalia had imagined. Just half an hour into a three-hour Bible study session, Thalia struggled to feign interest. If she'd had more time, she would've eased her way to the topic of witches, but she had to be proactive.

"I was hoping we could study from the book of Exodus," she announced to the circle.

Tammy, a freckly girl with short curls, smiled. She was always smiling, though, so Thalia didn't take anything from it. "An interesting choice. Is it special to you?"

Raina was at the snack table piling pretzel sticks onto her plate but had turned to Thalia.

"Some of you might have heard this already," Thalia continued. "But a boy I used to love . . . he broke my heart. He became a witch—" She braced herself against the gasps. "And tried to kill me."

Another girl named Elizabeth rushed over to rub Thalia's shoulder. It would've been sweet if she hadn't said, "Damn those witches to hell!"

Yeah.

"You shouldn't say that," Tammy whispered harshly. "We should be praying for his return to God."

Raina approached the circle on the floor, still balancing those pretzels. "There is no such thing. Once a devil is made, it cannot be unmade. Isn't that right, Annie?" She passed out cups of bright red fruit punch and handed out plates of junk food. Honestly, the snacks were the one thing Thalia didn't hate about Bible study.

"Yes," said Thalia.

"Did you love him?"

Thalia forced a pathetic laugh. "He was my first love. I find myself needing to be reminded that his path is drenched in hellfire, and I cannot help him."

"That's true. It's as God says . . ."

Thalia inhaled slowly. "Thou shalt not suffer a witch to live." She felt an itch on her wrist where a hidden tattoo lived. "I saw a strange flyer at the bus station. Is there a witchtown around here?"

Elizabeth wrapped her arms around herself as if a sharp chill had passed through. "I don't even really like saying that word, honestly."

Raina rolled her eyes. "Saying *witch* isn't going to turn you into one."

"You don't know about the power of manifestation, Raina! I'm just being careful."

Thalia clenched her jaw, trying to think of how to steer the conversation back. She expected Raina to mention Thalia's own crimes here, but she only picked at her snacks.

It was Tammy who inadvertently helped her. "There *is* a town near here where some witches live, actually."

Thalia shivered. "How strange, so close to a godly place like this. And judging from the flyer, it seems like a few witches haven't been accounted for. You don't think . . . they could have come *here*, do you?"

"Annex is godly because our pastor works tirelessly to make it so." Elizabeth's wide doe-eyes sparkled with pride. "Witches know not to set foot into our clean town, unless they want to be stoned." She said this all with a smile.

Raina looked pleased. "Who wants to read first?"

Okay, that was a flop. They read from the book of Exodus for an excruciating hour. Thalia nodded and reacted with solemnity when she had to and forced tears into her eyes as if the memory of her lost witchy love was too much to bear.

She was half-asleep by the end of it. They closed their books, but before everyone said their goodbyes, Raina asked Thalia to stay.

"There's something I think you should know." She swallowed. "I know how you feel, being targeted by a witch."

Keeping her mask on was harder here than it had been at her parents' house. Not because Thalia thought Raina might pick up on a quirk that would tip her off, but because in some ways, the tables were turned. Raina was hardly an innocent victim, but in this situation, it was Thalia who had taken from her.

"Oh?" Thalia muttered innocently. "I'm so sorry. Can I ask what happened? If that's okay, if you feel comfortable!"

Raina gave her a teary smile. "Everyone around Annex knows the story. You might have heard about Pastor Abraham's daughter who is a witch."

Thalia nodded, acid in her throat.

"He tried to help her, but a witch can never really be changed from her ways." Raina tilted her head and attempted to blink away the tears. "And she took it out on us. My brother died. She almost killed my sister and me, too."

Is that how it happened? Thalia wanted to ask. She offered Raina her hands instead.

Raina took them immediately. "I feel like I lost my sister, too. My parents separated, and she wanted to go with my dad. I decided to stay here with my mom."

"This witch, do you forgive her? Because I don't know that I've fully forgiven my ex-boyfriend."

Raina shrugged. "Maybe someday. But right now, all I feel is anger."

That, Thalia did understand.

She prepared to ease back into a question about the disappearances, but Raina pulled Thalia into a hug.

Thalia's insides twisted. She wanted to wrench free of this, but Raina held firm.

"I do have one last question, Annie," Raina whispered. "Does this hurt?"

Raina made a jerky movement, and Thalia's world flashed white with pain.

Whatever Raina had jabbed into Thalia's side sent blistering heat throughout her entire body. She twisted violently from Raina's grasp and tried to run, but everything was loud, hot, and dizzying. Had Raina's eyes always been so full of hate? How had Thalia not noticed her sneer when she looked at her? Her too-late witchy senses blared, *run, run, run*. But Thalia could only watch as she slumped. Raina ran her hands up over Thalia's jeans, then up and down her back. Horrified, Thalia felt Raina slip out the wand that she kept strapped against her back.

"Up you go," Raina said.

Thalia's limbs felt like liquid as Raina hoisted her arm over her shoulder. Thalia's mask was slipping. Her face buzzed with her witchery's attempt to keep the disguise.

"You always did have a savior complex." Raina's voice was strained from Thalia's weight as she dragged her out of her living room and into the backyard. The shed at the end of the yard grew closer and closer, though Thalia couldn't quite feel her legs moving.

"What . . . did you do . . . to me?" Thalia whispered. The pain had dulled, but she still couldn't tell her body what to do. And her witchery felt distant, retreating so far back into her consciousness that she couldn't reach it. But she knew this wasn't just blackthorne. That stuff hurt, burned, bit, scarred. This was a dreamy sort of lull, and for that, Thalia was somehow more terrified.

"Patience is a virtue; you might be the devil's spawn, but I know you remember that. Let's get you settled first."

Raina kicked down the door to the shed with surprising strength. She let Thalia go, and Thalia stumbled awkwardly to the ground.

Raina flicked a light switch, and the shed buzzed with electricity and heat. All around Thalia, she saw tiny potted blackthorne plants under grow lights, and the air stung against her witchery.

Flat on her back, Thalia settled onto her elbows. She could only watch as Raina pulled up a chair in front of her.

Thalia let the mask slip. There was no use. Whatever was about to happen, Thalia would make Raina look upon her true face as it did. As she felt her features slip back in place, Raina looked on with diabolical anger.

"He was my best friend," Raina said.

Thalia didn't answer. She tried to reach her magic, but the blackthorne plants kept her from focusing.

"I spent weeks in the hospital, did you know that? I almost didn't make it." She lifted up her shirt and her sleeves, revealing scarred flesh and mottled skin. "Look at what you did, Tallulah."

And Thalia did look. She wouldn't cower from her own sins. She felt something worse than fear. *Guilt.* It started in the pit of her stomach and warmed her face.

Raina dropped her shirt.

Thalia stopped to take a breath. "If you wanted me here . . . you didn't have to . . . kill witches . . ."

"Oh, there are no missing witches." Raina was trying to sound light and smug, but the tears and the strained voice didn't afford her that cool. She wasn't a Bloom, or a Strigwach, or even the old Raina that Thalia used to know. This was a girl cut so fully by pain that all she had left was sadness and a need for vengeance. Raina wiped her nose and pulled a very large knife from the tool counter.

"Witches respond to money the same way mundanes do, you know?" She tapped her index finger against the blade point as she spoke. "I told a few of them to get lost for a few months, and they did. And your wicked mother, hmph. I had a feeling that she hadn't cut ties with you like the good pastor had. She did most of my work for me, telling you all about the disappearances nearby. It was easier than I thought, which is nice, because I really didn't want to hurt anyone."

Thalia forced a scoff. It hurt, but it was worth it to see the annoyance in Raina's face.

"Really, Tallulah. I'm not a hateful person, and I don't want to murder witches. But I do hate *you*."

The lights flickered above them, the blackthorne plants twitching. "What did you stab me with?"

Now Raina did smile out of pride. "Regular old rat poison. Actually, it was in your drink. I just stabbed you because I wanted to."

Weirdly enough, this was the most that Thalia ever understood Raina. "It was an accident," she spat. "A mistake."

"And did you atone? Did you ever even apologize?" Raina lurched forward and held the blade right in front of Thalia's face. If Thalia moved, she'd slice herself up. It was already hard enough to breathe in the vicinity of all these blackthorne plants, and now she had a very sharp knife a good two inches from her eyes.

The blackthorne.

Thalia felt a twitch in her distant witchery. She had never grown any herself, for obvious reasons, except on that night in Haelsford Cemetery, against her will. Now looking at them, she felt an odd sense of peace. She didn't have her wand. She didn't have her needle. But she was still a greenwitch with the Gift of the Earth.

And blackthorne was a plant, just like any other plant.

The plan forming in her head was very, very risky, but she was out of options. "You know, when I look at you, I see myself."

Raina threw her head back and laughed. "Please don't say that vengeance isn't the answer? That I'll regret this?"

Thalia didn't have the energy to shake her head, so she just said, "No. I do believe that there are times where violence is the answer. Obviously."

Raina's laughter died with that.

"You're here to get your revenge. I get that. Problem is . . . I am, too." With all the strength she could muster, Thalia jolted toward the blade.

Raina acted tough, but the sudden movement left her scrambling. Blood seeped from the jagged cut on Thalia's cheek. The blade hit the ground dripping red.

She'd gone deeper than she needed to, which would have to be a problem for her future self. Right now, she shook her head back and forth, letting the droplets splatter on the dark green leaves. They twitched, they bristled.

Thalia dropped her head and cried out. *Come on, baby, come on.*

Her witchery flickered, and then went out.

Raina finally broke from her own trance. Thalia lunged for the discarded blade, but Raina got to it first and swung it with eyes closed.

The new cut across Thalia's chest bled fast.

"Thanks," Thalia seethed, wiping the blood with her hand and flicking it onto the plants. "I think that does it."

With desperation and rage, Thalia reached for the roots all around her and pulled hard on her own witchery. She called to the earth. The magic in her blood answered with a resounding cry, and the blackthorne plants bristled with life. The now unhidden sprouts in Thalia's flesh twitched with new energy.

Raina dropped the knife. Her eyes were wide with wonder and terror.

"You can't beat me, Raina. You could've, once. But I'm not scared of who I am anymore."

Thalia snapped her arm toward Raina, and the blackthorne followed her command, bursting out of the pots in thin, wiry stalks. Raina's scream caught in her throat as they snaked around her legs, her wrists, her neck. She was brought down onto her knees, struggling against the grip of the vines.

But Thalia hadn't thought this through. The more energy she gave the blackthorne, the more their power grew. It was a horrible game of tug-of-war, her feeding the very thing that was hurting her.

She felt a sticky wetness in her ears, her eyes, and her nose. Whatever Raina was seeing, it put the fear of God into her. The girl sobbed as Thalia ambled toward her on weak legs, black blood dripping from the cuts.

"It's not fair," Raina whimpered. "Why do you get to win? How do you get to do what you did and walk away?"

Thalia was too tired to make her voice anything but the shaky, unsure thing it was. "I thought the same thing about you every day that whole year. And what did I win? A new life, a horrible secret? I didn't even get to keep my name."

"My brother died!"

"And you all nearly killed me!"

Raina blinked. The exhaustion worked both ways, it seemed. While anger danced in Raina's eyes, she only groaned.

They were both silent for a few moments, nothing between them but the flickering lights and the sound of their own ragged breaths.

Finally, Raina said, "Are you going to kill me?"

Thalia blinked. "What? No."

"You should," Raina spat with new conviction. "This isn't the end."

"I know. 'One day, *I'll find you.*' That's what you're thinking, right?" She knelt down to Raina's eyeline. "You're making a promise to yourself and to me. You're going to accept this mercy I'm giving you, and once I'm gone, once you're free, you're going to get *stronger.* And then . . ." She lifted Raina's drooping head with a small touch to her chin. "When I least expect it, you'll strike."

Raina didn't speak, but the anger in her gaze said enough.

Thalia shrugged. "I look forward to it." She pulled her wand from Raina's pocket. *"Night-Night."*

Outside, Thalia ran her wand over her wounds, whispering healing incantations and purging the poison from her blood. With the connection to the blackthorne severed, she felt like she could finally breathe again. Thalia didn't bother wiping away the blood and gore on her face as she limped back to her old home. This would be the last time she ever set foot in Annex, and Raina wasn't the only one with a reckoning on her mind.

Even if Abraham Turner hadn't been kidnapping witches, there was retribution to be paid.

35

trent

The day passed with mind-numbing slowness. Maybe it was because his witchery was looming in the back of his subconscious like a bad habit he was trying to break, or because he hated this place, or because Thalia could've been walking to her death for all he knew.

Annex's library was nothing like Haelsford's. Its cramped size didn't bother him, but the books were untouched and uninteresting. It didn't even smell like old books or ink, so what was the point? Still, he trudged through the too-neat shelves, waiting for Thalia to signal that she was okay.

As the sun fell, Trent decided to head back to the motel. He hoped that Thalia was there waiting for him, ready to get back home. It was a lofty wish. Her determination was like nothing he'd ever seen before.

But there was someone waiting at the door of his room.

The woman's eyes popped at the sight of him. She clutched her chest. In worry or shock, Trent wasn't sure, but he knew from one look that this was Thalia's mother.

"H-hi," he blurted. "You're—"

Fiona Turner nodded, still dazed by the sight of him. She glanced over her shoulder to the empty breezeway. "Annie's still not back? She said she'd be back by eight to say goodbye."

Trent's heart plummeted. He shook his head.

Fiona rubbed her forehead. "I'm sorry, uh—"

"Trent," he whispered. "Hogarth."

Fiona looked him up and down. Her smile was thin, but warm. "My husband got a call and took off with a suitcase. I don't know if it was a work thing, or worse—" She swallowed hard. "You should come with me. I don't want you two spending your last night here."

A trail of witchy heat sped across his chest. Fists clenched, he held it back. "Thank you, let me get my stuff."

"Of course." She seemed relieved. "Thank you for being Annie's friend. I'm sure she's home now, waiting for us."

Trent gathered his things quickly. He'd only brought a large backpack's worth of clothes. He tucked the amplyfyr in his pocket with a darkly humorous thought. *Like old times.*

"You must go to Hammersmitt?" Fiona asked quietly on the way over. "That's the other school there?"

"Yes, ma'am."

Fiona's eyes grew wet. "Forgive me. I don't usually get to do the normal stuff like this. Meeting her friends."

Trent's heart tugged. "Maybe one day you can meet the whole crew."

"She's mostly told me about the girls, but I can see why she likes you. You've got a calming energy."

Trent's face warmed. "I'm lucky to have her, Mrs. Turner."

302

"Aren't you charming? Cute, too." She chuckled. "Your mama must be proud."

Another flicker of witchy heat. "She was."

Fiona led Trent to a nice-sized cottage with a perfect lawn. Trent tried to picture Thalia growing up here, but that felt like a betrayal. Thalia never reminisced about this place, not with how horribly her time here ended.

"She's not back yet," Fiona said, guiding him to the small living room. "Want a cup of tea while we wait?"

Trent smiled. "Tea would be lovely."

"Make yourself at home."

She left him then. Antsy, Trent walked around, trying not to think about the pulsating heat in his chest.

He eyed the framed pictures on the sideboard, Thalia's presence a notable omission among the small collection of photos. A young white man smiled to the camera, his arm around a younger Fiona. Trent grimaced at the sight of Abraham Turner and the gray eyes he'd always associated with comfort.

Behind it, there was another picture of Fiona from years ago. She smiled freely, a glint of trouble in her eyes and a peculiar silver bracelet wrapped around her left hand that separated into rings on her fingers.

Invisible flames seized Trent's limbs. Recognition twisted in his mind. He grabbed the picture, knocking the others away in his haste. He'd seen this woman before. *No.* No?

She just reminded him of Thalia, surely.

No, he recognized her.

But how?

The fire of his latent witchery raced through his thoughts, burning through them, eating away at something there. Trent winced. His memories blurred and unblurred, then focused. He saw his mother in a video on a small computer. Her expression dropped at what she saw just off-screen—

There was a woman. He'd seen her on the tapes; he remembered her now. She'd waved Lourdes over with open arms.

Silverhand.

A heavy blow landed on the back of Trent's head, and the photo slipped from his grasp.

36

mathew

Rebecca flicked on his bedroom lights with little care for his sleep-laden eyes.

"Matty, why are *you* napping? I was the one out battling demons, not you."

Mathew groaned. "Yeah, but *I* was waiting up, worried sick."

"Awwww! Poor widdle baby, sitting around, worried sick!" She gagged, miming a barf. "You're gonna be late for your little date."

At that, Mathew flung away his covers. He checked his phone. There was a missed call from his father, and a text from his mother, both of whom were taking separate luxury *wellness retreats*. He swiped them both off-screen; Iris had texted him as well.

meet me at the Mesmortes chapel at 7.

His skin flushed. Thankfully, he still had an hour and a half before meeting her.

"You're *welcome*," Rebecca sneered. She was wearing a plain tank, her death mark visible. "I should curse you for your bad manners."

He chuckled. It was nice to see her embracing her witchery. Looking at her now, he felt foolish for keeping the truth of his own death marks from Iris, who had welcomed Becky to the world of necromancy with open arms—or mostly open arms. Whatever the equivalent was for Iris. As much as he wanted the world's simplest date with the girl he was crushing on, he decided then that he would tell Iris about what he saw when he touched Chloe. There was no way around it. Three touches, three visions. He'd kept it from her for too long, and now felt ashamed for stalling. He wasn't her tether, but he was her Runekeeper, and he had to trust that whatever came next, they would face it together.

And maybe with Rebecca, which was annoying, but *fine*.

"I gotta get ready," he said, shooing her away.

"And I have sixteen episodes of *Bad Witches Club* to watch. Have fun!"

On his way toward Mesmortes, he stopped by Soma Café and texted Iris.

Left my sunglasses at Soma, you want anything?

"Mathew?"

He lifted his head, then blinked. Seeing Chloe sitting at a table in Soma was odd. He worked three shifts a week, and never once saw her there. She was out of place, like seeing a teacher at the mall, or a summer camp friend at school.

She rose from her seat to stand by him. "This place is cool, you come here a lot?"

Mathew wasn't in the mood to try and force pleasantries, as nice as Chloe was. "Yeah." He managed a smile. "I work here actually. Sorry, one sec." He stepped behind the counter, said hi to Jin and Kristine, then grabbed his glasses off the syrup rack.

Chloe waited for him as he did. Mathew briefly remembered a strange feeling he'd had at the party. It wasn't about the vision, but he couldn't quite parse it.

He checked his phone. Iris declined anything from the café but did threaten him about being late. He smiled, then looked up to Chloe. "I've got a thing, but nice seeing you."

Chloe nodded her goodbye, but Mathew felt steps behind him as he exited the shop.

There was a car waiting in the empty lot outside the café. The boy in the driver's seat must've been with Chloe. Mathew remembered seeing him at the party. Brett or something.

"Let's go for a drive," Chloe said sweetly from behind him. "Get in the car, Mathew."

Mathew glanced over his shoulder to look at her. "What is this?"

A soft wind passed, pulling Chloe's hair away from her face. Mathew had never seen such a severe expression on her usually soft features. "Get in the car. Becky would appreciate it if you did."

That's it. Chloe had mentioned Rebecca by name at the party, though Mathew couldn't remember ever sharing that detail with her.

"What about Becky? She's—"

"At home, watching episode eight of *Bad Witches Club*. Also, on her second bag of chocolate-covered almonds. Would be a shame if someone interrupted her. And your house is *so* pretty, but a blackthorne-laced smoke bomb through the window would be kinda hard to explain to Ainsley and Frances."

Mathew's pulse pounded in his ears. "What do you want?" he whispered roughly.

The boy pulled the car up to them and threw open the passenger-side door.

Chloe nodded toward the car. "Not here."

Mathew cursed under his breath. Sliding into the car, he realized that the party wasn't the first time he'd seen this kid. He had a rough scar on his right arm, the same one he'd used to stab Logan.

Chloe slipped into the seat behind Mathew. She patted his shoulder jovially.

"Where are you taking me?"

"You'll see!" She winked at him in the rearview mirror. "Go, Blake."

The boy hit the gas, and they peeled out of the lot.

Blake drove them to a secluded spot just outside Haelsford city limits, the offshoot of a trail or campsite. The trees were large and thick, and Mathew wondered how the hell his day had gone so wrong that he found himself being kidnapped.

Blake parked in a quiet spot under a tree. He pulled Mathew out of the car and held him against the passenger-side door.

"You're a pretty good liar, Mathew." Chloe's voice was low and sharp as she leaned on the car. "But I'm better."

Mathew kept his hands at his sides. In front of him, she pulled out her phone and showed him the screen. The images chilled Mathew through. There were some of just him and Iris, and another of them with Becky. The second one was near the house in Port Barrow just a few days before.

"What the fuck?" Mathew said plainly. He angled his head over to Chloe. "What. The. *Fuck?*"

"We heard you the first time," Blake quipped, finally letting him go.

Palms opened before him, Mathew turned to face Chloe.

Maybe Chloe was a good liar, but Mathew didn't miss how her eyes flicked over him. Then she smiled. "I thought you weren't into witches, and here you are, hanging around two of them."

"I never said I didn't know a witch," Mathew said. He stepped closer, the movement surprising Chloe, evident from the little hitch in her breath. "Tell me what you want, Chloe." Mathew lowered his gaze to meet hers. "Or do I already know?"

He heard Blake move behind him. Footsteps crunching, an annoyed slamming of his hands on the hood of the car. "We want a witch."

Chloe nodded, breaking the gaze between them. "And lucky for us, you know two of them." She placed the phone on the hood of the car.

Blake pulled him backward and held him over the phone. All Mathew wanted was to hit the guy in the face, but seeing Iris and Bex before him pulled the nerve out of him.

"The ritual happens tonight." Chloe's voice was easy and sweet, as if she were speaking of a dinner party. "If not tonight, then we have to wait a month, so we're in a bit of a time crunch."

"Ritual?" asked Mathew.

"Stab a witch on a full moon night and let her blood wash over you. Makes a mundane witchy."

"Yeah?" Mathew laughed, even as his fear made him nauseous. "Where'd you get that from? Some desperate hexeater online? You're all fucking delusional."

Blake slammed Mathew's head down against the car. A burst of pain left the world dark for a moment. As the blood dribbled down his face, he grinned. "Ouch."

Blake looked like he wanted to do it again, but Chloe stepped in front of him. "Not the face." She winked conspiratorially. "So, between the two, your sister or your..." She glanced at the picture and tapped Iris's face, zooming in. "Who is she to you?"

Mathew's heart pounded. "Nothing."

"You look pretty cozy," Blake sneered.

"She's a friend of my sister's." He swallowed hard.

"The ritual involves the transfer of one witch's magic into thirteen mundanes. And we're letting you choose because... she's not gonna make it." Chloe's eyes were glossy with excitement.

Is this how it happens? Mathew wondered. He wanted to offer himself up. He was no witch, but he'd put his body before Bex if he was asked, and the thought of leading Iris to these wackos made him sick.

But looking at the two hexeaters, he knew they were too far gone. They wanted witchery. They wanted power. And though no ritual would ever give it to them, their desperation had convinced them that this was the way.

Mathew shook his head slowly. The sardonic smile was gone, and all that was left was stony anger. "You'll die tonight." He spat blood. "It's your death wish."

"The next thing out of your mouth better be *Where do you want me to bring her, Chloe?*"

Mathew glared at her from behind blood-soaked eyelashes.

"We're friends, Matty. That's why I'm letting you choose." She reached over, pushed his dark, damp hair away from his eyes. "Or. We can go get Becky ourselves. Up to you."

He raised his hand slowly. He didn't want to frighten Chloe, he just wanted to touch her hand. And for the first time, this awful power felt useful, and the vision . . . comforting. His mind whirred, a horrible plan forming. It was the only way to ensure both Iris's and Rebecca's safety. "Where do you want me to bring her, Chloe?"

37

jailah

Olga Yara's Trinity spells were legendary for their difficulty to incant. Iris and Jailah had managed one themselves, and Jailah considered their survival to be a matter of both determination and luck.

Now this. For severing bonds.

Olga put tricks in her spells. *Convergence* had left Iris and Jailah in pain, and they saw visions of futures, of deaths, of destinies. In *The Culling*, a spell misspoken triggered death of those around the caster. For *Excavation*, there was a sly riddle scrawled in the corner of the page.

For the most fearsome,
The most hungry,
The wronged and the blighted—
I give you a spell to make old slights righted.

Jailah hadn't a clue what that meant, but she was terrified, and *hungry*, too.

The muck of the Swamp was unsettlingly warm. With what she knew now, it was the one place in Haelsford where Jailah felt safe, especially to do some forbidden magic.

Vero sat against a mossy rock, her legs stretched out, the tips of her Converse knocking against each other in an anxious rhythm. Jailah appreciated that she didn't ask her if she was *sure* about this, even though Vero was watching her every move with concentration. Heat prickled up Jailah's neck.

There were two parts to the spell. First, Vero had to drink a strong concoction for locating illness; Jai had to raid Thalia's cabin for that and was happy to see she left her mini fridge stocked "for emergencies," according to the note taped on the door. She'd also left a color-coded guide for each one, and Jailah chose the one that T had noted as the most potent.

The potion made Vero's eyes fuzzy. She hiccuped, and a trickle of inky-green goo remained on her lips. Still cute, though.

Vero wiped her mouth with the back of her hand. "Last words?"

Jailah stiffened. "If you're having second thoughts, tell me now."

"Psh." Vero lifted her head. "I'm ready to have my magic back, all of it. Are *you* ready?"

Jailah reached out and touched her cheek. Vero's eyes went soft. "You're my tether," said Jailah. "This is what I'm supposed to do."

Stunned, Vero only nodded.

Jailah turned back to *Wicked Works*. Ten minutes had passed since Vero drank the cleansing potion. Now she could begin.

The beginning to *Excavation* was wordless. First, Jailah pressed a sacrificial needle into the center of Veronica's chest until a tiny dot of blue-green blood seeped out. Veronica clenched her teeth, and Jailah wondered if she should've brought a towel or T-shirt for her to bite down on. They were in the Swamp, at least. No one would hear her scream.

Where the incantation for *Convergence* was a whole story, *Excavation* used a chant of six phrases.

Betrayals, Forsaken.
Bounties, Baited.
Corruptions, Starved.
Corrosions, Carved.
Slights, Weathered.
Bindings, Severed.

As she chanted, white, dreamy puffs grew from the end of Jailah's wand. They were like clouds more than smoke and smelled acidic. Jai was reminded of blood, but with a touch of too-sweet decay. Rotting fruit, sugar-scented death.

Veronica started to slump. The blue-green blood seeped quickly into her clothing, and her eyes went glassy.

Jailah forced herself to keep her voice calm and steady as she chanted. Vero squeezed her hand. "I feel it," she gasped. "The hexbinding—it's working."

Jailah chanted faster, watching the neon liquid trickle out of Vero's body, the Council's binding magic made solid. It pushed and scratched against Jailah's witchery.

Vero's grip tightened on Jailah's hand. With every chant complete, she grew radiant. Her eyes danced with excitment, glowing amber under the light of the moon. Her aura burst back to life, and the gem at her neck lifted up in levitation. As Jailah chanted, Vero threw her head back and laughed.

But when she lowered her eyes to look at Jailah, fear cut into her gaze.

Jailah looked down and saw that her own white shirt was dotted with that sickly, vibrant blood. And as the stain grew, the wound in Vero's chest began to shrink. Jailah's breath stuttered, the chant slipping away. She felt dizzy. The world turned. Had she always been lying down? Vero's aura grew and grew with every second that she regained a hold on her magic, and Jailah felt hers slipping away.

If Jailah were the type with a sick sense of humor, she would've laughed.

"It's me," she muttered. "I performed the *old slight*."

Jailah's health, her magic, was being given to the one she once wronged. She watched helplessly as the expelled curse spread and seeped into the already decayed Swamp. She didn't think the earth here could grow further corrupted, but the mucky Swamp dried up under the touch of the drained binding hex.

Jailah wasn't the only one who'd wronged Veronica. A whole Council had voted to take Veronica's magic. Mesmortes and Haelsford had cast her out. Yara's curse would come for them all.

"I don't want this!" Vero screamed, her witchery growing and growing.

Jailah's skin felt tight. She ran her hands over her body and felt bones where she never had before.

"Jailah!" Vero cried, dropping to her knees. "Fuck! Stop the spell!"

She couldn't, though, not when she could hardly lift her wand. She hadn't known she would be giving up her health and her witchery for Veronica, but it was fine now.

"Jailah, please!"

Everything was fine. The only thing Jailah wanted now was to sleep.

"Jai—"

Vero's final cry died in her throat. Jailah forced her eyes open and saw a blurred Veronica looking to the distance in horror.

Jailah heard a growl, low and ferocious.

Trampling feet and the stench of blood.

A flash of yellow hair, a flurry of movement, a burst of golden light.

Get away, she wanted to say. *It's not safe.* All she could manage was "Don't."

Had Logan heard her? Delirious, Jailah wanted to smile, but it would hurt too much. Logan wasn't the same baby witch she once knew. She was making progress, she was a proxy, and she had . . . something new about her.

Several red beasts circled them with curious anticipation. Vero threw herself onto Jailah protectively—*adorable*—but not a single one lurched forward, not one Wolf tried to devour them.

Logan was talking through something, something that stole Veronica's attention and quieted her cries. A Wolf kept close to Logan's side. It had gashes for eyes. Another Wolf stepped forward. This one was bigger and had rows of teeth.

"You taught me this one," Logan announced.

She did something with her hands that Jai couldn't quite see, and when she pulled her hands apart, Jailah was hit with a wave of magic that sizzled sweetly against her. If Jailah hadn't been watching with her own eyes, she wouldn't have believed that this was the magic of Logan Wyatt.

A great, shimmering orb grew around Jailah and Veronica, encasing them in yellow light. The curse inched up the barrier, rolling up and crashing down like waves on a shore. Logan contained it, keeping it from seeping farther throughout the Swamp, but Jailah was still trapped inside, drowning under the poisonous manifestation of Vero's hexbinding.

"This was a horrible idea," Vero spat, tears running down her cheeks. The wet drops landed on Jailah's face. Jai savored it, her senses relishing the touch.

On the other side, Logan shouted a command to the great Wolf.

The Wolf bolted into the barrier, taking on a snoutful of the rot. It whined in pain but burst forward. Veronica screamed as the Wolf took one of Jai's legs into its massive mouth.

It yanked Jailah out hard, bubbles of rot dripping behind her, Logan's barrier keeping it inside the protective orb. Vero was pulled out next, leaving the orb full of sickly green decay.

Jailah tried to breathe, but the air felt too thick. Vero pressed her head onto Jailah's chest as she whispered a desperate incantation. Her crescent moon gem was hot against Jailah's skin.

The air thinned. Jailah gulped down breaths. "Logan," she muttered. "If you break the orb—"

"I know. I learned from you, remember?"

Gingerly, Jailah lifted her head to see the Wolf yowling in the middle of the orb. The rot she'd created stuck onto its fur, burning it away, satiated by the sickness and corruption presented to it, dictated by the spell. Green veins pulsed through the Wolf's body as it took the full weight of the rot.

"That was so freaking silly, Jai!" Vero was furious, but her voice trembled with relief. She grabbed Jailah's hand, held it against her heart, and swooped down to kiss her. Dazed with glee, Jailah kissed her back with every ounce of energy she had left. The feel of her mouth was like honey, an easy softness when their surroundings were so dark and cruel.

It was familiar, the way they broke apart and kissed again. Tethers, once. Tethers, again.

Jailah couldn't wrap her head around this. Logan. The Wolves. The *kiss*. "How did you find us?" she gasped. "Are Thalia and Trent back, too?"

Logan looked just as perplexed as Jai felt. "I had to leave early, and when I got to Haelsford, I just felt it. I saw you through the eyes of my pack. They called me here. I don't know what this is, if it's like having a ton of familiars, or something else, but I'm grateful for it."

"Thank you," Jailah whispered. To Logan, and to her Wolves.

Logan released the orb. The Wolf staggered backward, convulsing. When it hit the ground, the others howled in mourning, the eyeless one standing protectively at Logan's side.

38

mathew

He showed up at the creepy, dilapidated Mesmortes Chapel in a casual band tee and dark jeans. His face hurt. The greenwitch at the town infirmary healed his wounds with a serious side-eye.

Silly fight, he'd said with a shrug, not wanting to think about how much worse the truth was.

Anxiety swirled in his stomach. He ran his fingers through his hair. If Chloe and her little minions were watching, and he was sure they were, they were probably growing impatient. He'd been out here for ten minutes now, trying to think of a way out of this. But at the end of every imaginary scenario, he saw himself mourning Rebecca. She was just a baby witch, how could she protect herself from a network of hexeaters that had slithered into Haelsford?

His visions of death didn't show him what happened after Iris killed Chloe. But he knew he had to be ready to protect Iris. He got them into this, and he would get them out.

When he opened the door to the chapel, his heart jolted into his chest.

"Surprise," Iris said with a deadpan sneer. "Happy horse prom! Or whatever."

She waved her wand, and multicolored scraps appeared out of thin air and into the macabre scene. There were black streamers, a table set with food, and a blown-up picture of Ruby running across a field.

Mathew held back nervous tears. "Iris."

"So, I don't actually know what your little banquets look like, but I know you like Ruby." She pointed to the poster. "And you also like fancy white people food, so—" She held her hands out to the table of food. "I ordered from Rizzo's. Ta-da!"

"Any snails on little lettuce leaves?" Mathew managed, voice tight.

Iris smiled. "Ugh, hell no."

Mathew was frozen at the sight of her. She was wearing a sleeveless black dress that billowed out around her feet, and her arms were draped in tight black gloves that reached her forearms. Mathew had always loved her impossibly dark eyes, but now, with her eyelids washed in brown glitter and lined with black liner, he thought he'd very much like to drown in them. Even more, he liked how her braids were pulled up and away from her face so that not a single strand hid her cheekbones, her skin, her lips from him.

She held out her hand.

"I look like an asshole next to you," he whispered, finally making the long walk up the aisle. "I thought we were going to go see a movie or something."

She shrugged, then turned to the speaker set up against the wall. Mathew was sweating for more reasons than one. Getting her out of the chapel was going to be harder now that she'd done all this. What he wanted, more than anything, was to stay here in utter seclusion with her.

But his phone vibrated, and he knew who it was.

"What do you want to listen to?"

"Anything." He was stunned, he was breathless. "Anything."

She looked up at him wistfully. How was this possible, to be looked at like this, by her? He swallowed his desire, even as her eyes traced the outline of his lips. Even as her eyes lingered there. "I'll put on something slow," she whispered, her breath kissing his cheek.

She's going to hate you, Mathew thought sadly. *She will never forgive you for this.*

Mathew slid his finger over the underside of her glove and lifted her hand to his shoulder. She moved closer, carefully, closing the space between them. He could hardly hear the music under his own frantic heartbeat, but this was everything. The press of her body against his, the feel of her silk-wrapped skin, the way she rested her head on his chest in silence, as if savoring him, too. It was she who pulled him tighter, closer, and the mental list of every single thing he loved about her grew.

"Mathew?" She looked up at him in confusion. "What is it?"

He inhaled quickly. His phone buzzed again. "Nothing."

"You stopped dancing."

He searched for the words, but only managed a slow shake of his head.

Iris placed her gloved hands on either side of his face and held him like he was precious. She lifted onto her tiptoes.

Mathew thought back to their moment in the Green, the scene he'd revisited thousands of times in the few days since.

And here she was before him. Hands caressing his face, eyes pleading, her mouth turned up toward him with the certainty that she would kiss him back.

Mathew bit down on the bitter knob he'd been holding under his tongue.

"I'm sorry," he whispered.

"Kiss me," she whispered back.

Mathew brushed her lips with his thumb before pressing his mouth to hers.

39

iris

She was drowning in his touch.

He seemed to be all over her, *those hands*, all around her.

Or was that just her imagination? Just what she craved?

"I'm sorry," Mathew murmured again.

She kissed him harder, unable to get enough, fueled by every touch. Soft, his finger brushing her cheek, his breath against her mouth. Every nerve in her skin buzzed, electric. He tasted like black tea, so bitter, but his lips were warm—

And the bitterness grew like smoke, harsh and cold against her throat—

Iris jerked backward but remained in his dreamy grip.

His fingers stayed on her cheek. His gaze went distant, like he was trying to hear something far away. "It's okay," he whispered sweetly, almost laughing with delight. "You'll be okay."

Iris wanted to rip his tongue out of his mouth. "What did you . . ." She choked, exhausted by the effort. "What did you do to me?"

"Iris, I need you to listen to me. There are people that want to hurt you, but there's a way out . . ."

As he spoke, she fought back, clawing at his face. She screamed every curse to damn him. Or so she thought. Her fists only flopped awkwardly against his chest. Her curses caught in her throat, coming out as garbled, harsh mutters. Her vision was going dark. Her witchery subsiding, like it was being sucked into an airtight box. She was helpless.

"I won't let them hurt you," he whispered, lips brushing her forehead.

I hate you, she thought, over and over again.

I hate you, I hate you, I hate you.

Iris came to on a slab of cold rock.

She wasn't alone. There were distant voices chattering excitedly as she looked around, trying to get a hold on her surroundings. She tried to sit up, but her hands and ankles were restrained against the cool rock.

She blinked away the tears that were still in her eyes and found herself looking around at a mausoleum. This was Haelsford Cemetery. Iris was in a cemetery in a nice dress, bound to a rock like a sacrifice. This was as infuriating as it was terrifying, but at the very least, the blackthorne was wearing off.

That reminded her.

Beaumont.

The kiss.

Hate rushed into her with an angry blaze. She jolted to her left, straining against the restraints. There he was. That motherfucker. Mathew Beaumont looked at her with sick sadness in his eyes, and all Iris could think was *I'm going after you first.*

But she couldn't do anything just yet.

"She's awake!" someone said.

Iris was rushed by a group of mundanes, most of them around her age if not a bit older. They were a diverse crowd, but all were giddy with joy. Some were even *applauding*.

The girl who'd alerted all the others sidled right next to Iris and squealed. "Oh my gosh, I'm so happy to finally meet you. I'm Chloe."

There were a lot of things that Iris wanted to say, but she settled for "Get *the fuck* out of my face."

Most of them did back away from the slab, but Chloe only frowned. "I'm sorry this is happening like this—"

"Let me go!" Iris struggled again.

"It's just what the ritual calls for."

At that, Iris looked her up and down.

Oh my god.

Being captured by hexeaters was something that happened in cautionary tales or witchy bedtime stories. In a delirious moment of shame, she wondered if she was dreaming. Iris opened and closed her fists. No, this was real. Would Death save her this time? She couldn't be sure and couldn't chance it. She had to break free, and quick.

"I said, let me go!" Iris thrashed against the restraints once more. She felt a loose rock or stone poke at her leg.

"I *can't*. We'd have to wait until next full moon, so it's gotta be now."

Iris bit back the childish urge to mock Chloe's annoying-ass voice. The fear was starting to win out now that another girl appeared behind Chloe with a curved blade.

Something else was happening, but Iris couldn't see with Chloe blocking her view. Iris heard Beaumont's voice along with another boy's but wasn't sure what they were saying.

Iris refocused. "Killing me won't make you a witch, it only makes you a witch-hunter. I thought you people loved witches."

"We do," Chloe said with that same annoying cheerfulness. "And we love witchery enough to want it for ourselves. Why should it be you? Why not me? Why do you get to reap the rewards and privileges of something you were merely born with?"

Iris closed her eyes and cackled. *Funny thing for a white girl to say.*

"Chloe!" Mathew had broken free from whatever struggle he'd been in and pleaded breathlessly. "Take me instead!"

Chloe wrinkled her nose. "*Cute*, but you're not a witch."

Mathew opened his palms, revealing those small death marks. "But I can—"

Seeing the death marks stole Iris's attention. Mathew's hands weren't just splayed outward. He kept gesturing toward his leg, running his palms against his pocket.

There's a way out. The blackthorne had muddled Mathew's warning, but she remembered now. *I'm sorry, Iris. You can hate me as much as you want, but right now I need you to trust me, because I know how this ends.* He'd slipped off her silk gloves, dropped something into her pocket, and hoisted her arm around his shoulder.

Iris fidgeted with intention this time. The protrusion on the slab wasn't one at all. It moved, a small stone in the pocket of her dress. Slowly, she inched her fingertips toward it and pulled it into her grasp while Mathew had their attention. Her wand was missing, but her knuckles brushed against her sacrificial needle. A boy walked over and punched Mathew hard in the stomach.

Iris ran her thumb over the rune and cursed.

Ten thin lines. A rune that cost years.

"Let's get on with it!" the boy said, eyeing Iris.

Sweat dripped down her face as she desperately jabbed her thumb.

Chloe climbed atop the altar. The moon rose above them, its light glimmering over the blade's handle.

"No!" Mathew screamed suddenly. "No, get—get the fuck—off me!"

A soft wetness bloomed on Iris's thumb. Heart racing, she watched Chloe raise the blade in a vicious arc.

"It's time," Chloe whispered. "Let us know the power of the earth's magic."

Iris's chest pooled with icy energy, a delicious surge that enthralled her as much as it terrified her. A million synapses opened up in her witchery and connected to auras in the ground beneath her. An explosion of death magic so intense, Iris's world flashed black.

Before Chloe could bring down the blade, Iris giggled.

Chloe faltered, eyes angry. "What's so funny?"

"Why . . ." Iris choked on her laughter. "Why would you bring a necromancer . . . to a *fucking graveyard*?"

A skeletal hand burst out of the ground, wrapped its bony fingers around Chloe's head, and twisted.

40

mathew

It didn't matter that Mathew knew Iris wouldn't die here. As he watched Chloe raise the blade toward Iris's chest, he felt the burst of pain as if it were his own.

"*No!*"

He rushed for her, and it must've been predictable, because Blake lunged for him. Mathew dodged and managed to hit him squarely in the jaw.

Blake slammed him into the wall. Mathew didn't bother fighting back. If he'd misunderstood what he'd seen and Iris was gone, then it didn't matter if Blake beat him into a bloody pulp.

But then Blake turned, distracted by the laughter as the others were.

Iris, tied to the altar, guffawed maniacally.

She said something Mathew didn't catch, and then a half-rotting hand punched through the wall and grabbed Blake by the throat. It pulled him in hard, slamming him into the rock.

Mathew scrambled away as hell broke loose all around him.

Sharp screams echoed up and down the mausoleum as bodies burst through the dirt and stone. Mathew was frozen, compelled to move only when a hand caught his ankle in its effort to pull its buried body out of the dirt.

A black heel stepped onto the hand, crushing it into bits of disassembled joints and metacarpal. Iris looked down upon him, a menace, a goddess, angry and beautiful with murder in her eyes. Three skeletal bodies staggered behind her as if waiting for orders.

She had her wand once more, having taken it off of Chloe's body. She twirled it with a sinister playfulness, then lowered her face to Mathew's and hissed, "I'm saving you for last."

"Iris, wait—"

She glided away, her magic propelling her out into the graveyard. The hexeaters scattered, ducking behind headstones for shelter. This seemed to amuse Iris. She raised her wand, a dark conductor to an unholy symphony.

The dead obeyed.

They lunged for the hexeaters. Mathew saw the body of an old man jolting, with inhuman fury, for a girl. Another creation of pure skeleton threw a boy into a headstone. Everywhere he looked, there was flesh and blood, bone shards, and the sounds of mundanes begging for mercy.

Mathew turned and found a bloodied Blake limping out of the mausoleum. He had a knife in hand and was focused on Iris.

Mathew threw himself at him. They clashed, and Mathew felt searing pain bloom in his left shoulder before the adrenaline numbed him so completely that all he knew was the sound of Blake's bones crunching as he slammed his fist into his face.

"Enough!" Iris cried out suddenly.

Every single member of the awoken dead stopped. Mathew removed himself from Blake. The boy was still breathing but was near unrecognizable from his injuries. Mathew's whole body hurt, and his arm was wet with blood.

Iris hovered a good seven feet above the ground. The death marks on her hands shimmered red. She held her wand to her throat.

"Listen up!" Her voice reverberated through the graveyard. "I know what you look like, and I will never forget what you did. If I ever see you again, I will kill you. You try something like this with another witch, and I will kill you. Every single move you make, I'll know. Why?" She popped her eyes open and grinned. "Because the dead are buried *everywhere*."

The hexeaters scrambled away, tripping over one another to flee Iris's wrath. Blake staggered away, wincing under the pain of his injuries.

Iris drew her magic back, and the dead slunk back to their resting places. Mathew watched Iris float back to earth, rolling her shoulders and taking deep breaths.

She turned to him, right before he was going to say her name.

Clutching his shoulder, Mathew dropped to his knees, the exhaustion hitting him all at once.

With narrowed eyes and a harsh incantation, Iris healed his wounds. Still, Mathew remained there, bent before her.

"You let me be taken by hexeaters," she said with an even steadiness that felt more terrifying than anger. "You *brought* me to them."

"I know."

She pulled out the rune and dropped it at his side. "Am I supposed to forgive you because you made this? Because you tried to warn me?"

"No. I don't expect you to forgive me at all."

Iris's face wrinkled with disgust.

"They threatened Becky." His voice cracked around the words. "I didn't have a choice—"

"Oh, *fuck* off—"

"And I knew you would survive the night. Even if they killed me, they were never going to harm you."

"I am not invincible!" Iris's eyes blazed with anger. "How could you know that? How could you be so sure that I'd get the rune in time, and that I could do all this?"

Mathew jerked his head up to look her in the eye. "Because I checked!"

"You. Checked?"

"My marks aren't just scars. I've been seeing deaths when I touch people. It happened with a man I met, and he died by a heart attack that I pictured. And then Chloe—" Iris twitched at the sound of her name. "I saw you kill her. I just didn't know how or why."

"And you didn't tell me?"

He dropped his head. "I thought I could fix it myself. I kept hoping the vision would change, and by the time I realized that it wouldn't, it was too late. These hexeaters had this whole thing planned out, and I couldn't stop it. So, I checked."

Iris closed her eyes. "You touched me."

"Yes."

"You saw my death."

Yes.

She looked at him once more. "What did you see?"

"Do you really want to know?"

She turned away. "No. I guess not." A moment passed before she added, "But I do want to know when you made the puppeteering rune."

Mathew let out a pained laugh. "After I caught you reading about it in the Green."

He brought himself to his feet. She didn't reach for him, and he didn't attempt to close the distance between them.

Mathew's heart ached, but that was okay. He took comfort in a vision of her, wrinkled and gray, cloaked in black, scythe steady, reaching willingly for Death's extended hand.

41

thalia

The lights were off at the Turner home. In spite of the great full moon, the cloudy night was a thick blanket of darkness.

Thalia opened the front door slowly, her wand in a tight grip at her side. She felt an unfamiliar presence against her witchy aura. It settled into goose bumps against her back.

As she stepped deeper into the house, the still quiet was broken by a soft whimper.

"Help . . ." the voice said. "Please . . ."

Thalia's blood chilled beneath her skin. The door to her father's office was ajar, and she saw the subtle movement of shadow.

Heart in her throat, she pushed open the door.

Her father was splayed out on the back wall of his office, two massive vines protruding from his chest and pinning him in place.

His clothes were soaked red, and Thalia coughed from the stench of blood.

He couldn't turn his head all the way, but his eyes flicked over to her. And the hand he'd stretched out fell limp at his side.

Her breaths were anxious, noisy heaves. "Father."

If he didn't recognize her at first, he did now. His eyes widened. Gurgles escaped his throat. He was trying to move, to lift hands to her, but never quite got there.

"This wasn't me," she whispered. "But it should've been."

Her father choked. A thin stream of blood dribbled out of the corner of his mouth. "You . . . you *wretch*."

Even now, Abraham found enough hate in his heart to curse his daughter.

"Just like your mother," he continued laboriously. "She always . . . she always needed guidance to the light."

Thalia stifled her confusion. "I looked through your records. You knew I was in Haelsford this whole time."

His eyes rolled aimlessly.

"Why didn't you come after me?"

He laughed, blood spraying from his mouth. "You weren't worth the effort."

Hatred pierced Thalia's chest. Of course, to the man who made a fortune off people's pity, she was worth more to him as a runaway witch who might come back than a dead girl. But Thalia was relieved. She didn't have it in her to feign sorrow and forgiveness if he'd been repentant.

She looked into his eyes one last time. "Hey, Dad? Burn in hell."

She watched the life slip out of his eyes. It was ugly and messy. So much blood, the hideous shudder of his death rattle. But Thalia watched. And as she waited for the satisfaction of finally being free of him, all she felt was an empty ache and that lingering feeling of strange magic on her skin.

"Mom?" she called out, making her way toward the living room.

Thalia's heart leapt into her throat.

Fiona was lifted in the air by thick vines that swelled from her back and dug into the floor. Her arms were curved outward in a display of power. Her head was thrown backward as her dark, joyous laughter undulated in her throat.

Against the wall, Trent was tied to the wall in another maze of vines.

Thalia looked in awe at the tendrils that had broken through the back windows and curled around her mother. Mossy vines snaked through cracks in the walls, and dark red flowers bloomed in the corners of the ceiling. Thalia's stomach turned at the sight of Trent's blood pulsing through the vines like veins.

"Finally!" Her mother gasped in delirious satisfaction. "A debt is paid!"

Thalia shuddered a cry. "Let him go!" She should've run to Trent, but her feet were frozen in fear.

"Baby girl, look at you. *Look at you.*"

She wielded the vines like limbs. One of them pulled the antique mirror off the wall and held it in front of Thalia. Her own curls were limp with filth from the evening's madness, but tufts of silver streaks had sprouted from her scalp.

"We are free," Fiona said, still smiling.

"You were a witch this whole time?" Thalia was mesmerized, her mouth moving on its own.

"I couldn't," Fiona choked out, voice thick and raspy. "I could not speak of it. The bloodpact—"

"Bloodpact?" Thalia blinked. She couldn't have just heard what her mother said. There was no way, but of course, of course, that was the only way Trent's presence here made sense. "What are you doing to him?" she whispered helplessly.

Fiona pulled away from her foliage. She hugged Thalia close, her usual shea butter and vanilla scent replaced with that of dew and fresh grass.

She stroked Thalia's head tenderly. It wasn't just a display of affection. Thalia's vision was blurred with tears, but it also felt like she was seeing through another's eyes.

A memory, sent down from her mother, and so palpable that Thalia felt her mother's fear, grief, and desperation.

A sticky Florida summer, a broken hex. Twenty-year-old Fiona prays at the grave of her first love, comforted only by a friend he left behind. Abraham Turner, three years older, is a kind man. He holds Fiona tenderly as she sobs and looks upon her with care. "We'll get through this," he promises.

"He did love me, then." Thalia could hear that her mother was smiling. "Loved my magic, too. I had no one else. He had money. He kept me safe."

They are young, bright, and optimistic, with dreams of healing the world of its ills. Abraham, a godly man. Fiona, her healing hands. He speaks scripture, and she uses her greenwitchery for good. She's special, blessed with a knack for solving the strangest medical mysteries and breaking the strongest hexes. They go town to town, turning skeptics into believers. Abraham brings the sick and helpless forward, and they call her a miracle, sent from God himself. But with every person healed, Fiona feels more like a blood bag than a saint.

All day long, she gives pieces of herself away. Her time, her freedom, her own blood. She gets few hours of sleep and often wishes that the sun will never rise.

But the lines of desperate folk never stop. Some have traveled across the country, others have traveled overseas. She is their last hope. The guilt eats away at her personal desires.

Pain twisted in Thalia's gut, but it wasn't hers. She felt her mother's helplessness and fury, two feelings that she knew well.

She wants a break, a change of scenery. But Abraham insists that they go south, to a town of witches. "Maybe you can heal this treacherous town," he says. "The people are suffering, and you've healed everything else."

In a hexed witchtown, Fiona finds a wonder of magic. She can't heal its Swamp, but it's worth it to spend long days curing ailments just to be around others like her. Abraham doesn't like it. He believes that a witch who uses magic in any way but to help others, no matter how simple and harmless, is an affront to God.

"Perhaps you can convince a few to join us," he suggests.

Fiona agrees, though she has no intention of doing so. She is planning to stay here, whether Abraham is at her side or not.

After a long day pricking her thumb, she buys a ticket for the Haelsfordian Coven Troupe. She couldn't remember the last time she had used her witchery for pure fun. All the healing leaves her too drained to do any sort of magic.

Then she meets the firewitch.

Against the wall, Trent stirred. Thalia tried to shake away her mother's embrace, but Fiona wouldn't let her go just yet.

"This is important," she cooed.

"Lourdes DeVry," the firewitch says proudly. "You must like the show, 'cause I've seen you in the front row every night. You're that greenwitch with the healing hands, yeah? Heard all about you."

Fiona stands there, utterly speechless. It's taken her weeks to work up the courage to approach Lourdes, and now she doesn't know how to explain what the performances mean to her. Lourdes is a few years older, radiant, with a beautiful husband and a perfect son. Fiona feels a pang of jealousy . . . until she shakes her hand and feels Lourdes's cells rebelling. Lourdes smiles, oblivious to the sickness running through her.

The friendship blooms quick and easy. Lourdes listens to Fiona's every frustration, soothes her every anxiety. Lourdes is no elder witch, but she seems so experienced and worldly. Fiona makes a promise to herself and to Lourdes that she will figure out a way to cure her.

"Thalia . . ." Trent whimpered, eyes fluttering.

She wanted to run to him but forced herself to stay focused on the memory.

Weeks and weeks of sleepless nights have not brought Fiona closer to understanding this illness that feeds on Lourdes's witchery. Though Lourdes is gentle with her, Fiona can see the anger she holds back every time she asks about an update and is left wanting.

"I'm not all-powerful," Fiona explains, twisting her rings.

"Then become all-powerful," Lourdes begs. Her witchy aura has thinned, barely palpable. The strength of her physical body is next, Fiona knows. "Save me, please, Fiona. I have a child. I'll do anything."

Fiona's heart hurts for her friend. "Lou, I can't bring back the magic that the sickness took, but I'll do whatever I can to keep it from taking your life."

Thalia glanced up at her mother. Fiona looked dreamy, unbothered by a past filled with so much misery. But she saw herself in the memories, in Fiona's unwillingness to give up, in her messy notes, experiments, and trials. Two greenwitches who believed they could find cures. And when Fiona cracked it, Thalia felt the joy ripple through her, too.

"I knew you could do it, girl." Lourdes's eyes are wet with gratitude, though her witchery is gone.

It's a bittersweeet evening in the tent. There's no room in the troupe for a firewitch without magic, and Damien is ready to move them to London to settle down. Abraham wants to move on as well, and though Fiona pictured herself staying here in Haelsford, she can't imagine herself without Lou.

Fiona never drinks, but tonight, she makes an exception. "Woulda saved your magic if I coulda," she says shamefully. Though Lou smiles, Fiona senses the sadness in her. Lou was made to be a performer and speaks of witches with such love and reverence. Though Fiona tired of her own witchery, seeing Lourdes without hers was painful. Guilt washes over her. Godly work or not, Fiona spent so much time feeling burdened by her magic that this just didn't seem fair.

Several cups deep, Fiona feels like her future is closing in around her. Lou spoke often of her hopes and dreams, but Fiona can't see herself doing anything but toiling for others. The more people she healed, the more word spread, and the more word spread, the more she doubted she would ever be free of her reputation, no matter where she went.

She grabs Lou's hand. "Take my magic." Though her mind is fuzzy, her excitement grows heady and intoxicating. It seems so obvious now that there is a way to give them both happiness.

Lou laughs, refilling both their cups. "Don't tease me, girl."

"No, I mean it!" Fiona urges. Half-drunk and eager to impress, she squeezes Lou's hand harder. "I have an idea."

The more they drink, the more it makes sense. And though Fiona's pleased with her idea, she knows better than to make this exchange permanent.

Lou pricks her thumb. "I agree to the terms. Your magic for that of my first-born. In ten years, when Troy receives his blessing, his magic is yours."

Through the open tent entrance, Fiona sees the boy running across the field and into Odeah DeVry's arms. "Your firstborn witch," she amends quickly. "And you will have children until you bear one that is blessed." A bloodpact usually involves some threat, but Fiona trusts Lou. To promise the magic of her own child was painful enough.

For a moment, Lou hesitates. Fiona can't read her eyes, but she wears something close to a proud grin. "Of course, yes. My firstborn witch."

"However long it may take."

Lou leans back, eyes glassy. "I'm not trying to trick you, Fiona."

"Of course not! I know you wouldn't. But we have to be specific."

In the silence, a ripple of unease passes between them. But when Lou offers her blood-slick hand, Fiona accepts it.

Fiona's hands drifted to Thalia's shoulders. Gently, her mother led her to the wall where Trent struggled against the vines, then slumped.

"It was so freeing, at first," said Fiona wistfully. "I thought Abraham would be upset with me, but he liked me more as a mundane, even if he couldn't use my magic to spread gospel. For so long, I thought it was what I wanted, but I realized that my solution wasn't one that brought me joy. What I *really* wanted was to be free of the guilt in using witchery as I pleased. Still, I abided by the pact and waited, even as my attempts to contact Lourdes went ignored. She tricked me." She lifted her head, heat flickering in her eyes. "She had no intention of offering up Troy if he were a witch, or any witch she might have mothered. Lourdes concealed her children from my gaze with *my* magic. I looked and looked, but it was like they'd all been blotted out of the world. Until today."

"Is that why I went to Mesmortes?" Thalia could hardly manage a whisper over her despair. "Not because it's far away, but to find him?" She turned to look into her mother's eyes. "You *wanted* me banished from Annex!"

"No, baby," Fiona said gently. "When you were born, you became my whole world. And when Lourdes died, I took that as my peace and moved on." Her voice hardened. "But when you needed a place to run to—"

Thalia squeezed her eyes against the tears.

"I thought it was a great bit of luck. And a few months ago, I felt him. Finally, finally."

Thalia turned to Trent. His hard breaths where softening, more time between each rising of his chest. "You're taking his life, too."

"I did not dictate the terms. His mother did. His power is mine—it's ours. Greenwitchery and firewitchery together. Like nothing our kind has ever seen. No witch, no mundane will ever be able to hurt us now."

Frantic, Thalia shoved her away from him. As Fiona stumbled, Thalia levied her wand at her mother. *"Roots of the Earth!"*

Sinewy brown tree roots broke through the floor and snaked up Fiona's legs. She laughed. "That is a good one, Tallulah!"

It wouldn't hold long. Thalia hacked at the vines around Trent with all the power she could feed into the *Cutting* spell.

Trent's body twitched. "T . . ."

Behind her, Fiona cursed. As she cut away one tendril, another took its place like a weed. "His mother owed a debt!"

"He's done nothing wrong!" Orange-red blood spurted from the vines Thalia cut. "And if you want to hurt him, you'll have to kill me first!"

My line, she pictured Trent saying with a smirk. All she wanted was his smile aimed at her, the two of them safe, far away from here.

With one hand on her wand, Thalia slipped her hand into his, relishing the unnatural heat there. Her hand was covered in his blood. "Trent," she pleaded. "I need you to call your fire. I know you're weak, and you've never done this before, but you have to try."

His eyelids flickered. "The . . . fleur."

Fleur? Flower? Thalia kept *Cutting*, but the knots and layers of her mother's blood-infused vines seemed never-ending.

Trent's head bobbed. "Left . . . left side."

Thalia didn't understand, and she was out of time to try. Behind her, Fiona dug up her *Roots* with a stronger set of branches of her own. She looked upon her daughter with a heartbroken stare. "You cannot defeat me, my love. Step aside."

Trent released her hand and pulled his blood-slick fist into his pocket.

Fiona looked pained but not enough to keep her from raising her wand. "You are an incredible friend, but this isn't your fight, Lullah."

At first, Thalia thought her mother had stopped speaking. But her mouth was moving. An incantation or more placating nonsense, she wasn't sure, because she couldn't hear her under the weighty drone of her own heartbeat in her ears.

A hot blaze of magic slammed into her, knocking her away from Trent and onto the floor. She scrambled for purchase, desperate. "Leave him alone!"

Her cry fell apart under her gasp. The whole room was alight. Thick orange flames seeped out of Trent's skin like lava from his pores. They raced up through the vines, green smoke billowing out in their wake.

Fiona released a bloodcurdling cry. The vines around her drooped lifelessly. The silver in her hair fell away in dead strands.

Trent, free from the vines, approached Fiona with slow steps. His entire body was covered in flames, but that didn't concern Thalia as much as the feel of his energy. What was that in his hand? Not a wand, but a stone.

Thalia launched to her feet. "Trent! Stop!"

Trent's eyes were furious, his witchery a firestorm. He looked soulless, ruthless, completely divorced from the boy she knew and loved. He raised a hand, revealing a glowing blade of fire.

Thalia whipped her wand toward him, but the vine that curled around his wrist only burned away. The amplyfyr remained tight in his grip.

Thalia hurled herself in front of her mother as Trent brought down the blade.

She felt little pops up and down her arms and all through her body. Her sprouts multiplied. Like well-tended wildflowers, they thickened as they grew from her flesh, dousing much of the flame.

But the fire fought back. The fire ate through a layer of her Swamp-touched barrier of sprouts, flames licking dangerously close to her skin. Trent's pained expression broke Thalia's heart, but she had to stop the amplyfyr's grip on him. With a roar, Thalia pushed her magic, throwing everything she had left into it. The sprouts stiffened, then grew out of her flesh in thick bursts of foliage. Thalia saw dots in her vision.

Her sprouts extinguished the remaining flames, engulfing Trent's flaming body entirely, wrapping him up in a cocoon of wiry tendrils and pillowy petals.

Half-dazed, he fell into the thicket with a soft sigh. "Shit."

Thalia gasped a sob. "Are you okay?"

Though he was lying in her lap, she had to push away a layer of sprouts to see his face. His eyes fluttered open. He nodded.

Behind her, she felt her mother move away. Fiona retreated to a window and used the ledge to pull herself to her feet.

"I'm a witch, by the way," Trent muttered.

Thalia smiled. "No way, really?"

He moved his hand under the foliage. Thalia met his fingers with her own. Before she lost her nerve, she gave in. She swooped down and kissed him quick. It was nothing more than a sweet peck, but Thalia's whole body went hot.

Trent grinned. "So, you *are* trying to kill me."

Gently, she lifted herself away from him. The mass of foliage stayed there, releasing from her body with tiny snaps. She was left with thousands of little sprouts embedded in her skin. With a deep breath, she drew her power in, and the sprouts retracted into her flesh.

At the window, Fiona's head was bowed. Thalia slipped a hand onto her shoulder, then hugged her mother as she cried. She didn't know what to say. Maybe there was something to be said about the corruption of seeking revenge, but it sounded hollow in Thalia's mind.

"You can't stay here," Thalia said finally. "Let's go somewhere else. I can leave Mesmortes behind. We can start fresh."

Fiona patted Thalia's hand. "Abraham's dead. You don't have to fear him anymore. I want you to have the normalcy you always craved, and you can't do that once they start looking for me."

Thalia felt a guilty twinge. "I'm not going to let that happen."

Fiona looked over at Thalia.

"A witch attacked a mundane man yesterday and left him in the alleyway outside the church. When they find Abraham's body, they're gonna look for her, and they're never going to find her *or* Annie Swift."

Fiona quieted, considering this. "I need to stay. Give a few statements about the witch who attacked my home and killed my husband."

"Then you run."

Raina was a wild card, but Thalia was telling the truth when she said she saw herself in the girl. Like Thalia, Raina was going to want to handle her, and only her, on her own.

Thalia wiped away her mother's tears.

Fiona glanced at Trent, who was dusting green bits from his clothes. The amplyfyr rested in its sanctifum once more. "You love him, don't you?"

Thalia swallowed. She nodded.

"Oh, Lullah." She kissed the top of her head. "Be careful."

after

August

Haelsford buzzed with life. The summer tourists were heading back to their haunts, and students were coming in for the new semester. The air was vibrating with witchery, and Trent took in a deep, satisfied breath.

Thalia opened the cabin door. Her silver-streaked curls danced in the wind. They mesmerized Trent for a moment, and when she smiled at him, his skin flooded with a totally unwitchy heat.

Inside, Thalia's desk was lined with little patches of Swamp-dirt in glass bowls. He stood next to her, then pulled out his new wand.

The feeling of Trent's magic eased Thalia's nerves. It was so strange to have him stand here with a wand and his own magic, especially considering what almost happened to that magic. She and Trent hadn't talked much about their mothers' history after leaving Annex, but not out of shame or pity for each other. They simply understood the choices Lourdes and Fiona made and didn't feel like there was anything else to say.

She lifted her wand. "I'll go first. Once I finish incanting, hit it with fire."

He nodded. His excitement was so adorable, Thalia had to hold back a laugh. "I'm ready," he said with a wink.

Thalia drew her witchery outward. The sprouts under her flesh bloomed, warming her skin pleasantly. *"Cut Out the Rot!"*

"Ignis!"

As Thalia's spell pulled the Swamp's hex out of the dirt, Trent's flames burned up the separated decay. She was right that the key to cleansing the Swamp was a powerful greenwitch . . . but one with a firewitch at her side.

"Trent?"

He turned to her.

"I'm excited that you're part of the coven now. But I've always just been happy to have you as a friend, too. Witchy or mundane. It's never mattered. I've loved you all the same."

The wonder and surprise in his gaze knocked Thalia's breath away.

He brushed a curl from her face, then held his hand under her chin. "Yeah, but I loved you first."

She chuckled and rolled her eyes. "It's not a competition!"

"If it was, you'd lose."

He lifted her mouth to his and kissed her the way he'd wanted to since that day he saw her at the library, coming in from the rain.

---•••❖••••---

Logan arrived at the Haelsford library carrying two large strawberry Fraps with glowing hands. Her supplies levitated behind her: a stack of grimoires, spellbooks, old notepads, and assorted Mesmortes pamphlets. She felt

Shadow waking up in the Swamp, saw him through his pack's eyes. As their connection grew stronger, so did her witchery.

She looked around the first floor and found Bex Beaumont glaring at her from a window-side table. Her legs were crossed casually, and she was balancing a pencil atop the desk with a finger on its point.

Bex popped an obnoxiously large bubble from the gum in her mouth. "Where's Iris?"

"Unavailable, so I'm here instead." Logan dropped the stack of grimoires, notebooks, and supplies atop the table, then pushed one of the Fraps toward her. Looking at Bex now, Logan saw that she'd made some adjustments to the Mesmortes uniform. The slacks were rolled up from her loafers, and the white shirt was tied up, revealing a subtle swatch of Bex's pale skin and the ring in her belly button. She looked straight out of the pages of a magazine, perfectly aloof in a way that felt effortlessly cool.

Logan dragged her eyes away from Bex's bare stomach, her face suddenly warm from an unfamiliar mixture of intimidation and allurement. She sputtered, "You can't go to orientation like that, by the way. You'll get a warning even though school hasn't started."

Still balancing the pencil, Bex drew her lips into a smirk. She leaned in and examined Logan like she was a fascinating thing, eyes snagging on the scar across her eye. "You're the Wolf Girl, yeah?"

Logan's nerves buzzed under Bex's gaze. She glanced over her shoulder before saying, "Iris told you?"

"No. Matty did. He's very excited about pulling me into all this witchy stuff." She flicked her gaze to Logan's supplies, unamused.

Gingerly, like not wanting to startle a jittery cat, Logan sat across from her. "Here's all my first-semester stuff. You can borrow books from the Mesmortes media center or from here, but it's always nice to have your own copies to write in. I've left you my notes, too. I wasn't any good at magic, but I took really good notes." She met Bex's skeptical eye over the stack. "I also brought you campus maps and elective pamphlets. Try to get into culinary arts if you can. Professor Singer lets you eat everything you make. And here's a list of on-campus jobs for students in case you, uh, need one."

Bex grimaced.

"Um. Any questions? Oh!" Logan pulled a wooden case from her knapsack. "Sacrificial needles. Self-sterilizing. I have a ton. And my wand, if you want an extra. I don't need it."

Bex twirled a dark strand of hair around her finger. "You don't have to give me all this 'cause my parents cut me off. I think I can handle myself."

Logan shrugged. "I'm trying to help you, baby witch."

Bex's smile twitched. She ran her teeth over her bottom lip in a way that made the hair on the back of Logan's neck rise. "I can do some magic. I'm not like *you* were."

"Ouch." Logan pouted sarcastically. She didn't feel the sting, not anymore. All her past weaknesses and mistakes had made her a witch that she was now proud to be. On top of that, she could sense Bex's insecurity simmering under all that played-up nonchalance. "Iris told us about the work you do for Death, but you need to know how to do normal spells, too, *trust me*. Have you even used a sanctified needle before?"

Bex looked at the needle between Logan's fingers. She popped another bubble before meeting her gaze. *"Fine."*

Dramatically, Bex yanked up her sleeve, laid her arm across the table, and presented her open hand like it was a gift. Under the table, her leg brushed against Logan's bare knee.

"Why don't you show me?"

With each dip and wave, Iris tightened her grip around her knapsack. The waters were rough, but thankfully this ridiculously over-the-top deck boat was much sturdier than the rowboat she usually rode into Sun Harbor. The plush seats were nice, too, she had to admit.

She watched Mathew at the helm, the wind blowing through his hair. She'd asked him to come with her as an olive branch but didn't expect him to offer up the Beaumont boat. Iris wasn't one to forgive and forget, but things weren't as awful as they had been since that night in the cemetery. For as much as Iris wanted to hate him, the death connection they shared transcended their mortal desires.

As if hearing her thinking of him, Mathew glanced at her over his shoulder. "Are you okay?"

She nodded.

"Good, 'cause this is my first time driving this thing. Really hope I can dock us without crashing—"

"Beaumont!"

"Joking!"

Mathew pulled the boat to the dock and watched as she gathered her things. She'd already warned him that the house wouldn't let him enter, but the fact that she wanted him here was enough. Maybe she'd never love him again, and he'd finally heal from the heartbreak. That was okay, as long as they were still in each other's lives.

The upcoming school year was bound to be a tough one, with Bex effectively disowned and Mathew unwilling to cast her aside. He'd stay at the Hammersmitt dorms as usual, crash at Bex's dorm during breaks, and try to keep them both afloat with his savings from working at Soma and whatever he could sell this boat and his car for. If their parents ever came to their senses, maybe Mathew would listen. But for now, this new independence was an unexpected pain and an immense relief all at once.

Mathew felt the energy from the Gothic house like oil on his skin. He was hit with a strong need to turn back and winced.

Iris laughed. "I've never seen a mundane experience the protections before, wow. You good?"

"Eh." He rolled his shoulders. "Just feels like I'm walking toward my death and my body's yelling at me to stop. I'm used to it."

At the wrought iron gates, she looked up at him. "Thanks. For coming."

He nodded. "Of course."

"I don't really know how these runes are going to work, but if you hear screaming or something, maybe call for help."

He paled. "Please tell me you're kidding."

Iris grinned, a perfect thing. Full lips, wide eyes; he felt a tug in his chest that was nothing like the tether they once shared.

He leaned forward just slightly, giving her the opportunity to turn away. When she didn't, he slipped his arm around her waist. "Your parents can't see us, right?" he whispered.

She chuckled. "I still don't forgive you. No matter how good of a kisser you are."

With a sly grin, she pulled away from him and pushed through the gates.

"Sounds like a challenge!" he called after her. "I'm good at a lot of things!"

Face warm, Iris trekked up to the door. She refocused and pulled out the scythe-marked runes that Death had given her.

When she entered, she felt the familiar touch of cold, the smell of dust, the presence of death magic.

"Honey," she said with teary joy, *"I'm Home!"*

Veronica Dominguez waited at the mouth of the Cavern with a look like murder. "Damn. Come *on.*"

Jailah shrugged, still dressed in her Mesmortes archery blues. "Tryouts ran late. As captain, leaving early would've looked bad."

"Ooooh, captain," Vero scoffed. "You fancy, huh?"

The reignited tether between them twisted comfortably.

A month's worth of blackthorne consumption had led to this. As they descended toward the tunnels, Jailah felt its awful buzz against her witchery. Wordlessly, Veronica took her hand.

"You all right?" Vero asked.

Jailah laughed. She'd pretty much blown up her future with the Haelsford Witchery Council, almost died performing a rogue witch's spell, and was now willingly trekking toward a giant blackthorne bulb. She still wasn't used to genuine concern in Veronica's voice and nudged her gently. "Yes. I'm perfect."

It took twenty minutes and three breaks to reach the bulb under the heart of the school. Looking at it now, Jailah felt all the anger she'd tried to get over come back up to the surface. She wanted to see the whole thing burn. She wanted every school's inhibitor destroyed. Cutting a chunk away would probably make no difference in anyone's power, but for now, she'd have to settle for this little defiance that the Council wouldn't notice.

But first—

She angled her head to Vero's and pressed her soft mouth against hers. Her tether was warm and familiar, from the taste of her lips to the feel of her hands caressing her neck.

Vero pulled away with a satisfied smirk. "Blackthorne makes you hot, got it, gonna remember that."

Jailah laughed. "Go on. You take the first swing."

"Don't mind if I do."

Vero drew out her witchery into the shape of a great sword, and her necklace buzzed with energy. Its magic skittered pleasantly against Jailah's skin. She watched with pride as Vero hacked at the bulb.

As the blackthorne rustled from the impact, a wayward flower floated into the air. Pretty, pink, utterly out of place.

Jailah caught it in her hand, then crushed it in her fist.

acknowledgments

I was warned that second books are hard. It's something I'd heard since before I got my book deal, that writing that first book under deadline is a whole different beast. Did I listen? Sort of. I was so excited to get the chance to write a sequel, but *wow*. Yeah. I was wholly unprepared for what it would be like to actually draft and revise this story in a fraction of the time I spent working on *The Witchery*. But while this book fought me in so many ways, the joy I felt when it finally matched the story in my head is one I'll never forget.

So first, to the readers, the bloggers, the librarians, and booksellers— your excitement for a sequel kept me motivated on those impossible writing days. If this is the last we see of Iris, Thalia, Logan, Jai, Trent, and Matty, I thank you for taking a chance on these characters that I love so much. Your support means everything to me.

To my brilliant editor, Jody Corbett—thank you for helping me wrangle all my ideas into this book! I'm grateful to have you in my corner, and this book is all the better for it.

Endless thanks to the entire Scholastic team and everyone who played a part in bringing this book to life: editorial assistant Kassy Lopez; production editor Melissa Schirmer; Brooke Shearouse and Victoria Velez in publicity; Erin Berger, Rachel Feld, Avery Silverberg, and Daisy Glasgow in marketing; Lizette Serrano, Emily Heddleson, Sabrina Montinegro, Maisha Johnson, and Meredith Wardell in library and educational marketing; and to the sales team: Kelsey Albertson, Holly Alexander, Julie Beckman, Tracy Bozentka, Savannah D'Amico, Sarah Herbik, Roz Hilden, Barbara Holloway, Brigid Martin, Liz Morici, Dan Moser, Nikki Mutch, Sydney Niegos, Caroline Noll, Debby Owusu-Appiah, Bob Pape, Jacqueline Perumal, Betsy Politi, Jackie Rubin, Chris Satterlund, Terribeth Smith, Jody Stigliano, Sarah Sullivan, Melanie Wann, Jarad Waxman, and Elizabeth Whiting.

To artist Thea Harvey and designer Stephanie Yang: If you could've heard my squeal of delight when I first laid eyes on this cover! Thank you for bringing the coven to life so perfectly once again. And of course, massive thanks to David Levithan and Ellie Berger. I am so happy we got to do book 2!

Special thanks to Laura Rennert, my incredible agent, and the Andrea Brown Literary Agency for all the support.

To the writer friends and non-writer friends: I could not have done this without your endless encouragement. Thank you, thank you, thank you to Maya, Linda, Candace, Flor, Sunshine, Kelsey, Rachelle, Chalice, Jin, and Kristine. Publishing is hard! Y'all make it not suck as much!

And to my family: It's totally cool if you don't read this book. But you do have to buy a copy. Or three. Love y'all.